THE SPY
ACROSS
THE WATER

THE SPY
ACROSS
THE WATER

JAMES NAUGHTIE

HEAD
of ZEUS

An Aries Book

First published in the UK in 2023 by Head of Zeus Ltd,
part of Bloomsbury Publishing Plc

9 7 5 3 1 2 4 6 8

A catalogue record for this book is available
from the British Library.

ISBN (HB): 9781784080235
ISBN (XTPB): 9781784080242
ISBN (E): 9781784080228

Typeset by DivAddict Publishing Solutions Ltd

Printed and bound in Great Britain by
CPI Group (UK) Ltd, Croydon CR0 4YY

For Vidhi. Welcome to the world.

April 1985

THIS IS FICTION, BUT THE BACKGROUND TO THE STORY IS real. In early 1985, the British and Irish governments were negotiating their first constitutional compromise on Northern Ireland, where thousands of British troops had been deployed for many years against the armed campaign of the Provisional IRA. The private discussions were sensitive, largely secret and often fraught. Only six months earlier, the IRA had tried to kill the prime minister, Margaret Thatcher, and her cabinet by bombing the Grand Hotel in Brighton during the Conservative Party conference. During that same spring, London was reaping new benefits from its most successful long-term intelligence coup against the Soviet Union, from an agent with a vantage point at the heart of the incoming regime of Mikhail Gorbachev in Moscow. Away from the public eye, these secrets collided in the British Embassy in Washington. This is the story of what *might* have happened when they did.

One

W<small>ILL</small> F<small>LEMYNG</small> <small>THOUGHT NOTHING COULD DISTRACT</small> him from the open grave. He was wrong.

His eye picked up a figure on the edge of the crowd, and the shock pulled his gaze away. Around him, the rain that had arrived before dawn had drenched the grassy slope where Hannah and the children were huddled in grey and black, and he was consumed by memories of the kid brother waiting to be lowered into the ground, about whom he was reminded how much he didn't know. But his attention shifted in an instant. Although Flemyng gave no sign of alarm, excitement crept across his skin like fear.

He looked towards an old man, standing alone, who had an awkward, twisted frame. If he had once been tall, now he had folded inwards. His oversized glasses were shining in the wet, and an antique black homburg made him look to Flemyng like some funereal accompaniment, a mummer among the mourners who might have been hired to stand in a tableau of grief when the priest had finished, and Abel was gone. His hands were deep in the pockets of his dark coat. He was motionless, unflinching in the gusty drizzle, and Flemyng thought at that moment that his stillness was as threatening as any weapon.

Why was he there?

Flemyng knew immediately who he was, although they had never met. The face of a legend had materialised at the graveside and with a hint of magic, too, because Flemyng hadn't seen him arrive, although he'd scanned the crowd for friends and was alert to any sign of recognition from someone standing near Hannah who might want a hand or need a word of consolation afterwards. No. He hadn't been there, and then he was.

Flemyng thought of the scene in church an hour earlier. He had been in the front row beside Hannah and so engaged with the melancholy choreography that he had taken too little trouble to identify everyone there. Now he regretted it. Had the old man been there, perhaps concealed by a pillar? Maybe he'd wanted to hide, which is how he'd spent much of his life.

In the cemetery it was difficult to hear the priest. The Brooklyn traffic was close by, and the air was so heavy with damp that nothing was clear nor sharp. Manhattan was a cloudy blur. Flemyng was accustomed to putting on a public face and he could deal calmly with enquiring looks, the small gestures of recognition made from respect that demanded a response. But he was confused, and disturbed by the fact – indisputable, overwhelming – that the unexpected visitor had swept from his mind the picture of his brother that he carried to the graveside.

Though not, certainly, from the question that had tormented him for more than a week. How exactly did Abel die – what had his last hour been like? And why?

Flemyng knew none of the pallbearers who lowered the coffin, letting the cords fall into the grave with a rattle on the wood as they stood back. The priest was finishing. 'Lift us from the darkness of this grief...'

Heads were bowed. He had not known that Abel would choose to be buried in the old way, and was pleased by how much it consoled him. After the prayer, he approached the priest, who put out both hands. 'Ambassador...'

Flemyng hugged Hannah and the children again. He would go home with them, to a house with no husband or father, but first he had to dispense comfort at the graveside. When he stepped back to let others approach as if he was in a receiving line, he turned naturally, without displaying anxiety, to look for the old man.

He had gone.

Puzzled, Flemyng got into a car with Hannah and the children and it took them slowly towards the gates. A few cars followed them, in a small procession that would make its way across the river to Abel's house on 20th. The driver pulled up at a stop light just outside the cemetery. As he did so, a black town car pulled out from the line behind them, the driver choosing just the right moment, and slowed down alongside in the next lane. Flemyng saw the rear window slide down, and a face turn deliberately towards him. He had his second shock of the day, this time in slow motion.

Red-haired and lightly bearded, with features thinner and stretched by the years, his face was as familiar as a family photograph. Their eyes met, then the window went up again. That was all. The rain on the glass let nothing stay in focus. The traffic light changed and the car was away.

For two hours, Flemyng offered comfort to the family, spoke about his brother to neighbours and friends, saw a few of his own. He had a few minutes on the phone to Francesca, in London with their two young sons who were changing schools, and she consoled him. He wondered about Maria, Abel's workmate and his own confidante, marooned in Poland or Czecho under the pretence of a journalistic life, but on the prowl. A new story was starting for him, he was sure, but his alarm didn't show to anyone who was there.

Concealment was his nature.

A couple of hours passed smoothly, helped along on the tide of sadness, then lifted at moments when the necessary release of tension allowed them to laugh. He had left his driver in town and made his own way to the cemetery with the family, leaving the instruction that he would see it through without an official presence at his side. 'No rigmarole, today of all days. Please.'

He had also made an unusual arrangement for his return to Washington. They would drive all the way. The day was always destined to be difficult, and he preferred the privacy of the car to anything else. Now, dipping into the Lincoln Tunnel, he thought of the decision as providential. A few hours of undisturbed thought, and solitude.

Before they settled into silence and the slimy Jersey moonscape, his driver repeated the sympathies he'd offered that morning. He asked how the funeral had passed off.

'As well as it could have, Gus, thank you,' Flemyng said. 'But a strange day indeed.'

The driver said he understood. 'A sad one.'

'No, not just the sadness,' Flemyng said, with the sharpness his colleagues knew well. 'You see, I've encountered a ghost. And not just one, but two.'

Two

A FEW MILES ACROSS THE SAME CITY, ON A BARREN STREET running straight towards the East River, any passer-by could tell that if the Star of the Sea had ever possessed a certain allure, it had evaporated. The place no longer pretended to offer a welcome, and instead set a stony face to the world, which as far as it was concerned consisted of a bleak corner of the South Bronx.

Once upon a time you might have wanted to visit the bar. A few traces of happier times remained. Splashes of faded colour here and there spoke of lost days, even festivity, but the steel door to the street now had a peephole, and a mosaic of black graffiti stretched from lintel to step. The old vessel had been stripped of all her dignity. Shutters covered all but one of the windows, and the beer signs had lost their fluorescence, with only a single shamrock still giving out a lurid gleam. The pub was sandwiched in the middle of a row of tailors' shops, ramshackle stores and the one deli that had resisted desolation, but it was an irretrievable dump.

Nonetheless, smooth Sullivan turned up there as an

incongruous customer on the appointed days, according to a rota decided by him, although, if truth be told, he had long since forsworn strong drink.

He was there on the day after Abel's funeral.

He never parked his car directly outside, but tucked it into the basement of Flory's Garage round the corner where he paid a boy to mind it, because he was a person of habit who refused to be anything other than himself. He would walk to the pub wearing his lawyer's uniform of dark suit, white shirt, sober tie, today under a belted raincoat. He had jet-black hair, slicked back and shiny, and a pink-cheeked, well-fed look. He usually carried a briefcase, apparatus that any of the other customers would be embarrassed to own. With Sullivan it completed the picture of a Manhattan man of affairs. He preferred to be recognised.

The door was opened for him from the inside before he had to bang on it.

A few men had arrived separately within the previous half-hour, one of them much younger than the others, who looked just like the kind of boozers you'd expect to meet on a midweek afternoon in the Star of the Sea. Bound for nowhere, and determined to be unhappy in their own way.

Above a launderette across the street, behind a window with cardboard taped across the cracked glass, Rodden was sitting alone, and bored. He had a camera on a tripod, a notebook and a few paperbacks for company. The room had an old sofa with a floor lamp behind it, two chairs and a sink with a kettle and some cups. Apart from a scruffy carpet smelling of mildew, there was nothing else. He noted down the time of Sullivan's arrival. He had four other names that were familiar, and below them he'd put question marks against two individuals he had never seen before.

Rodden gathered the facts, and seldom thought about them again. People came and went; he did his job. It was his turn for the four-hour watch, his next was probably a month away – it amused him that his own schedule was determined by the vagaries of Sullivan's life – and he checked the time to see how soon he would be gone.

From his perch he looked straight across to the window of the upstairs room in the pub. It was a dank afternoon and a light went on. Rodden knew the blind would be pulled down, so he kept his camera pointed at the front door through a small hole in the cardboard.

He would take a picture of Sullivan when he left, to add to the library, although there were so many of him that it hardly mattered, and get some extra shots of the youngest man who had turned up, the one he could be sure he hadn't seen before, because his blond hair was nearly white and would make his tall figure stand out in any crowd. The chance didn't come for more than two hours, which was unusual. He and his colleagues who shared the shifts at the window knew that these gatherings seldom lasted more than an hour, so he underlined the time when he noted it down.

Sullivan came out with the young man. Slim and startlingly fair, he wore a brown leather jacket and jeans, hands in pockets. There was no sign of the other unknown figure, whom Rodden had pictured from the back earlier, getting from a taxi to the front door. Sullivan walked to the corner beside the younger man, who was taller and fitter. Rodden noticed him taking his hands out of his pockets, as if Sullivan had told him off. He took half a dozen shots in profile, having captured him head-on coming out of the door, his white hair like an explosion in the gloom. He noticed that Sullivan, who in his experience was rarely demonstrative, was talkative and engaged. Making another short note on his pad, he was glad to have something to say.

Later in the afternoon he delivered his film, as usual, to a midtown office that was an outpost of the Bureau's vast field office in Federal Plaza, and two hours afterwards copies of the prints were picked up by a young man from the British Consulate near the UN building. He followed the procedure that he and one other junior had learned, putting them straight into a thick envelope with the copy of Rodden's note, without any contribution of his own, and marking it for the Washington bag. Placing it inside his own briefcase, he locked it with a key and, despite the rain, began to walk the four blocks to his own office.

At the embassy the next morning, Patrick Keane spent a few minutes flicking through the prints, and looked up Sullivan's thick docket, though he knew most of it by heart. His friends, his travels, his FBI interviews, some financial statements from his law firm, the transcripts of two criminal court cases in which he gave evidence for the defence. His public denials that he'd ever met a gun-runner. Of the white-haired young man beside him in the street, Keane could find no trace in his file of photographs. The older man who had joined the group, but hadn't come out of the bar afterwards, was pictured only from the back, and the hood of his waterproof jacket was pulled up against the rain.

Keane prepared a request for London and Belfast, attaching the pictures to a note with his queries. He wondered if the unknown young man had been responsible for the Tuesday meeting taking longer – much longer – than usual.

Bubbly, fair-haired and stocky, and noticeably young for a man in his position, he didn't discuss the contents of the envelope with either of his two colleagues who were working nearby that day. There was no obvious reason to raise an alarm; no red flag nor an atmosphere of particular urgency – and for him, just as it had been with his junior colleague in New York, the task was routine.

Besides, his relationship with his next-door workmates, one of them his own age and one a good decade older, meant that easy-going exchanges about workaday matters had given way to stiffer conversation. The atmosphere had cooled on the unexpected and unlikely promotion that had come his way. As leader of the team, at least for now, he was required to work his passage back to full comradeship.

It would take time.

Working alone, he marked the file of photographs and his comments and questions for the morning bag, and made a note of phone calls he would make to London after they had been logged and filed. It would be next week before he could follow up. He left a message with the secretary of one of his counterparts at the FBI to see if they might have lunch soon. Then he turned to other affairs.

Will Flemyng had been preoccupied and absent in recent days, leaving embassy business to senior colleagues, and Keane had to be ready with a full briefing to bring the ambassador back up to speed on his return. He set to work on a pile of messages. For certain, Flemyng would miss nothing.

Going through them, he was interrupted by his acting deputy, the title that infuriated Guy Cotton. Tall and sinewy, with hair as black as Flemyng's, he was a thoughtful dresser, with a reputation around the embassy for his gentleness. It had helped to make him popular in the sports club as well as the office, and Keane knew Cotton had a social ease, in his mid-forties, that he was still struggling to achieve. His soft northern voice, which had no hard edges, helped to complete the picture. He hadn't expressed directly the disappointment he felt about the office reorganisation, but both knew their friendship was on edge. Cotton hadn't challenged him, but Keane, who liked to plot ahead and never fly blind, was planning to spend some time on a mission to bring them together again.

As he worked, Cotton knocked softly and stepped in.

'You wanted me.'

Keane closed the folder on his desk and slid it away. 'Sure, Guy. I wondered if you might be around at the weekend for a quiet drink. There's quite a bit to catch up on before we all go mad about the prime minister's visit. Weeks away, but the whole joint's jumping. If you've got an hour or two, let's slope off. Sink a beer.'

'I'd like to,' Cotton said, without smiling. 'When's the boss back? We haven't had a note.'

'Tomorrow. He's taken a decent break. I've got to get a briefing together. He'll want to leap straight in.'

'And he'll be in one of his gloomy states,' Cotton said. 'Can't blame him, but in the general way of things it doesn't help.'

Keane said. 'We're lucky, remember. We run our own ship, and mostly he lets us. Doesn't always happen, especially when there's someone with his history running the place. I'll ring you about Sunday and suggest something. Late afternoon?'

'Fine,' Cotton said, and closed the door behind him.

A gloomy Flemyng was what Keane expected, too. He would have to cheer him up, somehow.

Alone, he stared at the empty desk.

Distracted, he took the file of photographs from New York from his drawer. Looked at the faces and wondered if he might meet any of these men. But where, and when?

Three

Rain was streaming down the windows when Flemyng prepared to return to his office three days after the funeral, a long stretch away for him, telling everyone how deeply he'd been affected. The dankness had lifted briefly while he'd been absent. Now it was back. With the dark still down, he spoke to Francesca in London. She lifted his spirits for a few minutes, and they talked about her return the following week.

At just before seven, the sodden trees in the gardens where he liked to walk at first light were unwelcoming and dark. At least inside there was warmth, promising cheerfulness. He had two pots of tea in the first hour, while he dealt with the overnight traffic from London that required a same-day response. His diary secretary got fifteen minutes at the desk and left happy, ready to cancel several drop-in promises for evening parties and keep the rest of the week clear of most interruptions. A congressman wanted a call, and a business delegation would visit for tea, but Flemyng had asked for as much time as possible. Routine meetings were reassigned, guaranteeing the deputy chief of mission a crowded week. Alone, Flemyng prepared for the senior staff meeting at ten.

Any caller might have concluded that after the personal upheavals of the past ten days a comforting normality had been restored.

Except for Lucy.

She could read Will Flemyng like a favourite book, knowing each page by heart. So she understood.

Behind the easy routine, restored after the funeral, lay a jagged nervousness. The dark lines that defined Flemyng's long face had deepened and told the story. She detected the worry, and understood. As a private secretary bred and trained by the machine, she had a position unique in the embassy. Neither pure-white official nor favoured friend, she had been planted on pleasingly solid ground.

Flemyng had prepared it for her. In his time as a minister, she ran his private office in the hot days of the crisis in London nearly a decade earlier that had been the most tumultuous in his short time in politics. They were also the events that persuaded him that the attractions of the political game failed to move him as much as the excitements of his old trade behind the lines. And when the unexpected ambassadorship was thrust upon him, at another moment of alarm when he was summoned to steady a wayward ship, he regarded it as a benefit almost heaven-sent that Lucy Padstowe was already working in the embassy, having got away from London to a Washington posting before he did.

He was able to insist that a place in his outer office be shaped for her, power of access guaranteed. No one in London could find an objection. He had her by his side again.

It worked, too, because there was a relationship between

Lucy and Francesca that was precious to him, in part because he didn't fully understand it. 'We three', Francesca would say, and it was true. Often, they managed him.

On that morning, after the staff meeting where Flemyng had put on a performance of business-as-usual that convinced most of his colleagues and had only a couple of spiky moments, Lucy asked straight off what was wrong.

'Quite a bit,' he said. No smile.

'Tell me,' she said.

'A face haunts me,' he told her.

'Losing a brother is an awful thing,' Lucy said.

He shot back immediately. 'Not Abel.' His tone told her that she shouldn't ask for more.

Then, an unexpected request. 'I need a reason to get to Chicago as soon as I can.'

She started writing on her pad. 'Any particular reason?' Immediately, she regretted her question.

'Unfinished business. It's where my brother died.'

'Of course,' said Lucy. 'I'm sorry. You want to tie things up. I understand.'

'But we need a different explanation,' Flemyng said. 'Float the idea to the mayor that I might get the prime minister to fit in a visit when she's here – which, of course, is never going to happen. But he'll wet himself with excitement. A sitting PM has never set foot in Chicago before. I checked. He'll fling open the doors.'

Lucy spoke carefully. 'Am I right in thinking that your brother's death is still... not known in the city for what it was?'

'More or less,' he said. 'Our friends in this town have been helpful. The people Abel worked with in his secret world aren't even a blip on the radar, they're buried so deep. And obviously his name gave no hint about me, being different. As far as most of them in Chicago are concerned, it's being handled as a common street fight that caught him up in its coils. But the police chief – they call him the superintendent there – is an exception. I'm told he's secure, believe it or not, and he was helpful. An innocent traveller strayed into the wrong place at the wrong time. Crossfire from some gang fight on the West Side. Unknown assailant. Witnesses fled in fear. Very sad, though unsurprising.

'All balls, of course. But publicity has been minimal, and no one has made the connection with me. Neatly done.

'The mayor knows, because we needed his help, but he's got no interest in stirring it up. Quite the reverse. Bad for business. Curiously enough, it means he may be glad to see me.'

In another mood, he'd have laughed at that point, Lucy knew. Not today. 'I'll find a way,' she said. 'Private reconnaissance trip, two or three semi-official meetings. A drink in the mayor's parlour. Drop in at the consulate to see the boys.' Flemyng said, 'And you'll come with me, please. I'll need you.'

After lunch, at his desk in the library of the residence where he liked to work, he said he'd catch up on correspondence that had piled up in his absence, but he wanted to see Keane in the late afternoon.

'If he's not poking around in the FBI or somewhere, ask him to come around five,' he told her. 'We need to talk.'

When Lucy gave Keane the message, she warned him that he'd find the mood in the ambassador's office hadn't lifted, despite his time away from them all.

Each time he saw Keane, Flemyng was tempted to change Francesca's phrase to 'we four' because he knew, as his wife had put it to him with mock primness, that Lucy and Patrick had started to see each other. Many in the embassy didn't yet know, because of the obvious sensitivities – between them, they knew nearly everything – but she accepted from the beginning that Flemyng had to be told quickly. The ambassador said firmly, almost formally, that he gave them his blessing. If that was patronising, so be it. He wanted to make the point, acknowledging that part of him remained traditionalist.

Keane was close to his own picture of his younger self. Hitting his mid-thirties, he was at the age when Flemyng had first roamed Europe on his clandestine adventures, with all the dash that he treasured in those days. A contrast to Flemyng's slim and dark figure, certainly, but his ambassador was vain enough to think, and now relaxed enough to admit, that they had a physical appeal in common, and Keane knew it, too.

Flemyng recognised a restlessness in him and an incipient wildness that touched him. It was common enough in his old life, although he was of the breed that had been taught to conceal it from outsiders. As a youngster, when it came to hearties and aesthetes, he'd tended to the latter. By instinct Keane leaned the other way. So, because he enjoyed engineering balance around him, Flemyng had been happy to insist that he should be made acting head of station when the embassy's chief spook went sick – ill enough, Flemyng knew, to be unlikely to return. Guy Cotton had hoped for preferment, or at worst expected some elderly fireman in a shiny helmet to arrive from London as temporary H/Washington on death watch for his ailing boss, but none arrived.

So Keane acted up, and would surely succeed as station chief in due time. Agreed reluctantly in London, but nonetheless accepted because it was at Flemyng's asking. Not done as a favour for an ambassador, but rather for an old boy of the spies' parish who'd held onto his fishing rights in their pond.

Now Flemyng could test Patrick Keane. As he pushed away a sheaf of London cables and signed the last of a pile of letters at his desk – a brief note of thanks to an octogenarian senator who'd entertained him the previous week – he was reminded how, with the passing years, he was finding it easier to confide in younger rather than older men.

Late in the afternoon, through which he'd been left alone, there was a solid knock on the door before it opened, and Keane, whose natural gift was a set of antennae that could tune in quickly to any atmosphere, realised as he sat down that they were to meet alone. Outside, the rain had settled in for the day. It was grey and implacably wet, with no hint of spring sun and an early dusk spreading. He gestured to the window.

'Grim. Easter gone, and it's like this.'

Flemyng ignored the weather.

'So, you're still in one piece, Patrick? No one stabbed you in the back yet?'

'Nor even in the front,' Keane said. 'So far.' He was smiling, a creased and rounded figure whose charm didn't lie in conventional good looks but in the aura of warmth that he carried. He had always found it an advantage to give the impression that he didn't have to try very hard, although Flemyng knew the truth.

But he noted how Keane was becoming comfortable in taking the lead, when he asked straight away, 'How can I help?' as if he knew.

Flemyng had been careful in Washington to play by the

rules, only rarely tinkering with day-to-day operations behind the locked doors on the floor where Keane and his colleagues operated, although he saw more of the traffic from Moscow and a few other places than any of his predecessors had done, a fact of which Keane was aware. Flemyng's history travelled with him like well-worn luggage.

Keane, like all his generation of spies, knew his office as the Barracks – the source of all their fellow-feeling, and a camaraderie they could never fully share with others, and the home of all their frustrations, too. It was there he'd learned the stories that Flemyng had trailed behind him, banners inscribed with the names of secret victories.

'I need your help,' his ambassador said coolly.

As their conversation began, each was wondering who was the more vulnerable. It was habit. They had been trained to look for weakness rather than strength. Keane's first controller had told him that you often learned more about someone by watching than by listening, and he studied Flemyng, conscious of his movements and his eyes. The strains of the past week were obvious. He noticed that when Flemyng smiled, the expression didn't last long but came and went in a moment. There was an unusual firm line to his mouth, and consequently a sternness that usually didn't show. And in his right hand he was jiggling a fountain pen that he wouldn't let go.

'Patrick, I'm going to confide in you. I saw a couple of faces at the funeral,' Flemyng went on, 'and they won't leave me alone.'

Keane was thrown. 'Family?'

'No,' there was fierceness evident in Flemyng's voice. 'Why would that be?' He sighed, showing an unusual sign of embarrassment at the atmosphere he'd induced.

'Look, I'm going to take you back to some events I can't discuss openly here. At least that I never *have* discussed, to be more accurate, because I don't want to. There would be difficulties – misunderstandings, gossip and so forth. We all know how it goes.'

Then, changing his tone, in a more familiar, intimate voice that convinced Keane of his seriousness, Flemyng said, 'You can tell Lucy what I'm about to say, and please make sure you do. In this affair, however it turns out, we're going to have to be together and should keep no secrets.'

Keane, taken by surprise by Flemyng's bald announcement that a game was afoot, knew he was being led by the hand into a labyrinth, as dark as the gardens outside the window. His alertness was sharpened by a sense of mystery. He had no idea what he was about to hear, assuming only that Flemyng's 'no secrets' promise was for show and couldn't hold.

Flemyng got up and took a few steps, then settled in the corner armchair, with the black fountain pen still jumping in his hand. It was a commanding place, more so even than the high-backed office chair behind the desk, and with the window beside him, the grey light emphasised his dark complexion, the sharp line of his profile and the youthfulness that he'd managed to preserve.

'I'll say something about Abel first. My late brother. You may know'– his eyes were fixed on Keane – 'that he was naturalised here. He took our mother's surname – it was Grauber – and he was happy as an adopted American. And, moreover, he was connected to your business. Deep in the shadows. I assumed you knew.'

He paused and stroked his cheeks in the gesture all his friends knew, picking out the lines that gave his face its character.

Keane inclined his head, which could have been a yes.

'I'll be straight with you. I had dealings with Abel over the years in a few operations involving us both. Allies in competition, you might say. He from Washington, me from London. And it's not always easy to mix office and family, as you will certainly be learning, but eventually we did find a closeness that had been missing for a while. Knew each other better again.' He clasped his hands, fingers intertwined.

'This has been a bad week, the worst, and there's the extra sadness that my older brother Mungo is stranded at home in Scotland. He's recovering from that heart attack and still can't fly. Missed the funeral. So, all in all, a bugger.'

He told Keane how grateful he'd been that Lucy had asked a BBC friend in New York as a favour to make a recording of the funeral service for Flemyng, which she'd sent to Mungo in Scotland. 'I'll get a copy of the tape here,' he said. 'Difficult, but I'd like to hear it all again.'

Keane said everyone always thought of Flemyng as a man to whom his family and its past were important. 'We know when you talk of the hills of home and all that, you mean it. Not everyone does.'

Flemyng went on, 'For a long time, home seemed quite distant. Out *there* somewhere, you know, despite all the precious things about it. Not just the house, which I do love a lot, and the hills as you say that do give me comfort, but the whole Flemyng story. Now I think I know how we all need a bit of extra sustenance as the years chip away at us, and that's where I find it.

'Mungo in his own way is the rock, even more now. For a historian he can seem a little bit innocent, you know, and I used to find that strange. Comical, even. But it's misleading. He has a feeling for what lies underneath. I needed him the other day and missed him because he steadies me when that's required.'

It was obvious to Keane that Flemyng, now leaning forward, didn't want to risk a diversion into a maudlin mood. 'Don't think that I'm angling for sympathy,' he said. 'I can manage. My point is different.'

For all the calm that he carried with him and that had become his badge, Flemyng's edginess was obvious. Watching him, and considering what bound them together, Keane also thought of the contrasts. Will Flemyng, brought up on that Scottish estate with an inbuilt confidence, was at home with a background that would have troubled Keane. Never had a suit that wasn't well cut, shoes of good leather. Spy, Minister, Ambassador. Keane was fashioned from a different mould with no family story to trail behind him, yet had been propelled into the fastest lane, to his surprise, even more quickly than the man who was now his boss. Not only a glittering degree, of the kind that his tutors stood to applaud when they pronounced him one of their own, but with the splash of eccentricity that recruiters could smell, like animals sensing fear in their prey. In his case, although Keane was a mathematician by discipline, his quirk was a passion for illuminated manuscripts he had managed to hoard in surprising numbers. And, unlike most collectors of incunabula, he played rugby enthusiastically and, Flemyng thought, not badly at all.

He knew that Flemyng would also be thinking about their differences, because although his smoothness had served him well, Keane was sure that secretly he wanted to be less perfectly formed. A little rougher. He had quickly decided when he had arrived at the embassy the previous year that as a young man Flemyng had been drawn into the shadows by that urge.

He was getting back to his story for Keane. 'At Abel's funeral, there were…' and he marked a conductor's beat with his hand to make the point '… episodes.'

A word that told Keane nothing. He watched Flemyng stare through the window, wondering what he could see.

Flemyng said, 'I want to give you the background, because Irish matters are your bag.'

It came from nowhere. Keane didn't ask why, stayed silent.

'I spent time on Ireland. Many of us did. This was more than a decade ago, before I had my time in politics. We've talked about that a few times, but let me take you back to the early seventies. Everything was boiling up, the Troubles at their height. Bombs everywhere, army numbers increasing, the internment nonsense that backfired and stoked everything up. Before your time, but you'll know that the Service was kept at arm's length because it was home territory and we were meant to keep out. Bureaucratic nit-picking in my opinion, and it lasted for far too long. That's now the accepted view, as you well know. Anyway, we still did… this and that… here and there. And I was involved in one operation that turned out to be quite important. I think it's fair to say that.'

Throughout the months that followed this conversation, and some of the events they all came to regret, Keane always looked to this particular moment, with the rain beating down on grey windows in a darkening afternoon, as the start of it all. The overture had ended, they were drawing breath, and the stage was set.

Flemyng stood at the window.

'I was a conduit. I had no background there, which was the point. No form that marked me out, because I was Berlin, Vienna, Paris in '68 and all the rest of it. In an odd way, you could say I was clean. Of course, I'm Catholic as you well know, so what followed was probably predictable. Anyway, I was pulled in to befriend an IRA character whom we thought had indicated – in a roundabout way – that he might be open to an approach. An outside chance, but at the time we were desperate. It was difficult, naturally. Sticky and slow.

'But we got there. He proved to be willing, despite all the struggles he had to go through, and it was the start of a long story that continues to this day. As you'll discover, if you haven't already.'

Keane was leaning forward, his expression intent.

Flemyng said he wanted to describe the operation that he put together. 'We met many times. There were the usual worries, plenty of alarms. You and I both know how it is. When he didn't make a rendezvous I wondered if his people were onto him. I thought more than once that he might be dead. If we missed an encounter, we fell back and tried again. All the usual rules, and he played fair. The next time he'd be there. So over time – I'm talking years here – we came to know each other well. I was doing other things. Spending time abroad, running errands – you know the way of it. I had no Irish responsibilities that anyone was aware of, but all the time I was in the middle of it. To my surprise, if I'm being frank. And this man – over time, we came to trust each other, because he was aware I had respect for his courage – gave us what we wanted. It's not the moment to explain exactly how it happened, nor why, about which I'm happy to confess to you I'm still not sure. But in the whole story – and you've been through the hunger strikes, God help you – what came out of it was a kind of victory. One that still delivers. With, I'm sure, the best still to come.

'He's the kind of source we dream about.'

After a moment, he said, 'It's maybe the greatest secret we

have.' Then he added, with a sideways look at Keane, 'One of them, anyway.'

Smiling for the first time since Keane had sat down, he said, 'It's good to know we still have some. If only to annoy our American friends.'

Then a tart question. 'Did you know about my adventures over there?'

'A whisper,' Keane said. 'That's all.'

Flemyng resumed without comment. 'For me this story is about the man I got to know all that time ago. Fishing in Fermanagh. Sitting in a weird bodega in San Sebastián, of all places. Standing in the wet on a bloody ferry to Scotland, more than a few times I can tell you. I knew him so well, because our encounters were intense, even when they lasted for just a few minutes.

'You've got to remember he was still a bomber trying to blow up Brits, especially in uniform. Of course he was, because that's the only way he could be himself. He was technically a terrorist target for us, but my mate, too. Just imagine it. He was born into the cause, could never shed that skin, but had his other side, and it pulled at him. I tell you, Patrick, there was trust between us. Nearly impossible to explain to outsiders, although not to you.

'A moral question of right and wrong? Hardly the way to look at it. I think we were both trying to get to a place where we could have that kind of discussion properly, instead of fighting it out on the streets. In the end, everyone loses there.

'He knew it, so he helped, and we've benefited to this day, although I know it wouldn't feel like that to someone listening to the news, nor to some of our innocent political masters.'

In the course of a few minutes, hearing Flemyng rekindle in his own mind the meetings and panics, the excitements and the times of frustration, Keane watched him change. It was as if in travelling into the past he'd taken on board the weight of years gone by, moved by a friendship built on danger. In looking back to his younger days, he had aged.

Keane saw darkness in the memories. Time for him to offer a thought.

'You said there were faces – *plural* – at the funeral. Whose? I'm still not with you.'

Flemyng's eyes brightened at Keane's sharpness. He said he would speak about one of them. That was enough for now.

And having listened to the story from his past, tracing the emotions etched on Flemyng's face and responding to his mood, Keane reached a remarkable conclusion. His ambassador, for the first time in his experience, and in a way that disturbed him with its unexpectedness, was scared.

But on the surface, Flemyng looked calm as he said in his elliptical way, 'If I could choose one scene from the other day, I would show you the picture of a friend's face without a smile. What would you make of that?'

Keane waited, said nothing.

'I want to know this,' Flemyng asked him. 'Why did my old Irish acquaintance turn up from nowhere at my brother's funeral?'

Always aware of the power of a theatrical pause, he waited.

'And how did he even know that Abel had died?'

Four

THE NEXT MORNING, FLEMYNG DISAPPEARED.

His long walks were part of his personality. He was known for them. At weekends especially, he'd leave the residence on Massachusetts Avenue and walk the city. Francesca let him do it, wanted it, and with her absence in London he could take even more time without attracting attention. In Georgetown, which emptied on Saturdays, he'd often spend a couple of hours on M Street and along the canal. Brunch at Nathan's with a pile of newspapers, some browsing in a bookshop, a walk down to the river and along the canal path, and then he would sometimes trek all the way home through Dumbarton Oaks, where he would sit under the trees and read for a while. So his wanderings were known, and with the shadow of Abel's death still clinging to him, no one was surprised when, after a few hours' work in the office and another hour of phone calls from the residence, he told Lucy and the rest of the private office that he was taking off for a while, despite the weather. They could cover his back quite happily. In London, it was evening and the messages would slow down. He expected to be back by five, and that was all.

Never mind the rain; on this Friday he needed to get out. He told no one where he was going.

In only fifteen minutes, he had walked the full mile down the hill to Sheridan Circle, where he found a mobile coffee stand nearby. After some observation, he decided he had seen nothing or anyone to put him on alert, and with his raincoat pulled up to shield his face he hailed a cab and took off for Arlington. With a mild feeling of absurdity, he took some trouble to disguise his voice. Without attempting a full-blown accent he softened the natural timbre that marked him out as a Brit of a certain class. He didn't encourage conversation. Feeling a touch ridiculous, he slipped down in the back seat and listened to a phone-in radio show with the driver.

Lucy was ringing Keane. 'Is he with you?'

She walked the corridors. No sign of him. The steward in the residence couldn't help. Lucy took a number of calls from colleagues hoping to find a gap in the ambassador's diary, and she covered for him. Business on the Hill that had taken him away. But since his driver Gus was seen coming in and out of the embassy foyer throughout the morning, and hanging out with the security boys, the word went round that something was up.

The city was grey, and although the streets were busy with traffic that promised a slow journey in the wet, Flemyng was across the river in fifteen minutes. The driver was unsure on the Virginia side, but Flemyng was able to navigate with confidence despite the destination being new to him. He had got the route clear in his head. They stopped at a park about half a mile away, and he walked the rest of the way. The rain had eased, and watery sunshine was breaking through.

Turning into North 33rd Road in Rock Spring, he found a street of houses in colonial style, generous in proportion but none of them grand. A few had Stars and Stripes hanging from poles sticking out from the balconies, but not the one that was his goal. Checking the numbers on the porches and mailboxes on their posts, he made no effort to conceal from himself his apprehension as he approached number 4814, set back from the slope and half concealed by trees. He savoured the feeling.

Afterwards, he thought it had been like the curiosity he might feel in a library or maybe the zoo, and knew he'd been perked up with the excitement of a schoolboy.

Stepping onto the porch, he rang the bell. Nothing. Tried again. Silence. Without any hesitation, he took the side path that led past the garage towards the back yard, under a spruce that dripped water on him as he passed beneath it. As he had expected, he came across a long glasshouse, bulging with foliage and early blooms, that seemed to take up half the yard. Dimly, he could make out someone moving among the plants and, without thinking about any reaction he might provoke, he walked to the door, tapped on it firmly and pushed it open. There was a bout of coughing, and a stooped figure took a moment to close the door of a wooden cupboard in the corner before turning towards him.

'May I say hello?' Flemyng said.

The old man, dressed in a loose navy smock, put down a small watering can, straightened himself as best he could, and smiled. He pushed his thick glasses up his nose, and held up a flower in a little pot, as if it were a gift.

'Indeed you may, Ambassador. Good to meet you. Of course, I knew you would come.'

That evening, having seen nothing of Flemyng in the afternoon, Lucy and Patrick went for a drink at Mr Smith's in Georgetown. The piano bar was crowded and the singing was about to start, so they went straight to the garden at the back. The rain had stopped and there was a lush green sheen on the plants hanging above their table, with freshness in the air. It was private, not because it was quiet but because of the background noise, and in any case they knew how to talk without using any names that might attract attention. They assumed some of the loud youngsters across the patio were staffers from the Hill – they were dressed in the gear – and Lucy thought she recognised a junior White House functionary.

They took care.

'He's not himself at all,' she said.

'He's given us that history lesson,' said Keane, having passed on every detail of Flemyng's story to her as instructed. 'Something's come back to life. Without warning.'

Lucy said, 'A straw in the wind – he lost his temper at the ten o'clock, about a stupid little thing. Unheard of. You saw. Everyone noticed.'

She put a hand over his. 'Straight question. Why do you think he's so anxious?'

Keane was looking her in the eye. 'The unknown. He can usually see ahead, and just now he can't.'

He said it would be odd if it were for Irish reasons, because he knew for certain that cooperation on the Troubles with the American authorities was improving all the time. Speaking in the carefully managed language they had to adopt out of the office, he rehearsed what she already knew. Compared with the experience of predecessors in his role at the embassy, closed doors were opening more often. It was public knowledge that an FBI operation had intercepted a shipment of arms for the Provos not long after it put out to sea from New York. There would be a trial. 'He should be happy about that, not worried. There's a change of mood. It's what everyone tells me. And he'll certainly get most of the credit for all that burrowing away on the Hill that's now paying off.'

He said he'd been monitoring routine stuff from New York – Boston and Chicago, too. Interesting enough, and passed onto the usual people at home, but no alarm bells.

'Exactly, and that's what scares me,' she said. 'What's got into him? The guy in the car at the funeral that you told me about earlier can't have upset him that much, when he was thinking about his brother. But we can't talk properly here. Let's go.'

He ordered two margaritas first. They spoke for a while about plans for the weekend, because it looked as if Saturday might be free for both of them. They'd find a movie. After a few minutes, Lucy asked him if he'd remind her about a call she had to make the next morning.

'You remember he asked me to organise a recording of the requiem mass to send to his brother? I have to remember to get a copy for him. I want to listen, too.'

They decided against another drink, but lingered in the front bar for a few minutes, in an unconscious effort to change their mood. One of the out-of-work actors in the group around the piano started to sing something from *Follies*, and one thing led to another. As usual at that time of the evening, the whole place was heaving, and the men who'd taken the stools from the start were floating off in their imaginations, with the honky-tonk rattling away. Keane smiled at the light rouge on the pianist's cheeks as it caught the light.

He whispered to Lucy, saying he might join in. 'I've done it before...'

'Don't you dare,' she said, close to laughter.

Light-headed and unsettled, she pulled him towards the door. Behind them, a young man leapt off his chair as if he'd caught sight of a spotlight, and sang about listening to the rain with a drink and wanting more, even a hurricane.

While they stood in the street, Lucy's coat draped over their heads, looking for a cab that would take them to Patrick's apartment, he said, 'Hurricane is right. I hope we have time to hunker down.' They asked themselves why, despite being together, they'd gone downhill so fast in the last hour. 'Maybe the funeral and all his dislocation has sucked the air out of all of us,' she said.

Patrick agreed for the sake of it, and they slid into the car to turn up Wisconsin. He ran fingers through her light-red hair, she squeezed his knee. But Lucy was convinced afterwards, although she was always suspicious of overheated spirituality, that they'd had a premonition. The phone rang soon after they reached his apartment, less than a mile from the embassy. Keane heard Flemyng's voice.

Looking at the clock, he was sure it was the latest call he'd ever had from him. 'Can you come round?' the ambassador said. 'Now, and it's just us. I'll be in the library. They'll expect you at the residence.' Nothing more.

He had attended a few social gatherings in the residence, next to the main embassy building, and before his elevation even a couple of formal dinners as one of the lowlier officials, but there had never been a one-to-one there. He threw on a jacket and tie because he'd worry otherwise, waited for a cab at the corner of Nebraska, and within fifteen minutes he was being welcomed by a guard at the door and taken under the looming Lutyens portico, along the chequerboard marble hall and through the double doors into the panelled library. Flemyng was standing by the white fireplace with a glass in his hand.

'Pour yourself a drink, Patrick. Please. And sit down.'

They were in deep, comfortable chairs on either side of the fire, which to Keane's surprise was lit and had obviously been burning for hours. Flemyng was a master of small talk, after half a lifetime's practice, but he didn't try to keep it going for long. He asked briefly if Keane was finding it easy to have a little time of his own, and that was it.

'Sorry to call you in. You'll be wondering why I've shouted for you in what's nearly the middle of the night. Thanks for coming.'

'The summit?' Keane said. 'Ireland? Trouble?'

'You're wrong,' Flemyng said, without a smile. 'Put that to one side. But I'll want to know, eventually, anything you've found out since we spoke this morning – I imagine you've been digging away. For now, I need to complicate your life a little more.'

'*Need* to?' Keane said.

The clock on the mantelpiece started to chime twelve. 'Yup,' Flemyng said, signalling that he was in familiar mode. 'I'm afraid it's your second history lesson of the day. As if Ireland wasn't enough.'

That allowed them both to smile.

Sitting down across the fire from Keane, Flemyng poured himself a slug of whisky, and splashed water into his glass. 'It's late,' he said by way of excuse. Placing the bottle on the table between them, he went on, 'You'll know this name, of course, but I'm assuming you haven't met him. Tell me if I'm wrong.

'James Jesus Angleton.'

Keane was startled. Of all the names he hadn't expected...

He said, 'I know bits of the story, obviously. But he's been out in the cold for so long I wasn't sure if he was still functioning. Or, frankly, even alive.'

'Oh, he is,' Flemyng said, 'although not in good shape. I was with him today.'

That was a cue for Keane to sip his whisky, out of nervousness, and settle down as if he'd always expected a conversation like this. First, he asked a question, in as neutral a tone as he could muster. 'Where do you stand on him?'

Flemyng replied, 'Oh, I've got no doubt he's as mad as cheese.'

So why had he been with him, Keane asked in a steady voice. 'Chance, or what? Forgive me, but start at the beginning.'

Flemyng spoke at the fireside as if he was reading a ghost story at Christmas. The flames were dancing beside him. It was the kind of scene he enjoyed; the creation of a few moments of calm in the knowledge that they would soon pass. The warm wood and the books lining two walls of the room gave the illusion of comfort and safety. There was an atmosphere of peace as he began.

'You'll know he was the guy inside the CIA who became obsessed with the idea there was more deception than honesty in our business. He turned counterintelligence into an inquisition. Spoke about a wilderness of mirrors that distorted everything. Ambiguity is his favourite word. So he spent years turning the Agency inside out looking for evidence of the great Soviet infiltration that, as far as anyone who's reasonably rational can tell, was a figment of his imagination.

'You'll also be aware that his sickness – because that's what I'm sure it became – was brought on by his own betrayal, thanks to our very own super-traitor. Angleton's drinking buddy in this town was Kim Philby when he was doing your job at the embassy around 1950, the master deceiver himself. You got the story like everyone else, served up with our mother's milk. He took everything from Angleton and gave it straight to the Russians. All of it. Forget the damage across the landscape, it was also the ultimate destruction of a friendship. When his dear Kim eventually disappeared to Moscow, leaving a trail of corpses behind him, Angleton lost faith in everyone.

'And here's the point – that meant losing belief in himself, too, because he'd been played for a fool. The perfect recipe for madness.

'An unkind word, but the one he'd use of others, so he can't really complain, can he? It was only about ten years ago that the Agency was finally able to boot him out, when they had to face up to the damage his witch-hunts had done – the search for non-existent traitors, and a secret blacklist in his lair at Langley that would have done Joe McCarthy proud. Not to mention his citizen surveillance operation that was certainly illegal and could have blown the Agency to smithereens, which it nearly did. That paranoia brought down many good men. I knew some of them. I'm told he still skulks around town. Fewer dry martinis, but the same old stories.'

Flemyng paused, and smiled as he raised his glass, and Keane, feeling he had to come up with something, said simply, 'And so…?'

'I know I'm sounding like a long-playing record… but he's another one who turned up at Abel's funeral.'

Keane laughed, which was a natural response in his confusion. 'The second face.'

'Exactly. I had no idea why,' Flemyng said. 'I needed to know of any connection he had with my brother, which would be news to me, so obviously I sought him out. Today. I got the address from an old friend at home. Angleton's over in Arlington. He spun me a good story, of course, and avoided answering my question directly. He still has charm, of a sour kind, but it was all disturbing. I got the feeling that he was laying out a jigsaw of hints, expecting me to put it together on the spot.

Keane answered in exactly the way that Flemyng had expected. 'Do you trust him?'

Flemyng smiled. 'Of course not.'

'So what did he tell you?' Keane said.

Flemyng deliberately waited a moment before replying. If there was to be confidence in Keane – a belief in his ability to take this walk with him – he had to judge this moment. Give it weight. Leave enough unsaid to challenge Keane but give him something to point him in the right direction.

Sitting by the fire, hearing the rain return in the darkness outside, he said that Angleton had managed to startle him. 'I was surprised. I'd thought that he'd be burbling about history – the boozy nights with Philby, the betrayal. I'd have enjoyed that – but no. He was horribly up to date.

'First of all, he knew some of the details of Abel's death.' Keane had known before the funeral about the story of a street fight in Chicago that had been concocted in case of publicity, but had never been required. The shutters had stayed down.

'That threw me. We've kept it so tight. But, and Patrick, I'm leading you onto dangerous ground here, he's aware of a name being known in this town that I'm sure you won't have heard. Or certainly shouldn't have. Our man in Moscow, and the best. I know about him, for reasons that go way back. But I can tell you that even our beloved all-seeing prime minister, who's been able to turn his information into gold dust, especially in this town, doesn't know his name. In Washington, where he's revered for what he's given us, he's Mister Anonymous. That's been the deal to keep the material flowing over here. Never to be broken.

'But Angleton tells me his name is now known.'

Flemyng took his turn to pour some more whisky into Keane's glass, and passed a jug of water. The young man appeared to be holding the drink well, though his nerves were obvious. He was sweating, and not just because of the fire.

'If Angleton's right, his name could leak. And that puts our man – let's be straight about it – in mortal danger. Nothing less. He'd be doomed.'

'Here's our problem,' Flemyng went on. 'We – *we* – have to find out how he's been identified, and what it means for all of us. And let me tell you that if we screw this one up, by making things worse, and the name surfaces *anywhere*, we're both stuffed. Indefinite home leave. Out.

'And I can't think of a more slippery character to have to deal with than Angleton. Can you?'

Keane's obvious anxiety forced him to get up from his chair. 'What do you want me to do?'

'Prove yourself,' said Flemyng, smiling again.

Then, in a move that Keane had no reason to expect, he stood alongside him and reached across to clink their glasses together. With anyone else it might have been an awkward manoeuvre, contrived or patronising. But Keane recognised it for what it was: an effort to bind them in an enterprise whose character he couldn't yet define.

'Don't you get the feeling that it's all happening at once?' Flemyng asked him. 'The walls closing in on us.

'You see, you've learned two things today – and each of them could get you killed.'

His face as he turned to Keane was hard to read. It had frozen in place. 'And all from one damned funeral.' He put a hand on Keane's shoulder.

'If I'm reading this correctly, time is very short. There are a couple of things I want you to do. In the morning, right away. We're heading for a long weekend. The longest. Don't go anywhere.

'I'm going to ring home, to talk to my brother.' His eyes were on his young friend. 'The one who's still alive, obviously.'

Five

The morning light brought life to the hills around Altnabuie. The water on the loch was bright, with some trails of mist drifting over the surface in the sun.

For many days, rain in the south had produced the same frustration that was afflicting Flemyng and his friends in faraway Washington. Francesca had told him that London was grey, although there was a flicker of comfort in the news from the north. It was an upside-down spring, because much of the Highlands had enjoyed the kind of clear skies that come along unexpectedly, when everyone elsewhere imagines that solid cloud and insistent rain are universal. For mid-April in Perthshire, it was a cheerful exit from winter, and all round the glen where the Flemyng house sat in the trees there were signs of change. The pines and firs seemed to have sprung out of a long sleep, and along the lochside the bare branches of birch were showing the first hints of fresh growth.

For Mungo Flemyng, given a pressing reminder of mortality a few weeks earlier, they were the signals he had longed to see. The lingering dark nights had been more wearying this year. A hospital stay, his first since boyhood, and then the crushing news – delivered directly by his brother early one bitter Sunday morning – of Abel's death in Chicago. The loneliness had been hard to bear, despite his robust good sense and all-round contentment, and the day of the funeral in New York had been the worst he could remember for many a long year.

He'd gone in the afternoon, at the hour of the burial, to the little church not far away where the family had always gathered and where he was still a regular in the small congregation that held quietly and determinedly to what Mungo liked to call the old religion. He stood for a while at the door, with not another soul to be seen, and looked down over the loch that ran west for miles, the steep hillsides in shadow and a stiff wind stirring up the water. Mungo thought it looked angry.

There had been some comfort for him inside, alone on a dusty pew. He remembered the last time Abel had come home and how the three brothers had spent half a day on a walk over the highest of the tracks above the house, ending up after a long trek at that little church where, from the same doorway, they looked over a scene that carried their imaginations away and encouraged them always to keep silence for while and lift their eyes to the high tops.

Now he was strengthened by the knowledge that – slowly, in measured expeditions – he could begin to get out again, as his health returned and the light and the air were a tonic and a challenge to get out and tread the old paths. His recovery would proceed in tune with the seasons as the sun got higher, and the promise of warmth came closer. So, day by day, he'd taken the trouble to walk a little more each morning. He would read and do a little writing on his research in the afternoons, but first thing, and again as the light began to fade, he would leave the house.

On this morning he was prepared for what would be, by his standards, a strenuous day. He had taken energy from Will's phone call the night before, later than usual and brief. But consoling. He'd sounded calm, but eager to hear the latest about his brother's health. After ten minutes, when they said goodnight, Mungo was content that nothing in Washington was troubling him. The funeral was behind them all. There was work to do, the embassy was busy, and that would consume him for a while.

So in the morning, Mungo was cheerful and ready for exercise. Soon after eight, his plump figure, swathed in his favourite green tweeds, could be seen moving slowly along the waterside, then onto the lower reaches of the hill to the south, into the woods and up behind the house along a glinting line of silver birches that would be in leaf in a few weeks now. It was cool and crisp, with a scraping of frost still whitening the fields behind the house, and he was glad they had set a fire for later. He took a longer tramp than usual, climbing slowly through the trees to the highest track and coming back by the far side of their loch, where he watched a familiar heron for a while and took a break on the old bench that gave him a view up the slope to home.

It was a mongrel house, its origins hard to define because the wings were from different times. The top floor was another addition that still looked a touch awkward, and there was no architectural flourish to speak of. She had a bent-backed look, like an old friend who was beginning to buckle under the weight of years. The three boys used to speak of her as a woman of character and experience, even Abel who'd spent the least time there in adulthood, and her familiarity had a kind of glory for them. Mungo looked to the first-floor room at the east end of the house, where their mother had painted long ago, getting energy from the morning light, and his eyes moved along to the room that would always be Will's bedroom, where he'd settle down again in the summer. Mungo would make sure his favourite books were there. A bird took off from the chimney, swooping down towards the loch, and he got up to take the slope home.

Later in the day, when he walked again after his reading time, he came back through the front door and spent a little time where he knew Will would want to sit when he next came home – with the brass and copper orrery, the machine that had fascinated his brother since childhood, with its meticulous replication of the planets on the move. It shone in the last of the sunlight filtered through the glass. Mungo liked to think it kept Will young at heart.

Mungo was tired now. When Babble joined him by the fireside, where the remains of a few small logs were glowing red in the ashes, he said he'd be taking himself to bed without supper. His old friend agreed.

Arthur Babb, hunched and thinner in his eightieth year but still with a defiant mop of dark-auburn hair, had known the boys since they were teenagers, his own youthful wanderings from London having taken him into the hills and eventually by chance to Altnabuie, where Mungo's father had taken him on as a handyman who connected in a natural way to the rest of the family. He had stayed. Why not? The young Abel had first called him Babble, and the name had stuck. Now, as Mungo felt the approach of old age, too, that companionship was showing its resilience. They took sustenance from each other. The fact was understood by them both, and didn't have to be discussed.

Babble said, 'The loch's looking as good as I've seen it for the time of year. There's a wee flicker of colour, the brightness of April. It's on the turn and a good spring's coming along nicely. And that wind is staying away for now.'

'We're lucky for the moment, certainly,' Mungo said. 'Don't I know it.'

'Should we have a dram?' Babble wanted to resume their habit of a turning-in glass.

'Better not. I've been doing well, and I won't spoil it yet,' Mungo said. 'You go ahead.'

They played a game of chess, quite quickly and without drama, and put the board and the pieces carefully away in their box. 'Abel always used to beat me,' Mungo said wistfully. 'You'll remember that.' Although it was the first mention of his brother's name that day, the lost sight of his thin, bronzed face with its mournful features, and that dark hair like their father's, had been in his mind throughout his walks, hovering just out of reach as it had been throughout the recent long days. He wondered if he'd ever learn the truth about what had happened.

But if Will didn't know, how could he?

Their fire died away naturally. Babble made sure everything was closed up, dropping the metal bar behind the front door, but leaving the back one unlocked, as he always did when they were in the house. It was only bolted when they were away on a trip, and that had been a while.

Darkness was down, and the air was sharp and still outside with hardly any movement in the trees. There would be a dusting of white frost in the morning. Far away, a car rattled over the hill and then the sound died quickly away. In his bedroom, Mungo opened the sash window a crack. There was no need to worry about a fierce wind, and despite the coolness he wanted a little air. The clock in the hall had just chimed nine o'clock, but he was weary. He took his pills, turned away from the books by his bedside, and slept.

About ninety minutes later, more than a couple of dozen miles away, two men walked across the car park behind Fisher's Hotel in Pitlochry. The younger and taller of the two went to the skip near the back door and pushed a newspaper deep down into the rubbish. Folded inside was a well-marked map. They had no need of it now, and he knew that by the morning the skip would have been carted away and the rubbish gone to nowhere.

They drove west, in a car that they had picked up from a friend in Glasgow early that afternoon. He had been happy to do his bit and lend his old banger, as mud-encrusted as any that might live on country roads, and therefore just the job for his mates. They had no interest in a shiny rental car covered in labels.

In the hotel bar they'd found themselves caught up in a Country and Western night that brought in a good Saturday crowd, and had taken advantage to sit quietly in a corner, letting everyone else make a din. They were hardly noticed as they sipped their pints, and they spoke to no one else, signalling the barman quietly for another drink for one of them.

It took less than an hour on twisting roads for them to reach the high point from where the road dipped down towards Altnabuie. They had passed the Pole Inn, its dimmed lights a signal of after-hours drinking in progress, and a mile or two farther on they stopped for a few minutes in a lay-by that was a favourite picnic spot for travellers wanting a view on a sunny day. Even in the darkness they could follow the contours of the glen, and pick out the roof of Altnabuie itself, just where they knew they would find it. From the house there wasn't a pinprick of light.

One of them lit a cigarette, cupping the match in his hand, and they stood by the car in the bone-dry cool of the night. They watched in silence for a while, and saw nothing moving. No other car could be heard on the road.

Driving on, after a few minutes they swung slowly round the last bend towards the open gate that was the entrance to Altnabuie. Turning the car round slowly to face the way they had come, the driver cut the engine. After waiting for a full five minutes in case of movement, talking quietly and keeping the radio off, they took care with the contents of a zipped holdall in the boot. When they were satisfied, they pulled on black woolly bonnets, and just as they passed through the gates, avoiding the gravel drive and taking to the grass, they pulled them down to turn them into balaclavas.

Everything was black. They looked like shadows under the trees. There was some distant barking from the woods, and nothing else.

The night protected them. But in case of a stray gleam in the dark, the taller man held his gun inside a pocket.

Steadily, taking all the time they needed, they moved through the trees and approached the back of the house.

Six

THE SAME SATURDAY, FOR FLEMYNG, WAS MEANT TO BE A placid interlude. He would have time to himself. But he couldn't put the Chicago visit out of his mind, and he knew there was more about Angleton that he couldn't keep from Keane for much longer.

He was calmed for a while by a walk in the park, having seen that there was nothing overnight from London to worry him. From Lucy, he got a message that one of his better White House friends wanted to meet, which could only be useful. An Anglophile senator, whom Flemyng knew was as dense as a clump of dogwood in his home state, was offering to help in the stand-off on visa rules, and that was a bonus. The residence was empty, and he could wander through quiet corridors, books in hand. There was a window in a little corner that caught the morning light where he sat unseen and read in the welcoming silence that filled the house. Soon, he'd leave for Georgetown.

The call from the Massachusetts congressman the previous evening had been presented as innocent, and Flemyng didn't care whether or not that was true. Charlie Farrell had suggested a lunchtime drink the next day. Unusual on a Saturday, and delivered with unspoken urgency, but all the more welcome for that. It was obvious, although Farrell was elliptical, that he had a message that had to be passed on personally.

Not, in other words, through an embassy switchboard with a long memory.

They met at his favourite Nathan's on the corner of M Street, where neither of them was worried about being recognised. A natural watering hole for both of them and their kind, and no one would be surprised. The Saturday papers were piled high on the bar, the brunch crowd was building up, and there was downbeat chatter at a weekend pace. The daily frenzy was absent. Official Washington in easy mode, with the crowd thinned out. The few who stayed in town enjoyed the calm that replaced the traffic and the rush and let much of the city recover its natural sleepy self.

He was in a tennis sweater and the congressman was wrapped in a green windcheater, topped with a Red Sox cap. They ordered Bloody Marys and picked at the weekend supplements for a minute or two.

'I've been asked to pass you a request, Will,' Farrell said eventually. Aware of Flemyng's alertness, he sent out some signals of nervousness as he went on. 'I should let you know that it comes from a family friend who knows the person concerned – the one who wants to get in touch. He isn't someone familiar to me. Not at all. That kind of connection – at one remove. OK?'

Flemyng, delighted by the circumlocution that promised a surprise, remained expressionless. 'Of course, Charlie. Anything I can do.'

'This individual says, I'm told, that he knew you a while back. There's some story about a rough crossing on a ferry by the name of *Antrim Princess*. I wrote it down, just to remember. I don't know if that rings a bell. Anyway, he'd like to see you. Catch up and so on, over here.' A pause. 'Which he is.'

Farrell had stiffened a little, his quiet relaxation evaporating as he delivered his message. He lifted the baseball cap on the table between them and then let it fall. 'But not in this town. You'll understand, I'm sure, when I say that this isn't really the place for him.'

'Completely,' Flemyng said easily, and nothing else. His mind was jumping ahead. 'Where is he?' He gave the congressman a friendly smile.

'New York, and I'm told Chicago, too,' said Farrell. 'Here and there, and I couldn't say which, right now.'

'I'm told that he's willing to take your instructions – your suggestion, I should say – about where and when you might meet,' said Farrell, throwing him a questioning look. 'Get together again.' A minute or two more and he would have been pleading.

Flemyng sounded enthusiastic, and there was no dissembling.

'Well, there's an opening that might work, if he knows Chicago. You know my life's a diary disaster. But on Tuesday night I could see him there. I'll be at the Blackstone'

Farrell cheered up again. 'Home of the original smoke-filled room, that hotel. Nice!'

'You should know. Maybe that's why I still like it,' Flemyng said.

The congressman smiled. 'You're a romantic, Will. Nineteen twenty convention. Wrong party. Worst president, so far. But we all enjoy our past, I guess.'

He was a beefy sixty-year-old who looked lazy, despite his reputation. The eyes were watery, his cheeks a dark blood-red, and there was a slight shaking in his hands. But Flemyng had concluded in recent months that he was an ally who would be useful in times to come. He had solidity, promising that a course once set would be followed, to the end. Flemyng noted that Farrell was careful not to make even the mildest enquiry about the circumstances, perhaps long ago, that had led the British ambassador to have a connection with the man on whose behalf he'd been persuaded to make a private appeal.

Nor had Flemyng offered a hint of explanation.

'I hope Chicago works for him,' Flemyng said, now sure of the answer. 'But Tuesday and Wednesday are the only days for a little while when I expect to be out of town. We've got some busy weeks coming up at the embassy.'

'He'll find you there, I'm sure, and be happy about that,' the congressman said, before slipping into unnecessary justification.

'I'm only the messenger. I knew a cousin of his, I think. So – family connections of a sort. All that.'

Flemyng thought the mixed-up storytelling was amusingly crude, although he gave no signal that might embarrass Farrell. He closed the deal.

'I have an assistant who'll be in Chicago on Monday ahead of me, at the Blackstone, too. A message to him there would be the easiest way. Patrick Keane. You'll remember the name easily enough.' The congressman smiled back. 'One of ours, I suppose. At some point, anyway.'

It was done. They talked about the morning headlines. State Department signals about politburo changes in Moscow, a presidential visit to Europe in the offing. Another indictment against a former governor of Illinois, already in jail for something else. News of the pre-season baseball trades. The conversations between London and Dublin were changing gear, Flemyng said. There would soon be a more public phase, and he wanted Farrell firmly in the loop for that.

'We need you and your friends, Charlie,' he said. 'Trust us this time.' Everyone hoped it might be the year of a big bend in the road, he said, the one some of them had been trying to get to for so long.

And, he did not add, that was precisely why he was so alarmed.

'Enjoy Chicago, Ambassador,' the congressman said, as a cab pulled over to take him up Wisconsin and home. Just before he yanked the door shut, he said softly, 'I'm told it's Michael, by the way.'

Flemyng almost skipped up the street. He dropped into the bookshop, noting that no one inside, nor at the window, seemed to have recognised him. He gave them another chance, saw no response, and after five minutes turned into O Street to set off diagonally across Georgetown through weekend-quiet streets in the direction of the embassy, where he would summon Keane later, and talk on the phone to Mungo.

When Keane arrived at the residence at around five o'clock, in sweater, jeans and trainers that he'd been told by Lucy not to cast off, he found Flemyng listening to Schubert's last sonata and reading a thriller. 'A contrast,' he said, looking at the book.

'Not at all,' said Flemyng. 'Blood and guts both ways. Now, sit ye down, young man. I've got a cocktail thing at seven.'

But Keane, embarrassed, said he hadn't made much progress. 'Out with it,' Flemyng said.

Keane replayed his lunch with an FBI friend, to whom he'd been introduced by Flemyng. Jack Whealdon, old-school, leather-faced and silver-haired, among whose long-time friends bow ties would never go out of fashion. And ex-CIA, which helped. 'I didn't mention our worries about a Moscow name,' Keane said. 'Naturally. But I did pump him a bit on Angleton, without mentioning you. Tried to make it sound as if I wanted to hear some old stories as an ingenu. Nothing much. He wanders around the old joints sometimes, Jack says, but only hangs out with a few friends from the past. He sees him on the circuit sometimes.

'Angleton takes long fishing trips to Idaho. Lonely ones, you might think. Turns up at flower shows with his orchids, trying to win prizes. Bizarre, but there you are. No longer knocks back the hard stuff like he used to, apparently, but smokes all the time and looks ready for the grave.'

He shook his head hard, trying to correct himself, too late. 'Sorry…'

Flemyng lifted a hand to calm his nerves. He said only, 'Did Whealdon ask why you were interested?'

'No,' said Keane. 'The only thought he offered was that the old man was still a pain in the butt. Can't stop spy-spotting, and looking for conspiracies.'

Keane then decided, because of the disturbance he detected in Flemyng, not to ask the question that Whealdon had suggested. With a look that was both friendly and sly, the FBI man had told him that if Flemyng wanted to know more about Angleton, he could always ask Maria. And that was all.

Keane repeated in his mind the question he'd asked himself at the time. Who the hell is Maria?

But Flemyng interrupted his thought. 'Ireland,' he said, without warning.

'It's half good news,' Keane said. 'I showed him the pictures. We have that young guy with the white hair here, somewhere – real name Cathal Earley, that's according to London overnight – but the Bureau has no idea how he got in. You've seen the New York photo, and you can't miss him, he's so fair. Nearly albino. Couldn't have been with his own passport, because it's on the list and he can't get a visa. They don't think he's here for an operation – no action on American soil is Rule Number 1, as we know. So they think it's more our problem, which it is.

'He's not somebody who can turn up at a fundraiser over here, even behind closed doors. Nobody's heard of him – and that's deliberate. He may be here just to get away from some heat at home. But judging by the New York photos, he knew Sullivan, and how he was expected to behave in his presence. An underling.

'And with that, I'm afraid I'm done. I'm sorry there's not more, boss.'

The few minutes that followed were understood by both of them as an effort at reassurance. Flemyng was determined to push Keane to the point where the younger man could demonstrate he had staying power – but to do it by means of encouragement. Keane, hungry for understanding but unnerved by the weight of Flemyng's history, wanted to respond without displays of the kind of hopelessness that had started to creep over him in the forty-eight hours just gone. He was the supplicant.

Flemyng responded personally, changing tack without warning.

'You thought it odd when you came in that I was reading Ed McBain and listening to Schubert. It doesn't seem unlikely to me, so I'm going to turn it around. How can you be seduced by higher maths – all that numbers mystique – and still be obsessed by manuscripts that were around before the whole business of scientific learning had got going? Off the wall at both ends, I might put it to you...'

'You're wrong, I'm afraid,' Keane was confident in how he could respond. 'Off-beam. Ancients knew more about the magic of numbers than anyone. You know that. When I was a student I thought that's what I was trying to rediscover. So it was natural to be obsessed by early books – pre-books, really – copying and so on. Illuminations. Block prints. Bits of parchment that survive from a time we hardly understand, at least in the way people went about their daily lives, and *felt* their world.'

'How did it start?' Flemyng asked.

'At a barrow in Clerkenwell Road, that's all,' Keane said. 'The guy on the stall let me have the corner of an illuminated page for a tenner. He had no idea. I worked out afterwards, when I'd learned more, that it was probably produced before about 1470, but it was nothing more than a torn corner so it looked a bit pointless. He was more interested at the time in trying to get thirty for a Wilkie Collins first that wasn't worth it. So I was lucky. Slid under his radar.'

'A steal,' Flemyng said.

'Exactly, and when you've got away with it once, you find you have to do it again.'

Keane said he had a modest haul at home – maybe twenty decent finds, and a few near-certain duds – but he knew that soon he'd be unable to afford anything that he *really* wanted. Hopes were disappearing beyond his reach before his eyes. But the excitement of the unexpected discovery never died. There would be fewer of them, but all the better for that.

Flemyng was enjoying him.

'I've got a couple of fragments that come from Scotland,

I'm fairly sure. One page that's nearly complete, and early enough to be serious. Can I give you one?'

'On loan,' Flemyng said, 'to the embassy. I'll treasure it.'

'That's kind, boss. Let's say it stays until one or both of us is gone from here.' Keane realised what he'd said.

Flemyng seized the moment. 'Which brings us to the here and now.'

There was background they had to get clear, he said, and news.

'We both know one of my main jobs here is to spread confidence that we're making progress in Dublin. Seriously, and for the first time. You know the Irish-American caucus on the Hill is starting to believe us, or some of them anyway. The guys who matter have pushed us hard, but they've moved, too. Much friendlier to me these days. We've got to keep sending the message – on both sides everybody recognises it – us, the bombers and all the Sinn Féiners, Dublin – that this thing will never be sorted out militarily one way or the other. Just can't be. Behind all the mayhem that's been obvious for at least ten years, but we know neither side can say it, for their different reasons.

'It's getting the connections in place that's the problem. When She's here – not too long now – I'm hoping we can persuade more of them that it's beginning to take shape in private and that this time we mean it. The Unionists in Belfast who'll resist any deal with Dublin are putting on the pressure, but fortunately London's brouhaha doesn't touch us here.

'You see my problem. If anything blows up – not literally, please God – and disturbs all that, we're back to square one. More blood in the streets, another generation poisoned. Failure stretching a long way into the future, and the costs, don't even think about them. That's why my experience this week, though I'm happy to have got the message, worries me. When someone like the man we're talking about is trying to contact me after years have gone by, my first feeling is that it's unlikely to be good news. Right?'

Keane agreed.

'And at the same time, *exactly* the same bloody moment, if you can believe the coincidence, there's an alarm bell sounding, rung by Angleton, of all the old rogues, about the one guy that we've got among the Russians who can tell us what's happening, just when the whole show there is on the turn. We both know that London's investing heavily in the new regime. Wondering how best and how far to snuggle up.

'We can't let that chance go. And we know more about Mr Reform in the Kremlin than we've ever known about his predecessors, thanks to our man – and, believe me, in the White House they're jealous as hell. They've got no source that compares with ours, though they don't like admitting it, and it drives them nuts. Fact. And when Herself arrives here in a few weeks, she's going to be able to boast like billy-oh about it. Politely, of course. And the old boy across town will have to lap it up, which he will, because he melts in front of her. So his people will have to do the same, most of them anyway.

'We're at the kind of moment when our lords and masters back home can see progress. Everything they're brought up to deliver, and put in their memoirs. It's amazing, isn't it, Patrick, how you can trump all the economic stuff – all the aches and pains of people's lives – if you can burble on about a tide of history that carries us along. Especially if you can persuade yourself just for a moment that you can command the waves. And, of course, all the better if you've got some secrets to boast about.

'It allows us to say we're not a post-imperial irrelevance, but the real thing. You could say it's a way of keeping a place at the top table. For a little while longer, anyway.'

He broke off to pour some treacly coffee from the pot he kept heated.

'Which is why you and I are finding ourselves in the biggest potential fuck-up either of us is ever likely to know. Our government's passport to Moscow may go missing. And back home, we might lose our chance to wind down that dirty war that's been rolling along for three hundred years, more or less.

'Because, on Ireland, something may have gone wrong, just when we were hoping it was turning, slowly, the other way. I'll tell you right now that I may get closer to the answer in Chicago. More of that later. There's a plan.'

Keane waved a hand. 'OK. I see the big picture. But on the Soviets, I can't see why Angleton has got you so worked up.'

Softly, because he wanted Keane to know he was confiding, Flemyng said, 'You're right. There was something I didn't tell you about him. It's why I got you back here.'

He had Keane where he wanted him, and leaned forward.

'It's not just that he says our man's name is known to some people here – which infuriates me, and which is a mystery we'll have to solve, because it's going to send the Barracks into meltdown – but something much worse. He tells me that the Americans may have sprung a leak – maybe even inside the Agency – that could lead straight to Moscow. So he claims. His message to me is that it means our man may be blown out of the sky.

'And all by our friends – an American administration that has hung on his every word, and a president who drools about what Brits can still bring to Washington. Think about that.'

'But Angleton sees Russian spies in every 7-Eleven,' Keane said.

'So he does. They dance around in his head, night and day,' Flemyng said, 'but how do I know he's wrong this time?'

'Sorry to be pedantic, but if our man were exposed, what would we do?' Keane said.

Flemyng was happy with a pupil at his feet. 'We'd have to get him out before it happened. Before he was tortured and, after a painful time, shot. Because, how much might he tell them about us – the people, the places, the methods – before the last walk to wherever they choose to do it these days?

'But we've also got to protect him. Gratitude, obviously, and because of the promise we gave him of freedom in the West. But – and I'm afraid this is even more important – if Angleton's right, the fallout will screw up our relations with this town, infuriate Herself, and undermine the reformers in the Kremlin. We'd be picking up the pieces for years.

'Imagine if our guy was blown, and it got out that he'd been betrayed by our dearest allies, who're not even supposed to know his name? Shit everywhere is a crude description. But apt.

'I should tell you that there's a rickety plan in place to get him out if we have to, detailed as hell and dreamed up years ago. "Exfiltration" in Barracks-speak. It was put together when we realised that he might end up near the centre of things, and become precious, which he has. The problem is hardly anyone thinks it will work. People I know think there's a one-in-ten chance that we could get away with it – a six-hundred-mile car chase, that kind of thing. And if we were caught at it... well, the whole thing gets even worse. Bad for us, and for the new guy in the Kremlin, whom we hope may turn out to be a friend.

'Get it?'

Keane raised the obvious objection to his gloom, aware that he was digging deep into his natural optimism. 'But why should we believe Angleton? He's a fantasist.'

'The problem, young man, is that we can't afford not to,' said Flemyng. He drained his cup.

'How are things back at home?' Keane asked as he got up, getting his breath back.

'Francesca's fine and dandy. She'll be there for another week at least. One of the kids is having settling-in problems at school. We spoke this morning. Thanks for asking. Mungo in Scotland seems to be happy with himself, and getting stronger day by day. I meant to ring this afternoon, but it's a bit late now. I'll give him a call tomorrow.

He looked up at the clock. 'It's nearly midnight in Perthshire. Lucky Mungo, he'll be having an untroubled sleep.'

Seven

THE NEXT MORNING FLEMYNG HAD A LITTLE TIME OF peace before the storm broke.

He went into the residence garden earlier than usual, not long after the sun came up. He walked for a while, thought about Chicago and what he wanted to bring back. He saw no one else for almost half an hour, walking through the trees, watching the chipmunks capering in the oaks and the Japanese maples, and turning to a paperback he took from his pocket. He sat on a bench near one of the beds filled with roses, their early buds starting to swell. He was seldom without a book when he was alone, and when he settled into his place in the garden anyone spying him from the house would mark him down as content.

He wore a light jacket against the cool of the morning, but the weather was on the turn, and there was cheering light and a hint of coming warmth. Spirits around the place would surely rise after the weekend. On getting up, he'd spent a few minutes sending a detailed message to Lucy – she expected them on Sundays, as on any other day – with thoughts about their Chicago schedule. He added a particular instruction that would puzzle her further, but he knew she would choose to wait for an explanation rather than push him now. In the meantime, she'd make the arrangement he wanted.

He had opened the doors from the house to the terrace and at eight o'clock, from inside, he heard the musical tinkle of a clock striking the hour.

It seemed to him that it was almost exactly on the last chime that his valet, in dress-down Sunday gear, appeared at the top of the steps, evidently ruffled. 'A call, sir. Foreign Office chief clerk.'

Stepping through the door, he felt an immediate onset of concern and the atmosphere around him changed. A flow of material would have arrived for his red box overnight, as it did each morning, rain or shine, but it was odd to get a phone call from London at that time on a Sunday. A foreign secretary panic at this hour? Unlikely. Something in the papers that would frighten the horses in Washington? A prime ministerial conversation later? It wouldn't be the first time, but it was rare to have no warning. Nothing on the front pages he had scanned when they'd been dropped outside his bedroom at six had caused him to prepare for trouble.

Resisting the urge to rush, he walked deliberately to the library.

The telephone console near his corner chair was blinking red. He sat and lifted the receiver.

'Good morning, Ambassador. My name's Heckler, Francis Heckler. Duty clerk in the office. Sorry to call at such an hour on a Sunday.'

'That's fine, Francis. Good morning. Washington's up and about,' Flemyng said crisply. 'What can I do for you?'

'I'm afraid, sir, it's personal.'

Flemyng knew on the instant that he would remember this moment. Everything around him seemed to take on an extra stillness that emphasised the calm he had been enjoying, and then turned it by some alchemy into a tingling threat. The walls, as he'd put it to Keane, were threatening to close in and crush him.

A rush of alarms. Francesca? The boys? Their faces floated in front of him.

He felt a shock that was making him tremble.

'It's your brother, sir. But I should tell you first of all that he's alive.'

This was hardly how Flemyng would have scripted the sentence for the young duty clerk, although it served its purpose. Mungo. Where and what? Another electric surge passed through him.

'Heart attack?' He found the words surprisingly difficult.

'No, sir, I'm afraid it's rather more complicated and unusual, if I may put it like that.'

Flemyng half wanted to tell Heckler, whoever he was, to get on with it, but he recognised something original in the word 'unusual' that suggested a character who – astonishingly – he was beginning to like for no identifiable reason, even at a distance of three thousand miles and after a conversation of less than half a minute. This was bad news of some kind, but he was listening to a young man and not a machine, one who was probably shaking as he held the phone.

'You'll have to explain,' Flemyng said gently.

'A physical attack, sir, I'm afraid. At home in Perthshire. Two men broke into the house. They were armed. For quite a time they held your brother – and the other man, Mr Babb, I hope I'm correct about that – as hostages, so it seems. They haven't been seriously harmed. Tied up roughly, and very shaken, of course. That's a concern, I'm told.'

'Hostages, you said?' Flemyng's shock was tangible.

Then, assailed by a jumble of images and unsure how to sort them out, he turned immediately matter-of-fact. Step by step. 'How did you get the news?'

'A parish priest – Father MacNeil, would that be right? – called at the house a little over an hour ago to see your brother, and enquire after his health. Apparently he's in the habit of dropping by on Sundays. Came across the scene. Helped as best he could, and got the emergency number for the office your brother was keeping to hand, which is a blessing. The priest was very disturbed, of course, but took charge with good sense and speed.

'The telephone line had been cut, inside the house, so he drove to a farm nearby to ring us. The neighbours were alarmed, of course, and went back with him. Tea and sympathy, lit a fire and so on. Within the last hour. I'm told an ambulance is on its way to deal with the two... gentlemen.'

'Police?' Flemyng said.

'We hope officers will be there by now. They were left in no doubt about the urgency, you can be sure. And naturally, we're discussing security arrangements at this end. It's an open line, sir... so...'

'Of course. We'll set up a secure call for a little later, but I need to know more about my brother. Will he have to go to hospital?'

Heckler said they would both be taken in to be checked over. Special Branch from Edinburgh – who'd be there in less than two hours – would reconnect the phone line and secure the house. Mungo was going to have to live with them now, Flemyng knew. Perhaps they would never leave.

Then after a pause during which Flemyng could hear him breathing hard, as if he was preparing to get to the point after dealing with preliminaries, Heckler said, 'I'm sorry to say, Ambassador, that there seems to be a terrorist angle.'

'I'm sure of it,' Flemyng said, wearily.

Heckler said that he or a superior would explain further on the secure call.

'No need to apologise for anything,' Flemyng said. 'Here's what I want to happen. I must talk to my brother as soon as possible, and obviously right now please pass on through the police my best wishes and my love – my *love* – if you can help with that. Thank you. A private line can surely be got up from the hospital if necessary. I'd be grateful for an account from Special Branch of what seems to have happened, as soon as they can. In case things go... badly wrong, I'll take the precaution of booking a flight to London tonight. Let's hope it won't be necessary. There are matters that require me to stay in Washington. And I assume you're informing security here at the embassy. They'll want to take coordinated steps.'

Heckler said that was happening as they spoke, and as if on cue Flemyng saw through the open door his chief security officer appearing in the corridor outside the library. Besuited, dark tie, glossy shoes, as if he'd been waiting for the word. He stopped at the door, giving a nod of reassurance, and stood aside to give an indication that he had no need to overhear a private conversation. Flemyng gestured him in, then pointed to the mouthpiece of the telephone. 'Chief clerk's office... come in, Tony.'

Back on the phone, he offered a thank you, and although it was unnecessary he said to Heckler, 'I'd like you to know that my brother is a gentle man, not one for the rough and tumble, and this will be awful for him. You have my gratitude, and he will be appreciative.' Thus leaving Heckler feeling thoroughly content with the way he had handled his task, he was promised an update within the hour. Dialling Lucy's number, he was not surprised to get no reply. He rang Keane's apartment.

'We have a problem here, Patrick. Personal, and serious. Now. I'm sorry, but could you both come to the residence as soon as you can? There are calls to make. Thinking to be done.

'I do need you here.' He said nothing more.

Before he turned to Tony Pringle to talk about security, he wrote down five questions. on the pad beside him. They were the first that would have to be answered. Top of the list was one word, with a query. 'Hostages?'

'Well, here we go,' he said. 'All change.'

Pringle, ex-military with a shaved and shiny head that looked like an armoured shell, was all-seeing around the embassy. He never seemed off-guard, and Flemyng trusted him without encouraging intimacy. Officer–men relations suited them both.

'Indeed, sir. At least it's Sunday,' Pringle replied. 'That helps. Dead quiet all around and nothing untoward seen on the streets. Yet. We're on top of it. But please, sir, no long walks today. That's out, and not just for now. We'll have a better idea of what's happened by the afternoon.'

'But I wonder when we'll know why?' Flemyng said.

'I'm worried about Chicago,' Pringle offered. 'Lucy says you're bound there on Tuesday.'

'And I still am, Tony, full stop,' Flemyng replied with no hesitation, and without any inflection implying he wanted an answer. 'We'll just have to cope. I'm sure you can handle it.'

Before Lucy and Patrick arrived, he made sure they would

be catered for through the day. They'd all have lunch together, and remain in the residence. Senior staff would come in the afternoon to plan the week. By habit, he began to establish a centre of operations, with his library as headquarters. In truth, the place needed little organisation but Flemyng got succour from the idea. The empty residence, without the rest of his family for more than a week, turned once more into a busy hive.

The plan for the days ahead began with breakfast when they were shown in. First, he said Lucy should book him on the six o'clock flight to London. 'Let's hope I won't be on it, but I have to be ready. More in a minute or two.'

Keane had tried to plaster down his hair. Lucy was in new blue jeans and a bright-red shirt. They looked as if they were ready for exercise. Sport. Flemyng sat them down, and gestured to the fresh pot of coffee. A table was quickly laid and a simple breakfast brought in, while they all waited in an edgy silence.

When the staff had gone, Flemyng said, 'A tricky story, and a bad one. Last night there was an assault at home on Mungo and his companion in the house, Arthur. Armed men. Provos, almost certainly. They weren't beaten, so it appears, but tied up. As for long-term damage to them, I don't yet know. But even in the summary from the office, I realise they're certain of one thing.

'This wasn't a robbery. Mungo was the target, personally.'

'The office called them "hostages".'

Keane was messing up his hair now, worrying it with his hands. 'What was the demand?'

'None that I've heard of, so far,' Flemyng said. 'That's my question, too.'

'A note?' said Lucy

65

'And that's my second question. No indication from the office.' Flemyng, as Lucy had seen him at other moments of crisis, showed no outward sign of alarm. Instead, his voice had softened. His eyes seemed even darker, the lines that gave his face its length stood out more strongly. He spoke at a gentle pace, as if he was trying to protect them from the feelings that were running through him. They watched him finding a rhythm that would stay the course.

'From what the office says – we'll have a proper team call in an hour or two, and I want you both on it – we're in Irish territory. After the last few days, what else could we expect? But why like this, exactly? If the Provos wanted to kill Mungo they could have done it easily. There's no one for a mile around or more and it was the middle of the night. They could be off and away and in Manchester or somewhere by now. But they seem to have wanted them both to survive. And Tony P says there's been no message here. No threat, ransom talk, nothing. They came and they went. Leaving a scared man – two scared men – who have no idea what this was about.'

'Have you?' Keane said.

'Not much. Except I know there's bound to be a Chicago chapter in this story.'

Lucy said something quietly. She was startled.

As was his habit whenever he began a long discussion, he took care to act as the host who would set the pace, and modulate the conversation. 'I'll have to set the scene for you,' he said. Leaving the table and taking the china coffee pot to the side table near where they now sat together on the sofa, he introduced them to the episode of Charlie Farrell and the Georgetown drink that had been so awkward for the congressman and such a relief to him.

'I don't know how Charlie was persuaded to get in touch, and how willing or not he was to get involved. But that's for later. He spun a yarn about someone who wants to be in touch. An old acquaintance. Naturally I hoped it was the message I've been waiting for since the funeral. Sure enough, Charlie produced a titbit from the past that was designed to convince me. A reference to an old ship that used to limp across from Larne to Stranraer. *Antrim Princess*. We met on her more than once. So everything looks kosher.

'It's him all right. Charlie gave me the wrong name, but that's my friend's protective instinct at work. I passed on the information about where I'm going to be on Tuesday. I expect him to be there. Wouldn't you, after all this?

'The question we've got to consider, although I don't think there's a chance of answering it right now, is whether there's a link between his approach to me, and what's happened to Mungo. We've got to assume there is, though it's not obvious to me what it might be. Notice the most important fact. They didn't kill him. Think about it. It would have been easy to push him over the edge. He's not a well man, with a dodgy heart. But they went away, and let him be. Apart from tying him up.'

Lucy, whose time with Flemyng dated back a full decade, stepped in with comfort. She recalled her times with Mungo in London – at another moment of drama – and gave Flemyng some words of comradeship that she knew he would want. Even more than Keane, she understood how deep the wound must be, and how raw. Flemyng's older brother was his responsibility: he had always felt so, maybe because of guilt. He hadn't wanted to hide behind the veil that had fallen between them when he slipped into the secret world in his twenties, but accepted the inevitable distance it put between him and the family. Mungo knew the outline of Flemyng's life, but none of the details of its rigours and pain. Though he did sense its moments of exhilaration, enough to be content about his brother and his world.

'Is he in good hands?' she said. 'Everybody cares about him.'

'Thanks, Lucy,' Flemyng said. 'You'd adore him, Patrick, incidentally. He'd love your collection, apart from anything else. I'll find out soon how he's come through this.'

One brother buried on Monday, the other held at gunpoint in the same week. Lucy was expecting to be asked what she thought it meant for him.

Instead, he said, 'Before we have this phone call, when I have questions to ask, we'll talk about Chicago.

'Here's my feeling at whatever it is – half past nine on Sunday morning,' he said, looking up. 'First of all, this trip is going to be quite different and considerably more complicated than I'd hoped. I'm happy about hearing from my Irish friend but we've now got to deal with the fallout from what happened at Altnabuie. I'm going to travel, absolutely, but I know Tony P and his boys will insist just as strongly on the kind of security I don't want. Not quite sleeping outside my bedroom door, but more or less.

'There's no chance that I can stop them. The office wouldn't stand for it. But I'm damned if I'm going to talk to Tony or anyone else about my friend. That's for me alone, and both of you up to a point. It stops with us, and that has to be our rule.

'There's too much at stake.'

'So, Patrick, I've got a fieldman's job for you. We need a plan. A clever one, if you please.'

Lucy mentioned the request she'd got from him the

previous day. Why did you want me to book a different hotel for myself?'

Flemyng was smiling. 'It should be even more obvious now. Before this personal security blanket was dropped over my bloody head, I was planning to have my meeting away from my hotel, just for safety's sake. You could give me your key. Long ago, Patrick, I wasn't just like you for nothing. Old habits. 'But it's going to be much more tricky now.

'You need to work this out, young man. How. If I'm right, I can only get to the root of this thing – Abel's death, the funeral, the old friend from nowhere, and I'm sure Mungo's troubles, too – if I can find a way to operate alone. I need help from you two, but if everyone gets involved, it'll fall apart at the hands of the machine. Inevitably. I – *we* – learn nothing, and we screw up the politics of our own ancient little war. The one we have to bring to an end, however long it takes.'

Keane enjoyed Flemyng on politics, from his delight in gossip from London to the pen pictures he liked to draw, in pencil as well as in words, of the cabinet. He'd taken some time to delve with care into Flemyng's few years as a minister. The cuttings, the stories. The legends of his smooth manoeuvres in the Whitehall jungle.

The political newcomer, with a past that was intriguingly shorn of detail, had risen fast at first, then become becalmed for a time when the speculation that he was heading for the top started to dry up, and just when his energy seemed to be flooding back, he'd found himself pulled out of government and awarded the embassy. Where, Keane suspected, he was happier. It had been a spectacular leap onto a different stage, bringing in its wake all the jealousy that Flemyng knew he would attract, but in Keane's short experience he'd begun to understand his boss. Not through ideological impulses that had to be satisfied, but by recognising an instinctively political animal who wanted to understand the mechanisms of persuasion and change, how ambitions and delusions could be turned to use.

Keane also believed that Flemyng, were he to be asked to get to the heart of it, would go back to the crisis, just about a decade earlier, that brought down one of his friends and killed him, ripping a personal network apart. A time that revealed bleakly the weaknesses and sometimes the venality of colleagues. The full story was only known to a few, and to most of them only in crude outline. Keane and his friends had been introduced to the drama, and its blood – with the important names changed, and some details omitted – as part of the folklore of their trade, fed to them to keep their appetites alive. Not as a warning, but for encouragement. And the greatest lure of all was to be reminded that in the outside world, even to most of Westminster, almost none of it was known to have taken place at all.

No wonder Flemyng wore his confidence so comfortably.

Once, when the boss had been talking to Keane about life in the Barracks in his time, he passed on a truth – no other word would do, he said – given to him by one of his early guides, whose coat he had held on the battlefield. It was Freddy Craven – he'd served in Vienna and later in Paris at his side, and loved him – who convinced him that the fascination of their trade, beyond any absorption in business on the street, was in watching and trying to explain what he always called the riddle of power. Freddy, long gone to his reward, thought that was the beginning and end of it. 'You'll discover it, too,' Flemyng had told Keane.

And here they were again, wondering why.

Sitting in the drawing room, with the shocks and excitement

of that Sunday beginning to crowd in on him, Keane was startled to realise that Flemyng had barely mentioned the central mystery, from which everything flowed.

What had happened to Abel in that Chicago street, and why?

Lucy often told them that she worked out when Flemyng's emotions were in a heightened state, and his concentration at its most deadly, not by looking at his face, which became impassive whenever he wanted, or even by watching the way he moved or spoke. She said it was when, by an instinct that pulsed outside his conscious mind, he reached to touch his scar, the one he'd got in Vienna two decades earlier, out in the street when it had all gone wrong in an operation planned by Freddy Craven himself, after which he'd limped back to the embassy in agony in the dark, wounded by a slash from his shoulder to his breast that could have killed him. It remained a stubborn scar, through all the adventures that followed, and a reminder of how close he'd stepped – in a moment that was wild but thrilling – to the edge of the abyss.

In the hurly-burly of that Sunday, with Lucy making telephone calls in the corner of the library, he and Flemyng throwing around some outline plans for Chicago, where he was beginning to be convinced they would be operating together, the history seemed to play across the walls like an old movie. He couldn't separate Flemyng's meticulous account of Farrell's conversation, and his musings on Angleton that interspersed their conversation in recent days, without thinking of the stories from the past.

Flemyng drew up thoughts for the staff meeting later, and Keane asked if he could absent himself from it because he'd arranged to meet Cotton for a drink. A repair job was needed. Flemyng agreed.

Keane took a chance.

'Can I tell him I'll be in Chicago with you, and he'll be in charge of the station?'

'Certainly. You're going first thing tomorrow,' as if there had never been any doubt in his mind.

He added, 'I want you out there before me. I'll tell you why when we get together after the staff meeting.'

Lucy came across from the writing desk where she'd been making her calls.

'There's news from Scotland.'

Eight

THE CHOREOGRAPHY QUICKENED. FLEMYNG HAD ASKED Lucy and Keane to step into the garden promptly while he took the waiting call. Now he beckoned both of them back into the library.

'I've talked to a doctor. He was as reassuring as he could be.'

Lucy asked if that meant Mungo was going to come through it in decent shape.

'Yes is the answer to that, as far as we can tell. He's been badly thrown, but hasn't been bashed about. No blood or broken bones or anything of that kind. They've wired him up and his heart seems to be pumping away reasonably happily.

'He's lucky.'

Lucy asked when Flemyng might be able to talk to him.

'That's where it gets frustrating, frankly. I've now got a phone number at the hospital in Edinburgh. I'm supposed to ring at one o'clock our time, so in less than an hour. But the doctor said two things that don't help us especially.

'One is that I shouldn't alarm him in any way – for reasons that I understand, of course – and two, judging by what Mungo has said so far about what happened and his reaction to it, that he doesn't want to go into detail about what was said by the intruders. That has to wait.'

When Keane appeared to hesitate before saying something, Flemyng intervened. 'I agree, Patrick. Unfortunate. I want to know how they approached him, everything they said and did, all the words in detail, the threats – which there must have been, surely – and, frankly, anything they said about me. Because I'm the point of it, obviously.

'I may be able to get something from him. A steer.'

'Of course,' Keane said. 'But your brother's health is more important right now.'

Flemyng, whom Lucy could see had darkened into what she knew was a mood with a hint of anger, said. 'Indeed, Patrick. I know that.'

Keane, less of a Flemyng student than Lucy, didn't know how to take the response. Resignation? Frustration? Bitterness?

Flemyng sighed. 'Here's what I suggest. There's a sandwich lunch or something going to be laid out next door. You get stuck into that, and I'll stay here. I imagine my conversation with the hospital won't last more than a few minutes. The doctor's going to be on hand, no doubt ready to jump in. So, we're back here at twenty past one.'

Then, as he turned towards the garden, he gave them work to do.

'Patrick, it's an early flight for you to Chicago tomorrow morning. Lucy, I want you to get the police chief – personally, preferably – to alert the hotel that Patrick's got to be given every assistance in making arrangements for me. As far as everyone in Chicago is concerned, he's a senior first secretary here who's looking after me on the trip. Nothing more than that. They'll oblige, I guarantee. Now – it's adjoining suites for Patrick and me at the Blackstone. Fix it. I know the hotel, a genteel old lady who hasn't changed much in recent years, and they have good small suites on the upper floors. Remind them of a previous visit when I had a good view of the lake, and thanked them for it afterwards. They'll have the letter on file.

'Lucy, I told you I want you elsewhere. Book the Hilton for yourself. Just a step down Michigan Avenue. All clear? Thanks both.

'Now, I'll get on with family business.'

Lucy said to Keane, as they closed the door behind them, 'You see the change? In an hour?'

Flemyng was alone. For half an hour he played with plans for Chicago in his head, writing nothing down but concentrating hard enough to sit almost immobile in the library, without ever reaching for a cup of coffee or a glass of water. He felt the outline of a plan.

He watched for the hour, and the switchboard was ready to put through the call.

'Ambassador, thank you for ringing. Mr Mackay here again, consultant. Since we spoke, you'll be pleased to hear that all has progressed as we would have hoped. Mr Flemyng is with me, well tucked up I should say, and anxious to hear your voice.'

'As I am his. Thank you, doctor,' Flemyng said.

After a pause – a thin, faraway voice.

'Will, I'm so sorry.'

'For goodness' sake – no, Mungo. I just want to know about you and Babble. No competitive apologies, old friend.

I'm glad they've got you… plugged in or wired up or whatever they do.' He could see his brother's smile.

'They have,' said Mungo, 'and apparently I'm ticking along at about the right pace. They'll let me home the day after tomorrow, all being well. But Babble's had a hard knock, Will. It was a terrible shock, and he feels a certain responsibility, which is daft but we can both understand it. We're all wondering why it couldn't have been different.

'They do say he'll be fine as long as he can get some rest. So we're lucky boys.'

Flemyng said, gently, that he didn't want to revisit the attack.

'But there's one thing I should tell you now,' Mungo said, without any prompting.

Flemyng said nothing. Waited while Mungo took his time.

'They seemed to know about dealings you had in Northern Ireland. The Troubles. But I could be honest with them, of course. I know so little. I did say you'd had a few fishing trips, years ago. Fermanagh, wasn't it?'

'Anything else?' Flemyng kept his voice as level as he could.

'They asked if anyone had visited you from there, years ago. I do recall one weekend – but it's been so long…'

'What did you tell them?' Flemyng asked, working to sound calm.

'Just that I couldn't remember any visit, which is true. Almost.'

Flemyng could imagine Mungo in his hospital bed, his familiar smile stealing back

'Did they push you?' his brother asked.

'A little,' Mungo said. 'But they weren't so much putting facts to me. They were fishing around.'

Flemyng said he knew how such conversations went. They

agreed they should leave a detailed conversation about the whole business when Mungo was safely at home at Altnabuie, but Flemyng did ask, apologetically, if there was anything else he needed to know about first.

'They asked if you had a spy across the water,' Mungo said. 'I remember the phrase.'

Flemyng said nothing, and Mungo spoke again, into the silence. 'Still there?'

'Yes, hearing you,' his brother said. 'How did you answer that?'

'I said I didn't know what they were talking about,' said Mungo. 'Again, almost true.'

The doctor came on the line.

'I'm going to ask you both to draw this to a close, if you don't mind. We need you to rest here, my Mr Flemyng, and we really must call it a day now. Ambassador, if I may, might I suggest a call tomorrow at around the same time if it's possible at your end? That would suit everyone here.'

'Of course.' Through the doctor the brothers said goodbye.

Flemyng stayed on the line for a minute or so, felt all the distance in the echo.

Soon, Lucy knocked on the door. 'How is he?'

'Remarkable, really,' Flemyng said. 'They're watching him. But home in a day or two. He's coming through.'

'That's good news,' Keane said. 'Anything I need to know?'

'Not yet.' Flemyng waved them away. Keane put his arm on Lucy's shoulder, and they walked quietly together down the long hall. In the silence, he felt her trembling.

Nine

GUY COTTON HAD AN APARTMENT ON 18TH STREET AND Keane met him round the corner at the Tabard Inn. They took two wing chairs in a quiet corner of the lobby, from where they could see the front door. The afternoon crowd was thin enough to give them privacy. Two beers were brought to them.

Tall Guy Cotton was relaxed and smiling, with no sign of anxiety. In jeans and loafers, with a striped rugby shirt, looking as if he'd been settled in the chair for an hour, a stranger might have thought that he was the host. It was Keane, scruffier and less easy all round, who was unusually on edge.

'Cheers,' Guy said. 'I'm glad I've got a chance to say something away from the office. I've been hit a bit by the changes, but you need to know, Patrick, that it's nothing to do with you. We carry on, and I'm happy for you. Genuinely.' He drank. 'I mean it.'

Keane had prepared a few words. 'We all get a hit from time to time, Guy. I'm sorry if you've felt as if you've been rolled over. I'll do everything I can to make it work. That's my job. Duty, I suppose, without wanting to sound pompous. We know each other well enough to come sailing through. Lots to do.

'You know that this week, you're in charge? From tomorrow. I'm off to Chicago at the crack of dawn.'

'With the boss?' Cotton asked. 'I thought it was Tuesday.'

'I have things to prepare,' Keane said. He added, 'Any games in play that you want to talk about? Anything promising?'

Cotton made a gesture to push it away. 'Not the moment, is it? Clearing the air seems a bit more important, for both of us. So, when you're back. OK? You'll be wondering about my relationship with the boss… after all this.'

Keane gulped his beer.

'I won't pretend we're the happiest pair,' Cotton said. 'He seemed distant on Friday. It's going to be quite hard to get back to where we were. And I'm afraid he probably knows what I think.'

'Which is?' Keane said.

'That sometimes – quite often, in fact – he's a prize shit.'

Avoiding confrontation, which was generally Keane's way, he said, 'I wouldn't take this episode as evidence of that. An awkward choice had to made, that's all. Couldn't please everybody.'

But Cotton, he saw, had come ready to open up. They ordered more beers.

'I know you want to be loyal, Patrick. Admirable. So do I, up to a point. But I've got some history, you'll remember. My secondment to cabinet office.'

'Working for Roland Saviour,' Keane said.

'The same,' Cotton replied. '*Sir* Roland, as of last month. You do know that there's no love lost there?'

'I'd gathered,' said Keane, who knew only one side of the story.

Saviour took shape in his mind in an instant. Rotund, and physically the largest man by far in the prime minister's circle, with a haystack of unruly grey hair and the pink cheeks of a much younger man. He had made himself Mr Security, so he was feared, as much for his cleverness as his power. He rolled into rooms like a bulldozer. Ministers were trained not to cross him, but he liked to cross them.

'Saviour fought against the boss getting the embassy,' Cotton said. 'Hard. I remember because I was in cabinet office at the time. Thought it was window-dressing. Said Flemyng wasn't the right fit. It's personal, for some reason. Spends a lot of time doing him down.

'Anyway, they're oil and water.'

Then Cotton added, 'And you know he's heading our way?'

Keane tried to conceal his surprise as best he could.

Cotton said, 'Week after next, I'm told. It's going to be worth watching. Two smoothies at each other's throats.'

Keane behaved as if nothing was new to him. 'Steady on, Guy. They both want the summit to work. They're both realists, on the same side.'

'True,' Cotton said. 'But I'm a student of Saviour. He's got a long memory. I wouldn't expect any generosity of spirit.' He smiled. 'We'll see what the boss is made of. Not a good enemy to have, I'd say.'

'From my experience, Saviour's quite an operator. Impressive. Surprisingly warm, when you know him. Obviously, we keep in touch.'

With Keane struggling to keep his discomfort from showing, and dampening down his rage, Cotton added,

'Everything else serene around the place? I'll drop in on Jack Whealdon at the FBI this week. Pass on your regards.'

'Anything Irish you want me to look at?'

'Nothing pressing,' Keane said. 'Worry not a jot.'

He finished his glass, and said he had to get back to the embassy. He walked all the way from 18th Street, trying to calm himself as he went. He was grateful for the time before he reached the embassy.

Back in his office, he went through the cables from London in response to his queries about the New York photographs. His colleagues at home were sure of their identification of the white-haired young man who'd left the bar with Sullivan as Cathal Earley, but it surprised them because they'd had no indication he was on the move. He was on every watch list. 'Hard-boiled,' the note from Belfast said, 'with a reputation.'

Another mystery remained – the man who had been photographed entering the Star of the Sea and hadn't come out. He'd been bent forward against the rain as he hurried from a cab and his face couldn't be captured. It was assumed he might be one of the regulars concealed under a coat, but his figure didn't appear to fit any of the pictures on file, which was puzzling.

When he and Lucy met Flemyng at six o'clock, the confusions were circling in his mind.

Lucy reported that everything in Chicago was ready. The mayor's office, even on a Sunday, had confirmed an appointment for Wednesday morning. The police superintendent's deputy would meet Flemyng at lunchtime on Tuesday to take him to the street where Abel was attacked.

'Where he died, you mean,' Flemyng said.

'Of course,' said Lucy, looking down. 'Somewhere on the

West Side, beyond Ukrainian Village. They'll have a proper briefing for you. Everything that's been discovered since.

'You asked about the Art Institute. If you want private time there, that's easily arranged after hours. There's a Hopper show. I've said we'll confirm on Tuesday.'

Flemyng was at the writing desk in the corner of the library. 'Now let me bring you both up to date. After the staff meeting, I spoke to the Special Branch inspector who's taken charge in Perthshire.

'It was odd to hear the phone ringing at home. For a moment it was as if nothing had happened.

'Anyway, he seems to be on the ball. From what I heard from Mungo earlier, and now from SB after his conversations, I've got a decent idea of what happened.'

Keane said, 'Can you take it from the beginning?'

'Two men, faces covered, both with handguns. Arrived between eleven and twelve. Pitch dark. Walked in, woke them both up, got them dressed and into the drawing room. I'm amazed one of them didn't pass out. Anyway, tied their hands with rope, snipped the phone wire and settled down to talk.

'Their accents left no doubt, apparently.

'A weird scene. They said no one would be harmed, but any funny business and they'd do what had to be done. Those were the words. Then they put Mungo through the wringer.

'Asked him directly about my dealings with Northern Ireland. Was I involved in action against the Provos? Was I army in disguise – can you think of a more pointless question than that? – and what was I up to in the early seventies?

'My brother couldn't recall precisely the sequence of questions. They did seem to know quite a bit about me, but Mungo, historian that he is, thought it sounded as if they'd just mugged up a few facts from public sources, or had a basic briefing. They didn't seem to *know* me, he said. Not in anything but the barest outline.

'And, of course, as far as my work goes, that's true of Mungo, too. Which is a sadness to me, but it comes with the rations I'm afraid, as you both know. Of course, on this occasion it was a blessing because there was genuinely nothing much he could tell them. He simply doesn't know.

'But we can tell something from their questions. They knew I'd visited Northern Ireland. Fishing trips, Mungo called them, and, of course, in a way he was right.

'The stickiest moment must have been when they asked if anyone from there had visited Altnabuie with me. Mungo dissembled – he does remember one visit, though he was away for most of it, and it sounds as if he batted it away with style. But it's interesting that they didn't have a date, far less a name. Mungo sailed through unscathed, it seems.'

'Conclusion?' Keane asked.

'They don't know very much. They have the scent and there's a hunt on in their ranks. Mungo said they asked him straight out – did I have a spy across the water?'

'Piquant,' Keane said.

Flemyng gave him a questioning look.

Keane added, 'Well, you're now the spy across the water yourself.'

'Just a different pond,' Lucy said, trying to lift the atmosphere, and failing.

Flemyng said, 'And so this brings us straight to our friend, whom I expect to see in Chicago.'

'We're going to be tested, boss,' Keane said, with an obvious relish that he half tried to conceal.

'And so is he,' Flemyng replied. 'Remember that. Please.'

There was a natural pause. Keane had been wondering

when to interrupt, and had decided that waiting would be worse. So he said, 'I've got some London news I need to pass on.'

Something in his tone excited Flemyng, who could see his discomfort. 'You can tell me now,' he said.

'Saviour is coming to see us,' Keane said.

Flemyng sat up with a start. 'And no one's told me? Hell's bells.' He slapped his desk hard.

'How did you find out?'

'Cotton heard on the grapevine,' Keane said, awkwardly.

So they had to talk about Saviour. He appeared to have created the post of security adviser for himself and become a gregarious presence in any Whitehall corridor where secret servants and soldiers might do business. Usually cheerful, with oyster eyes and that layered pile of grey hair, he had a tenor voice that rose from the depths of his substantial girth, and his memory was known to be near-flawless, particularly when it came to the intimate history of combatants who had tried, nearly always without success, to rein him in.

He scooped up the gossip from every embassy that mattered, entertained well at home in Primrose Hill, and seemed able to be at the theatre more often than anyone else, all without disrupting the rhythm of days in the office that began well before eight, there to start another day of political intelligence-gathering and manoeuvring across every flank of the Whitehall pitch. Saviour had matured and was at his peak – drinking well, as Flemyng liked to say. It was known by everyone who mattered that any hint of a problem carrying with it the faintest whiff of security would pass across Saviour's desk before the last judgement. More often than not it was he who wrote the verdict. In truth, there was hardly a minister who could match his powers.

The cast in his left eye was disconcerting, causing it to swivel down and away to the side while he simultaneously looked straight ahead with the other. But being unable to disguise the squint, he made it play to his advantage with jokes about skewed sightlines. To anyone with less bravado, it was another display of authority and an unanswerable putdown.

Keane said, with a slight hesitation, 'Can I ask you, frankly, how you assess him right now?'

'Same as I always have,' Flemyng shot back. 'Clever as a snake, and just as venomous.'

Keane was still showing signs of his short and disturbed night, with tie askew and an unironed shirt. Lucy saw, to her surprise, that he was struggling for fluency. She said, 'How much will you tell him?'

'I'd suggest that depends how much I know when he gets here,' Flemyng replied, unhelpfully. 'We've got ten days or so – if you've got it right – to get ourselves in order.

'On the other matter – Angleton and his witterings – I'm not going to make a fool of myself until I find out more.' Lucy noticed that Flemyng assumed that she'd been told the whole story by Keane. It was more evidence of the tangle of secrets that now bound them together. She knew of old that it was the kind of obligation he liked to impose. Turning them into a gang; he'd always wanted blood brothers around him.

Flemyng went on, 'So the short answer is that when Saviour descends on us the week after next for meetings about the summit I'll go with him to the White House to make his calls, and we'll look after him. We can expect a performance, and they'll probably enjoy it over there. He should coincide with that theatrical dinner – Lucy? – so we'll lay on a happy night. He'll dress up, you can be sure of that. Knowing him, he'll bring a tame minister, somebody who's getting a leg-up from him. Get the usual briefings ready.

'But why the hell haven't we been warned? Find out, will you? Say we've heard a whisper from the White House. That might even embarrass them, although I doubt it.'

He whacked his leather folder shut to send them off.

As they left, Lucy said to Keane, 'We're going to have to help him through this, you know.'

Keane replied, 'But I've never felt so young, nor so hopeless.'

Ten

MONDAY WAS THE DAY OF DISCOVERY FOR EVERYONE around Flemyng, when their illusions began to fall away.

Even while Lucy was making her delicate preparations for Keane's visit to Chicago in advance of Flemyng's arrival, she persisted in the hope – and her resolute optimism made it a belief – that the complications from Abel's funeral, and now the bizarre attack on Mungo, would begin to resolve themselves soon. Within a few hours, she was convinced of the opposite.

Keane had slept at her apartment. They hadn't settled their night-time arrangements yet, because neither had identified a moment when it could be done easily, and vagueness remained the one of his unlikely characteristics that she most liked, but he tended to spend at least two days a week at her place rather than his. She lived on a steep, wooded street in Cleveland Park, with the cathedral above her and the embassy an undulating fifteen-minute walk away, and she had filled its rooms with colour and warmth. One of Keane's framed manuscripts hanging just inside the door was a nicely startling welcome, its vivid pigments reflecting the spirit she'd brought to the place, just as its intricacies were a perfect partner for the dense foliage outside her windows that gave privacy and calm to her life.

Since her marriage had unravelled four years before – her young husband had found teaching in California too attractive, and skipped away with only a few days' warning and a parting blast at embassy life – she had patiently constructed a comfortable nest, with only a little regret. Flemyng himself came round regularly for a drink from the start of his time at the embassy, and she had turned it from a useful perch near her workplace into a home where she could close the door with a sense of release and satisfaction. Keane's pad, not too far away, was a contrast in mood. It had a late-boyish ambience, with trails of old socks, piles of trainers and overflowing drawers. The half-dozen manuscripts he displayed haphazardly on the walls gave the general detritus an atmosphere of high wildness, because he hadn't worried where they should hang. The story of a man who had yet to grow up.

And when he was out of the office, he knew it.

He had packed too quickly for Chicago. The cab dropped him at the National terminal just after six, and he was still coming round when he tumbled out, to the sight of the Capitol only a couple of miles away picking up the eastern sun and glowing creamy white. But at the counter, as he searched both back pockets for his ticket, he realised that for someone on official business – about to consort with the mayor, no less – he'd thought too little about smartening himself up. His first task when he arrived would be an emergency shopping trip.

By the time he was in the air, Lucy was already in the office and had been alerted that Flemyng wanted a private word.

She closed the door firmly behind her and faced him at his desk.

'Lucy, before we leave town, I've got to tell you that there's more to this affair. It's bigger than you may think. I can't tell you everything now because, to be brutal, it might put you in danger. I haven't told Patrick, for the same reason. I've decided for the moment that it's better for him to get on with preparations without an extra alarm bell ringing away in his head.'

He asked her if she was surprised. Lucy simply gestured that he should carry on, and kept quiet.

'After yesterday, and the Mungo business, it's only fair that I warn you now about the stakes we're playing for here. I can't tell you for certain whether the guy we'll meet in Chicago is running for his life yet. If not now, some day he will be. We can be sure of that.

'And I have to tell you, Lucy, this goes beyond him.'

She knew he was telling her because she understood him in this mood. His gaze was fixed on her, and she was aware of the intensity that had been growing in recent days. As so often before, she was reminded of the blackness in his eyes.

'The bit of the puzzle I can't let you see yet.'

She sat back on the sofa. Flemyng let a few moments pass.

'I'm sure he must have something for me that has consequences for all of us at home. This isn't about his trying to get a bit of help, but more than that, I'm certain. And for him, it's mighty dangerous.

'Here's the point, Lucy. This isn't history. It's the here and now. He isn't just a figure from my past, useful to us in the seventies. He's still in the game.'

No more emphasis was necessary. Lucy's concentration was obvious. She knew a door was opening, and she waited.

'He's trying to get to me for a reason,' Flemyng went on. 'I think I may understand why, but I'm afraid I can't tell you right now. Not until I'm certain, and even then it may be difficult.

'You'll remember it was I who suggested he met me in Chicago. You should be aware that to the authorities – a funny word for me – he's not a marked man. He's travelling on his own passport, still not on the red list, and over the weekend I confirmed as much, privately, through a friend in London. But he's bound to be lying low, because that's been his life, and he won't like moving around too much. So I deliberately told Charlie Farrell that I could only see him in Chicago. I was setting a test.

'There wasn't a peep afterwards from Congressman Charlie. So he's coming. I'm sure he came to my brother's funeral because he knew I'd be there, and he'll understand the significance of Chicago. He must assume I'm trying to find out more about Abel's death. So I come back to the question I've been asking myself since this started.

'How did he know Abel, and when did he find out about his death?

'We're still in the dark. But when we can answer that one, then I'll tell you more.' He paused again. 'If I can.'

Lucy spoke in a more serious tone than before. 'Shouldn't you have told Patrick more before he left? Made all this clear?'

Flemyng said he'd considered carefully how far he should go. 'To be honest with you, I disciplined myself, to see if he would draw the right conclusion. And understand my friend's anxiety to be at the funeral.'

'Another test,' she said. 'You do think Patrick's up to this, don't you?' Flemyng knew the look she was giving him, and it pierced him.

'The most honest thing I can say is – I hope so,' he said.

A downbeat Lucy, who understood the significance of Flemyng's account, asked him why his friend's name, whatever it was, didn't appear on the long list of people who triggered interest whenever they checked in for a flight to anywhere. She found it hard to believe.

'Let's leave that one for now, if you don't mind,' Flemyng said. He had his back to her and didn't look over his shoulder.

Not being a moment for small talk, she left the office quickly, went to her own desk and set to work on a queue of pressing phone calls, hoping they would clear her mind.

Keane, meanwhile, was checking into the Blackstone in Chicago. He spoke to the duty manager, in crisp black and white with a yellow buttonhole in place, who materialised beside the bellman a moment after he was alerted to Keane's arrival, and found that the requested adjoining suites had been arranged. For their convenience and as a courtesy, Flemyng's would not be occupied that night, and the ambassador would be able to check in early the next day, with no delay. 'Flowers, of course,' said the manager with a little bow. 'And champagne for your own suite today? Our pleasure.' He waved a welcoming hand. Keane couldn't resist.

'I'm Szymanski,' he said. 'Radek.'

Having thanked him, and riding the tide of goodwill, Keane asked for a private word in his office, where he made a request.

Meanwhile, Flemyng was talking to Special Branch in Perthshire.

'We've got tyre marks on the grass and on the drive, sir, but frankly we don't expect that to be much help at all,' the inspector in charge told him. 'The car will be over the hills and far away, as you might say. Ferries were watched from yesterday, flights obviously, but again they'll have taken care to cover their tracks. Around the house, there's not much. They were wearing gloves for much of the time, according to your brother, and although they were there for more than an hour and a half, we think, the chances of getting an identification are slim. We'll check locally if anyone saw a car in the night. But... to be honest with you, we wouldn't expect it. They've gone. Professional Provos, who knew what they were doing.

'Now, despite the fact that apart from a horribly uncomfortable night trussed up – strangely enough, they put blankets over them, which I suppose was thoughtful in its way – your brother escaped reasonably lightly, as well as Mr Babb. But it's been made clear to us from London that for the next little while, maybe longer, the house has to be kept secure and needs to be watched. We'll be talking to him in detail when he's out of hospital about what happened – and preparing him for what lies ahead. I'm afraid, sir, I must tell you this phone line is going to be monitored.'

'Of course,' Flemyng said, and made the request that had been in his mind. 'Inspector, I've talked to your people in the past about getting a secure line installed for the times when I'm at home. Now's the moment, surely. Can it be done?'

'Certainly, sir. I'm sure I can get permission today and the boys from Glasgow can have it rigged up pronto, I'd expect by tomorrow evening.'

'I'm grateful,' Flemyng said. 'It will be a comfort to my brother, too, for emergencies. By the way, is there any post at the house I need to know about?'

'Various magazines. A council bill. There's always one,

isn't there? And a package from New York that arrived this morning.'

The arrangement he'd made had slipped his mind in the chaos of the last two days. 'Could you open it, please. My brother was expecting it, so you can be confident it's safe.'

After a moment, the inspector told him that out of the thick envelope he'd pulled a reel-to-reel tape.

Flemyng finished the call, and before he turned to routine correspondence he punched the console to buzz Lucy. 'Have we got our copy of the funeral recording yet?'

She said it had been expected to arrive in the overnight BBC bag from New York and she'd check with their bureau on M Street.

Half an hour later, she rang Flemyng. 'It's in a cab, on its way. I think Guy Cotton has a machine that will play it.'

'Just when you can,' Flemyng said. 'I want to leave my desk clear for tomorrow morning.'

Keane rang from Chicago on the direct line, avoiding the embassy switchboard. 'I've checked in. The management is helpful. You wanted me to call.'

Quickly, without any time-wasting, Flemyng told him what to expect later in the day, and gave some brief, specific instructions. 'Understood?' No small talk. Keane rang off.

He started to map out Chicago. It was his first visit. He wandered through The Loop, marking out a likely spot for lunch, and at a discount store he bought a sober blazer that he judged would transform his appearance for any meetings where he'd have to accompany Flemyng and look reasonably senior. He backed it up with a cheap pair of shiny black shoes. Dropping his stuff back at the hotel, and picking up a leaflet for an architectural boat tour along the river in the afternoon, he was intercepted again by Szymanski in the lobby.

'Sir, a note for you.' The slight bow again. Keane kept it folded as he took the elevator.

Alone in his room, he examined the envelope carefully. His name was in block capitals. Pressing his fingers against the edges as if he were holding a small pane of glass that might shatter, he took the knife from the fruit bowl and eased up the flap, which came away easily. Inside was part of a picture postcard of Boston, showing the harbour. It had been torn in half, cutting an old sailing rigger in two, and Keane almost laughed.

A traditionalist at work, he thought. Do people still do this?

Written on the back, in a confident looped hand, was 'Kasey's Tavern after 9.' Nothing more.

He wrapped the envelope in a tissue from the box beside his bed and slid it into a zip-up pocket in his suitcase. The postcard went into the pocket of the jeans he'd wear later.

Confident that he now had some time for himself, he sallied out for an afternoon on the town, excited at what Chicago had to offer. First, he would walk north and find the Wrigley Building. The wind was coming off the lake, and he felt his energy level rising in a brisk easterly.

Back at the embassy, Flemyng had a clear desk at last. His deputy had mapped out the week's appointments, and, unless there was an unexpected intervention from nowhere, the ambassador was almost free of Washington. He tried to reach Keane at the Blackstone, but didn't leave a message when his call went unanswered. A phone call to Edinburgh told him that the doctor was with Mungo, but nothing should concern him too much. He relaxed.

Keane's call from a payphone a little later was brief. 'Just to say, boss, that everything is in hand.' Thanked him, and rang off.

Lucy didn't call for more than an hour, then said she had to see him.

Pulled out of a reverie, Flemyng was on alert.

'Guy Cotton's been helpful with his machine,' she told him, 'and we've started to play the funeral tape. It's very moving. I can imagine what it was like to be there. But...'

Flemyng realised that he had been expecting this, without knowing why. Was it hope?

'... the recording has picked up something I think you need to hear. Now.'

Eleven

LUCY BROUGHT COTTON'S RECORDER TO FLEMYNG'S office with the tape still wound on its spools.

'Esme at the BBC did exactly what you wanted. It's uncut. She was still getting herself organised at the back of the church when the priest came in. She apologises because the place doesn't have a sound system of its own, so she couldn't make a studio-quality recording. She just had to do her best from the pew with her microphone. But we can be grateful.

'Here's why.'

She pressed the start button and the spools turned.

Flemyng was taken back in an instant. His office took on the atmosphere of the church. Soft music. Bach. Mourners shuffling to their seats. Footsteps on the flagstones – perhaps his own? – heading towards the front pews. Some indistinct conversation, then an usher directing someone to an empty place in a louder voice, 'Please take your seat.' A bell ringing somewhere above.

He could see Abel's smile.

Then, after only a minute on tape, a voice he remembered so well.

Soft, polite, curious. Addressed directly to Esme and her microphone, and as familiar to him as yesterday.

'Are you taping the service?'

'Yes, for Ambassador Flemyng and the family. I'm an acquaintance, from the BBC. I hope you don't mind.'

'Not at all. He'll hear this?'

'Certainly, if my recorder does its job. Are you family?'

'No,' he said. 'I'm representing a friend who can't be here.' Flemyng could picture him leaning towards the microphone, making sure nothing was missed.

Then, a name.

On the tape, the voice of the priest sounded from the door as Abel's coffin was carried in, and there was the noise of the congregation standing to receive him. He could feel the hush as the feet of the pallbearers stepped in unison through the church. Flemyng's heart was full.

He gave a signal to Lucy. Stop the tape. He was quiet for a moment.

'I'll listen to the whole thing, obviously. Thank you.

'You heard that name?' he said.

'I didn't recognise it,' said Lucy.

'You wouldn't,' Flemyng told her. 'No one would.'

'Explain,' she said.

'It means nothing. But everything.'

Aware that it wasn't the moment to press the point, she nodded.

'He could always think on his feet,' Flemyng said. 'Even in church, it seems.' He was smiling now. 'Leave me with this. I want to listen through to the end.'

He pressed the button. She left his office to the sound of a hymn and closed the door to leave him alone.

By the time Flemyng had finished, the embassy day was winding down. But he was full of energy. He had reversed a decision to duck a party that evening. Everything was ready for Chicago, and there was no one to go home to at the residence. Tony Pringle took the front seat in the Jaguar, although they were travelling only two miles or so, but he said that with a heightened security level ordered for Flemyng from London there was no choice.

'Riding shotgun?' Flemyng said. 'I'm afraid so, sir.' Even when only Flemyng's driver was accompanying them, Pringle was a stickler for form and rank and never gave a thought to loosening the rules unless the two were alone and in the embassy. 'And tomorrow, I'm bringing young Mount with me to Chicago. The boy's unobtrusive, and he's got a sixth sense. Coming along well, I'd say. We'll keep a watch, and the superintendent of police is aware. He agrees, incidentally.'

Flemyng made no objection. He was dropped at a house at the corner of 31st and Dumbarton where he knew the party would be gossip-laden, and told them to wait. An hour should do it. Unfortunately, almost the first person to approach him was a correspondent for a paper back home. Flemyng spent ten minutes of friendly conversation diverting his attention from the summit, and made no mention of Saviour's likely visit. He turned it as best he could towards Westminster. Chicago wasn't even on the horizon, so far as the reporter was aware. He assumed the ambassador was planning a quiet few days in DC while he looked forward to the return of his wife the following weekend. Nothing Flemyng said was directly misleading, but he didn't leave a single ripple on the water.

But one later exchange in the course of the hour excited him, and was enough to let him feel his old luck flooding back. An editor from the Associated Press approached, introducing herself as a friend of Maria Cooney. 'I think you know her of old.'

Flemyng, amused at what he could tell her if he were able, said they were certainly acquaintances from former times in Europe. 'An age ago, Paris in '68 among other places.'

'When she was on fire! The old hands still talk about that copy.'

She had been kind in recent days, Flemyng said, in passing a message via the AP bureau about a family bereavement. Was she contactable now?

'Well, she's in and out of Prague – things are kicking off there again – and in touch with us mostly through cables. Public phones are a bad idea, even if you can find one, and the office and the hotel are monitored. You know that. But I can send her a message when she cables her copy overnight.'

Flemyng made his judgement in an instant and took the chance. 'Look, I'm in Chicago over the next few days. I may see a mutual friend of hers and mine. So it would be good to catch up while I'm there. Could you let her know that I'm at the Blackstone? Might your Chicago bureau be able to help?'

The editor's smile suggested to Flemyng that she might know more than either of them could say.

By the time he stepped down the wooden steps to where his car was waiting on the corner, about ten minutes later, he had convinced himself that, against the gloom that had often settled over him through the weekend, his gentle digging had revealed a seam of unexpected good fortune. Gold?

As Flemyng arrived back at the residence, Keane was preparing to leave the Blackstone. He was wrapped in a thick fleece and in jeans, looking as unlike an ambassador's sidekick as anyone could imagine. He zigzagged across Wabash and State until he found Kasey's Tavern, which was as gloomy as he'd hoped. Good beer, dark wood, low lights. A bar with four shelves of glistening bottles that ran from end to end of the long room. A sporting crowd, big enough to avoid any danger of anyone standing out, but it wasn't heaving with drinkers on a Monday. He chose a corner perch with a view, got a beer, spread out a couple of newspapers and waited. Nine o'clock.

He was spotted easily. Only one other customer was sitting alone, and he was in his seventies, grey and weary. So the red-haired man who pushed open the heavy wooden door twenty minutes later was able to make a quick and accurate judgement. He didn't try to catch Keane's eye, but got a drink at the bar, his face reflected in a set of polished golden beer taps. He was wearing a dark coat and had taken off a green woolly hat he was wearing against the cold. It was on the bar beside his beer. Soon, he moved towards Keane's table and asked if he could take one of the empty high stools beside him and glance at the sports pages.

'Sure. Be my guest.'

Without wasting time, when he took off his coat the man let the torn half of a postcard fall on the table like a scrap he might be discarding from his pocket. Keane slid his own half across like a cardsharp at work, with the picture hidden under his hand. Then he moved a newspaper to cover them both.

'C'mon. We're not in a fuckin' movie,' the man said softly, almost in a whisper. Unsmiling.

Keane waited, unsure whether the conversation would turn light or dark. He considered a joke about the Boston Tea

Party, and quickly discarded the thought. He could see the beer glass across the table was nearly empty.

'I'll be on my way quickly,' the man said. 'You'll understand why.'

Keane leaned over, sorting out his newspapers as if that was all that mattered. 'The bar across from the Blackstone on East Balbo. Tomorrow at nine.'

'He'll be coming?' the man said.

'You can be sure.' Keane said no more.

The man asked if he could take the sports section of one of Keane's newspapers, as if that's what they had been discussing, and as he left the table he raised his arm and said, quite distinctly. 'Thanks, my friend, I'm grateful.' In a moment, he was gone.

Keane stayed for a quarter of an hour. Watched the crowd. Saw nothing to alarm him.

In Washington, an hour ahead, it was still not midnight when he reached the Blackstone. He rang Flemyng from his room.

'Just to wish you a good flight, boss. Everything's ready in Chicago. Prepared.'

He sat by the window, a picture in his mind of the man he had met. Who was he?

Twelve

FLEMYNG DREAMED OF HOME.

Chicago was a world away.

He was back on the hill, on an early summer morning. There was blossom spread across the garden below, and around him alder, birch and larch bristling with green. The flowering chestnuts towered and seemed to swagger up the drive to the house, and along the path that curved down to the loch the white hawthorns looked as if a painter had streaked the scene with a river of warm white oil that caught the morning sun. A feast for the eye, and he smelled the scent of pine carried up on the breeze from below, the lingering tang of home. Above him, the line of the hill was sharp against the sky, and beyond it the high tops, misty and strangely insubstantial in the distance.

In the depths of sleep, he watched a kaleidoscope of muddled images, thrown together in a wild mix but each of them imprinting itself on his mind as the scene changed in a trice.

Thrilling, but mad. A disordered world.

The old orrery turning at an impossible, dizzying pace. The rowing boat on the loch, empty but driven fast towards the shore by some power of its own. The shiny bark on the silver birches sending out beams of light. Mungo with a rod and line on the little jetty, pulling fish from the water one after the other as if they would never stop leaping for him. A thin trail of smoke from the drawing room chimney pulled across the house by the wind and wrapping itself around the roof in a ribbon of fine silk. The dogs barking as they ran to the hill, the rattle of a tractor from somewhere behind, the sound of rooks and crows in the wood, getting louder and louder until they seemed to deafen him.

Suddenly, as if the whole merry-go-round had been stopped with a jerk on a lever by some unseen hand, there was calm. Everything was still. The woods, the loch, the house. Quietness returned, to set everything straight, and nothing had changed after all.

Then he was walking through the garden with his friend. It could have been a risk too far – one that in later years he would have been reluctant to take – but the lure of uninterrupted time had been irresistible. A day and a night felt like a week or a month, because on those walks together they could talk without worry about whom they might see or who might hear in their private wilderness. Nothing.

Mungo, after being on hand to offer a welcome which he regarded as a cheerful and inescapable duty, had taken himself off to Edinburgh, Babble with him. There was always teaching to be done. Abel, already in New York, knew nothing.

With his mother gone, the place was his. Hours of conversation through day and night let them come so far. Knowing what they could do together, and what they couldn't.

And, in the next chapter of his dream, all the exhilaration

– danger, deception, alarms – passed away, leaving him the gift of a peaceful sleep, burnished with the memory of moments that would last.

Just before four o'clock, when it was still dark, he opened his eyes and it was as if he had sprung from a hypnotic trance. Everything was as clear as the morning sky after a storm.

The images from his dream were sharp and fresh, and circled happily around him. He was prepared. Didn't have to think about when the car would leave for the airport; pictured Lucy arriving to join him, smart and alert to every obligation ahead; saw Keane in Chicago, in his nervousness thinking through the plan for that evening once more. Wondered what he would hear from the man Farrell had called Michael.

After a run of days during which he was conscious of how much he'd demanded from those around him he felt, for the first time since the funeral a week before, a man in charge of himself.

Showered and dressed, he checked the bag he'd packed the night before, and retrieved from the bureau in his bedroom a small keepsake from long ago, wrapped in soft paper, that he had decided to take with him. He put it in his briefcase, and placed the bags in the hall ready for the flight. Then, looking for fresh air, he walked into the garden. Encountering the night guard on the long path, they spent a minute or two talking about the obvious coming of spring, each of them enjoying the dawn chorus and waiting for the sun.

Flemyng had time to walk for a short while, alone with his thoughts about the day ahead. Then Pringle was there, as smart as if he'd been groomed and polished up by a valet, with young Mount beside him, sallow, thin and dressed in black. He'd dealt with the bags, and Lucy was outside. Gus was ready with the Jaguar and the three left for National, Mount following alone in a cab.

An hour later, they were taking off into the sun, then wheeling back over the city to head west.

Chicago in two hours.

Pringle sat next to Flemyng, with Lucy and Mount in the row behind them. She was buried in a briefing book, having first passed Flemyng his hour-by-hour itinerary on two sheets of paper. Omitting, naturally, any mention of the plans about which he'd thought about the most.

After the coffee cart had passed, Pringle returned to Mungo's trauma. As Flemyng knew it must, the story rekindled his own history.

'It hits me, sir, that we're still bogged down where we were. Three tours in Northern Ireland certainly left their mark on me.'

'Royal Signals, weren't you, Tony?' Flemyng said.

'Yes sir, saw it all. Enough, anyway.'

'Troubled memories?' Flemyng asked.

'Lost two mates in booby traps. One to a sniper. Got our own back in a way, I suppose. But ugly stuff.'

'We're hoping, as you well know, that we can strike out on a new path,' Flemyng said. 'But it's a long and hard one, that's for sure. The first step's always so difficult. Rocky. And if we trip up, more nightmares will soon be along.'

'You serve there, sir?' said Pringle, who knew Flemyng's story better than most.

'Never directly. You'll remember all the protocols.'

'Too well,' Pringle said.

They were leaving the Appalachians behind. For a while,

Flemyng didn't turn away from the window. Wondered about the name of the river he could see winding onto the plain that stretched westwards.

Pringle suggested that the visit to the scene of Abel's death was bound to be difficult for him.

'A relief, too,' Flemyng said. 'I need that, Tony.' He picked up his newspapers, and Lucy's notes. Scribbled some thoughts for her. Only when they began their descent over the lake towards O'Hare did they talk again.

'At least we won't be frozen stiff,' Flemyng said, looking down at the dancing glints of sunlight on the water.

'Don't bet on it,' said Pringle, tightening his seatbelt.

Two cars from the consulate were waiting for them on the tarmac, and they were led by a truck with a whirling light on top to an exit that led them straight up to the freeway. The city was silhouetted fifteen miles away, its heights making a zigzag on the sky, and despite the morning traffic they had an easy ride downtown. They dropped Lucy at the Hilton, where she disappeared through the door with Flemyng's red box as well as her own bag, ready to establish a temporary office by the time he had settled into his room in the Blackstone, one block north on the avenue.

Keane was waiting in the lobby, with Szymanski ready to step forward at Flemyng's arrival and escort him to the eighteenth floor.

'Now, tell me all,' Flemyng said the moment he and Keane were alone.

'I can't say we had a long conversation,' he said. 'And I couldn't honestly describe it as relaxed. Not a laugh to be heard. But the timing is fixed.'

He said he would walk to the Hilton and go through it with Lucy. Flemyng's dinner with the consul-general and his deputy was confirmed, at a suitably distant steakhouse, for eight o'clock.

'While you're out,' Flemyng said, as if it was something that had just occurred to him and maybe didn't matter much, 'can you pick up a bottle? You'll be lucky, but Talisker if you can find it. Macallan will do. Something decent anyway. Chicago's history with hooch should make that easy enough.' To Keane's surprise he felt a hand on his shoulder, and a squeeze.

'Here in ninety minutes, then police headquarters,' Flemyng said.

He started to unpack his bags.

After an hour, Keane and Lucy walked back from the Hilton. He was in his new blazer, but was conscious of how easy it seemed for Lucy to manage her wardrobe, at home or on the road. She was in a red and soft blue dress in wool that hung perfectly, and he realised that she'd probably given thought to which suit Flemyng was likely to be wearing. She had piled up her light-red hair but without making herself look severe. They would look well matched and serene, even at a murder scene.

The first deputy superintendent, Donato, introduced himself at the department front entrance on 21st Street. It was scarred and showing its age. Looking at the patched-up façade, Keane could see how much pride had been stripped away, leaving only the evidence of decline.

'My condolences, Ambassador. Welcome to the city.'

In his office, Donato explained *con brio* the depth and the character of the gang culture on the West Side, his own patch. Across the city, he said, they could identify about fifty groups. Some small, with a local grip on their own neighbourhoods, but a few operating like mini-corporations with eyes and ears everywhere. Sparing Flemyng the task of asking for the city's latest estimate of the murder rate, he offered a figure of between two and three a day. That was refreshing to Flemyng. They wouldn't now spend the next hour skating around a truth that was well enough known to be attached to the city's image as boldly as a heraldic device on its coat of arms.

He suspected that Donato was passing him a message. The official version of Abel's death, however confused it might be, was the settled story, and wouldn't have to change. They would leave it be. Good.

They drove due west in a convoy of three police cars. Crossing Goose Island, they drove through Ukrainian Village, with its painted domes and cupolas, until the first car turned south at Humboldt Park. Soon, they drew up at a parking lot at a four-way junction with a building site stretching westwards. One of the patrol cars led them onto waste ground that had evidently been untouched for years.

They drew up at a tall red-brick warehouse that had no windows left, as empty as a Roman ruin. The roof was gone, exposing a skeleton of rusty iron beams. Donato's officers parked the cars at the frontage, which looked as if a wrecking ball had crashed through it, and arranged them in a triangle to offer some makeshift privacy on the scrub and dirt. Flemyng got out and stepped inside the shell, standing on his own for a few moments with his head bowed. But quite quickly he turned back to Donato and asked for the story. Business-like. 'Take me through it, if you would.'

'It was a gang shooting,' the deputy superintendent said, smoothing down his uniform as he spoke. 'I'm sad to tell you that it was just by that pile of bricks over there that your brother's body was found. You've seen the pictures of the scene.'

Flemyng, though he understood well that looking for evidence after more than two weeks was pointless, scuffed the earth with his shoe as if he had to, and seemed to be trying to commit the scene to memory. Rough, bare, bleak. He poked around in the loose stones. What else could he do? Keane had said nothing since they arrived. He and Lucy remained together and a few steps away.

Donato gave his account. He'd worked on it with the skill of an old hand, having frequently had to give explanations that were as much about embarrassment as enlightenment.

'We got a tip-off. I think, sir, you're aware of that. A gang meet of some kind, right here.' He waved around the empty warehouse. 'But detail? Almost none.' Then, unconsciously imitating Flemyng's way of scuffing a foot in the dirt, he kicked away a stone, almost as if something might be revealed underneath and surprise him.

'One of the gangs was the Latin Kings, hard people. The others we didn't know. But there was some reason for an encounter here. Probably, we think, about a dozen guys. I'm afraid squad cars were a little slow that night. There was other stuff going on in the city – lots of it. So when they got here it was after midnight, and the business whatever it was – drugs, weapons, something – had wound up. Over and done. Things like this, they do quickly.

'The first cops passed a little way down the street as they arrived. Got away.

'And the six or seven who were left were jumpy as hell. Ran. There were some wild shots. My men returned fire. A mess. Panic. One of the Latin Kings' guys went down. Died on the way to hospital. And... I'm afraid your brother got swept up. The one thing I can tell you – and this is a certainty – it wasn't a police bullet that got him. Took his life, I mean. Forensics know that for sure.

'But he was caught in the middle of it, whatever it was, and I'm afraid there was nothing anyone could do. Just over there.' He pointed to the place where Flemyng had already had a quiet moment, and he didn't need reminding of it. 'But what I can't honestly tell you is whether it was accidental or intended. There's no way of telling.'

'Have you picked up anything from the street?' Flemyng asked. 'Any ideas what the deal was?'

'Not so far,' Donato said. 'But often it takes time. Might do yet.'

'And the tip-off?' Flemyng asked. 'Call traceable? Recorded? Exact words?'

More embarrassment.

'Payphone. Not recorded, I'm sorry to say. But the operator did take down the words. Just the address, then told us to get straight over there and we'd find gang business being done. No more than that.'

'And your boys were slow on that night?' Flemyng said.

'I'm afraid so, sir. Regrettable.'

'Ah well, crises aren't organised in advance, are they?' Flemyng replied.

He called Lucy and Keane across and led them into the warehouse. They were standing in a wide space, open to the sky, that had once been full of life. Men and machines, noise. Now the wind was coming through the windows, where only a few fragments of glass were left in the corners, and the floor was strewn with bricks and beams that had fallen from above. Keane could see Flemyng wanted them to experience all the emptiness that had taken over.

As the squad cars got ready to leave, Flemyng asked Donato, 'Have you picked up anything new about my brother's movements on that evening? Bars around here? Cab companies? The usual stuff.'

'We looked at a couple of bars on West Division, not far away. One German, one Irish, the most likely,' said Donato. 'We checked them, with his picture. Put the word out.' With hardly a pause, he added, 'Which we're pretty good at, incidentally. But not a whisper yet. I'm sorry.

'All we know is that he checked into his hotel, not far from yours in fact, two days before.'

'Two days?' Flemyng said. 'I hadn't been told it was so long.'

Donato said that they had been given help from Washington – for example, with the name Abel had used when he travelled – and his colleagues had known the name of his hotel, though not why he was there. But of his movements around the city, nothing.

'I'm not surprised,' Flemyng said. 'It's not as if he was a tourist. He knew what he was doing.'

Then he asked Donato the question he was certain he couldn't answer, but which had to be put, for the sake of it.

'So, why do you think he came here?'

'We were made aware from DC, sir, that we weren't expected to explore that… as… thoroughly as usual. In fact, there was an instruction, to the superintendent himself.' Flemyng was coming to enjoy his bluntness, which was bolstered by a stubborn pride in his uniform. 'None of our business, was the message.'

Donato went on, 'May I ask, sir, do you know yourself why he was here?'

'No,' Flemyng said briskly, shaking his head. 'I'm afraid I do not.'

They got into the cars. On the way back Flemyng thanked Donato for everything the department had done. Abel's possessions, even the photographs from the scene. Their help in discouraging awkward enquiries. His own gentility, against the odds.

After they parted, he had an instruction for Keane.

'Get to his hotel this afternoon. See what you can find. There's going to be something, I promise.'

He and Lucy went to her hotel, where Mount had made a nest in an armchair near the elevator at the end of the corridor, curled up like a black cat.

'Do you have any notion about why your brother came?' she asked.

'Not yet,' Flemyng told her. 'You know me. The trick is never to jump to a conclusion that leads us astray. I'm trying not to.'

She knew an exercise in self-discipline when she saw one. Flemyng was dark and still. Quieter than usual.

But then, in a moment that reminded her of crises past, his mood was transformed. Neither had expected it.

Keane called from the Blackstone. 'Front desk says someone's trying to get you,' he said. 'A woman from the Associated Press, with a message.'

'And?' Flemyng said.

'Maria Cooney wants to get to you.'

Thirteen

FLEMYNG'S RESPONSE SPOKE OF HIS CAUTION AS MUCH AS his excitement.

He told Keane to tell the AP editor that he could take a call at the Hilton in the course of the next hour. Maria should give the room number. Lucy would get the switchboard to put it straight through without asking for a guest name.

'Brief, of course, but worth it,' he said.

Keane set it up, and thought back to Whealdon's hint, that Flemyng could ask Maria about Angleton. Eventually, he'd decided to ask Lucy, but she had no more than a shadowy image from long ago of a figure close to Abel in Washington whom Flemyng trusted – had he loved her once, in Paris? – who moved in the shadows where he'd once lived, but nothing more. She'd never met Maria. A friend who had disappeared, having cared about Abel.

But Maria had never been far from Flemyng's mind through the years, and for him the question was simply how much she could afford to say.

He knew, first of all, where Maria was operating and how she had to live. Moving from the small, bespoke capsule of intelligence where she and Abel had managed some magic that even he couldn't decipher, she had slipped easily once more into the deep cover that had protected her when Flemyng had first worked the streets in Paris with her in a distant time. Now she was writing copy again like an old pro, at home with deadlines and days that stretched as long as they had to, but working like a demon on the side, and walking on a wider shore. Flemyng enjoyed the thought that some of her material was almost certainly finding its way, stripped of any identifying marks, to his very own office at home. Maria was a treasure, and there was nothing fake about her cover, because she loved it. The cleverest trick of all.

But Flemyng knew, if she was indeed anywhere within a hundred miles of Prague, there wasn't the chance of a phone she could reach where they could safely have one of their old conversations. A few words between them would set off a red light and ring a bell, and soon there would emerge questions that neither of them could afford to have asked, in London or in Washington.

But how much should he tell Keane?

He waited with Lucy. Fifteen minutes later, the phone rang. 'Hello.' As if she didn't know him.

The voice came not just from faraway, but from a different time. They had seen each other only intermittently in the last decade, but for Flemyng her presence always brought vigour. And she could see behind your eyes, he always said. She had loved Abel like a brother, all along the secret path they had to tread.

But none of that now, on a Czech phone line. Maria didn't use his name, and simply expressed a sense of happiness at speaking again. He asked her about Prague. She went through the routine – spoke of its beauties, even its joys.

'It's a quick call, but let me mention your relative,' Maria said. 'I want to let you know that the journey he made not long ago was all about giving you a surprise. You. He wanted to establish something that would make you happy, and help you, and thought he would succeed. I hope it worked out. I really do.'

She mentioned that a friend in DC wanted to have a drink with Flemyng soon, and would keep the conversation going. And she hoped to be home soon.

They trod water for a couple of minutes, improvising some old friends' talk, and rang off.

Flemyng looked pleased.

'She took a risk,' he said. 'But we're pretty clean here.' He stared at the phone as if warning it to keep a secret.

'How much can you say?' Lucy asked him.

Flemyng shook his head. 'Very little, I'm afraid. For everyone's sake. Except that I'm happy.'

'But she knew Abel well, and... his life?'

Flemyng was looking away by the time he answered. 'Better than I did, to be honest with you.' His voice trailed away.

Then he sprang into managerial mode, leaving that thought behind. Lucy had a list of routine calls and messages from the embassy, and he dealt with them in twenty minutes. They planned a staff discussion by phone the following morning, before they called on the mayor, and Lucy told the embassy he was hoping to be back in Washington late in the evening. Saviour's visit was expected to be confirmed before the end of the day. He'd arrive on Monday week, and Lucy had already passed on the news that a theatrical dinner awaited him. A star or two would be on hand for him to enjoy.

'I can't wait,' said Flemyng in a monotone.

Unusually, he said he wanted to take a nap. He'd been awake since four, and he wanted to sparkle at dinner with the consul-general. Outside the room, Mount uncurled himself from his chair and asked if they should walk together to the Blackstone.

'You'll like the steakhouse,' Flemyng said to him as they left the Hilton. 'The consul's arranged a table for the two of you, and work shouldn't stop you and Tony having a good time. You can keep an eye on me all the while.'

'Thanks, sir,' Mount said. 'That's appreciated.'

'Mind you,' Flemyng added, 'you'll probably see an old newspaper picture on the wall of a gangster gunned down in the restaurant, in the middle of his T-bone steak. Better than an even chance, I'd say. This city does like its old stories.'

Mount, unused in his day-to-day duties to being alone with Flemyng, said he hoped not. 'Don't worry about being a little less serious,' Flemyng told him. They took the Blackstone elevator, and Mount opened the bedroom door for him.

After he'd taken up station in the corridor, Flemyng rang Keane next door. 'Make sure Mount sees you coming out of your own room right now and knocking on mine. The adjoining door is locked, as everyone knows. OK?'

Two minutes later, Keane came out, carrying a brown paper bag that clearly held a bottle, and told Mount that he'd be as well to move to the downstairs lobby, where it was more comfortable. They wouldn't be leaving Flemyng's room until it was time for dinner.

There was no nap. 'The whisky's for later,' Flemyng said first, stowing the bottle in his wardrobe. 'Tell me about Abel's hotel.'

Keane described an old-style, medium-grade place,

anonymous in scale and position, filled with more tourists than business types, and usually well filled. As a hotel in which to be unnoticed, it was a five-star joint.

'You'll know he used the name Johnson, about as unmemorable as you can get. I checked. There were three other Johnsons in the hotel while he was there. Mind you, they had good reason to remember him afterwards – when the police came and cleaned out his room, and sent the dogs in.'

'What else did you find out?' Flemyng said. Keane was relieved he had a story to tell.

'I lounged around the lobby. Straightforward enough. There was a busload from O'Hare at least once an hour. New Yorkers, Germans, Swedes, all sorts. The lobby was never empty. Asked the bellhop if he knew a good little bar anywhere close, and of course he pointed me to the one all the staff use.

'I only had to hang out there for about half an hour, and in he came himself, at the end of his shift. Remembered me. Nice kid.'

Then Keane was able to tell Flemyng, with obvious satisfaction, that it didn't take him long to get the bellhop to tell the story of the murdered guest, not that Abel had been the first to fulfil that role. Less than three weeks had gone by, so the details poured out. Keane said he had an interest because by chance he'd stayed at the hotel in the week of the murder and wondered if he'd seen him.

He need hardly have bothered with his story. The bellhop was in full cry. 'The cops wanted to know it all. When we saw him, did he speak, where he was going, any funny stuff. Bring in any women? Get stoned? Same stuff as always.'

His boss, the concierge, recalled getting Mr Johnson

a ticket for a concert at Symphony Hall on the night he arrived. As for himself, he'd been unable to offer anything much, except that he had been a decent tipper and had asked him on the second night to hail a cab in the street about ten o'clock, which he had then seen heading west. The night he died, Keane knew.

But the bellhop had more. 'All the guys wanted something to give the cops. Natch. Best we could do was Bernie at the front desk – said some guy left a message for him. Day he arrived. Youngish, blond, foreign voice. Friendly, and obviously knew Mr Johnson, wanted to be remembered. Bernie said. But who he was – search me.'

'I wonder if he knows what happened?' Keane said.

'Nothing much in the paper,' the bellhop said. 'So maybe not. Sad.'

And that, Keane said, was all he had. 'Bernie, by the way, is in Vegas for the week.'

'It won't matter for now, Patrick,' said Flemyng. 'Thank you. I'm content.'

It was nearly seven. Flemyng wanted to shower and change. He'd be in suit and tie for dinner – the consul-general would want the restaurant to make a modest fuss of him. 'Half an hour? Just knock. Tony P should be here by then.' Keane stepped out.

Lucy had arrived in the lobby, watched by a smiling Mount, when Pringle took the elevator to Flemyng's floor.

'Come in, Tony.' Flemyng opened the door. 'Just getting a tie on.'

'Car's outside, sir.' Pringle went to the window, made sure that it was closed. Slipped into a routine that let him take in every detail of the room. Admired the flowers the hotel had sent up. And, just as he and Flemyng prepared to leave, habit made him press down the handle on the adjoining door to check that it was locked, which it was.

'Let's go,' Flemyng said, and in three minutes they were in the lobby. 'Patrick's looking after himself tonight,' he said. 'Lucky guy. But let's make this enjoyable. Lead on, Tony.'

The quartet entered the steakhouse through a passageway with glass-panelled cold rooms on either side, hung with vast sides of beef like a bloody honour guard, a few bright red and some darkening to purple. Whole carcasses six feet long were hanging on hooks, with haunches and shins laid out in rows underneath, surrounded by a collection of thick steaks in every shape and size, ready to be selected by eager customers who'd point at a favourite cut like children in a sweet shop. Lucy, who'd also been aware in the car that Mount was taking every opportunity to squeeze closer to her, didn't find the sight appetising, and settled in her own mind on pasta and a pile of greens. Flemyng, she knew, would play the game like the consul, and ask for Chicago's best, whatever it might be. Oozing blood, probably. Each time the swing door to the kitchen was banged open by a waiter with a tray, she could see flames and smell seared beef and smoking fat.

Fortunately, she knew that the consul, waiting at the table with his deputy and rising to greet their guests, was a fun-lover and full of stories. There would be good wine. Flemyng would relax and let him do the talking, and she would be able to enjoy the table. As a bonus, Mount was over at the other side of the dining room, sitting with Pringle under what she assumed was the head of a buffalo on the wall.

The men were carving their way through their beef, with Lucy fork-deep in a salad, when Keane checked his watch and prepared to leave his room in the Blackstone. He was in the bar across the street at ten minutes to nine.

At only two minutes past the hour, a cab drew up and delivered the man with whom Keane already felt bizarrely familiar, although he was setting eyes on him for only the second time. Standing for a moment in the doorway, in a rough tweed jacket over a sweater and brown cords, he was lit up against the darkness and still for an extra moment or two. Trembling a little, Keane felt his excitement grow – recognising the feeling he'd had with the bellhop earlier – and was conscious of a stage being set. He couldn't predict the moves that would follow, nor how the night would end, but he knew he would remember every hour of it.

He raised a friendly arm in welcome, and they were together.

'It's Michael, is it?'

'If you want.' When he smiled, Keane was relieved at the nervousness that couldn't be concealed in his striking blue eyes. The more intently they focused on him, the more they sent out a signal of uncertainty. Keane put him in his early fifties, but for a brief moment he looked older.

'Patrick.' He put a hand in his. The first time.

Beers poured, they talked about Chicago. It was clear he knew the city well and Keane confessed his ignorance. It kept them going for five minutes, and then, when they paused, he asked 'So?' Keane found his eyes difficult to avoid, and he found that his stillness put him on alert. Threatening or reassuring he couldn't tell, but he was compelled not to disturb it.

'Across the road,' Keane said. Paying up, he led him confidently into the lobby of the Blackstone. Too late for

Szymanski, though Keane had been ready with the right words if they had been needed, and they rode up to his room.

When they stepped out at the eighteenth floor, Keane took a moment to point out the service elevator. He explained how quickly you could get from the basement up the ramp into the alleyway behind the hotel, and how easy it was. In the room, when they sat on either side of a small table, Keane said, 'Let me tell you what's going to happen.'

He did, then produced two beers from the fridge. They found a basketball game on TV.

Just before ten thirty, they heard voices in the corridor. Keane listened at his door, and heard Flemyng say distinctly, 'Goodnight, Tony. See you at seven.'

He heard the elevator bell, then the doors open and close. Pringle and Mount were sleeping on the floor below.

They waited, in silence, watching the adjoining door.

There was a soft double knock from the other side.

Keane took a key from his pocket, found the lock, and turned it.

He pulled open the door.

Flemyng looked at them, his long face drawn. Then he smiled. 'Liam.'

Fourteen

KEANE SAID NOTHING AS HE LAID THE KEY TO THE adjoining door on the table beside Flemyng's bed. It wasn't yet the moment for talk. Before stepping back into his own room, he turned towards the window where they stood together with their backs towards him, looking out. They could have been watching for something. Waiting. In the distance, he could see swaying lights on the masts of the boats tied up at the lake, beyond the darkness of Grant Park. Liam had a hand on Flemyng's shoulder and Keane was moved by the private view he had of it. Night over the city, low lights in Flemyng's room, and a certain peace. But before anyone spoke, as Keane prepared to leave them alone, a feeling hit him without warning and with great force. He wondered, with an anxiety he couldn't explain, when and where he would see them together again.

Quietly, he left.

Flemyng took it slowly. He was aware that neither of them was in a rush, despite their shared knowledge that precious information would be exchanged and a deal done. Of what kind, Flemyng didn't yet know, so he did as he had trained more than a quarter of a century before and slowed the pace. Established a mood. It was clear to him that his old acquaintance wanted the same. Time. They shared a belief that their stories would come out when they were ready, and not before. An outsider would have found that strange, might have expected a race to the line, but for each of them it was natural not to hurry.

They'd been there before.

'Liam,' Flemyng said, as if it had been a long-arranged visit. 'I was thinking back the other day. The fishing in Fermanagh.'

His friend had still not relaxed, though he'd tossed his jacket on the bed, and Flemyng had produced whisky. There were red-flecked worry lines side-to-side across his brow, and sharp features of his face were more tightly drawn than Flemyng had expected. His beard was short and wiry, grey hairs starting to take over, and not at all as bushy as of old. Seven years had passed, and Flemyng saw a friend – it was the word that still refused to go away – who had aged with a speed that had once seemed unlikely. He had never been carefree, because the nature of their encounters made that impossible, but they had laughed a good deal. Each knew that it was worth the effort to treasure any fun they could have in their times together.

His face had been bright in those days. It was more shadowy now, taut and scarred.

'Enniskillen,' he said. 'I can see the lough. The trees on the bank where we spoke, sitting beside our fishing bags. That leaky boat we took out on our own.'

'I've never been a great fisherman,' said Flemyng. 'I can admit it now.'

'Well, you have plenty of patience. And that's half the battle,' said Liam, relaxing into a smile.

With a few sentences, they were breathing more easily. Liam's fierce blue eyes were no longer jumping here and there. He'd settled. Flemyng, whose own anxieties had been calmed, was ready to talk.

He opened the drawer of the desk and took out the keepsake he'd carried from Washington. It was wrapped in white tissue paper and when he took it out they both laughed. It was serving its purpose already. A china model of the monastic tower near Enniskillen where they'd once met, made for tourists who wanted to feel like pilgrims on a sixth-century journey for easier purposes.

Flemyng took them back to their first encounter. A deliberate signal that they would revisit the whole story from the beginning and take their time, because nothing else would do.

Flemyng said, 'I waited for you at the lough. I knew you were in the village, but not when you'd come. Remember? I'd been there the previous day as well, just in case.'

'I surely do,' Liam said. 'But you understood, and if you'd tried to push it too fast – well, we wouldn't be here today.'

'Two whole days, and I hardly caught a bloody thing,' Flemyng said. 'D'you remember the first conversation?'

Liam put a little whisky in Flemyng's glass, taking the lead for the first time. 'I remember asking how you'd found the way,' he said. 'We spoke about the roads in the North being what they were – patrols everywhere, your Brit boys at checkpoints along the way, waving rifles. The rough crossing from Scotland. All that stuff, and I'd no idea what you would be like.'

'And I had no picture of you,' Flemyng said. 'Why should I? I'd no idea who I was going to meet.'

And the reconnection began

Liam was breathing easily, at last.

They spoke about the time it took to get to know each other. The strange mechanisms for contact they had to invent, and the worries they shared when they couldn't find each other. The dozen times when encounters were cancelled or interrupted. Belfast, Spain, Glasgow, but never London. Phone calls so short they could count the words. The watching, always, just in case.

And the time it took for them to understand each other.

Above all, the danger that never went away. Liam the informer, and his enemy-friend Flemyng, for whom exposure would put him top of a target list, carrying a risk that would never go away, however long he lived. True for them both.

They went over it all, forgetting the time.

Eventually, Flemyng took them back to Scotland, well aware that although they had been talking for an hour and more he hadn't mentioned either of his brothers. It was a slow burn, of the kind they knew so well. 'It was only a couple of days at home,' Flemyng said, 'but you'll remember how much longer it felt.'

'And I was only getting you started on your Irish history by the time I left,' Liam said.

'Does anyone know?' Flemyng said, and he saw the fear pulling on his face.

'I'm sure not,' Liam said. 'Unless you know different.'

Flemyng shook his head, said nothing of Mungo. Yet.

They recalled the walks, and the house, where a whole night of talking had lasted until nearly dawn with Liam taking him into a life committed to the cause – and a brutal understanding of the price he was willing to pay for it – and then all the confusion and emotional solitude that came with his decision to try to loosen some of the shackles. The guilt he felt for things he'd done, and the struggle he'd taken on in secret.

'Remember this,' he'd told Flemyng sitting by the fire at Altnabuie. 'I can't share this with a bloody soul. Not family, friends, my brothers-in-arms. No one. I'm alone.'

'Except for you.' He'd spoken softly, some of his words fading to nothing.

His was the treachery that could never be forgiven, but running through it was an iron-strong belief that he could play both ends against the middle. Soldier and peace-seeker, too, who might help to bring it to an end someday, and all without betraying everything that had shaped his life.

Arrogance, or weakness? He confessed to Flemyng he couldn't know. And Flemyng's task in those days had been not simply to accept the gift he'd been given, but to understand it.

As they remembered, and time rolled away, they came back to Mungo, who'd been there when Liam arrived, but took off immediately for a visit to Edinburgh that had been arranged to give his brother privacy. Flemyng had watched for a signal from Liam, and seen none. So without warning, he said, 'Speaking of home, my brother Mungo has been attacked by your boys. Provos came to the house. Roughed him up.'

Flemyng was certain that Liam's reaction wasn't faked. He saw astonishment in his eyes, and a flash of fear.

'What? When?'

'At the weekend. He was at home in Scotland.'

'Bad? Is he... OK?' Those blue eyes were darting round the

room again. He rubbed a hand nervously and hard against a knee.

'More or less,' said Flemyng.

'Thank the Lord for that.'

'A warning of some kind,' said Flemyng.

'Obviously,' said Liam. 'Who for?'

'You knew nothing of this?' Flemyng said.

'No.' Emphatic.

Flemyng told him the whole story so far as he knew it – the questions put to Mungo, and the signal that he assumed it was meant to send to Washington. In doing so, he was leading them back to the reason for their encounter in this hotel room in Chicago, through the darkness he'd been walking through for three weeks, into the mysteries wrapped around Abel's death. They had needed time, and their conversation alone had given it to them.

'Time for me to talk now,' Liam said. He told the story of his recent years.

'I've been living over here for a while now. New York, and here. Friends have been good, and it helped that I wasn't on the banned list. I was lucky.'

'I know,' said Flemyng, smiling again.

'But I had to get out, and away from the front line, you might say. There comes a time when you've had enough, although it's hard to admit it to yourself. I had a wee cousin blown up by his own bloody bomb. Imagine that. One-off shootings, endless running and the feuds, the feeling that hiding away was all there would ever be. The funerals. War-weary, that's what I was.

'But I still work it. This is my cause. You know that, Will. The money, and sometimes the guns – I'm part of all that, quite a serious part to be honest with you. But I've also kept my side of our bargain. There's still contact. I don't know if you're aware...'

Flemyng shook his head. 'I'm not, because that's not how it works. But I'm glad to hear it.'

'Well, I truly hope it's been worth it.' His face showed the pain as he said it. 'A word here and there, or sometimes a name. You know – enough to be of use sometimes, but not so much it would blow me sky-high, or my friends. Sorry for the phrase.'

Both on edge, they smiled. Liam was enjoying the Scotch.

They shared stories for a while and let the night wear on.

Then they returned to themselves. 'I understand you,' Flemyng said. 'I think I did from the start. We'll always be on different sides – I've lost too many people down the years, as you well know – and I believe in what they stood for. Profoundly, just like you and yours. But we can talk, always have.'

Then, because a sudden change in the atmosphere wasn't just desirable but necessary, and he knew instinctively the moment had come, he said with no preamble or hesitation, 'Tell me, Liam, how exactly did you come to be at my brother's funeral?'

They'd let their conversation breathe. It was nearly three o'clock in the morning, and he saw Liam's face relax fully at last. He was smiling, his eyes crinkled, in the old way that Flemyng remembered from the moments when they were safe and alone. In the minutes that followed, he felt everything churning around him. The Abel Case, as he'd begun to call it in his head, turned upside down. And, like Lucy's expectations, his careful assumptions and calculations were cast aside. He was starting again.

Liam said, 'I was sent by my people. To spy on you.'

Fifteen

THEY HAD ONLY TWO HOURS BEFORE THE LIGHT CAME, and he would have to be gone. For Flemyng, the opening he had waited for. He was seeing more clearly and, as he realised afterwards, understanding that their history couldn't be parcelled up and laid to rest. It was alive again to carry them into the future, to an end point that neither of them could discern. Perhaps because they didn't want to.

But Liam's announcement was enough to make them laugh together.

'I didn't think there would be any surprises tonight,' Flemyng said, not truthfully but with feeling.

'You guys never know as much as you think you do,' Liam told him. 'Never.'

Flemyng was ready to admit it. He said he would sit back with his glass of Talisker, stay quiet and hear the whole story. Every detail. And he'd be grateful, first of all, if Liam could explain how he came to know Abel.

'I didn't. Never met him. Didn't know his name until after he was dead.'

'Your capacity to surprise me is never-ending,' Flemyng said. 'Tell the story in your own way, by which I mean start at what you think is the beginning – because I've got no idea where that is.'

Liam was a natural when it came to setting a scene. He knew he had enough time, and that Flemyng wanted everything. Not a summary, but a diary of his journey that would reveal his feelings and his fears. For that reason he wanted him to slow down, not to rush, and said so.

Liam began to talk.

'First of all, it was a relief for me to be able to come to America, and have the chance of staying put for a while. I had left home, and I'd had to admit to myself quite a while ago that I wanted away. That was difficult. When you struggle for something you believe in – to fight hard, as we both know, and see the blood – it's hard to accept that you want to leave it all behind.

'But I did. I had worries – you know this better than anybody – about the consequences for the people we were defending, and fighting for. A dead end, in more ways than one. If you don't have doubts about that, who are you?

'I didn't want you to win, but I knew that we couldn't either. So I started to talk to you. But that screwed me up just as much. Glad I did, but I was scared and worried.

'So you'll realise when I came here, with you in my past and the street stuff far away, I was able to breathe again. I could do my bit – we'll come to that farther down the road – but I had some freedom to think and be myself. Enough to pull me back from the brink – I thought for a while at home I might be going mad, whatever that means. As you well know, I'd managed to stay in the background in the North. Never mind what I'd done, my name wasn't bandied about too much, which meant I was able to get over here without as much trouble as I expected.

'I know I'm in the files – you've told me enough – but I was never thought to be a top guy. Not right up there.' He put an arm up, the flat palms facing down, as if he was touching the top of the pyramid.

'But I was bigger than many folk thought. Knew things – people, operations. And I was willing to help you along the way, here and there. And in one particular way, which we both know did turn out to be important.'

Flemyng didn't interrupt. He had wanted the story told in Liam's way, and he waited. They could hear the night-time traffic outside, but they felt alone. The room was still, the night-time giving them cover.

'So I was able to feel that I was still helping the cause, over here. I got the money moving, and to tell the truth there were lots of times when I knew exactly where it went – the people who got it, I mean – and what it bought. I could have told you about boxes that we managed to get onto a passenger liner as baggage – on the bloody *Queen Elizabeth*, would you believe that? – and they were picked up in Southampton with nobody any the wiser. In a week, the guns were on the streets in the North.

'I was out, but still in.

'I'll tell you, Will, I've enjoyed it often enough. There's no danger, not the kind I knew at home anyway. I'm not being followed, watched when I meet friends. I can go to a bar in Brooklyn or in Boston. Nobody's going to pull a gun on me, and I could answer any cop's questions – even the FBI – without much worry about leaving traces. And I have some protection, from guys who'll look after me, because of what I've done. I've got invisible campaign medals, and they know it.

'But there's guilt. I've been having it too easy, that's the main thing. I do worry about some of the stuff that our money buys – of course I do – but mostly I've been trying to explain to myself how I can still believe I'm a volunteer and a soldier, but never take a serious risk any more. It eats at me. Two women left me, I've lost touch with most of the family. I thought I'd come here for freedom, but I began to feel as if I was locked up.

'I suppose I should have felt most guilty about the what I gave you in the past – the betrayal, because that's what it is – but you know the bit that caused me the most pain was the sheer fact that I'd left the battlefield. I'd deserted, my friends might say, and some of them do. I know that.'

He spoke for a while – neither was conscious of time passing – about his American life. The people, the feelings that shaped him and the colour of his days. To understand why he'd used the funeral to make contact with him, this was the background Flemyng needed to know.

'It was pain that brought me back to you. Not curiosity, pain.

'I thought I'd escaped, but of course I hadn't. I learned that lesson here, in this city. Here's what happened.

'You'll know that we have plenty of friends around the place. I don't have to tell you how many Irish cops there are in Chicago. All we need is one guy in the right place, and word gets out. We hear things. You used to spend your life with your networks. Agents, whatever you want to call them. It's in your blood. Mine, too, I suppose. We got an important tip. There was no name, but the cops had got wind of someone who was interested in what we were doing here. It was tight, only a few FBI guys knew the story, but one of our friends passed it on. Danger.'

Flemyng spoke for the first time since Liam had started his story. 'Abel?'

'The man himself,' Liam said. 'It must have been. We knew the FBI was taking more of an interest generally. Changed days. It's been a worry for us and I suppose good news for you. But this was different. Somebody working in a little corner of spookland, a long way under the radar, was poking around. A guy we can rely on told us to keep watch.

'Then something else turned up in Chicago that got Fergus Sullivan into a wild state back in New York. He's a hard man when he's angry, and you can imagine what happened when one of our cops told us they'd heard from Washington that a lot was known about our group here. Bad news, because this town is important. It's full of guns, for a start. To be honest, that means it's been a happy hunting ground. You know fine that we don't need much – three dozen good pistols keep us content for a while. The heavy stuff comes from elsewhere, as you know. What we get here just slips into Canada, then away like the wind. So we were worried about leaks. Sullivan got it into his head there must be an informer.'

'Something you understand,' Flemyng said.

'You'll appreciate my reaction, right enough. And just like everybody else I was panicking. In my case, not an act. The network here is fairly efficient, and if it's bust open there's big trouble. Court cases. Publicity, the last thing we want. And then all the noise from home: hard men asking, how did we manage to screw up?

'So we were on the watch for trouble before the handover three weeks ago. We'd done a deal with one of the gangs who had good stuff for us. Your brother had been hanging around, so there was bound to be suspicion. New York was telling us to watch out for an informer, so...'

'Any stranger was suspicious,' Flemyng said.

'You bet. And then he turns up at the handover. Our guys go to get the stuff, and the cops arrive. A wee bit late, thank God. But somebody shouts that he must be a spy. There's panic, and shots.'

'And my brother was left dead,' said Flemyng.

'He was, and I'm so very sorry, Will. By whom, I don't know. And that's the truth.'

Flemyng said that before Liam got to the aftermath, and the events that led him to be at Abel's funeral, there was a question they had to answer. 'If he knew about the handover, where there would obviously be guns around, why the hell did he turn up himself? It was madness to take the risk.'

'I agree,' Liam said, looking away. 'And I don't have an answer for you.' He offered nothing else, and Flemyng could see that he was uncomfortable in the silence that followed – more uneasy since the moment they'd met at the door.

Flemyng was sitting low in his chair, and stroking the scar on his chest with the habit he couldn't resist when he was gripped by high anxiety, said they should leave the speculation about Abel's motives – and the decision to mix with the two gangs, which he thought inexplicable – until Liam's story was finished. 'Keep going. I want to hear what happened afterwards.'

Liam described how he was summoned to a meeting in New York. 'They were hushing it up here in Chicago, but the word came to us the next day after from a cop friend. Panic. The dead guy was the Brit ambassador's brother.

'Imagine my feelings when I heard that.'

'I think I can,' Flemyng said. He saw the pain on Liam's face.

'But I've learned things from you,' Liam said. 'I could see a way of turning all this to my advantage, and maybe to yours. They were all over the place, but I kept my head. I said I might be able to help. Compared with some of them, I was clean – background boy. So I made a suggestion.

'I could go to the funeral. See what I could learn.'

'Who had to give you permission to do that?' Flemyng asked. It was so quiet they could hear each other breathing.

'I probably don't have to tell you much about Fergus Sullivan.'

'You don't,' said Flemyng.

'You'll know he pulls all the strings. Knows where every cent has gone, could tell you every shipment that's gone across the water. I told him I could be useful, when he most needed it. They'd get a pair of eyes and ears at that funeral. Something might be said that could help us. There might be somebody there from Chicago that I recognised – they showed me photos of our guys in case there was a snitch who was so stupid he'd go to the funeral – but there was no danger to me. Nobody would know me. If someone asked, I could spin a story about having met him in Washington: with friends like your brother had, who was going to check that out? He lived in the shadows. So it was safe. And I might bring back some useful dope.'

Flemyng said, 'You've never lost your appetite for a risk, have you?'

Liam smiled. 'I never will.'

So permission came from Sullivan himself. Liam would go to the funeral, say nothing, watch and listen. It had been easy to find out details. Cop friends again.

'And I knew for a certainty I would see you, which is what I wanted. If you can believe it, all the while Sullivan thought I was helping him.'

'What happened afterwards?' Flemyng asked.

'I met some of the boys the next day at the bar they use in the Bronx. Sullivan in charge – sharp as a dagger, and ruthless, as you'll know. He got me to describe the funeral, and I told them the truth. No details about Chicago, just regret at a cruel accident. Not a word about Abel's work. In other words, nothing to trouble us. I told them about your eulogy. Warm, eloquent.' He was starting to smile again. 'I didn't say it was a masterpiece of deception.'

'Did anyone know what really happened in Chicago?' Flemyng said.

'This is where I have to introduce you to the Viking,' Liam replied. He enjoyed the look of anticipation he'd produced on Flemyng's face.

'He's the man. Gets his name because he's blond, nearly white. There aren't many like that among friends of mine. He stands out, not a good thing considering that he's an assassin. He's over here because he had to get out, fast. Now in Chicago, lying low. But he was at the New York meeting the day after the funeral.'

'In touch with Abel?' Flemyng asked.

'Didn't say, but I think so. He was there for the handover. According to him, he ran when he saw the first blue light – he's used to that – and didn't see the shooting.'

'Did you believe him?' Flemyng asked.

'To be honest, he's smiley and friendly a lot of the time. Even a charmer. But I wouldn't trust a word that comes out of the Viking's mouth.'

'Name?' Flemyng said, giving no indication that he'd made the connection with Keane's photos from New York, which were as clear in his mind as if they had been lying on the bed in front of him.

'Cathal Earley,' Liam said. Confirmation.

Flemyng asked if he had another identity.

Liam couldn't say, but would have been surprised if he'd been able to enter the US under his own name, given what was known about him. Then, as he had done so often in the past, he offered a gift. 'He hangs out at a bar called the Old Cork. His crowd's always there.'

As he spoke he tore a sheet from the hotel notepad on the desk and wrote down a phone number. New York area code. 'Mine, in the evenings, when I get back.'

'It won't be me, obviously,' said Flemyng. 'But thank you.'

He got up, because they both knew it was an important moment. He went to the window. The first light was leaving streaks on the eastern sky, and the lake was picking up the low sun. Time to wind up, with the cloak of darkness lifted. Without turning round, he asked Liam the question that had been in his mind all night.

'And why did you *really* want to make contact again? Was it about Abel, or me?'

'You, of course,' said Liam.

Flemyng took him back to the funeral. He said he'd listened carefully to the tape, and Liam's words.

'When I heard your voice speaking to me – directly – I was swept back. The years rolled away. Believe me, I was moved.'

Liam knew what he would say next.

'On the tape you used the name.'

'I did,' Liam said.

'A name,' said Flemyng, 'that I haven't heard anyone else utter, since you and I made it up, long ago'

All that had passed between them, taken them through the darkness to dawn, crystallised in that conversation when they were bound together by Liam's pain and Flemyng's grief, and by the knowledge that lay open between them. A commitment was renewed, because so much depended on it, and Flemyng believed long afterwards that it was never better demonstrated than in the words they now exchanged.

'It's why you're here.' A statement, not a question.

'Yes.'

'Do you believe he's in danger?' Flemyng asked.

'I'm sorry to say it, but I do,' Liam said.

Flemyng leaned across to put a hand on his arm. 'And so do I.'

They spoke for a little while longer, seriously, into the dawn.

Sixteen

KEANE, WHO HAD SPENT MUCH OF THE NIGHT IN THE Hilton imagining the conversation between the old friends, was not surprised by Flemyng's first instruction in the morning.

'You're staying in Chicago.'

When he'd got back to his room, the adjoining door was locked again. He waited until he heard Tony Pringle arrive outside on the stroke of seven and joined him in the corridor. Flemyng answered the knock to let them in, and managed to give the impression that he'd had a good night's sleep. Pringle said he'd have breakfast sent up and left to make arrangements. The moment he'd gone, Flemyng told Keane that he wanted him to stay in the city.

'Move hotels, obviously. Organise some cover. I have a job for you. Your disgruntled friend Cotton can mind the shop at the embassy. Are things improving with him, by the way?'

'I think so. We had a clear-the-air the other day,' Keane said, and before he could say more, Flemyng had moved on to Liam. 'I assume he was able to make a quiet exit after he left me?'

Keane said, 'Nothing was left in my room. No message. He'll have taken the service elevator I showed him, and the quick way out of the basement. At that time of the morning, there are only a few kid breakfast waiters crashing around. Zero suspicion.

'What did you learn?' he asked Flemyng.

'A great deal, I think,' Flemyng said. 'But I don't want to take it too fast. For a start, I want to look at the New York photographs again – with you. You did give them to Lucy?'

'Sure. They're in her box,' Keane said. 'Sealed. She doesn't know what they are.'

Flemyng told him to ring the Hilton and get her over.

Within a few minutes the room was busy. Pringle accompanied the breakfast trolley and Lucy arrived with Flemyng's box. After a table was laid, and Pringle had left with the waiter, she said, 'I had some papers from the consulate overnight. More details about Saviour's visit, just to cheer you up. And I've got the briefing for our call on the mayor. City Hall, fifth floor, at eleven. I've cancelled the staff call as you suggested. There's no need.'

They drank coffee and picked at some toast for fifteen minutes. Flemyng went through the morning newspapers, Keane shovelled away some scrambled eggs.

Flemyng asked her to step outside. There was some business with Keane that it would be better for her not to hear. 'Why don't you take this to the manager? Give us ten minutes, that's all.' He handed her the key to the adjoining door. 'Thank him. It's been useful.'

Alone with Keane, he opened the box and found the sealed yellow envelope with the pictures taken at the Star of the Sea on the day after Abel's funeral. Sullivan; the skinny young man with white hair; the hunched figure in the raincoat ducking out of the cab and through the pub door.

'It's obvious now, isn't it?' Flemyng said. 'That's Liam under the coat. I couldn't be sure when I first saw the pictures. From the back, no face. He's thinner, shrunk a little, and he used to have more of a swagger. Time takes its toll. But it's him.'

'Did he tell you about that meeting?' Keane asked.

'Yes, up to a point. He volunteered the fact he was there, though obviously I didn't tell him we had photographs. It's the white-haired guy you're going to have to remember, and we know his name all right. These are quite good shots.' He laid out three prints on the glass-topped table, spacing them out with his long fingers. Two were in profile, one head-on. 'My friend said you couldn't miss him in an Irish bar. He's the only one who'll be bleached blond, like a Scandinavian.'

'At a stretch,' Keane said.

'Anyway, that's why they call him the Viking. And remember what we've learned – he's a killer.'

In silence Keane replaced the pictures and resealed the envelope which went back into the box.

'Find him,' Flemyng said. 'Or his people. Then tune in. That's all.'

Keane said, 'Give me a clue, boss.'

'The Old Cork pub.'

Keane smiled at him. 'That's it?'

'Not quite. Don't even think about talking guns, even the money trail. You'll get nowhere, and you'd be a marked man in two minutes.'

Keane said he was mystified. So why track down the Viking?

'You're a man for atmosphere. Drink it up. Listen to them.

Find out what they think about what they hear from Belfast. Something will come your way. Promise.'

Despite himself, Keane was irritated by Flemyng's smile.

Then Lucy knocked, and Keane let her in. 'Now, to His Honour,' said Flemyng.

They spent half an hour thinking through the courtesy call on the mayor, and in preparing for Saviour's visit, now brought forward and due to start on Monday. Five days away. He wanted a long call with Flemyng from Washington the next morning. 'Give him an hour at eight o'clock. That has the advantage of buggering up any lunch he's got in London. So I bet he'll ask us to change the time.'

When they arrived in the consulate car at City Hall on La Salle, ten blocks away, there was a welcome party at the entrance behind its neoclassical columns. A Union flag hung between the Stars and Stripes and the flag of the city over the door, and the quartet, with Pringle as sentinel at the rear looking every inch a plainclothes cop, were led to the mayor's ornate private elevator, its Art Deco brass and oak shining inside as if it had been lit for a photo shoot, and they rose to the fifth floor. There were handshakes, and a photographer did indeed emerge from the wings.

Flemyng spent a few minutes alone with the mayor in his inner sanctum – more than double the size of the prime minister's office at home and grander by far, Flemyng noted – and it gave him the opportunity to express the city's condolences to the ambassador. Condolences, of course, that no one else in the city knew were due.

'We do live in terrible times. A scourge of violence in every city you can name,' the mayor said, relying on context for protection. 'I can only hope that the way we've handled this awful event – the privacy we've been able to afford you – has eased some of the pain.'

'It has been a comfort, and I'm deeply grateful,' said Flemyng, thinking that the mayor was certainly not aware of how profoundly he meant every word.

And he was assured once again that the privacy organised by the police superintendent down the hall would be protected, for all time.

They joined the others after a few minutes and talked about the city. Flemyng said he hoped to go to the Art Institute in the afternoon, and they spoke about the street sculpture recently commissioned by the mayor, large enough to be seen from the high windows where they sat.

Feeling unexpectedly mischievous, Flemyng said he knew of no other city outside Europe that had such a commitment to public art and architecture against the odds, because it had always seemed to him the perfect answer – a contrast of spirits – to the culture of gangsterism and violence in the past. He stopped himself from adding political corruption to the list.

The mayor acknowledged the compliment, and broached the notion of a prime ministerial visit, the lure that the embassy had dangled.

'You'll realise that these things can sometimes happen in the course of a trip, but everyone's nervous about overfilling the programme,' Flemyng said. 'It's a heavy agenda – all the Russian upheavals – and you never know whether White House time is going to stretch.'

'Don't I know it,' said the mayor. 'Watching the Soviets right now, I often think that we're more like each other than people think. When my time comes, my successors will be round my deathbed, too. And they'll be watching each other, not me.'

'The perils of life at the top, Your Honour,' said Flemyng. 'Well, I'm going to try to help you on this one,' he went on. 'I'll make a pitch for the claims of the city. Capital of the Midwest, breadbasket of America, you name it. The embassy will be in touch in two weeks or so to report how we get on. There are a couple of speeches to be made, and it might be possible to schedule one here.'

The mayor said that if that could be arranged, a red carpet would be waiting. 'A Chicago welcome. The fatted calf, as we say.'

They left just before noon, mission complete. There would be no loose talk.

Lucy had organised an escorted tour of the Hopper show at the Institute and Flemyng spent the next hour and a half with his mind cleared of the jumble of thoughts and strategies that were beginning to take shape. Afterwards, he felt in better shape to face the questions he had to confront.

Meanwhile Keane moved hotels, choosing a place faded and old-fashioned enough to fit in with the feeling of anonymity that he wanted to put on like an overcoat, and began to think of a cover story. He cast off the new blazer to dress down for the next few days. He'd tracked down a shop calling itself the best second-hand bookstore in the Midwest, and that's where he would spend the afternoon hours.

Back at the Blackstone, Flemyng and Lucy planned the rest of the week. The ambassador's formal duties had been devolved to his deputy – preparing for Saviour was the official reason – so much of the regular traffic from London hadn't been passed on from Washington. The consulate had only sent round a few telegrams it was thought he should see.

All that done, Flemyng said he had an amusing encounter for her to arrange. 'Lunch with James Jesus Angleton. I'd like it to be Friday. Anyway, it needs to happen before Saviour swans into town, and certainly not while he's there.'

'Amusing?' she said.

'Definitely,' said Flemyng. 'But important as well. And I'm not going to meet him in town. It would end up in the Style section of the *Post*. So he needs to come to me. Funny, isn't it? When I want no one to know, I invite him to the embassy. Anyway, make it the residence. I don't want him getting a sniff of the office, or anyone there getting a sight of him. On the terrace if the weather's fine.'

'And don't circulate it.'

He dug around in his briefcase for a moment. 'Here's his card with a home number. I notice he's reached the stage where he's no longer even concealing his address. He won't be hard to persuade. For the first time in his life, he's craving company. The right kind, anyway. You can call him early. He's a dawn riser.'

As they prepared to leave, Lucy took a moment to say that the last two days must have been draining for him, and to sympathise.

'I haven't had time to feel sorry for myself,' Flemyng said.

She asked more openly than she had for a long time about the brotherly bonds that had been snapped. She'd first met all three nearly a decade earlier, and the relationships had fascinated her ever since. Flemyng's caution about Abel, his protective love for Mungo, the strength of their mother's presence, as if she was still painting at the window in Altnabuie, looking down to the loch and up to the hills.

'Abel's commitment,' she said. 'Mungo's innocence. You must be feeling that so much has been lost.'

'I've always known it would happen,' Flemyng said. 'Life is decay.'

Lucy said that she'd been affected – hit – by the malign chance of his two brothers caught up in the same crisis. 'Even though they were targets in such different ways.'

'Different?' Flemyng looked up sharply from his papers.

'Yes, completely,' she said. 'Isn't that obvious?'

He didn't reply, and she could see he had slipped into a familiar mood. Dark. More intense than a moment before. For two or three minutes he was entirely still, his eyes unfocused on the room and far away. Business done, she packed up his box and summoned the consulate car.

It was late rush hour when they left, and they were slow out to O'Hare. Flemyng was quiet for most of the way and Lucy, alongside him in the back of the car, amused herself at the honking horns from truck drivers rolling alongside who spotted the small Union flag fluttering over the bonnet. Most of them seemed friendly.

As they were approaching the airport, Flemyng said, 'Did you speak to Patrick before we left the hotel?'

'Sure. He's checked in somewhere on the North Side, near the consulate where he can pick up messages. I'll get you the details. He sounds happy enough.'

'Really?' said Flemyng, turning to her as if he was surprised. 'Yes, I suppose he will be. But this won't be easy. And I should tell you now that it's quite dangerous.'

When Pringle and the driver got out at the terminal to deal with the bags, Flemyng took the chance to say a few words to her quietly. 'Thank you for everything you've done here, Lucy. And especially for something you said a little earlier. You've cleared my mind, remarkably I'd say.'

Within the hour they were taking off. Evening in the city

meant that the skyline looked from the air as if a string of lights had been draped along its whole length at the lakeside, and they flickered on the horizon. As they turned towards the east, and the dark, there was a splash of livid colour from the sinking sun in the west, painting an orange and indigo stripe across the sky.

'Chicago makes its own drama,' Flemyng said.

Minutes later he was asleep.

Seventeen

BOTH SAVIOUR AND ANGLETON PLAYED THEIR PARTS according to Flemyng's script. By the time he'd walked over to the office soon after seven there was a note beside his first pot of tea telling him the call from London would come at eleven instead of eight. Saviour's lunch hour would be protected. And little more than an hour later, Lucy arrived with news that the old spook apologised for being unavailable on Friday but hoped the ambassador wouldn't mind him suggesting today, on the off chance.

'He cast his fly, and he knows I've taken it,' Flemyng said. 'Get him round.'

He wasn't expected to take the senior staff meeting, but he read a few telegrams that Lucy had copied to his box and, with Saviour in mind, reread the transcript of the last prime minister/president conversation from two weeks earlier. He'd been on the line throughout, with Saviour and two others in London, and three more in the White House, and he always enjoyed going through the meticulous transcript line by line, with each hesitation and pause carefully reproduced, because the effect was to prevent him compressing the exchanges into a crisp summary in his mind, and to reveal all the caution and careful probing that characterised even a brief call. Not to mention the rambling. The cleaned-up versions always lost the flavour. Away from the podium, politics was often so tentative and unruly.

He kept three boxes of transcripts close to hand in his office. They were always worth rereading for diversion.

Before Saviour's call, he asked Lucy to get a private message to Keane at his hotel – without using his office or the Chicago consulate – asking him to ring in the evening from a payphone to the direct, unlisted number in the residence.

Then, family business. Francesca, for whom a week of Saviour as a house guest in the residence seemed torture of a high order, had floated the idea of remaining in London to avoid it, and Flemyng agreed. The boys needed her there for now, he would say, and no one would think anything of it. They spoke happily for half an hour, each aware without addressing the truth directly that there were tumultuous days ahead in Washington.

Mungo next. A call to the hospital established that they were happy for him to be driven home that afternoon. He would be at Altnabuie by early evening. Flemyng scribbled a note on his pad that he must ring before bedtime.

Preparing for Saviour's call, he reread the overnight traffic from Moscow, routinely circulated to him, which he had been enjoying week-by-week for months as if he was readinga favourite Russian novel in serial episodes. An ailing patriarch loved by no one, an heir who'd over the past year become the target of jealousy and suspicion, a Kremlin court that was touched by fear and consumed by plotting. And unlike even some surprisingly senior colleagues, he was aware of how much his government knew, and why. None of that would have been obvious to a casual reader of the telegram in front of him. But where it mattered, it was known.

Lucy joined him for the call, but it had been decided that otherwise this should be private, without a cohort of officials taking notes at either end. Saviour was punctual.

'Will, my dear chap. Can't wait to be with you, in these stirring times. I hope Monday works.'

'Roland, you're always welcome here. I'm glad it's a whole week. I've got a full roster of visits and conversations for you. Lucy has sent a draft list, I think.'

'Indeed she has,' Saviour said, 'and with her usual efficiency. Such an asset to you.' Flemyng knew, looking at Lucy across his desk, that she was experiencing a shiver.

'And, of course, I have some of my own, to add to the programme.'

'Naturally,' said Flemyng. 'There will be old friends, and so on.'

'And some new ones,' said Saviour, practised at getting the last word.

He would let Flemyng know. They parried for a few minutes, Flemyng imagining himself in the middle of a tennis match where the ball kept coming back over the net where you least expected it. Relentless. Exhausting.

They discussed the current White House batting order and, since it was a secure call, the president's latest speech. The intention was to have a detailed plan for the summit in place by Thursday. Flemyng asked him for his own assessment of Moscow and its machinations.

The reply took nearly ten minutes. It was elegant and sharp, but it was Saviour himself who was at the centre of the story. Flemyng disagreed with none of it, but told Lucy afterwards that he could have done the job in a two-minute summary, adding, 'I must stop this. I really must.'

With Saviour, he went through the diary plan for the week, for which his senior colleagues had devised an impressively complicated series of transfers, from the Pentagon to the Hill to State and then round the course again. There would be back-to-back meetings for three solid days. 'But I do have some relaxation for you,' he said, 'when it's winding down.'

'*Henry IV*, isn't it?' said Saviour, whom Flemyng imagined consulting his crib sheet. 'Power politics. Just what we need.'

'Indeed, and I'm glad to say that we've been able to organise a late supper in the residence with the cast. You can relax.'

'I shall,' said Saviour. 'And I should mention that I'm bringing along Arthur Livesey, for a couple of days anyway, to give him a taste of the Washington circuit. People he should know and so forth. He's just been raised to minister of state level, as you know, and as a result in touch with all your old chums. New territory for him. I can tell you they like him, very much I hear. A coming man, I promise you.'

Flemyng had expected it. His view of Livesey was, as he put it bluntly to Lucy, less creepy. Quite apart from his reputation as a groper, Flemyng knew he was a wild gossip, and his ambition undisguised. So – play it carefully, and straight.

The effect of Saviour's call, which finished just before noon, was to leave him feeling washed out. He needed a walk in the garden before lunch.

Half an hour later, a red and white cab with Virginia plates drew up outside the residence. Lucy had been watching for it from the portico for ten minutes and had stepped into the street by the time Angleton emerged from the back seat. Touching his arm, because she sensed frailty, she led him inside.

She hadn't noticed a yellow cab that had pulled up five minutes earlier outside the Chancery building next door. It had come the other way down in the hill on Massachusetts Avenue, and deposited Guy Cotton at the security gate a few yards away. He stopped there for a cigarette and while he had a smoke beneath a tree he saw Lucy, preoccupied and unaware of his presence, coming out to greet the arriving guest at the residence entrance.

Cotton, who enjoyed the romance of his trade, recognised Angleton in a flash. The fabled rogue of Langley, in person, and come to see Flemyng. He threw away his cigarette and went inside.

Flemyng was in sports jacket and his favourite moss-green tie, but Angleton wore a dark-grey suit and a lifeless tie that had seen too much service over many years, and he seemed to be wanting to make the point that nothing had changed, although everything had. He was the man he used to be, he was saying, his eyes still magnified by the oversized glasses and the cut of his jaw giving him the look of someone always looking for a fight. Waterspout grey hair parted in the middle. Yet he was smiling with hand outstretched when he reached the terrace, and there was warmth in his greeting.

'Ambassador, it's wonderful to see this garden again. Truly.'

'It's Will from now on, please.'

'Jim,' said Angleton. 'And here we are.'

'I've taken the liberty of organising martinis. OK with you?'

Angleton said that he was trying to cast off old habits – strong drink at lunch, and cigarettes the whole day long – but was discovering that, like life itself, it was a losing battle. He threw up both hands in acceptance, and they took their drinks into the garden.

Walking among the maples, Angleton said, 'I knew this place long before you were invented, young man. Before that Chancery building next door, not a favourite of mine, was even put up. In the late forties, everyone was still cocooned in here.' He turned and gestured at the Lutyens roofs and tall chimneys, the red brick and pale stone. 'Little England.'

Then he moved closer quite deliberately, head thrust forward, as if he was having trouble focusing his eyes. Flemyng had noticed the habit when they had first met, and understood how threatening it must have seemed when he commanded his troops from a corner room at the Agency with the blinds always down and excess light kept out. 'I suppose you might like to talk about that history.'

'I should, very much, if you'd like to – but shall we start with the here and now?' Flemyng said, interested in Angleton's eagerness to reminisce.

He turned towards the house and they walked together to the steps from the garden, and then to the table where a simple lunch had been laid out. They wouldn't be disturbed. Another martini stood beside Angleton's place.

They sat down. His voice was softer than it must once have been, but it still came from the throat, rasping rather than smooth. 'Tell me what you made of the story I gave you last week.'

Flemyng had prepared carefully. 'I took it seriously, of course. If you're right – and I don't doubt your sources – that our man, our prize asset, is known by name to some people in this town, then it's a problem that London will find very troublesome. I'll tell you right now that I took a decision, after considerable thought, not to frighten the horses until I'd seen you again. It's a delicate moment, as we all know, and until it's obvious that this breach of confidence poses a threat, it's a political embarrassment, and no more. So I waited.

'To be frank, Jim, I can't operate on the assumption that your old agency has become so leaky that this will go straight back to Moscow. Because I've got no evidence. They know this is as super-confidential as it gets. And without proof of a leak – let me be blunt here – why should we spring the best spy we've ever had in Moscow, at a moment when he's more useful than ever?'

Angleton had reached for a packet of cigarettes, and Flemyng passed him matches to give his approval.

'And who is not in Moscow as we speak,' said Angleton, his face lit up with a wide smile.

Flemyng was thrown. Like only a handful of others, he knew that Britain's most precious agent had been posted from Moscow to be KGB chief in the Soviet Embassy in London, from where his delicious flow of information would swell even more, and be more easily collected. The idea that Angleton had access to that information was another shock.

'I can't confirm that – I'm a mere ambassador as you know,' Flemyng said with a smile.

'I told you last week,' Angleton said in a style that Flemyng thought was veering towards the pedagogical, 'that the Agency was determined to find out who the hell was giving you all this great stuff, from which we get some rich pickings that look so good on the desk in the Oval Office. *Amour propre*. They wanted to know. Understandable. And they succeeded. Took a long time, but they padded patiently along the trail and got there in the end. It follows that they're tracking his movements, doesn't it?'

'But what I need to know from you,' Flemyng said, 'is why you're so convinced that the Soviets will get the name.'

Angleton took a long draw on his cigarette, and blew a cloud of smoke.

'If I may translate that, Will, you are asking if I'm still suffering from paranoia about the Soviets and their penetration. The one that got me booted out, and trashed my life's work.'

Weirdly, as it seemed to Flemyng, he was smiling again.

'I'd never call it paranoia.'

'Obsession, then?' said Angleton.

'Perhaps.' Flemyng put both hands on the table in a gesture that might have been one of surrender.

'It's hard to let something go when the evidence that you're right is all around,' Angleton said. 'I know they're still recruiting, and I'll tell you this. They're not only looking for ideological traitors, the screwballs who believe in a land of milk and honey over there, but they're starting to pay good money. Big bucks. That's what I've learned in the last few years. In my isolation, I still hear things, you know, and I can still put two and two together. So here's my argument. That even if your instinct is right and there isn't anyone on the inside who's sold his soul politically – I don't have your confidence, but let's assume for a moment it's true – there will be somebody who's taking the money. Doesn't want to go to Moscow, doesn't give a damn about Lenin. But wants a more comfortable life than public service in this country can ever give him.

'There's a lot of bitterness around, and I should know.'

He lit up again. 'Of course, I hope I'm wrong, and you don't have to believe me. But if I were you, I'd get a warning out there. It could happen, and when it does you're going to have to get him out fast. I hope you have a plan.'

Flemyng said he wouldn't know. Those days were behind him.

Angleton laughed. 'If you say so.'

'Well, you've delivered your witches' warning, Jim, and I'm grateful. I'll decide how best I can pass this on, and when.' A sinking feeling about the inevitable conversation with Saviour was threatening to drag him down. 'But, of course, there's something else I want to talk about.'

'Your brother,' Angleton said.

'Last week,' Flemyng went on, 'you said you had known him a little, and that's why you turned up at his funeral. Then we got bogged down in Moscow talk. I want more. Please. It wasn't enough to make sense to me.'

Angleton was now in a cloud of smoke. Behind the glass doors, Flemyng's butler was waiting at a distance for any signal that might come. He was ready, at Flemyng's nod, with another martini.

'You know, I'm sure, how your brother was recruited by a friend, a very good friend, of your mother's. That was how he became, in practice, an American.' He drew deeply on his cigarette.

'I'm aware,' Flemyng said. 'The family knows the story, and it still touches me.'

'And you surely also know,' Angleton went on, 'that in recent years his work – so productive for us – was all done in a sub-section, little known, and tucked away…'

'On L Street,' said Flemyng, who couldn't resist.

'Splendid. Well done, Will,' Angleton said. His laugh became a cough. 'That is indeed correct. And unless I've lost the last of my marbles, it's still there, or very close by. What you may not know' – he was watching him carefully through the smoke – 'is that it was my invention. I conceived it. Got them to set it up.'

Flemyng, for whom this was the latest in a series that

had turned the previous forty-eight hours into a cataract of revelations, had to pause for a moment to think of the right response.

The best he could manage was, 'It's odd for me to imagine you as a kind of godfather to Abel, but I suppose you were.'

'I like that,' Angleton said. 'Yes, I do.'

He went on to explain that he'd had little day-to-day influence on Abel's outfit after the late sixties, let alone control of its operations, but he retained pride in the principles on which it operated. It represented his obsession with detail, his belief that deception was the human instinct that could never be expunged, and his relish for taking the battle to the enemy.

Flemyng knew that Abel's approach had not been Angletonian. He had no exaggerated fears of Soviet success in penetrating Western intelligence, and had little time for the rigour of the original cold warriors. He thought of them as unbending prairie preachers with an obsession for the fight and too little interest in the question why. So had Angleton known him well?

'A little, no more. He was a model of discretion, as you are aware. And, I'm told, one of the bravest. That's all I needed to know. Loyalties matter. He was a graduate of my academy, if I can put it like that, so I mourned him.'

'And it gave you a chance to make contact with me in a discreet manner,' said Flemyng.

'Indeed it did, and here we are.' His lined face was creased with a smile.

They had eaten, and Flemyng led him down the steps. The garden was sunny. The early magnolias were in flower, and a riot of tulips greeted them along the walkway from where they could get the best view of the residence.

'You spoke about everyone being in there, before the new building,' Flemyng said. 'Take me back.'

'You want to talk about Philby,' Angleton said.

'Of course.'

'You know how hard I find it to mention Kim's name. For years, I couldn't. We shared everything in those years. Every secret. Some women, too, I may say. If anyone had taped our lunches at Harveys, right next to the Mayflower – the place is gone with the wind now – they'd have an intelligence archive to match the best. But you know, in the end it was just currency to him. Nothing more.

'You know what my first codename was, during the war? It was "Artifice". I'm not kidding you, Will. Can you imagine anything better? And Philby taught me that it's the structure of our lives. It was from him, of course, that I learned about betrayal. The worm that burrows so deep, and lies there unseen, but never stops eating at you.'

'He was misguided,' Flemyng said, 'we know that. But was he selfish?'

'We both know many good men died because of him,' Angleton replied. 'That's bound to be selfish, and cruel beyond my understanding.'

'Sure,' Flemyng said. 'He sold out friends, and we can't forgive. A former friend of his described him to me as a copper-bottomed bastard, and I wouldn't argue with that. But I've known betrayers who've wrestled with the dilemma. A commitment to friends and a commitment to another future – they're not all the same.'

'I don't believe he gave a fuck,' Angleton said, suddenly angry. 'He sold us like slaves.'

'I certainly agree about his Russian fantasies,' Flemyng said. He told Angleton a story, given to him by a veteran

British journalist he knew in Washington who'd worked in Beirut in the late fifties at the same time as Philby. It was after his dismissal from the secret service, but before his formal admission of guilt with his flight to Moscow. Years later, his old newspaper friend was posted to Moscow and one night, in the mid-seventies, was at the Bolshoi. In the interval, a hand touched his shoulder. He turned round and saw Kim Philby.

They spoke awkwardly but increasingly happily for a few minutes, and it became clear that the tie hadn't been fully severed. But Philby said they couldn't meet again, even to renew a private friendship. His people, as he called them, wouldn't allow it.

As they parted, he told Flemyng, his friend asked Philby if he was happy in Moscow. Looking back over his shoulder as he walked away, the old renegade's last words were, 'What do *you* think?' And then he was gone.

It had been, so Flemyng's acquaintance told him, a moment of electric sadness.

'As a man who believes in a permanent state of ambiguity,' Angleton said, 'I understand the expression that must have been on his face at that moment. A face I knew, and almost loved. The irony for him is that one of the greatest spies the Soviets ever had was so good, so productive for so long, that when he went across it was as if he was too good to be true.

'Here's the thing – if I were running counterintelligence in the KGB, *I'd* think Philby was a plant.'

'Wow,' said Flemyng, feeling dizzy, which he knew was a common response to Angleton's company.

'I haven't had this conversation often,' Angleton said. 'But my life has been about betrayal, so it's always there in the background. When you've experienced it, you can't forget.'

'But we have to use it when we can,' Flemyng said. 'When

people come our way. That matters if we want to preserve what we care about, when there's a struggle. It's right.'

'Like you in Northern Ireland,' Angleton said, without warning.

Stiffening a little, Flemyng didn't change his expression. 'Perhaps.'

'I hear from a friend of your brother's that he had an interest in these matters,' Angleton went on.

'Gun-running?' Flemyng said.

'No. The FBI do all that. More the conflicts of loyalty that are at work, and how they're playing out over here, well below the radar. Terrorist politics. Someone I know mentioned it at the funeral. That's what Abel had been trained to look for, after all.'

They walked quietly for a minute or two until they were in the trees, hidden from the house

'I'll tell you another Philby story before I go,' Angleton said.

'You know that in his disgusting memoir in the sixties – brimful of deception and poison – he told the story of burying his secret camera and bits of Soviet spy equipment before he had to leave this town in a hurry? When Burgess and Maclean flew the coop.'

Flemyng said he remembered the passage.

'He claimed that he put them in the trunk of his car and somewhere up the Potomac to the north – about four miles from Key Bridge, he said – he buried them on a hillside in the woods on the way to Great Falls. I believe him. We had family picnics up that way a few times. Would you believe it, I've looked for the place. Somewhere close to what they call the gold mine trail. It's one of his stories that just might be true. I've taken that road again and again, with a metal detector, like some civil war nut looking for battlefield scraps. Nothing yet. But one day I'll uncover that secret little hoard. And then I'll die happy.'

'Why?' said Flemyng.

'Simple. In the wilderness of mirrors, I'll have broken another one. The one with my face on it.'

They turned towards the house. 'You've been a gracious and stimulating host. Thank you,' the old man said, taking his hand and holding on to it. Flemyng felt his dry skin, the eagerness of his grip.

'My pleasure,' said Flemyng. 'I've learned a lot. My car will take you home.'

Lucy was at the gate.

Flemyng watched as she took him to the car. Before Angleton folded himself into the back seat he put a hand on the roof to steady himself and turned to look at the building. Flemyng saw him scanning the windows, where he might catch a flicker of so many memories.

He watched until the car disappeared, climbed the steps and sat on the terrace to think for a while, about the lonely agent far away who would soon face the decision that came to them all. When to run.

Eighteen

An hour later, lifting the phone to ring home, he wondered how he would react to Mungo's voice. They couldn't pretend that the previous few days had been wiped from the record, nor ever would be, and he couldn't imagine Altnabuie – the house, the hills and the loch, swathed in the colours that flowed around them like a river – without going over again the attack that despoiled the scene. An act for which he felt a responsibility, because his past never left him. Sitting in the study in the residence, where he'd decided to remain for the rest of the day, he felt as if a storm was stirring up and bringing dark disturbance to a landscape that he depended upon for calm. He pressed the buttons on the console

'Invergarry two-two-oh.' Mungo said it in the old way, though the local exchange was long gone.

His voice was softer. Flemyng sensed a hesitancy, then accused himself in the same moment of inventing unnecessary worry. Why interpret evidence that didn't exist? Maybe Mungo was back on form and none the worse for it all.

'Will.' No surprise or alarm. It was almost a sigh.

In natural harmony, they let the moment spread a little.

'You're home. I'm so happy.'

'And I am, too,' Mungo said. 'The police were kind, you know. They drove me back from Edinburgh, with Babble. He's fine on the surface, Will, but hard hit. There's no point in pretending otherwise. I'm concerned, because I see a proud man who's taken a blow that's left a mark. However, we're here, and we press on.'

Flemyng noted that he was more worried about his friend than himself, and said he wanted to hear about the house. He'd determined that he would revisit the events of the previous Saturday when he was satisfied that Mungo's confidence had been restored. Only then would there be questions.

'It's all calm. We have a fire on. The wind's cold, you see. There's going to be a late frost in the morning, and I need to remember to switch on the little heater in the greenhouse. I don't want to lose the tomato plants I've got going in pots, and I'm starting a lot of blooms all the way from seed this year. It's been bright, and when we were coming over the hill there was hardly a cloud in the sky. We had the view you love. The hills will be clear, and I'll try to have a decent walk in the morning, up to the high track and back again. It's going to be bright. The fishing starts next week, so that's a date in the calendar.

'I'll take a stroll down to the water before I go to bed. Unfortunately, of course, I'll be accompanied.'

'I'm so sorry,' Flemyng said.

'There's nothing we can do about it. No point in moping. The police are settling in happily. Now tell me about yourself, because you sounded low when you phoned the hospital.'

'I was upset at being so far away,' Flemyng said, 'and not able to leap on a plane. There's a logjam in the embassy at the moment.'

'Francesca?' Mungo said and Flemyng promised to pass on his good wishes. 'London for a few more days, then it'll be good to have her back here.'

Mungo's understanding of his brother was acute. He said that Flemyng was preoccupied.

'I hope you're not too worried on my account. I'm going to be fine. They gave me a good going over in the Infirmary, wired me up, and it seems the old ticker is repairing itself in the way hearts do, so they tell me. Now, I'm thinking you'll have some questions for me.'

Flemyng said he had, when the time was right. Mungo's reply was a relief, and the prelude to a story told with such flavour and feeling that it gripped his imagination and would remain in his mind as an uplifting, helping hand towards the truth.

'First of all, I want to give you my own recollection of the whole saga,' Mungo began. 'I suppose it's the historian in me, trying to get everything in the right order, sorting out the important from the trivial, but it's also a way of putting the emotional side of it in context. I need that, for my own peace of mind. It was a shocking night, but illuminating, too.'

Flemyng pictured him smiling at the end of the phone, his well-upholstered figure nestled by the side table in the drawing room in his old tweed trousers, feet crossed before him and the fire dancing alongside. It was the Mungo he loved, who now said to his younger brother with a smile in his voice, 'If you're sitting comfortably, then I'll begin...'

That Saturday night had been quiet. His evening walk was longer than usual, because he could feel his strength coming back. The chess game with Babble made a comfortable, routine end to the day. They wound down together. Babble had a whisky, but he didn't. Keeping the window open a crack, because he judged it wasn't too cold, his feeling that he wouldn't pick up a book that might take him into the small hours, but try to sleep instead. His thoughts after he put his head down, about the garden and the coming fishing expeditions. He'd taken his pills, and expected to sleep soundly. He said he believed it was Abel who was probably uppermost in his mind as he slipped under. In recent days the youngest of the boys had never been out of his thoughts.

'Neither of us heard a car,' he said. 'The police think they were careful in managing it so that there was as little noise as possible. They walked the last bit to the house, on the grass. The back door wasn't locked, as usual when there's anyone here. The first I knew of anything was when I woke to find a man in my room telling me to get up.

'The odd thing was that he had a softer voice than you might expect. I recognised an accent, obviously, and knew it wasn't a neighbour. But looking back at it now, the extraordinary aspect was the lack of drama. It was only when I had shaken myself awake properly, after a few moments of confusion, that I saw the gun.

'I was confused more than fearful. The pills will have helped. He said he had no intention of hurting me – what was I supposed to make of that? – and wanted me to have time to get out of my pyjamas and dressed. So he let me put on my dressing gown, take my clothes to the bathroom and get organised. That was strange. I had an armed intruder in Altnabuie, but he was respectful.

'It meant when I got downstairs with him, I was mainly curious. He wasn't like any burglar I'd ever imagined.'

From Washington, Flemyng risked a quick interruption. 'What did he look like?'

Mungo painted a clear picture. 'Tallish, slim and six feet at least. Black hair, as dark as yours, well-kempt. A climbing jacket, that's what I'd call it, and a thick jersey underneath. Black jeans, and walking boots. But gentle hands, Will. He had gloves, but they came off after a little while. There weren't any rough edges. His nails were carefully filed – funny how you remember these wee details. Late twenties, perhaps. My first thought was that he looked like one of my students. In fact, I wondered for a minute or two whether this might be some kind of prank. A kidnap for charity or that kind of thing. It's happened before.

'But when we got into this room, I realised it wasn't. Babble was here with a rope looped around his wrists – though not too tightly – and that was a shock. The second man was a little more of the kind you might expect, though I don't know why I say that. Shorter, dark, too, but with a rougher edge. Calloused hands. A face that had seen trouble, I'd say. He was the quieter of the two – that was true throughout the whole business – and the younger one was clearly in charge. He asked the questions, and his friend deferred to him. They didn't use names, of course, when the questioning started.'

'About me?' Flemyng asked, then apologised hastily for making the story about himself.

'But of course,' Mungo said. 'The young man said they wanted information. He said I must have realised where they came from, what they represented. No one would be hurt if I could help them. He said the phone line had been cut, and we were alone. They told us they'd disabled our car, let the tyres down. The curtains were tightly drawn so no light could get out. I asked – silly question, really – how long this was going to take. As if it was an exam paper. They both laughed at that. Then he began.

'It was obvious to me, having spent so much time with students, that he had the ability to concentrate. Did I remember how often you had gone to Belfast or anywhere close by in years gone by? Well, I told them the truth – that it was difficult to remember, but I'd known of a couple of fishing trips, where to I didn't know – Fermanagh maybe? – and I was aware that you had been there a few times, on the ferry. That was all. He asked if I knew what you did, day-to-day, before you got into politics. I said Foreign Office, naturally. He waved that away, as I suppose you'd expect.

'This went on for a while. They could both tell pretty quickly, I think, that I knew nothing in detail. But they did get to Altnabuie itself, as I said before. Had someone from their place ever come here with you for a visit, and when? They didn't offer a name or a description or anything. As I told you the other day, I said I couldn't remember anything of that kind. He pressed me for a while, but realised it was going nowhere. That maybe I was telling the truth, I suppose. Then it became much more interesting.'

'How?' said Flemyng.

'Well,' said Mungo, 'I obviously wanted to talk about history.'

Far away, his brother smiled. This would be good.

'I said I had no doubt about where they'd come from, who'd sent them, and what they thought about people like you. Working for the British state and so forth. I'd begun to think of the older one as a kind of Dickensian ruffian, short on words but probably good with his hands if violence was required. He didn't participate, but the young one did. With enthusiasm, I'd say. I asked him for his view of British–Irish history.'

'Mungo, my dearest friend,' Flemyng said, 'are you seriously telling me that, sitting in the room where you are now, with two armed men from the Provisional IRA in front of you and your hands tied with rope – or at least about to be – you started to conduct a seminar on whatever it was – Parnell or 1916 and partition, and all the rest of it?'

'I suppose, in a way, that's just what I did,' his brother replied, and laughed down the phone. 'You're right. I hadn't been tied up yet, and he didn't seem troubled by that. We spent quite a while chewing over it all. Sure enough, he was bright.'

'I'm not going to forget this,' said Flemyng.

Mungo described the conversation, telling the two men that in case they didn't know it he'd been teaching history all his life. He told them, and he thought not in an ingratiating way, that he understood Irish nationalism very well, and believed that if he'd been born in nineteenth-century Ireland there was no doubt about where his heart would have been. As it was, he thought it was a tragedy that a hundred years earlier Home Rule efforts had failed – he'd have been egging Mr Gladstone on if he'd been around at the time – and that a sorry century of civil war and division might have been avoided.

'For good measure, Will, I told them that you certainly held the same view.'

'Thanks for that,' said Flemyng, only half joking. He was unable to decide whether he should think of Mungo as clever or naive, or simply as ever-curious and master of a good conversation.

'The younger one was interested,' Mungo said. 'As I've

said, he was bright, knew a good deal. But by this stage, Will, I'd come to a conclusion of which I was pretty confident.'

'And that was?' Flemyng said.

'That they had no interest in hurting us. Maybe that was foolhardy, but I still think I was right. They wanted information, not blood. There was no sign they would harm us – seriously harm us. It's a strange thing to say now, but they were gentle, and that told me something.

He knew I had been ill. I think he was aware that he didn't want to push me too far. That's interesting, too, isn't it? They let me live to tell the tale.'

Flemyng said, not for the first time, he thought that in another life Mungo could have been him. He was a natural.

'They wanted to establish some facts. But you know, I don't think they expected detailed answers from me. If you were operating in the professional way they assumed you were, they'd understand that I would know almost nothing. You wouldn't have blabbed to your family. So it was all about sending a message.'

'Letting me know they're on my trail,' Flemyng said.

'Something like that,' Mungo replied.

He said he'd felt able to ask the younger one about why he'd chosen the path of what he'd call the armed struggle instead of a democratic fight, but the argument wasn't taken up. He'd made his choice, the youngster said, and it would never change.

'I asked him whether it mattered where that would take him,' Mungo said. 'Without even blinking, he said no.

'I talked about how many people had died on both sides, the carnage. Made the obvious point about innocent young soldiers from over here doing their duty. Children of his people trained in violence that could only bring them misery.

Folk going about their business on a normal working day, and never going home to their families. The pointlessness of trying to blow up the whole British cabinet six months ago. Where was that going to get them?

'By this stage, we almost half knew each other. Babble and the other man were astonished, I think. But it came to an end. They said they'd leave. They tied my hands. But they gave us blankets, built up the fire. A strange scene, not least because we discovered afterwards that they'd tied the ropes deliberately loosely. Between us we were able to free ourselves after a little while when we'd recovered our wits, as they must have known we would, but not until after they were well gone. That was a gesture, I suppose. And, of course, the phone was out and the car useless. Neither of us fancied a two-mile walk to raise an alarm. They knew that, warned us to stay put until the morning, and they were off and away.'

Flemyng said that in a life that had encompassed many unexpected encounters and dangers, he'd almost never heard anything like it.

'You were so brave, old friend,' he went on. 'I just want to take you back for a moment, to the questions, before you managed to divert them into history – you really are a star performer, Mungo – and ask you if there was anything else in particular that they wanted to know, apart from journeys and dates and so on.'

'Yes! Will, I was giving you this in strict chronological order. You know me, so let me finish. There was indeed one query – maybe it was a demand – that came just before they left. The most important moment, I think for some reason. The youngster came over to me, up close – the concentration in those eyes was remarkable, as I've said – and put something to me quietly but exceedingly clearly. A name, and he was watching for my reaction. Straight into my eyes. I couldn't help him at all.'

'Tell me,' Flemyng said.

Mungo did.

Of all the names in the world, the one Flemyng least wanted to hear.

Keane was preparing for a return visit to the Old Cork, and he was pleased about what he could share with Flemyng before he did. As he sat in his hotel, in a room registered to Patrick O'Neill, and paid for upfront, he spent a few minutes with a map of the campus of the University of Chicago on the South Side of the city, where he had decided he was a post-graduate student in maths engaged on a two-year course. Anyone trying to break that cover in conversation would soon be lost in a theoretical maze that was safe as could be, where Keane could duck and weave with impunity. And he had spent the afternoon walking in the neighbourhood, so was ready to drop the names of a few cafés and bars – he'd had a sandwich at Valois – and the street where he had decided he was renting a room.

He was confident it would pass muster with Flemyng. Since he'd been in the city he'd become more keenly aware of how much he wanted to perform for him. Not just to protect his position, though he was honest enough to admit the anxiety, but from loyalty that he felt more strongly, day by day. He knew how useful crises could be. Just before six he went to the payphone with the folding door that stood in the lobby and called collect to the unlisted number in the residence, where he knew Flemyng would be waiting.

'Get over to the consulate,' he told Keane. 'It's safer for a long conversation, and we have a lot to talk about. I've arranged a secure room for you and no one will ask questions. Ring in half an hour.' That was all.

When he rang, Flemyng sounded tired.

'All well, boss?' he asked him.

'Thanks, Patrick. But it's getting stranger by the day rattling around in the residence on my own. I miss Francesca, and I had a long talk with Mungo a little earlier that I suppose made me feel distance from family even more.'

'I'm sorry,' Keane said. 'I hope he's recovering, and I can cheer you up a little.'

'Mungo's grand. Fire away.' Business-like.

'Well, I found the Old Cork last night,' Keane told him. 'A fine bar. Quite big, and the real thing. There's an IRA hat from the old days – the broad black brimmer, like in the song – in a glass case above the bar. Flags everywhere, raffle tickets to raise money for widows and orphans. The usual. I bought two books.'

He tried a joke. 'On expenses, naturally.'

There had been music. Good quality, Keane said, with an excellent fiddler. He'd fitted in easily and joined a crowd of guys about his own age.

'Your cover?' Flemyng said. Keane went through it all and seemed to pass the test. 'Accent?'

'My mid-Atlantic seems to get me by,' Keane said. 'So far. I'm not pretending that I haven't been living in London.'

'Awkward questions?'

'Nothing I couldn't handle. But I did have one surprise.' He was listening carefully for Flemyng's reaction.

'Good news or bad?' Flemyng said.

'Good, I assume,' Keane replied. 'Liam turned up.'

Flemyng's silence convinced him of what he had already concluded. No surprise.

'He was discreet, meaning he did everything by the book. No sign of recognition. Introduced himself. Spoke naturally to me at the bar, got my name, joined in the same crowd. Asked me just what you'd expect – where I came from, what brought me to Chicago, where I was living. Everyone could hear. It gave me a modest respectability. A new acquaintance for the gang, and he introduced me to a couple of the guys.'

'You'd almost think he'd been trained,' Flemyng said. Keane could imagine his smile.

'But I assume it didn't go any further than that, at first?'

'No. We talked about rugby for a bit. He mentioned as he left, after just about half an hour, that he might see me around tonight. So, I'll be there. I was able to tell him quietly which hotel I'm in.'

Flemyng said, 'I know I don't have to repeat what I said to you the other day, Patrick, but I will. Keep it natural. No probing. No obvious curiosity. Politics if that comes up, definitely, and go with the flow. But nothing else.

'Liam, as you now know him, is in a mood to be quite bold, I suspect. Follow his lead, if that's how it goes, and don't doubt the fact that he's tough. Brave.'

Keane said he would call from the consulate at eight the next morning.

'You'll probably need to be there through the weekend, Patrick. Let's take that as it comes, but we've got the whole Saviour fandango kicking off on Monday, and I certainly want you here for some of it. You won't want to miss the show, and I may need you on hand.'

Keane rang off, promising a full account of happenings at the Old Cork.

For Flemyng, the day had been draining. Mungo's adventures had been a revelation, but had also given him unexpected enjoyment along the way. He was aware of an emotional charge that complicated the obligations – and sheer bureaucratic manoeuvring – that would be required in the coming week. Saviour's visit would test his capacity for calm, the quality he'd always especially prized, and which he'd tried to wear as his badge. Being honest with himself, he worried more about that than the deft political footwork he'd have to deploy, for which he'd formulated a strategy. He was arrogant enough to be sure he could carry it off.

One piece of timing on other matters, however, still eluded him. His plan wasn't ready.

To move on from the strains of the day, he took a favourite book from the shelves. He often found it difficult to explain to friends why he returned so often to *Moby-Dick*, with entire chapters devoted to the slaughter and dismembering of whales, and much blood in the water. He went back, again and again. A plunge into the unknown and a fight with elemental forces was hardly, for him, a psychological mystery. It was quite natural, and he knew his attraction to the dark was inescapable. Like Ishmael, he had to find a way of driving off the spleen and regulating the circulation when it was 'a damp, drizzly November in his soul'.

He lost himself with the book for a while, the curtains still open as darkness came, and his feet up on the sofa where he felt he might lie for hours. He was away, with a threatening sea pulling him down and forcing him to fight.

Then Lucy was at the door, Tony Pringle behind her with an expression of obvious solemnity, his polished bald head gleaming like a signal of alarm.

'I'm afraid we have difficult news,' she said.

Flemyng was on his feet in a moment.

'Saviour's office wanted us to get this message directly. They tell us there was a raid today. A house we've been watching for a while in London. One arrest, no weapons or explosives. But a list, unfortunately. Of possible targets, it's assumed. Familiar stuff – a handful of MPs, military top brass, three former ministers. But…'

She was walking towards him.

'I'm afraid Francesca's on it.'

Nineteen

FLEMYNG'S IMMEDIATE RESPONSE TO THE SHOCK WAS TO take charge.

He kept his feelings to himself. Within a few minutes, a plan was in place. Police had already been despatched at Pringle's request to the basement flat the Flemyngs kept in a Pimlico square, from where the first report from outside said there was no sign of disturbance. It was nearly three in the morning, Francesca was awake and well and had seen nothing unusual in recent days, but a decision had already been made that she should be moved before first light. Two officers took up station in the living room, which was dominated by her piano, and cars from the diplomatic protection squad were placed outside, one at the door and one at a corner fifty yards away. Flemyng was well aware of the firepower at their disposal.

Police were also on their way to a school on the South Downs to keep watch on the boys.

'Let's be realistic,' Flemyng said, when it was all done. 'There are loads of these lists around, and there's no reason to believe – especially if it was a house occupied by one individual – that this particular one suggests an imminent risk. There were more than twenty names on it.'

But then he added, 'Of course, we can never be sure.'

He spoke to Francesca after about ten minutes, Lucy and Pringle having stepped outside the study.

She was calm and matter-of-fact. The threat was theoretical rather than real, and she was heading for a safe place. It was Flemyng who sounded more distraught on the phone. Friends, unconnected with the office, would certainly offer her a home for a few days in the country, and wouldn't ask too many questions. They had been on standby once before. Flemyng would ring them in a couple of hours.

'I'd rather have you there than put you on a transatlantic flight right now,' he said.

They spoke intimately for a little while, about the boys and Mungo. Themselves, and what might lie ahead. 'I'm sorry,' Flemyng said more than once.

He opened the door for Lucy, and she discovered him dark and drawn.

'I'm afraid this changes everything,' Pringle said.

Flemyng rehearsed again the argument that his perch in Washington gave him unlikely protection against attack. 'It's a cardinal rule for the Provos,' he said. 'Nothing happens over here that might turn opinion in the wrong direction. It's an advantage – a weapon – they'd be mad to throw away. I'm sure that offers some protection for Francesca, list or no list.'

He looked at Lucy with sadness, and some perplexity. 'So what's going on?'

Pringle, literal as ever, said that they had to assume there were elements on the loose who hadn't got that message. 'There's no other explanation.'

It meant an extra layer of security in the embassy, for which plans were kept ready, and restrictions on his movements. Lucy knew how that would affect him. On top of it all, Saviour would soon be on his way to Washington.

And Lucy mentioned Patrick. She suggested she call his hotel to ask him to ring on the direct line. Flemyng looked at his watch. 'He won't be in yet. I know he's at a bar. But leave a message that he should get in touch, however late. I'll be here, after all. I'll give him the details when we speak.'

Pringle, brisk and energised by events in London, said he would post Mount in the residence overnight. 'Sleep well, sir, if you can. I'm sorry about it all.' He disappeared.

Lucy poured a whisky for Flemyng. 'Water it down well, if you will,' he said. 'We may have a long night.'

She rang Keane's hotel from the corner of the room and left her message for Mr O'Neill.

'Now,' she said to Flemyng, 'what have you got to tell me?'

She was in command; he had to respond. First, the call to Mungo, and his story. Flemyng told it again from the beginning, and spoke about his surprise and admiration for the calm his brother had managed to display. 'I wonder what I'd have done?' he said.

'The *sang-froid*! They even decided in the morning that there was no point in going for a long tramp to raise the alarm. Sensible. Most people would have panicked, but old Babble wasn't up to it and Mungo knew. So they made breakfast and waited for Father MacNeil with his car. He drops by on most Sundays.'

Despite the alarm they both felt, sensing a tingle in the air that wouldn't disappear, they enjoyed the idea of Mungo's history seminar. 'He was lucky with that young guy,' Flemyng said. 'It could have backfired, if that's not the wrong word. They couldn't have sent anyone better suited to the job.'

'My own thoughts exactly,' Lucy said.

'From everything Mungo said,' Flemyng went on, 'I'm certain that this was never going to be a violent attack. If you were going to categorise it, you'd put it down as an intelligence mission, wouldn't you?'

'I think so,' said Lucy. 'So do you know what they were after?'

Flemyng walked across the room to replenish his glass. 'Possibly, but I may be wrong.'

'You've got to let me in,' she said.

'Not yet, Lucy. There's a point beyond which I just can't go, even for you. It wouldn't be fair, I promise you, nor safe. But I can take you a little way down the road.'

He took her back to the funeral recording. 'You'll remember the message left for me, that name on the tape.'

'I do,' she said. 'You said it meant nothing, and also everything.'

'Which was true, and still is.'

Flemyng said he couldn't explain his obfuscation. But he could pose a question that he had to answer, and which she would find intriguing.

'How much does the name mean to them? That's the beginning and end of it.'

The phone rang. It was Keane, from the payphone in the lobby of his hotel.

'Find a phone in the street,' Flemyng said, keeping it brief. 'Somewhere quiet. Ring me on this line – with coins, don't call collect – and give me the number. I'll get straight back to you.'

It took ten minutes, but then Keane was back with them.

Flemyng signalled to Lucy to pick up the extension. 'There's news from London,' he said, 'but first of all I want to hear everything from you in Chicago. From the beginning. I should tell you...' Lucy knew what was coming '... that I've had a lesson in storytelling from Mungo already today, so I'm counting on you to measure up, Patrick.'

Keane began. 'The bar was busy. A different band, and a good crowd. I spent about an hour just shooting the breeze. Our friend Liam turned up just before ten – the place stays open later from Thursday night. He was more relaxed than last night, leather jacket and so on, maybe because I looked as if I was comfortable with the gang of boys that he knows. Mainly the ones who were around last night.

'With one exception.'

Flemyng looked at Lucy across the room. She couldn't know what was coming.

'The Viking,' Keane said, with satisfaction.

'Describe him,' said Flemyng, as if he'd never seen his photograph. 'Skinny, that's the main thing,' Keane said, who was so conscious of his own weight. 'Fit, I'd say. I wouldn't like to run alongside him. His hair's even whiter than it looks in the pictures, and you can see why people mark him down as a Scandi. Voice light, accent not Belfast I'd say, but you'd know better than me. And, just as we were told, good company. Smiles and laughs a lot. Life and soul. But there are dark moments – his face can change in an instant.'

'Did you get the impression he's living in the city?' Flemyng asked.

'Yes is the answer, and I'm certain. I spoke about an apartment I share on the South Side, if you follow me, and he was happy to tell me roughly where he is on the West Side, along with at least two of the others who come to the Old Cork.'

'As far as they're concerned, where does that mid-Atlantic voice come from?' said Flemyng.

'I didn't make the mistake of inventing a background that they might see through. So London, second generation, when they asked. Don't know the home country at all well, to my regret.'

'Good,' said Flemyng.

'But I do know the politics. So I was able to get them talking, in the way you'd expect. Bar talk. And I was sure that they weren't sizing me up, watching for mistakes or anything. That was a relief. I was just a guy a long way from home who was glad to run into some friendly souls a bit like me.'

Lucy couldn't help herself. 'You're describing your natural habitat.'

'I didn't know you were on the line,' he said.

'What did you expect, Patrick?' Flemyng was focused, with his thoughts organised. 'The politics. Give me a flavour.'

'There was talk about the cause, obviously,' Keane said. 'Stuff about the army, patrols, searches. Two of the guys had come over quite recently, and they were full of it. Glad to be away, they said. Then the collecting tin came round, so that gave me a chance to ask a little about what was going on. Somebody spoke about the Brighton bomb. Bad luck that it hadn't done the job properly, was the view. I agreed, which is what you'd want, I assume.

'And the Viking got into his stride. Liam was encouraging him, I could see. He's clever, as you know. Just a little nudge here or there to keep him talking. And I think it was obvious what was churning away underneath. Big-time frustration. It was Liam's presence, I'm sure, that let the conversation take this turn, and the fact that he behaved as if he knew me quite well. The Viking felt safe with him. Gave him respect, but felt free to talk.

'You'll appreciate that the last thing I wanted to do was to let them think that I wanted to know more. In fact, I suggested once or twice that one of the things I liked about being in Chicago was that all this stuff was out of sight and out of mind. The Viking said that I needed to remember that it was closer than I thought. Had to be. I was getting sensitive, thinking I might be showing too much interest. So I backed off. But it was worth it.'

'Yes?' said Flemyng.

'He said there would be much more, soon. Brighton would be forgotten, because it was going to get better. At least he hoped so.'

'What do you think he meant by that?' Flemyng asked.

'Just this,' Keane said. 'There are voices arguing for different tactics. Fewer big bangs. Less activity on the mainland. He wants the opposite. More active service units in place – I was amazed he used the phrase. Liam agreed, and pumped him up a little further. He even took the trouble to say that I was secure. Could be trusted. It's obvious that the Viking rates Liam, and feels able to talk in front of him.

'He said they were at a turning point in the struggle, and everyone needed to know it.'

Flemyng, Lucy could see, was concentrating on Keane's every word. His inflection, his asides, his reading of the Viking's mind.

'Liam – I feel I know him now, and he knows where I'm staying – gave me a look that I took to mean that it was time to steer away from heavy politics, because it risked getting us too deep. He led me onto different territory. I followed happily. Not long afterwards, I said I had to go. An overdue paper to finish in the morning.'

'And you waited for a bus heading for the South Side, I hope' said Flemyng, like a teacher.

'Of course,' Keane said. 'Talked about which was the best route. That's why I took so long to call you.'

'And let me ask you this,' Flemyng said. 'Any mention of Abel, or anyone like him?'

'Not a sausage,' Keane said.

Flemyng said they could surely both see what he had meant when he described Liam as brave. 'Patrick, that's been terrific from you. Thank you.'

For the next few minutes he described the alarm surrounding Francesca, and Keane was moved enough to sound thrown off balance, for the first time. 'It's important you know about it,' Flemyng told him. 'I want you to stay put in Chicago, until Sunday morning.

'Get some sleep now,' he continued. 'Ring in the morning. Well done indeed.'

Midnight had gone. 'I want to walk in the garden,' he said.

Lucy walked down the black and white marble floor between the pillars in the hall, arriving at the chair where Mount was stationed near the front door. He confirmed that extra guards were at the gates and others were patrolling the perimeter, so a walk would be fine so long as he could watch from a vantage point on the terrace. He was in walkie-talkie touch with the men outside – his handset crackled on cue to prove the point – and he'd be able to hear the phone if it rang inside. He smiled in his boyish way, and said it was a nice evening to be out.

Lucy and Flemyng went down the stone steps and soon they had walked out of the pool of light cast from the terrace.

It was a clear night. About two miles away, through the trees and towards the south-east, they could see the white spike of the Washington Monument, its red warning light at the top like a distant eye keeping watch on them. The city around them was still, with nothing nearby to prick the calm. They took one of the pathways that offered them a circuit back to the house. Flemyng spoke about Francesca, as Lucy had expected.

'She's strong,' he said. 'But this is tough, not knowing if it will ever end. I think the risk right now is tiny, but it's the long stretch ahead that gets you.'

They walked for a little in silence in the dark, crisp night, coming round behind an old oak tree to face the residence again. They could see the black figure of Mount against the lit windows, erect and still on the terrace and looking towards them.

As they walked in his direction, Flemyng said to her, 'A week of pure politics ahead. We'll have to navigate it with care, for everyone's sake.'

They approached the terrace, where Mount waited for them like a sentry.

The lights picked them up as they got closer, in step and walking slowly.

Mount had a message for them. 'A call a moment ago, sir. Mr Keane would like you to ring.'

They looked at each other. Lucy dialled the hotel from the library, and Keane answered on the first ring. She handed the phone to Flemyng.

'Liam wants to meet me in the morning. It sounds urgent.'

Twenty

By first light Flemyng felt he had slept for only two hours or so. The night had been a series of arguments with himself as he'd tried to make the right connections and avoid wrong turnings. Although he knew he had switched off two or three times and lost consciousness, he could hardly call it sleep. When he woke, he was exhausted. But as he showered and began to plan his day he convinced himself that light was beginning to shine, and he let its energy flow.

Firstly, he'd realised the significance of Lucy's routine observation in Chicago about the fates of Abel and Mungo being different, an obvious statement of fact but one that lodged in his mind and remained there stubbornly, working away at him. Why had it intrigued him so much? He decidedthe answer was simpler than he'd been tempted to imagine.

Secondly, he now saw Angleton's wholly unexpected intervention in his life as a stroke of good fortune. He well understood that he would soon be obliged to ring an alarm bell in London, which would bring disapproval and official scepticism because of its source, unless he could conceal it. The risks were obvious, and trouble would certainly ensue. But at that moment it was the broad alluring pattern the old spook had painted for him that moved him more. He was convinced that somewhere just beyond his understanding was a connection that would help him to make sense of Abel's death and the resumption of his dealings with Liam, quite separately from the awkward journey that Angleton had obliged him to undertake.

As a result, he was more cheerful than he had expected when he asked Lucy to get the Downing Street switchboard to find Roland Saviour, wherever he might be. He was quickly summoned to a phone.

'Saturday, Will! There must be news on the Rialto.'

'The obvious, Roland. Your people gave me news of that target list. You'll appreciate my anxiety.'

'Of course. Of all people, Francesca!' Saviour made it sound as if Flemyng might have swapped wives quietly, without telling him.

'Yes, a threatening message to me. And as you may know, it follows an unpleasant incident involving my brother. My surviving brother, that is. Were you aware?'

'A whisper, that's all,' Saviour said, which could have meant anything. 'I was sorry to hear it, and wanted to get the whole story from you on Monday. How serious do you think all this is?'

'Quite,' said Flemyng. 'We can't afford to think of it any other way.'

Saviour was in the country, and Flemyng could hear a distant lunch party. 'Proper security in place, and Francesca safely in seclusion, I hope?'

'For the moment, yes, thank you,' Flemyng said. 'There's background I can give you, so I'll carve out some time on Monday evening. I simply wanted to alert you. Something's starting.'

'And I can brief you properly on Irish matters from my end,' Saviour said. 'You need to know it all, and you will understand – as you do instinctively, of course – why nothing must be allowed to derail the progress we are making, gratifyingly fast. Nothing.'

'We're approaching the most tricky stage. Ultra-sensitive.'

Flemyng said, 'Ultra, of course. I'll look forward to a proper conversation. We should have it alone.'

'Splendid,' said Saviour. Flemyng could picture him raising his glass in the garden. 'Until Monday, then. And, please, my fondest regards to dear Francesca. A precious part of the team.'

'I'm grateful, Roland. You'll be most welcome here.'

Flemyng ordered tea, and asked Lucy to sit with him. He put the phone call behind him.

'You remember I asked you in Chicago why you'd said that the attacks on Mungo and Abel had to be thought about differently?'

'Indeed, you did,' she said. 'I couldn't see why you found it odd.'

He said, 'I realised that the most important fact about Abel's death is that no one knew he was my brother. Mungo got involved because of who he was. It was the opposite with Abel. The New York people were shocked to find out the truth about him when he was dead, after they got a leak from the cops, but I'm now sure he wasn't recognised in Chicago either. I had been assuming the opposite, without justification, just because it helped to explain the fact that he was attacked.

In fact, if he *had* been known to be who he was, he might still be alive. Do you follow?'

Lucy was tentative, 'I think so.'

'If you start with the fact that he was anonymous until after he was dead, which is such an unnatural thought for me, I think his activity – maybe the extent to which he was able to find things out – starts to look different. And it may explain why he found himself – physically and perilously – in the middle of a transaction between two gangs, which is a position he would never have allowed himself to get into alone. I couldn't make sense of it.'

Flemyng said he was still working it through in his mind, but he was more hopeful than he'd been in Chicago.

'Now, I wonder what your young man is up to.'

As he spoke, Keane was walking along the lake shore to freshen himself for the day. His summons, as he considered it, had come from Liam in a call from a payphone to his hotel, near midnight. Brief, and crystal-clear. Liam would be on one of the benches in Union Station just before noon.

Keane had walked for an hour. He was in a red fleece and jeans, and as his curly blond hair caught the wind and his cheeks got pinker, he looked even younger than his years. A student walking off the night before, perhaps. He didn't look at all like a hiker, nor a jogger warming up, just someone determined to enjoy the spring weather in the quiet of an early Saturday and walking without purpose. But he had planned his route with care, and, heading north to meet the river where it joined the lake, he swerved westwards at the breakwater to follow the waterway around the curve that brought him eventually to the great bulk of the station, a pillared monument to twenties' optimism. And where better for a meeting than a travellers' playground, where they came and went all day, bumping into each other, passing the time in brief conversation? A place where strangers couldn't help but meet.

He'd allowed time to find his way round the building, because it was his first visit, but still hadn't expected its scale. Desperately in need of love and attention, long-promised and long-delayed, the vaulted roof in the great hall was crying out for an exhibition to be spread out beneath it. But he still thought it thrilling. High and wide, with secret echoes. A field for private adventures. The light poured in from above, and he walked diagonally across the vast space, picking up the figures on the wooden benches, high with rounded backs in the old style so that they gave comfort to quite a number of men who had spent the night there, and he assumed always did. There was no sign of Liam. Half an hour to go.

Wandering the galleried halls, he picked up some timetables, and, in case any of the cops lounging at the corners asked him a question, he went to one of the old-fashioned ticket windows and took out insurance against an enquiry with a round trip to Kankakee, about fifty miles down the track to the south. Eventually, just before the hour, he reversed his route from corner to corner across the great hall and there, hunched down at the end of one of the benches on one side, was Liam. Keane sat down about four feet from him.

After three or four minutes, he produced the packet of cigarettes he'd bought for the occasion and leaned over to ask Liam if he had a match. He took out a lighter. They smoked together, like travellers the world over, two strangers falling into a chance conversation.

'I'm taking a risk with you. You know that?' Liam said quietly. 'I've told the guys in the bar that you're trusted by me. That matters, because of who I am. If this goes wrong, there's hell to pay. OK? *Hell.*' He let the word sink in.

'But I need to use you to get back to your man. I can't do it myself, so you're a messenger boy.'

Then, to Keane's surprise, there was a warmer smile than any he'd given him before.

'I don't mean to put you down. Your man told me to trust you. That's enough for me.'

Keane was looking straight ahead, smoking as if he was used to it. 'Is there a particular message?'

'Of course there is,' Liam said. 'And listen to me, young man, there's something else just as important. No American fingerprint of any kind on it. Not a trace. Understood?'

He faced him along the bench, a twist of smoke drifting over his shoulder. Keane noticed that the nervousness he'd diagnosed on their first encounter had given way to seriousness. His expression was set and determined. Keane saw ferocity, and felt the power of it. He was beginning to understand the variety of Liam's moods.

'Tell him this from me,' Liam said, speaking slowly and facing directly ahead. 'There's a unit getting ready for an operation right now, and if your people can find them they'll understand its importance.' He drew on his cigarette, then named a north London street and its postal district. Repeated it. 'I don't have a house number but it's where the boys are. They're into final preparations, and it's big.'

Keane said he understood, and no more. He was shaking a little. A few travellers crossed the hall, but there was no one sitting near them. Aware of what he had heard, he took in the scene as if it was a photograph that would be imprinted on his memory and always carried with him. The silence was broken by an announcement. A train for Memphis was boarding.

The hooter sounded.

Getting up, Liam said. 'You stay here for a few minutes.'

Then he turned back as if to say goodbye. Leaning towards Keane, he said softly, 'No one at the bar knows anything. Nothing. Remember that. See you there tonight.'

He walked through one of the high stone arches towards the suburban platforms and was gone.

Keane read his timetables, and finished the cigarette. Leaving the station through the doors to the bridge over the river less than five minutes later, he was soon back in The Loop and walking northwards towards his hotel, faster than before.

He made the call from the lobby payphone. Lucy answered immediately. 'I need to speak to him from the consulate,' Keane said without any preamble and using no names. 'Can you make sure someone lets me in? I'll be there in less than ten.'

He picked up his small rucksack from his room, poured coffee into a paper cup in the lobby and went into the street. A passer-by would have noticed nothing unusual as he stood on the next corner with his cup, watching the weekend traffic building up and enjoying the sun. But Keane's nerves were on edge. He was trembling.

His experience had been that long conversations, after hours of planning and waiting, sometimes produced a tasty hint, and occasionally a morsel of information that allowed him to complete a pattern, or open up a new line of thought. But you usually had to work hard for little reward. Often, it was only later that the significance of a word or two was revealed. Being frank, he had never been the recipient of anything like Liam's gift, dropped into his lap with almost no warning. For a moment he wondered if he deserved it. Then, realising that he was at risk of embarrassing himself, he zipped up his fleece, dropped his coffee cup in a bin, stepped quickly and deliberately across the walkway on the corner and turned towards the consulate on the next block.

A security guard was on hand, expecting him, and he went to the room on the second floor that he knew. Locking the door, he used the unlisted phone to ring Flemyng's study. 'I'm in the consulate. This is secure,' he said.

'Thanks, Patrick. Perhaps Lucy shouldn't hear this – depending what you've got to say – but in all the circumstances I'm going to keep her in the room, though not on the line. Something's up. What exactly?'

Keane had rehearsed his story to keep it simple. 'It's for you. He's given me a specific piece of information, without any warning. About an attack, imminent he says, being planned in London. He gave me the name of the street – he doesn't know the house number where they are. It's meant to be big. That was his word.

'And it was just as important, he said, not to let it be known where this emanated from. No American fingerprint. He was emphatic, very serious.'

Flemyng said. 'I can understand that.'

To Keane's surprise, he added, 'So what do we do?'

'I assume it can't come from you. Right? Keane said. He could imagine Flemyng's expression of concentration.

'Correct,' Flemyng said. 'He's concerned that if there's any American sourcing of this, it'll spread through the system, and leak out. Let's be clear – he believes that would be life-threatening for him. I agree.'

'For the same reason, I don't think we should feed it through the station here. No reflection on Cotton, but we need to use a back door.'

'So what do you suggest?' he asked him directly. Keane's nervousness, which he'd felt pulsing through him since he left Union Station, rose further.

'You mean I have to find someone?' he said. 'A cut-out.'

Flemyng said. 'Yes. And quickly. Imagine if we didn't deal with this now, and there was an attack tomorrow. Ring me back within twenty minutes, no more. Bye for now.'

Keane had the ability to clear his mind of the unnecessary. When he was enjoying himself in the realms of number theory, his satisfaction came in part from discarding any thought that didn't help him follow the trail he'd mapped out. He could cut out any interference, and push the rest of the world away. He did it now, focusing sharply on ways of protecting Liam's information and refusing to be diverted by thoughts of Flemyng or Cotton or the boys at the bar. He pulled up a list of names in his head. Knowing he should use Belfast, within five minutes he had a plan. As he might with a robust equation of style as well as purpose, he looked at it from every angle. It would work.

He picked up the phone.

Flemyng said, 'Eleven minutes. Well done.'

'OK, boss. I won't use a name, but here's my thought. I have a friend in a city that we both know, who's been helpful. He's in our partner agency, so to speak. We've cooperated often enough in the past. I can give him the story we've been given, and tell him it comes from someone I've used before on that patch, whom obviously he would never expect me to name. It would be natural for this source of mine to come to me with a tip like this, even though I'm over here, because these relationships are so personal, as we know. Man to man. I'll say he's doing a favour for me.

'So, as it happens, I can offer a favour of my own by giving my colleague the information and letting him pass it to London. He's been having a rough time. You'll know about the upheavals in his organisation, and they're fairly brutal. This is bound to put him back in the good books. It's a gift, and it will suit him very well not to involve me, especially with me being seen as the opposition in the turf war on the other side of the water. When I ask him to keep me out of it – too many complications, too far away and so on – I can count on him. It's wholly in his interest to make this his own show. It'll help us both. And he'll never know.'

'I'm aware of some of the scene-shifting in Five,' Flemyng said, choosing not to dissemble.

Then, 'Who is he? I think you can tell me...'

Keane hesitated. 'I have obligations...'

Flemyng reminded him they were on a secure line, that in any case he'd fought the same bureaucratic battles in the past, and moreover he was his boss. 'I need to know.'

'Johnny Silvester.'

'Ah well, you're on safe ground there.' Keane could imagine Flemyng smiling.

'Know him?' Keane said.

'No. But there was an uncle, a long time ago. I'll tell you sometime.'

'I think it will work,' Keane said.

'Good,' Flemyng told him. 'I'm happy with that. Ring me later.'

The nervousness that Keane had felt since his meeting with Liam had given way to clear-headed concentration. He checked the time. Just after six o'clock in the evening in

Belfast. In the bottom of his rucksack was a cloth-backed notebook with his friends' telephone numbers. A chance visitor to these pages would find it of little use in chasing up those among them who were in Keane's line of business, in one way or another. All their numbers were disguised by a simple code that would confuse everyone else. And the names that mattered had been changed.

He found the entry he was looking for. Dialled a number in south Belfast.

'A friend calling for Johnny,' he said. After a slight pause, the voice said, 'He'll be here in fifteen minutes.'

'I'll ring back,' Keane said. He remained in the room, picking up an out-of-date copy of *The Times* from London and starting the crossword on the back page.

He found a couple of clues to get him going, and started to make progress.

'*Rebel creating revolutionary stir in countries.*'

Taking the pencil, he wrote neatly, '*INSURRECTIONIST*'.

He enjoyed himself for a while, and liked having the unsolved clues floating around in his head, knowing they would make a happy landing a little later in the day.

Opening his notebook, pencil in hand, he dialled the number again.

'It's Patrick.'

'Where are you, my friend?' It was a conversation in which each of them would speak with care, and brevity. They didn't need instructions.

'Well, you know, I'm pretty settled in Washington now. Still interested in the old place. I need to have a quick word in private. Can you do that?'

'Give me ten.' He read out a phone number.

A quarter of an hour later, Keane rang it. 'Johnny, how are

tricks? Sorry about all that. Saturday night and everything, but I've got something for you.'

'Two minutes first,' his friend said. 'How are you doing out there? Must be interesting to have an ambassador who knows everything about your game. And you'll know we're up to our eyes in London–Dublin stuff. All going a bit faster than we'd expected, and happily under the radar most of the time.'

'And you,' Keane asked. 'How's your office? I hear things. I know the changes haven't helped your lot.'

'I'm afraid that's true. We've got a section boss who doesn't get it all, the context. He can't stand your people. We'll bring him round, but it's irritating and it eats up our days.'

'Well, old friend, maybe I can help a little,' Keane said.

Johnny Silvester was a decade older than Keane, and had been in Belfast for longer than he'd hoped. He'd been promised a move after three years, and time was stretching towards five. His family were living in the Home Counties and he was lucky if he saw them once a month. The strains were telling on them, too, with his children in their early teens. Silvester was popular with his security service colleagues on the ground – he'd been marked down as an obvious lifer from the earliest days there – but he was a man of habit, often abrupt in manner, which meant you had to understand him to get to like him. In office politics, he found himself struggling to a degree that mystified him. Prematurely grey, he wore a look of sadness that Keane had watched develop over the five years or so when they'd known each other, and worked the same terrain for their different masters. Now Keane could help to puncture the cloud of disappointment that seemed to have settled over him

'Johnny, I've got a tip. For your use alone. This is from my past, not my present, if you follow me. No Washington link. An old contact has passed me something hot. He got onto me, although I'm a long way away these days, because we've had reason to trust each other in the past, at nasty moments.'

'I get the picture,' Silvester said.

'So, listen to this. He tells me that there's a big operation in preparation in London. An attack of some kind, though I don't know the target. Imminent, that's the point. Hours away, who knows? It's one for you.'

Keane gave him the name of the street and the postal district. He could hear Silvester's breathing down the phone, because he had a smoker's throat, and the way it stopped for a second or two.

'No more than that, Johnny. But this is Grade A stuff. My source has gone to ground, as you'd expect, and I can't offer anything from here. Poor bugger is terrified, I expect. But I wish him well. Keep me out of it. I've got enough to keep me occupied here. Just get it into the system, pronto. Over to you.'

They both knew that Silvester had been given an opportunity that he wouldn't miss.

'Thanks, old friend.' He spoke with feeling.

Keane rang off. He knew what Silvester would be doing. From his office, secreted in a government building in a wired-off compound with armoured cars at each corner, where the Barracks also had one of its Belfast outposts, he could send a secure message to London. A trusted source had come good, handing over a little packet of gold dust. A fire bell would sound, and there would be an immediate response. Special forces, Keane knew, would be out in north London within the hour. He had a vague picture of the street Liam had named, which could be scoured quickly from end to end. And even if there was high drama, his name would never be attached to it.

He rang Flemyng. 'It's done.'

Only mid-afternoon, but he needed some sleep. He was spent.

Flemyng spoke to Francesca, who had their boys for the day. They postponed the conversation about when she might return to Washington because each of them wanted some days to pass first. Their friends in Dorset had a piano she loved, so that was a solace. Flemyng said he couldn't wait until she played for him again. From the room next door, as they spoke, he heard the older of the boys picking out a simple tune. 'Time for a lesson,' she said with a laugh, and they rang off.

Flemyng asked Lucy to join him in the garden. 'Because of what Patrick has learned, there may be an operation in London tonight. You probably worked that out from the phone call earlier. It's an important one, possibly, but it's vital that our hand in the business is hidden. I do want to know if something takes place, but I don't want any enquiries to be logged from the embassy. We're bystanders. Can you handle it?'

Saturday night, Lucy pointed out, wasn't the best time to go on a fishing expedition on the phone without leaving traces.

'I'm sure you'll think of something,' he said.

He wanted to go to his favourite bookshop, and Lucy got Pringle to drive him.

At her desk again, having thought for a while, she rang the duty clerk. It was Heckler, back for the second Saturday in a row. 'You've certainly drawn the short straw,' she said.

'Never mind,' he said, 'I've got a thick novel and the world seems a little quieter this weekend. How can I help?'

'You may or may not know that we've got Roland Saviour here on Monday. There's material galore from the office about summit preparations, but I'm helping to get an Ireland brief of our own together, putting it in the context of this town. State of play in the draft agreement talks, and all the rest of it. I just want to make sure – I'm going to write this all up by the morning – that I'm up to date. It would be embarrassing if Saviour found us behind the curve. Can I count on you? If there's anything fresh on that front, could you throw it my way? Anything at all. I'll be working half the night because I have to get this stuff right.'

'Sure,' said Heckler. 'I'll check what's been incoming.'

She said, 'By the way, what are you reading?'

'*Life and Fate.* Grossman,' said Heckler. 'I like the Russians, for some reason.'

And, glory be, thought Lucy when he rang back two hours later, what an inspired call that had been. Young Heckler was happy to be of service. He spoke for five minutes, and she said the ambassador would be grateful.

Flemyng met her in the study, and she joined him for some tea.

'A raid,' she said, 'about an hour and a half ago. They found them fast. Corner shop proprietor knew everything about comings and goings, and thought there was something not right about the house. Lad on his paper round had a bad time at the front door. The boys went straight in with no ceremony, and they panicked. Bomb squad on hand in numbers. The good news is, although there's massive activity – house sealed off, neighbours moved out – it doesn't seem to have caused particular excitement. No cameras. Cover story about a drugs factory is holding for the moment. Nobody local is surprised by that. Meanwhile they've got them at

Paddington Green and they have two days to question them without going public, so there's time. And although Heckler was coy he did say the word was the target couldn't have been bigger.'

Flemyng was looking through the window into the dark.

'Well done,' he said. 'Tell Patrick that was brilliant work. He'll need his wits about him in Chicago tonight. But he's used to it. This won't be our last alarm.'

Lucy, having plucked up her courage during the garden walk, asked if he was worried about Liam.

'I have been from the beginning,' said Flemyng. 'Fear is built in.'

Lucy asked him how long it had taken to reach properly across the divide that separated them.

Easier than he had expected, he told her.

'You see, solitary men get comfort from being alone together.'

Twenty-one

HAVING PRESSED THE BUTTON, KEANE WAITED FOR THE explosion.

He accepted he could have no contact with London without breaking Liam's rule: no American trace. So he was stuck in ignorance. After his afternoon sleep, another exercise in the concentration he'd worked on from the moment he had changed time zones with his move to Washington, he felt restored. But he was jumpy. He spent an hour or so with the book of medieval illustrations he'd found in the second-hand bookstore, and it took him off for a while. But after he shut the covers, wondering how he'd fit the heavy volume into his bag for the journey home, he was still so unsettled that he couldn't decide whether he wanted coffee or a beer, knowing that neither was a good idea at that moment.

After a restless hour in his room, he rang Lucy at home and caught her soon after she'd left Flemyng in the residence. It was ten in Chicago. He couldn't know how much Flemyng had told her: there was no reason to expect any news. It was solace he sought.

Her news shook him. From her apartment, she didn't want to talk in detail. 'There's been activity in north London in the last few hours. Decisive. I thought you'd want to know. Are you going out tonight?'

Keane's edginess was such that he was almost overcome by her cryptic message. He felt his words tumbling out. 'All over? Yes, I'm out later.'

'Successful, yes. Relief all round.'

He asked, 'Quietly, if you follow me?'

'To the extent that's possible, yes,' she told him. Then, 'When are you back? There's a wild week ahead. He'll want you here before our visitors arrive.'

'I'd planned for tomorrow afternoon,' Keane said. 'But I'll wait until tonight's over. Who knows?'

'I hope you're back safely for tomorrow evening,' Lucy said. They said their goodbyes.

Keane prepared for his evening. He had his bag almost packed for the morning, and he checked that he was leaving nothing behind. Aware of the company he was keeping, he took his passport and his embassy security pass and slipped them underneath the Gideon Bible that had been left in the drawer by his bed, as in every American hotel room he'd known. The Lakeshore didn't stretch to a security safe in every room. He was amused that neither had it invested in electronic key cards, and still dispensed old-fashioned brass keys emblazoned with its name in a cursive script. He liked them because they were difficult to lose.

Zipping up his fleece he felt the heavy key in an inside pocket.

The walk to the Old Cork took him a full half-hour. He was working off his excitement, aware that a mistaken word or a misjudged question could wipe everything away. Even more heavily than before, he felt the weight of his obligation to Liam, who'd set off down a hard road with such a burden on his back.

Keane's most difficult challenge was in not showing too much understanding, let alone sympathy. He knew nothing, just a passer-by who felt some communion with the guys in the bar and shared at least a few of their sentiments. There were sharp eyes in the group, and he knew enough to be sure that the Viking's ear picked up everything.

When he walked through the doors, the place was full with the late-Saturday crowd. The band was singing a favourite rebel song.

Where are the lads who stood with me when history was made
Oh Ghrá Mo Chroí, I long to see the boys of the old brigade...

Noise and smoke, drinking and singing. It was hard to hear anyone talk.

He looked around. As he turned away from the bar, past the banners draped on the end wall and the huddle of people round the little stage where the band sang behind a row of pint glasses lined up like footlights, he saw Liam at the door. There was an accordion and a skin drum hanging from the roof above him. The lights were picking up the grey in his hair, and Keane thought it wasn't just his imagination that made Liam seem weary, a tired figure who just at that moment, standing on the edge of the crowd apparently unsure about whether or not to join, looked lost and alone. An illusion surely, because hands of welcome stretched out to him even as Keane looked across, and the smile that he'd enjoyed earlier in the day wiped away the sadness that he'd seen etched there. But underneath the back-slapping, Keane could see the mark was there.

He waved across the room.

After a few minutes, because Liam went first to the table where the Viking and four others were sitting, they found themselves squeezed together at the bar. Liam was wearing the battered brown leather jacket that gave him the look of a man of the road. Keane noticed he'd had a haircut and carried a coolness that was missing in the rest of the sweaty throng. His eyes were dancing, scanning the crowd. 'There's a party later,' he said quite loudly, because it was hard to be heard. 'Come along. Just follow me when I go.'

Then, heaving into him as if he'd been pushed forward by the crowd behind and might fall over, he spoke into Keane's ear. 'Any news?'

Keane winked, and raised his glass. They drifted apart in the crowd.

Keane enjoyed a bit of singing, and spent a while at the Viking's table, where he learned nothing.

Soon after midnight, Liam waved him to the door. 'A bunch of us are going to carry on.' Seven of them piled into two yellow cabs and headed west.

He had worked out on his previous visits that the Viking lived with at least three others. It was into their apartment that they decamped, and there were more of them. There was plenty of beer. The Viking produced a wooden box, and rolled some joints. Liam said no, which everyone accepted without argument, but Keane joined him and a few minutes later they were alone on a sofa while the others followed a guy who'd got out his guitar in another room.

'I haven't even told you my name, Patrick,' he said. 'It's Cathal.'

'Sure,' said Keane. 'Someone said.'

They smoked.

The Viking said, 'I suppose it's peculiar for you, coming from London and all that, to find yourself with us. Surely?'

Keane said not really, because he'd so many Irish friends at home and he felt comfortable hanging around in the bar. 'Identity's a strong thing.'

'Aye, that's true enough,' the Viking responded. 'But you'll understand that it's hard for me with Brits, even if they've got a bit of the blood in them.'

'No other blood, in my case,' said Keane.

The Viking's voice was rising a little. 'But you don't feel the anger. Maybe you think you do, but it's not the same.'

'I'm sure that's right,' Keane said. 'If you're not there, you can't know. *Really* know. What brought you over here?'

He knew the question was a step closer to the edge, and the reply confirmed it. 'Why d'you ask?'

'No reason, except you're a long way from home and you care about it all so much.' Keane was grateful for the joint, because they were both relaxed and getting woozy. He had to work hard not to push the conversation forward too fast, because his inhibitions were falling away. Dangerously.

The Viking's, too. 'I'm a fighter, all the way,' he said. 'I had to get out.'

Keane risked it, because that was his mood. 'Orders?'

'You could say that,' the Viking said. 'If I was you I wouldn't ask so many questions, though. We learn that, where I come from.' But he was still smiling, as he had been from the beginning.

'I don't mean to, Cathal,' Keane said.

'You see, here's the problem,' the Viking continued. 'We get people who try to find out too much, things that don't concern them. We've had signs recently. New York, other places. Fucking FBI, as well.

'You're a student here, you said. So the Brits are probably in touch, a London guy away from home, on some scholarship I suppose. That consulate will know all about you – maybe watching. I'd be telling a lie if I said that didn't worry me a little.'

The smile had disappeared, then it flashed back for a moment.

'No need to worry about me,' Keane said.

'Well,' the Viking said. 'You're getting on well with Liam, right enough, and that's good. He's one serious man, with a lot of respect. He'd spot danger if there was any, I can tell you. You know that?'

Keane felt as if he was taking a deep breath, but pressed on. 'You guys haven't had trouble in this town, have you?'

The Viking took a long draw on his joint, and soon he was surrounded by sweet smoke. He picked up his bottle. 'That's a good instance of the kind of question I'm talking about. You don't know about it, do you?'

'Nobody's mentioned anything to me at all,' Keane said, wondering if he was about to head round a bend at high speed.

'Well, that's good, because the answer is yes,' the Viking told him. Keane could see that his caution was dissipating. He sensed that he was beginning to talk to himself as much as to him.

'A complete fuck-up three weeks ago. There was a deal going on – if I told you what it was, my life wouldn't be worth living – but somebody turned it over. And we found out there was a spy there. There's no other word for him. A Brit agent, on the spot.'

Keane made what he hoped was a sympathetic noise. He asked how they found out.

'We were getting suspicious. Then when the deal was happening... well, the cops turned up. That it was it for us. The slug must have known we'd blown him.

'So he got it in the neck. Well, in the back. It was a mess. Chaos. We were all running.'

'There was shooting?' Keane said, as if the thought had never occurred to him before.

'He got in the way of a bullet. That's all.' The Viking went quiet, fiddling with another roll-up.

'But how did he find out you were all there?' Keane said.

The Viking had subsided, lying across the sofa, his head on the armrest away from Keane. 'I wish I knew.'

Recalling through the fug, and his own state of pleasant disorientation, the bellhop's account of the blond-haired visitor to Abel's hotel, delivering a message on the day that he died, he steeled himself to ask the next question in the right way. A statement instead. 'Somebody obviously told him to be there.'

The Viking was looking at the ceiling, a joint sticking up from his lips, his hands now limp by his side.

'Maybe. But what I hear is he was asking too many questions, so we're well rid of him, and all his kind.'

'Questions about what?' said Keane. 'Not that I want to get into all that.'

'You're not going to, don't worry,' the Viking said. 'I'll just say this. I'm told that he knew too much about some of my friends at home. Too much for his own good. And he ended up in a place where he obviously didn't want to be. And he was right, because that's exactly where he did end up. If you get my drift.'

A brief smile again.

'I do,' Keane said. 'Look, I'm fond of you guys, Cathal, but I'm not at your level. I won't blab. That's not me. I'll forget everything, don't you worry. I'll be out of town for a few days, anyway. Good luck.'

'Where ?' the Viking asked.

'North for a few days. Over the border to Canada,' Keane said. 'Hunting trip.'

'Good for you.' His smile disappeared again. The Viking had dropped a smouldering joint from the floor below him. Keane picked it up and threw it into the bucket in the fireplace. 'I need some fresh air,' he said.

It was a tall apartment building with a wooden stairway to the street. Keane pushed back the rickety screen door.

Unsteadily, they stepped together into the dark.

Twenty-two

KEANE SAT ON THE BOTTOM STEP OF THE STAIRWAY, IN THE cool of the early hours. The Viking was beside him on the scrub grass in the front yard, legs out and his back against a wooden fence. Still smoking. The streetlamp above him cast a dim light, and they were both wreathed in shadows.

A siren sounded a few streets away, then faded. It would soon be the city's quietest hour, and for a minute or two they were silent.

Then Keane asked him, 'Did everyone get away afterwards?'

The Viking's mind, as he knew, was still in the warehouse. 'The cops didn't know what they were doing. Thank God for that,' he said. 'Chicago's finest, my arse.'

Keane said it was obvious the guy must have been an idiot to get mixed up in the gang encounter, whatever it was about.

'No.' The Viking's voice was louder than before. 'I told you already. He wasn't stupid. He was too clever... while he was alive, anyway.'

Keane, aware that he was talking too much, still felt his words pouring out. Trying to stop himself, he failed.

'You might be imagining it,' he said. 'Who was he, anyway?'

'Listen to this,' said the Viking. 'A friend of ours told us the next day. The Brit ambassador's brother. Jesus, Mary and Joseph. Shit was flying all over the place. So it was obviously an operation, and his brother must have been running it, from fucking Washington.'

'How do you know?' Keane said.

The Viking took a long draw on his joint.

'Because he's got a past.'

Keane, his head swimming, smiled towards him.

'Well, that's Will Flemyng for you.'

In that instant, they froze.

For Keane, the darkness suddenly deepened. It was as if a door had slammed shut, leaving only a heavy silence.

The Viking's eyes were on him, finding a laser beam from somewhere, and didn't flicker.

Then he spoke. One word.

'Bastard.'

Keane had no choice. He jumped up and ran.

The gate to the street was hanging open on one hinge, and he grabbed it as he dashed into the street, sending the frame clattering to the ground. There was no traffic, and only one or two shining windows in the houses ahead. Another lit up as he ran.

Breathless, in panic, he had taken fewer than a dozen strides when he heard shouting behind him, then a sharp crack. A thud beside his ear told him that a bullet was now embedded in the trunk of one of the lime trees along the street. By instinct, he ducked as he speeded up, and almost fell flat out on the sidewalk.

Take cover, or keep running? Memories from his last handgun training course flashed in his mind. He'd never been required to take aim since, but he remembered one of the rules of combat his instructor had told them they must never forget.

At anything more than about ten feet you needed a fat slice of luck to hit a moving target with a handgun.

So, run.

Don't look back.

He tried to weave a little, as if he was on the rugby field, and almost dived headlong for the corner. But not before there was a sharp stab of pain across his cheek, and the metallic screech of a bullet whizzing off the fire hydrant ahead of him. On his face, he could feel the warmth of his own blood.

The bullet had strafed his cheek, and he felt as if he had been stung by a whip.

Lucky Patrick.

He massaged his face, getting his fingers pink with blood. It was a short street and he could see a crossing ahead, with four cars waiting at a stop light. He scrambled there in less than a minute. At the junction, he had to decide which way to turn. Darkness to his left, but to his right he could see the lights of a twenty-four-hour pizza parlour, and a gas station just beyond. His best bet for a taxi.

He reached it in a couple of minutes and looked behind him for the first time. There was no one else in the street, except two guys standing together, pulling apart a pizza to share. He could smell it from where he stood and took notice that neither of them had blond hair. 'I'm losing it,' he said to himself immediately, shaking his head as if to wake up. Then he remembered what he'd left behind, and jerked himself straight.

His red fleece was still on the back of a chair in the hallway of the apartment, with his old-fashioned brass key in the inside pocket. On that key was the name of the hotel, with his room number engraved underneath. And inside room 2035 in the Lakeshore, under the Gideon Bible in the drawer by his bed, were his passport and embassy security pass.

He assumed the Viking would find the key. But Liam had been in the kitchen, must have heard the shouting and the shots, and he might have been able to delay him a little before he set off for the hotel.

But not for long.

So, keep running.

He was out of breath, his heart thumping fast. But there was no time to sit down. Stepping onto the roadway, he could see a taxi pulling up at a red light maybe a hundred yards away. Probably his best chance. He stood in the middle of the road and waved both arms, as if he was trying to flag down a train.

'I'm on a job, buddy, sorry,' the driver told him as he pulled up beside him and rolled down the window. But Keane produced two twenty-dollar bills from his pocket.

'OK. Get in.'

'Fast,' Keane said. 'East Erie. Lakeshore Hotel.'

'Not hospital?' He'd seen the blood.

'A scratch. It's nothing.'

No more questions. A Saturday night in Chicago.

He was thrown back on the ripped back seat as the driver did a U-turn. There was no sign of a pursuer.

Did the Viking have a car? Would it be a taxi that would come after him?

He checked his watch. Almost three o'clock.

At each junction, the change from red to green seemed to take longer, and the quiet streets made the waiting worse. Then on the east side of the river they came upon three police cars, their revolving lights flashing red and blue and saw an ambulance approaching. A man was being held on the ground by two officers, one with his billy club at the ready. The hint of violence shook Keane in a way he wouldn't have expected.

He fingered his cheek, and realised for the first time that next morning he'd have a gash. The bleeding seemed to have stopped, but there was a red trail down his shirt.

The driver had done well. Nearly there. 'Keep the forty,' Keane told him, handing him the bills. As he looked back from the hotel door for fear of a following car, the driver was staring after him in astonishment.

Everything had to be fast. Straight to the desk, where the night clerk had snuggled down in his armchair with a book propped up on his knees.

'I've had a bit of an accident,' Keane said, rubbing his cheek. 'And I need to clean myself up, but I've lost my key. Can you let me into my room? You can check my passport photo.'

He was glad about the blood, because it got the clerk out of his seat, and Keane was already holding open the door of one of the elevators with the button pressed for the twentieth floor. It was slow progress in an elevator that seemed to be dying of old age, but there were no other floors lit up on the panel of buttons. No one else was coming or going.

On the twentieth floor, he moved at speed. He retrieved his passport and security pass, showed the night clerk that he was the same man and slipped him a ten-dollar bill. Why should the clerk worry if the passport name wasn't the same as the one recorded in the register? It didn't occur to him to double-check.

Before he'd closed the door behind him, Keane was zipping

up his overnight bag and checking nothing was left that might identify him. He slammed the door and almost ran to the elevators. There were two of them, and a third for staff to use for service. He looked at the lights above the doors. One was heading down, just leaving the fourth floor. That would be the clerk, soon to be back at his post.

Then he saw something that made him touch his passport in his back pocket in alarm. Above the door of the second passenger elevator, the light was showing that it had just left the lobby and was travelling up.

Just as slowly as the other one, he hoped.

2…

3…

Keane had no doubt the elevator was carrying the Viking.

He pressed the button in the service elevator, which he saw had stopped at the floor above. The doors opened a few seconds later. It smelled of clean laundry, and he breathed in deeply as it began to go down. Making the assumption that all the lifts were equally slow, he did an instinctive calculation. If the Viking was now passing the sixth floor on his way up, their lifts would cross at the thirteenth.

Unlucky for whom?

14…

13…

It would be tight. The Viking would get to his room before Keane reached the lobby. He would know in a few seconds that it was empty, if his bird had flown. Would he guess that Keane had beaten him by little more than a minute? He would certainly think it possible, and get down as quickly as he could. Taking the stairs from one of the top floors would be even slower than the elevator, so Keane guessed that he would already have pressed the button.

Keane was at 5. The last floors passed excruciatingly slowly.

When the doors opened he saw that the Viking was already on his way down, and had reached the twelfth. The service elevator, as he'd feared, was even slower than the others.

The lights flashed, one by one.

11...

10...

The Viking was catching him up.

As he ran across the lobby to the door, he made a plan.

7...

6...

Outside were three cabs. Two drivers were leaning together against the bonnet of the second car. 'Hi, guys. Quick run to Union Station? I've got the earliest train you've ever heard of,' Keane said, loud enough for both of them to hear.

He threw his bag along the back seat, and in less than a minute they had taken a left at the first stop light and were out of sight of the hotel.

'Change of plan,' Keane said, talking through the glass partition, 'if you don't mind. I'm going to take you out to O'Hare, OK? I think it's going to make more sense for me.'

The driver, who was never likely to complain about an airport ride, was happy to change course. The next light turned green on cue – glory be, Keane thought – and he swung right to head west.

He looked in his mirror, and said to Keane, 'Been in the wars?'

'Nothing much. Bit of a scratch. I'll get cleaned up at O'Hare.'

They were crossing the river, and the city around was at its quietest. It was sturdily handsome in the dark, a few lit-up office buildings reflected on the water, strings of street lights marking out The Loop, and the forest of towers in Downtown reaching for the sky. Nighthawks were making their way home, and the first street sweepers of the day were out. After the river, Keane could just see, away to his left, the arches of Union Station. For the first time in an hour, he allowed himself a smile.

Outside the Lakeshore, the second taxi had already left. The Viking had come through the door in just as much of a rush as Keane. He told the driver he was going to have to catch up with his friend – the one who'd just gone – because he'd been held up, retrieving something from their room.

The driver was ready. 'Sure. Union Station. Let's go.' So the Viking knew that he'd missed him by only a minute or so, and he asked the driver to give it a push.

He'd find him.

But Keane, though aware that the effect of the joints the Viking had rolled was more long-lasting than he'd expected, looked at the first streaks of light in the sky with the relief of a prisoner freed from his cell. He knew that many problems would flow from the events of the past two hours, but, as he ran a finger along the wound that was beginning to firm up along his jaw and his cheek, he knew he'd make it home.

And he would see Lucy before he had to face Flemyng.

When the second cab reached Union Station, it was still quiet. In the cavernous hall where Keane had met Liam only the day before, there were a few sleepers on the benches that they used every night. Each had his own patch, and respected the others' territories. A few early passengers were gathering for the first train south to Kansas, and there was a train arriving hopelessly late from Detroit that delivered an unhappy crowd into the early morning. The Viking could cover the ground quickly in his search for Keane.

He could see from the board that no train had left in the last fifteen minutes, and he got to the track where the next one was filling up, to check the coaches. It was thinly populated at that hour. Easy.

Nothing.

He visited all the rest rooms. Still nothing.

Fifteen minutes later, he was an angry man. Gate by gate, he made sure that he'd covered every corner of the station. He even took the risk of describing Keane to one of the attendants at a ticket counter, though not to any of the cops who were standing around.

Not a sign.

The station was beginning to wake up for the day, and the Viking was getting even angrier. He knew that through Keane's mistake he'd obtained information that his people would treasure, but that wasn't enough. He wanted revenge.

But quickly he knew there was no chance. Somehow, he'd been cheated.

Walking out of the station, he was gripped by fury.

He stroked the gun in his pocket, remembering as he did so that daylight was coming and he needed to take care.

But the Viking needed release. His hatred of Keane was now intense. It welled up inside him.

Walking up North Canal, the street still deserted, he looked down at a dozen tracks leading from the station, spreading in a fan of rails, each finding a different way out of the city. The sight of a train pulling away from the station brought him to a stop, still angered by the way he'd been tricked, and desperate to finish the job.

Leaning over the low concrete wall he gazed down on the

rails, watching the silver coaches slide slowly into the tunnel to turn south. The last one disappeared, and the rumble on the rails died away. His eye picked up the movement of a rat, scuttling along one of the tracks, and breakfasting on rubbish as it went.

The Viking's instincts kicked in, and his hand went to the gun. With only a quick glance along the street to make sure he was alone, he took it from his pocket.

Crack!

One shot.

The animal lay dead on the track.

Twenty-three

FLEMYNG'S FIRST ACT OF THE DAY WAS TO CALL AN EVENING council of war for six o'clock, before he knew anything of his head of station's bloody scamper through the night.

At O'Hare, Keane had patched himself up in a men's room. He looked at himself sideways in the mirror, preparing for the worst, but the wound was less dramatic than he'd feared. He was more worried about Flemyng's reaction to his blunder.

First he had to clean his tubes out, as Lucy had put it crisply when he rang her as early as he dared. It was only after he confessed how much he'd smoked that he told her what had followed. He had no reason to suppose, he told her hopefully, that could link him directly to the embassy, despite having blurted out to the Viking that he was aware of Flemyng.

But how long would that last?

Their first thought would be to connect him with the consulate, maybe as the agent for someone who worked there.

But Flemyng's name, and their suspicions of him, would point directly to Washington. He'd be lucky to keep them off his trail.

Days? A week? How could he know?

Lucy booked an eight o'clock flight for him and offered the sympathy he needed. But as he waited at the gate, he concluded that he hadn't felt so low since he had arrived in Washington. His horizons had darkened in the course of one night, and he wondered when the light would break.

Lucy decided to say nothing to Flemyng about him. He would have to tell the tale himself.

Flemyng himself made his usual early call to Francesca and spoke to the boys. They were hazy about the reason for her temporary relocation, but were learning quickly that the life into which they'd been born could never promise predictability. Flemyng finished the call feeling as untroubled as he could expect to be.

And then he rang Mungo.

'Our Sunday call, just like old times,' his brother said. Flemyng could hear that his voice had recovered its rhythm. He sounded confident, the air of bewilderment of the past week evaporating. Mungo was enthusiastic again.

'You'd have enjoyed the walk this morning so much, Will. Early apple blossom down by the gate towards the loch, and my bees are flying. The willows at the waterside are starting to fill out. The herons are nesting on the west side, and it all tells me everything's coming back to life. Going up to the high track – I do it most mornings now – there's a proper canopy in the trees that wasn't there two weeks ago. I hope it's not long before we're walking there together.'

'Me, too,' said Flemyng. Then, 'What about the police?'

'Fine and settled,' said Mungo. 'One of them's here most of

the time – young Alex – and two when they do a check round the house in the evenings. Plainclothes – naturally – and helpful. To be honest, I think they're enjoying it here. Alex has made himself a comfortable lair in the back bedroom. I don't know how long it will go on. We haven't had that conversation yet, and I'm not going to start it, at least for another week or so.

'They're thoughtful about me and this place, and that's quite touching to be honest with you.'

Flemyng asked how heavily the events of only a week ago were preying on him.

'I have moments of sadness more than anger or any such thing – and no real fear, which is maybe what you mean. But, of course, it's Abel I think about the most, more than the strange night itself. It hits me at different times, but every day. He'll never again walk to the hill with us both; never take the boat onto the loch, with the old rod in his hand and pa's fishing jacket on his back.'

They shared silence for a moment. Then Mungo said, 'I've been going over my last conversation with him.'

Flemyng was pulled up short. 'I don't think we've talked about it,' he said gently. 'When, exactly?'

'I suppose about two weeks before all the business here,' Mungo said. 'A weekend call, anyway. We haven't been speaking regularly, just from time to time. I could tell he wanted to tune in, just in the way you do yourself. I'm afraid I should have told you about this earlier, and I'm sorry, my boy. But to be honest, I had a bit of a block on it. Partly instinctive, I suppose, blacking it out after what happened, but I probably just wanted to put it away. Because it involved listening to our little brother in my head.

'How could I know I'd never hear his voice again?'

'I understand,' Flemyng said after a pause. 'I feel it, too, believe me. Please don't worry on my behalf.'

He could hear the relief in Mungo's voice. 'Thanks, Will. It's all come back in the last day or so, as clear as day. I can hear him now. The first thing to say is that this is connected with my... visitors last Saturday night. That's why I'm a bit guilty, to be honest, about having pushed it away. You'll remember I told you that I got into a rather strange discussion about politics with them, sitting there with the guns and everything. My understanding of what we've always called the Irish problem on this side of the water, for obvious reasons. Well, it was the same with Abel, so we spoke about it. Why not?'

'Indeed,' said Flemyng. But he added, 'That must have been a surprise.' He was sitting forward in his chair in the study in Washington, alert in a way that he hadn't been when they started.

'It was,' Mungo said. 'But there had been a bombing on the news, which I mentioned to Abel because it was such a depressing thing, and he wanted to talk.'

'You know how proud he is of you. Like me. He spoke about how much time you must be spending on Irish matters, because he knew that there was a big change of gear coming along, politically speaking. I've never asked him about what he might be doing at any moment – because the old rule we've followed for years still seems the best way. "I know but I don't know" – that kind of thing. So I never pry or probe. The same with you.

'But he did want to talk. Unusually, as you'll realise. He said he was spending a lot of time on Irish–American matters, and finding it engrossing. Apart from the folk who work through the established parties, and keep away from the hard men, he spoke about the difference between the ones who were determined that the IRA was justified in doing more or less anything, and the others in the same camp who wanted a different way forward. Not armed-struggle types by inclination, you might say.

'He told me he'd learned much more about the tensions. Especially from the hardliners who were suspicious that they were being undermined. That was the thing that had grabbed his imagination, he said, and the pressures were coming from places you mightn't expect. I talked for a bit about my teaching friends in Dublin – we had a good conference on the 1840s at the back end of the year in Edinburgh, by the way – and how I could see their problem. How far was it right to go to set the history straight? The endless question, without an easy answer.

'Maybe that was what encouraged him to go further than he might otherwise have. He said he saw the same among Irish–Americans who thought we'd been pig-headed over here for generations – I could hardly argue with that – but couldn't stomach the bombs either. I suppose I pushed it a little far, but anyway I asked him whether he had any reason for hope.

'He said he had a little. Abel the cautious.'

'I know,' Flemyng said, but that was all.

'Then he got back to the subject of you,' Mungo said. 'He was hoping he could help. I hadn't often been brought into these conversations about how the two of you might cooperate, for reasons I well understand, but I was sure that he wanted to let me know that he saw this as a moment when it might happen.

'I may have a gift for Will,' he told me.

Flemyng took his time. He wanted to be sure that Mungo

had reached a natural stopping place, which he had, and asked the question with which he'd wanted to interject for a while. 'Do you think he meant you to pass on a particular message?'

'Not really, or I would have done it on the spot,' Mungo said, his voice betraying a hint of hurt. 'Of course. It was more an expression of hope about what he might learn, I'd say.'

'That's what I would take from it, too,' Flemyng said. 'Please don't worry, Mungo. It's obvious that you were able to get him talking, for the reasons you've explained, so he was willing to give a little more than usual.'

'And we have to remember,' said Mungo, with a sureness that took Flemyng aback, 'he didn't know he was going to die.'

Flemyng said, after allowing a few beats to pass, 'That's exactly the point.'

The exchange marked the end of a difficult confession on Mungo's part, and an onset of excitement in Flemyng. With each conversation, a little more light was creeping in. But he now needed time on his own, to think.

They spoke for a few minutes about Babble, still finding it difficult to emerge from the shock of the previous weekend. Flemyng sent his love, and got Mungo to finish the conversation by going to the window and describing the view down to the loch and up to the hill in the light that was beginning to fade. 'I've got time for a stroll along the edge of the wood,' his brother said. 'I can feel the wind stirring. Branches are waving, fast ripples on the water.' He would get his police escort.

Flemyng said goodbye, and sat in silence for a full five minutes.

He rang Lucy. 'Can you ask Tony P to come round? I need to go for a walk. Patrick?'

'Landing at National in less than an hour, I hope. I'll get him rested and ready for six.'

Then she added, 'I'm afraid he has some difficult news that he needs to explain for himself. I'm sorry.'

Five minutes later, with Pringle walking just behind, Flemyng set off for Dumbarton Oaks. There, in the trees, he could pretend to be alone.

Twenty-four

AFTERWARDS, LUCY THOUGHT THE GATHERING IN THE library a perfect picture of Flemyng's way of working. Everything was in character. When the others were speaking, he listened without interrupting except to pin down quickly any assertion of fact that wasn't quite clear, and hardly moved in his chair. When he held the floor it was obvious that he had established his storyline in advance – there were no detours, no reverse turns – and had settled the sequence of questions that he thought must be answered before they left the room. By nightfall they would know precisely where they stood, and what needed to be done

His demeanour, she thought, was also pure Flemyng. Sitting half in shadow, he was wearing what she knew as his serious face. Long, dark, defined by the twin clefts that she always imagined deepening at any sign of trouble. He wore a blazer over his pink shirt, he was tieless, black hair well groomed, and had the air of a man who was comfortable in the face of trouble. Ready. If he was worried about the outcome – for family, friends, government or himself – he gave no sign. He was simply a man determined that they shouldn't lose sight of the objective.

Both Lucy and Keane knew these were the conversations that would set the course of the next few days, and their futures.

He sat them down, thanked them for steadiness in the course of the weekend he'd stolen from them, and signalled the start. 'Before we leave, I want us to have a picture of where we are. Then we'll see the road ahead. A dangerous one, as you both now know.'

In the silence, he leaned back, hands together, his feet crossed in front of him, and said, 'So, Patrick, what's happened to your face?'

'I'll explain. But let me start at the beginning, with the Viking.'

'No,' Flemyng said firmly. 'You first.'

Keane had never been more aware of his apprentice status as he began his confession.

He painted the scene in the bar, his encounter with Liam, the invitation to the apartment, and the Viking rolling the joints. Step by step, he described the journey there, their conversation, Liam's behaviour, and his exchanges with the Viking.

Lucy watched him treading water, wondering when he would find the courage.

'I was obviously worried that he was suspicious,' Keane said. 'He asked about my background and so on – but I could see he needed to unload. It was getting too much, and I was there to help. I'd spoken to him on the three nights I'd been in the bar, and he was starting to confide. It was enough that I was a listener, sympathetic enough to give him licence.

'So I'm afraid we smoked quite a bit.'

'Joints, I'm assuming' said Flemyng, who'd watched Keane's rising embarrassment.

'Yes, and I'm afraid I cocked things up a bit.'

'Out with it,' said Flemyng.

'The Viking was banging on about your brother. Their suspicions. The panic when they found out afterwards who he was. They thought it was an operation run by you...'

'What?' said Flemyng loudly. But he didn't laugh.

'... and I'm afraid I let slip that I knew your name.'

The silence reminded Keane of the moment his defences had fallen at the Viking's feet.

Expressionless, Flemyng asked, 'Does he know who you are?'

'Not yet. I can't see how he could.'

Pointing at him, Flemyng said, 'And your face?'

'A bullet. I was lucky. A scrape.' Lucy had never seen him look more miserable. 'I was running. It was close.'

Quickly, he went through the story.

Flemyng got up and walked to the window. 'I'm sorry,' he said. It seemed to Keane that he paused for a long time. 'You had a bad night, Patrick. I'm relieved you survived it.'

Turning back, he said, 'But this changes everything. They'll assume you've confirmed their suspicions about me, ridiculous though they are. And it puts you in a difficult spot.'

'Just how difficult?' Keane asked. Lucy thought he looked as if he might be about to be kicked out of the door.

But Flemyng was kind. He spoke softly. 'You're safe for now, and there's no reason to doubt your position here. Obviously you'll tell the Barracks what's happened, and if there's any trouble, you must let me know. I'll back you up. Meanwhile, we have to plan. There's the summit coming up here and the Dublin negotiations are in a sensitive state. We have to find out more about what's going on with Sullivan and his friends.

'After what you've been through, Patrick, you'll have to be careful. But you're going to have to see Liam again. First of all, let's go back to your conversation with the Viking. Describe him properly.

'Wiry and tough. Nervous, only just under control. Skin so smooth it's scary. Misses nothing, clever. Articulate and ready to pick up any stray word. Eyes that follow every movement. Oddly enough, he smiles most of the time.'

'Why oddly?' Flemyng asked.

'Because he's serious,' said Keane. Not a frivolous man.'

Looking at Lucy, he continued, 'So I suppose I have to explain how it was that he spent half the night smoking himself into a stupor, and definitely gave more to me than he meant to.'

Flemyng said nothing, but, without seeming to notice, began gently to massage the scar under his shirt. He didn't try to hurry Keane.

'I think he's under hellish pressure,' Keane said. 'He smiles to conceal it, but he's ready to snap. So when the chance comes, he escapes. Needs to. I was lucky to be the guy he wanted to take away with him on a Saturday night.'

'Your conclusions?' Flemyng.

'Firstly, their nerves are shot to pieces,' said Keane, aware how agitated he was himself.

'They're panicking about FBI interest – increasing – and the security of their operation. Obsessed about betrayal from inside. The Viking made it clear that their suspicions about Abel – remember he'd sprung from nowhere – were confirmed in their minds by the cops turning up when they went to meet the Latin Kings in the warehouse. They put two and two together.'

'And made five,' Flemyng said.

'Of course,' said Keane. 'There was no reason at all for your brother to blow up an operation where he was going to be present. He'd be putting a target on his own back.'

Realising what he'd said, he began to show more signs of agitation, crossing his legs, and losing the thread of his story.

Flemyng said nothing, but signalled with both hands. Settle down. Continue.

'It's obvious they tie you, personally, to Abel's arrival in Chicago. They're so nervous about penetration – discovery – that when they got his identity from one of their tame cops after it was over, they went into a tailspin. As I've said, they're convinced a Flemyng is operating against them.'

'And that's it.'

'Not quite,' said Flemyng. 'Did the Viking kill him?'

'Sorry, boss,' said Keane, shaking his head vigorously. 'I don't know. He was hazy. It's obvious that whatever they were doing was interrupted by the cops, and there was panic. They drew the conclusion that Abel was an informer and in the confusion somebody – maybe the Viking, maybe someone else – pulled a trigger.'

'Go back,' Flemyng said. 'What exactly did he say about the kinds of questions Abel had been asking?'

'No detail,' Keane said. 'Just that he knew too much about friends at home.'

'You've done well, Patrick. I'm grateful. Please don't be too upset about what happened. They'd probably have rumbled you in the end anyway, given the edgy state they're in. Let's hope they associate you with Chicago, and not this town, and it stays that way.' He was as serious as before. 'Lucy?'

'I want to know who phoned the police,' she said.

Looking back towards Keane, Flemyng asked a different question. 'How was it left with Liam?'

'He gave me a phone number, in New York,' he said.

'I've got it, too. So we think he's there now, or will be soon,' said Flemyng. 'It would be the last moment to walk away.'

He asked Lucy to deal with drinks. He'd have tea.

'First, the north London arrests. I've got a full account here. He took some folded sheets from his inside pocket.

'Good news in two ways. No connection with this embassy whatsoever. Patrick, your clever byways remain a secret, at least for now. That's something, I suppose. Second, the police operation on the ground seems to have been efficient. Unusually so. Assuming that charges are laid, there won't be much public detail at this stage about what the gang was planning. That'll wait for the court case, which certainly won't happen until next year. So this won't interfere with the politics of the moment.

'Saviour will have all the background, of course. Except our part in the story. So, please – no clues, not a hint. No knowing smiles.'

He looked at Keane.

'We'll express general satisfaction. That's all. Now, I'll bring you up to date with what I've learned from Mungo. He's given me details of his last conversation with Abel, a couple of weeks before he died. You'll be intrigued to know – I certainly was – that they spoke about Ireland. There was a bombing that was on Mungo's mind. Abel seems to have opened up to him, to an extent that, frankly, I wouldn't have expected.

'Mungo says Abel was interested in the strains among those Irish-Americans – I'm waving a broad brush here – who're sympathetic to the Provos. That is, the ones who think constitutional nationalism is a dead end. Abel was obviously making progress, in his own mind, following the struggle going on between the true hardliners – the bomb-the-Brits-to-hell brigade – and the others, who're willing to go along with "armed struggle", but in their hearts want it to end.

'Mungo told me that Abel might have a gift for me.

'Now, to me, that means something more than some clever political analysis. He knows I can dial one of those up when I like.

'It ties in with what Maria Cooney – Abel's old friend – said to me on the phone in Chicago. She couldn't speak openly, but said he'd told her he was hoping to make me happy in some way. We can assume that Abel thought he might be able to change the game. But I can't know what it was, nor – and this is important for you two to ponder – how he came to be looking for it in the first place.'

Then, in the kind of pirouette that Lucy had seen him perform so often in a logjam, he announced, 'It's time for me to tell you about James Jesus Angleton. Patrick, you need to know I had him in here for lunch alone, out on the terrace. Good stories from the distant past, of course. You'd have loved it. And plenty of evidence that he's an old man in a great hurry, who wants to talk.

'He made me think, which I suppose is the function of any ancient mariner who stops you in the street, and he gave me one quite unexpected bit of information: it was he who set up the very intelligence outpost that Abel worked for.' He paused to speak directly to Lucy.

'By the way, as far as security is concerned, you know enough of this already, and I'm deciding on my authority that your clearance covers all this stuff, which doesn't go outside this room. Stay.'

He resumed his tale. 'So Abel's outfit was an Angleton operation in the sixties, therefore focused on counterintelligence, tracking infiltration and so on, which as we know has been his lifelong obsession, stoked up by his own betrayal at Philby's hands.

'He told me that in his last years in the Agency he had no operational control of Abel's lot. It took on its own character. But he felt a certain loyalty to any of its people who fell in the line of duty, as we might say, so he came to the funeral. Besides which, as he was happy to admit, it gave him a Byzantine way of contacting me. He never goes through the front door if he can help it. He wanted me to know that Abel was trained in his techniques, and of course that got me thinking about what my brother might have been up to with Liam's friends. More of that in a moment.

'Then there's the Moscow stuff from Angleton, which brings me to *Sir* Roland, our arriving guest. I'm going to have to fill him in, which won't be fun. But that's my function, I suppose.

'About Chicago, I'm going to say as little as possible to him, and I'll have to set my own boundaries. But I want you to give me your thoughts about where this leaves us, what our next move should be. And I want you both to think about how Angleton's story touches – or, rather, casts light on – our other interests right now.

'Lucy?'

She said, 'Angleton's Moscow warning – or whatever we call it – has nothing to do with Liam or that set of troubles. How does it cast light?'

Her reply delighted Flemyng. He clapped his hands together.

'Remember what it's about,' he said.

'A name,' Lucy said.

'Exactly,' he said, as the phone rang behind him.

They watched, saw him smile. 'Really?' he said into the phone, 'that's good news. Thank you.' When he rang off, he gestured to Lucy to pour him a drink, pushing his tea to one side. 'More of that call in a moment. First, let me tell you where I think we are, and what happens next.'

For both Lucy and Keane, the next few minutes cleared the landscape. But when it was over, they also knew that a storm was lying just over the horizon.

'Abel died because he was trying to help me,' Flemyng said. 'How his operation began, or why, we don't yet know, but he told Mungo and our mutual friend Maria that he hoped it would benefit me. He had made enough progress to have made a discovery. Now, what do we know about his enquiries? That he wasn't interested in guns or money, but instead people and the disputes among them. That was his own story, and the Viking confirmed it to you, Patrick.

'We also know that the Provos were concerned enough after Abel's murder to put pressure on Mungo. That was organised in Belfast, not New York, because there's no operational control from over here. But obviously it started with a word from here after they discovered who Abel was. They needed information from Mungo. About me. And interestingly they had reason to revisit the past. What was my involvement in the Troubles? Did I have a spy across the water?

'If we try to put this together, we have to conclude that the questions Abel was asking were troubling their American friends a great deal. After they found out who he was, they had to put pressure on Mungo, and therefore on me. They thought I knew *something*.

'Well, what specific line of enquiry was so worrying that

they had to go through that quite complicated and risky business with Mungo – undertaken by someone whom I'd guess from Mungo's account to be one of their more delicate operators – and start to threaten me? This was much more than a generalised worry about people chasing the gun-running or the money-laundering, which is a constant to and fro.

'Simultaneously, we got a valuable tip about the bombers in London. Knowing what I now know about their target – I can't give you that now – the leak will have spooked them further. They'll be asking themselves if anything is secure any more.

'Now, imagine that in their high command there's a serious dispute about tactics. Not just about operation x or y but about long-term strategy. They know the London and Dublin governments are working on an agreement – a first step to more grown-up relations. A break with the past, thank God. For hardliners, of course, it's the start of a sell-out either by Dublin or London, depending where you stand. Our hope lies with the ones who think quietly that it's the beginning – or the beginning of the beginning, if you see what I mean – of bringing all this to an end. Years away, but without a start we'll all be dead before anything changes.

'If you don't want it to be different, of course, you'll want to blow this out of the water. I'm sure that's what they're trying to do. We've got to stop them. Now. Because the evidence from north London on Saturday night is that we may not have long. If there's another plan in place and it works, we're back to the worst of the bad old days.

'I think the key is over here. But there's desperation in the air, and a mistake on our part would start a spiral of violence that would take us with it.'

He got up again.

'You asked me, Lucy, why I said the Angleton business casts light on this problem. I'll tell you both. The old man's story has been nagging at me in the last week. Now I know why. Think about it. He wants me to warn London that our Moscow man's name has been uncovered by our American friends here – not out of hostility, but because curiosity is their business just like ours. And he thinks there's a risk – in his mind, it's a near-certainty – that it will soon get back to Moscow, in which case our source is blown, he dies if we don't get him out pronto, and our relationships in this town are turned upside down.

'Apply that to our own problem. Imagine that in finding out about the arguments among the people who're funding and organising the current Provo campaign – Abel uncovered information that damages us instead. Unintentionally, but disastrously. Think about it. If it became clear how much we know about their internal arguments, then in London, and in Belfast where we know the gossip level is sky-high, there's a risk that any advantage we may have could be rubbed out. The consequences would be disastrous. Here's why.

'Forget about the public. The Provos' Army Council would crank things up, and hardliners would have an excuse to go for more bombs. And the atmosphere would make it politically impossible for our ministers and Dublin to sign the agreement that's nearly ready. We'd be back in the deep freeze. The political progress that we want, quite desperately because we need it? Gone.'

Neither Lucy nor Keane said anything, sensing that Flemyng had more to give.

'There would be other consequences. Meltdown in Liam's crowd. Trouble for my family. I think I'd no longer be spared the attention of the wild boys who'd come after us, and I'm sure both of you – up to your necks in it – would be in their sights. Especially after what happened to you in Chicago, Patrick. All bets would be off. They'd find you in the end, have no doubt.'

Turning back, and leaning over the sofa where they both sat, he said, 'We have to hold closely onto what we know, because I'm afraid Roland, and that twit of a minister who's arriving in his wake, could easily turn all this into a weapon, directed at us. Even while they convince themselves they're being helpful.

'Put it like this. If our adventures here become known in detail either to the Provos or our own bloody government at the wrong moment, the balloon goes up. And who would want to help us? We'd be alone.'

Keane, he suggested, had a mind that would be pleased with the symmetry that he'd found between Angleton's storytelling and Abel's fatal quest. 'There's a pattern that in another context might be pleasing,' he said.

Lucy, because she always went back to unanswered questions and the piece that hadn't yet been slotted into the puzzle, said. 'You've talked two or three times about a name as the key to it all. 'Whose?'

'All in good time,' Flemyng said, and turned away. 'Let's survive Saviour's visit first.'

Neither of them was ready to interrupt any more. Each felt that silence was appropriate.

Over his shoulder, Flemyng said, 'You wondered about that phone call earlier. It was good news.

'Maria Cooney's coming home.'

Turning to Keane, who was raising a glass, he said. 'She'll be here the day after tomorrow. You're going to love her.'

Twenty-five

THE EFFECT ON KEANE OF FLEMYNG'S WARNINGS WAS SUR-
prising, even to Lucy. He was propelled into a reorganisation
of his apartment that had been postponed a dozen times and
more. Down from the walls came his manuscript fragments,
copies of early illustrations, and his precious illuminated
letter 'A', which he always considered the cornerstone of his
collection because it marked the start. He conceived a new
arrangement on the walls, and in a wild burst of activity before
he left for the embassy at just before eight, only half dressed
throughout, he produced in his living room a brighter aspect
than before. There was order, and a fresh storyline on the walls
which he thought he might use someday to explain to Flemyng
the nature of his enthusiasm.

Surveying his work, and filling his washing basket to
overflowing from the piles of stray clothing in the corners of
the room, he put away his duster and experienced a rush of
freshness, as if he'd dived into a crystal-clear pool of water,
deep and cold.

He and Lucy had gone home separately after the Sunday

night meeting, both agreeing that sleep was more important than anything else. But before turning in, Keane had felt the urge to take the apartment in hand. It was a displacement exercise, and his mind needed to be directed away from embassy affairs which, in the course of little more than a week, had become labyrinthine and threatening. He was filled with excess energy that had to find an outlet and, while Lucy listened to some of her jazz collection into the small hours, sitting in the dark with a glass of wine, he turned his mind to the transformation of his room to try to reflect the sharp seriousness that he'd discovered in recent days, even in the mistiness of the Viking's haze.

As he bustled about, he could see that face and hear his soft voice. The unexpected smile wouldn't leave him. His energy was still flowing, when he finished his task and slammed the door shut on an apartment that he hoped might astonish Lucy, perhaps even that evening, Saviour permitting. Then his mind turned to Guy Cotton, the first order of business.

'All quiet on the eastern front,' Cotton said when he sat down opposite Keane, who wondered again how he could contrive to be so effortlessly irritating. At least he smiled. His length, because he was slim and supple, gave him a comfort that Keane had often seen missing in tall men, and the softness of his voice – spared the Yorkshire bark that might have spoiled it all – made it easy for him to relax in any atmosphere. Keane often wondered why he himself quite often felt less comfortable. Cotton said, 'There was nothing much I needed to trouble you with in Chicago.'

He spoke of a good morning's schmoozing at the FBI on Friday. Whealdon and others had been welcoming. There were two telegrams from London in the course of the usual traffic that he'd thought it best not to forward via the consulate ('not that there's anything dodgy going on there, perish the thought') simply because the sensitivity was exceptional. Keane knew it was one of Cotton's favourite words.

'North London was a good operation, though obviously the praise will fall on our brave colleagues on the other side of the river, like manna from Heaven. Never mind, they did pull it off with gusto, on this occasion anyway.'

Keane skimmed the sheets that he passed across the table, and confirmed that there was no reference to Washington, nor the smudge of a fingerprint. Not a scintilla. And Cotton didn't know a thing.

The burden of the song that he read, however, confirmed Flemyng's account on the previous evening. There was good reason to suppose that a second active service unit was holed up somewhere, no doubt fired up by the arrests and the scuppering of Plan A, and ready to try to do better. 'Anything from the Feds on this stuff, Guy?'

'Not a peep,' Cotton said. 'They'd barely caught up with the north London business, and weren't awfully interested, to be honest. But I gave it the full treatment. The fight goes on, we've got them on the run, et cetera.'

'I'd have expected nothing less.' Keane said, and offered an apology for having left Cotton in charge at short notice. 'I'm grateful, Guy.'

'My pleasure. So what was going on in Chicago?' Because of his height, it looked as if Cotton was springing forward.

Keane was ready. 'Following up some things. A couple of people who may turn out to be useful. The boss has good political contacts, so it was worth being there to look at the landscape. I'd never been there before, and wanted to get my eye in. You?'

'A couple of times,' Cotton said. 'Love the buildings.'

'I took a tour,' said Keane, treading water.

'And how was he?' Cotton enquired.

'The boss was fine, though it was obviously raw and emotional for him. We went to the place where his brother died. The very spot. But the good news is that the great city of Chicago has no interest whatever in letting anything about the affair be known. None. As we can all understand.'

'Anything else?' Cotton said.

'Nah.' Keane stretched himself. 'Here they'd call it a boondoggle.' Then he took Cotton back to the FBI. 'Did Jack Whealdon have anything much to say?'

'Mostly routine. Gangs in Baltimore; too much cocaine; Teamsters stuff. The usual. There was only one remark that I didn't expect. He said his friends over in Langley were getting excited about our Soviet material.'

'Excited?' Keane said, as if he was puzzled. 'So what's new?'

'I did get the feeling that something has changed. He said we've been providing such good material for so long. Exceptional. But for some reason they're talking about it more – I assume because Kremlinology's everything at the moment.'

'Probably,' Keane said. 'Anyway, I may give him a ring.' He left it vague.

Cotton stood up. 'Meanwhile, we'll all be on best behaviour for Roland. Mid-afternoon arrival, I see.'

Keane looked at his watch. 'On his way now.'

Flemyng's equivalent of Keane's spring cleaning was a phone call to Mungo. He wanted to think of home for a while, before politics took over. Time to break out. 'It's the perfect moment,' his brother said. 'I'm back from the afternoon walk.'

Flemyng reassured himself about Mungo's health, then asked about the house and the glen.

'There's still a chill in the air, and I'm sure we'll have a blowy end to April as usual and most of the new growth will kick in. But, you know, there's a brightness around that wasn't here two weeks ago. You can feel the days lengthening, little by little. Will, you'll be so happy with that copse that we planted years ago, the three of us on that weekend, just beyond the rise before you get to the high track. The birches have shot up – you'll remember how good they looked last summer. They're going to give the entire wood a different look one day. And everything's nesting. I haven't seen so many blackbirds and thrushes for years. The swallows aren't back yet, but I expect we'll see them up at the house in a couple of weeks. And, by the way, Tiny says he's seen a kingfisher on the lochside, under the willows. That would be something. We've known the whole place, you and I, since we were wee boys, but I do think it's slipping quietly into a new phase. That's how I like to see it. Old trees looking their age and gracefully, if you follow me. Young ones bursting through. A different time of life.'

'Like us all,' Flemyng said, recognising in his brother a man who wanted to restore order. Recover what had almost been lost.

'Well, speaking for myself, I'm aware I've stolen some time,' Mungo went on. 'It could have been different. The doctors say I've come through pretty well, but I get the feeling that they weren't quite so optimistic when my attack came along. It was a jolt, and I think there was a certain amount of panic. Never mind, it's behind me for now.'

'I hope through your recovery you're not brooding too

much about your Saturday night adventure,' Flemyng told him. 'A nasty business, but you know, Mungo, I have a feeling that it wasn't so much luck that got you through it. Oddly enough, as you told me, they seemed to be looking after you, guns or no guns.'

Mungo said, 'I think I said they wanted me to live to tell the tale, and that catches it well. Which I suppose makes it all the more peculiar,' Mungo said.

'Or not,' said Flemyng. There was silence on the line from Washington.

Then, after a pause which was long enough to strike Mungo quite powerfully, his brother added, 'Who can say?'

They resumed as if there had been no interruption, although both realised they had experienced one of the moments that so often marked their conversations, when the unspoken intervened. Mungo knew better than to ask his brother to explain, and pressed on.

Babble's quietness and apparent frailty were a concern, he said, because he'd always assumed that his old friend was indestructible. Now he could see that life in the house would change. 'The days of him chopping all the logs, and both of us heaving away for hours in the garden, are probably behind us. Well, we'll just have to adapt. As long as we can walk, we'll still enjoy the old place, and we can always get in some extra help.'

He said that with the start of the season on the water in a few days he was going to get his Special Branch minder, Alex, onto the loch. 'He's no fisherman, but he can't wait to try. We're going to lay out the rods and the nets at the weekend.'

They spoke for nearly half an hour. Flemyng didn't take him back to his time with the intruders, but they did return to Abel.

'Do you have any idea how he was going to help you?' Mungo asked.

'No,' Flemyng said. 'I'm having to use my imagination.' Risky though that might be, he said to himself. 'But an old friend of his is coming through Washington this week – you've heard me talk about Maria, years ago – and I'm hoping she may be able to help. I gather they've been talking while she's been ploughing away in eastern Europe, and anyway she knows his mind. They were always birds of a feather.'

'I hope she can help,' Mungo said. 'It would be good to know what was on his mind at the end.'

The unintentional brutality of his words, coming from a man who carried his gentleness like a warm cloak on his shoulders, stopped them both short.

'I think I can say,' Flemyng said with a slight hesitation that Mungo picked up instinctively, 'that he believed on his last day – what a terrible phrase that is – he was helping me and others. He was a builder, never a destroyer. We know that, and I think it was true to the end. He still believed in his purpose. I think I may soon discover what it was.

'And that's a comfort, isn't it?'

'Certainly,' Mungo said. 'I'm glad he had no cause to lose that faith.'

'If I'm right,' Flemyng told him, 'that was absolutely the case to the end, whatever others might have imagined. Like you, I can't help trying to put myself in his place. But we've got to accept, both of us, that we can't.'

'Yes,' said Mungo, 'sadly, that part of our story is over.'

He looked out from the hall in Altnabuie through the open front door and across the dip in the garden, his eyes following the path to the gap in the stone dyke that eventually led you down to the loch. It seemed to him that a shaft of sadness had darkened the scene. But as he watched, he found the spirit of calm that lay underneath. The boat tied to the jetty was moving almost imperceptibly on the water. Everything else was still. The birds had taken to the shelter of the wood, because the light was starting to fail and the breeze coming into the house was colder even than when he had picked up the phone to Will. Coolness and quietness were coming. Time for a fire.

He told his brother that he'd spent some time with the orrery the previous evening. 'I gave it a little touch of oil last week, and there's not a squeak. Moving perfectly. Your planets go up and down as they always did, and at least to me the sun and the moon look as if they're in perfect order. Aligned as they should be. Harmonious.'

'I'm sure. A happy note to end on,' Flemyng said.

'You'll be sitting alongside that machine before long,' Mungo told him. 'And the time can't come soon enough for me.'

With a few last words, they rang off. Flemyng felt a gush of relief, and underneath it a ripple of excitement that caused him to think for a while at his desk, forcing himself to work at it. He hardly moved, as his mind swung from the drawing room at Altnabuie to Abel's hotel in Chicago, and out to the bleak ruin of the warehouse where his brother had died. Round and round, fitting the pieces together in different ways. Trying a line of thought like an attack on a chess board, then turning back and trying another.

Eventually he settled in his mind on his next move, realising that it had been lying in wait since he left Chicago.

He was bent head down over some correspondence when

Lucy knocked. 'Sir Roland has landed. Tony Pringle's on hand, and the embassy posse will soon have him in the car and away. Traffic from Dulles permitting, they should be with us in an hour.'

Flemyng smiled and stretched out his arms. 'Wish me luck.'

Twenty-six

KEANE COULD SEE THE GATES OF THE RESIDENCE FROM HIS
office window, and he watched Saviour's arrival. As the
Jaguar drew up, Flemyng stepped out from the portico where
he must have been waiting. With Pringle holding the car door
open, Saviour swivelled onto his feet in one easy movement
and Keane, ever sensitive about his own weight, admired
the balance of a large man who could still manage to make
an entrance like a dancer. He raised both arms in greeting
towards Flemyng, who waited just inside the gates, giving
his welcome a touch of formality. Keane watched the two
men shake hands, with Saviour the more demonstrative. He
placed one hand on Flemyng's shoulder and squeezed, and, as
they turned towards the doors and Keane lost them, he saw
Saviour speeding up, happy to display his enthusiasm.

The familiar hypocrisies of office, Keane thought. How
they all love them, until they turn into obsessions and start
eating at you.

An hour later, Saviour having showered and changed
in the rooms on the second floor that he always occupied,

Keane joined half a dozen colleagues for his briefing. Flemyng introduced him warmly. 'You all know Roland, of course, always so welcome among us, and I can promise you an exhilarating week. We're here to help where we can, although he hardly needs a guide in this town, and of course he will be helping us all to prepare for the summit. These are days of opportunity for the embassy and the government, as we know.' He turned to Saviour and smiled. 'Now, Roland, inspire us.'

Keane watched the performance intently, following every gesture. Saviour was impressive. Hanging his jacket on the back of the chair, and with his cuffs turned up as an extra signal of relaxation, he spoke for about ten minutes on his objectives for the summit. Making a precise distinction between his own role and that of the private secretary for foreign affairs in No. 10, he succeeded in appearing sensitive to the boundaries that had to be respected, while simultaneously placing himself centre stage.

'A different era has opened in Moscow, with a funeral as the inevitable prelude,' he began. 'Our thinking on defence and security as we deal with the new regime is our highest priority. We are watchful, but hopeful. I shall have conversations this week, many of which I'm sure I can share with you, that may prepare us for a summit meeting that, I think I can say, will lead us towards some new and fertile ground. Purpose in all things. Whatever our opponents say, they can't deny us that.'

By the time he was in full flow, the Italian pomade that he favoured for his hair was giving the whole room an odour of sweet spice.

Flemyng listened in silence with everyone else. Saviour was sharp, anecdotal, funny in little bursts.

248

He took down two ministers on the way, built up a couple of others. Keane admired the perfectly engineered analysis and the fluency with which it was laid out. Saviour spoke without notes, and never faltered. No one round the long table was in any doubt of his command and, despite the flourishes that he used to flavour his material, the seriousness of purpose. Keane was pleased that he made only the briefest passing reference to the north London arrests, didn't mention the suspicions about a second active service unit, and – of course – said nothing about the quality of the Moscow material coming from the Barracks, which improved his own standing in Washington rather more than he would have cared to admit. It wasn't his style to acknowledge too many helping hands.

He took questions for about twenty minutes, without a stumble over the name of any of Flemyng's colleagues, leaving what a visitor might have believed to be a glow of goodwill. Keane knew, however, that they were a sceptical bunch, who would dissect and analyse the performance with no sense of obligation to Saviour. His skills were admired, and envied by most of them, but for those round the table that was less of a reassurance than a warning.

Flemyng took him for a drink in the library. 'I've arranged supper for us. No interruptions. Important, don't you think?'

'Will,' said Saviour. 'I'm delighted to be in your hands.'

They sat down an hour later at a table set in Flemyng's private dining room. There was no need for him to rehearse his usual introduction to the paintings on the walls. Saviour remembered them all.

He passed on some inconsequential No. 10 gossip and turned to Moscow.

After listening for a few minutes, Flemyng said, 'Roland, I'm afraid I have news I must pass on, touching on the matter you've been laying out. Not for circulation, obviously. It's important.'

Saviour, whose bright-blue shirt seemed to emphasise his high colour, was beaming as if he were the host. His wayward left eye seemed to be roving across the table as he fixed Flemyng with the other. Instead of putting on a serious face, he gave an enquiring look with his smile intact as if he were about to hear something amusing. He turned the golden signet ring on his fat little finger.

'Trouble?' he asked, and his smile broadened.

'Yes,' Flemyng said. 'Something that should worry us, without any doubt.'

Pouring himself another glass of Burgundy, Saviour settled back. 'Surprise me.'

'I think I can,' Flemyng said, accepting the challenge. 'I've picked up a hint that I think may alarm you. It certainly disturbs me.'

He reminded Saviour that for reasons deep in his own history he knew more than any of his fellow ambassadors about the star Moscow operative recruited by the Barracks nearly a decade earlier. For years their most fabled source. 'It's a privilege,' he said, 'that has come my way. By chance, I suppose you could say.'

'Indeed,' said Saviour. 'Some of the less charitable would describe it as luck, but not I.' He drank. 'Tell me, Will.' His springy grey hair lay like a little cushion on his head, and he tried to pat it down.

'The Americans know his name,' Flemyng said simply.

Saviour took a few moments to respond. In every conversation, he liked to measure his pace so that his command never slipped. Not too much eagerness; seldom a sense of surprise, unless it served a useful purpose. This time, it did. He stiffened visibly, then let out a long sigh. Whatever his feelings, he fashioned them into a theatrical moment.

'Oh, dearie, dearie me. That is awkward indeed.' He gave a sigh and his good eye held Flemyng's gaze. 'Have we got a leaky old ship over here?'

He was tapping two fingers on the table, marking time.

'Hardly,' Flemyng said. 'I'm certainly alone in the embassy in knowing who he is. A function of my past life, as you know. Keane, who's acting up well as station chief, by the way, and handling some material he hasn't seen before, is obviously outside the circle with access to his identity.

'I take it that at home those in the know are still a tight little group?'

'Indeed so,' Saviour said. 'None tighter, I'm told. I would never breathe his name, even in my own office.' He was still tapping time on the table. 'As we know, curiosity killed the cat.'

Flemyng was aware that their Moscow super-source was handled by two – maybe three – old colleagues, who might as well have been operating in a sealed container with no windows. Almost no one else knew the name, and he would be surprised if even Saviour had it.

But he only said, 'You can easily imagine how it came about. Sheer jealousy, to be frank. We're getting a worm's eye view of the Moscow transition, and we're better prepared than anyone else. We know these people's thinking as we've never done before, and their foibles, too – who's up, who's down, who's sleeping with whom, who's dying, of course – and this has been the story for years. We're ahead of the game, and the Americans know it.

'Naturally, as you well know, we share the material – enough of it, anyway – with our friends in this town. I play my part in that. But they've been getting more curious about our man. Jealousy's involved: they ask themselves why they don't have someone of their own who's as good as this.

'That's why they set about tracking him down, so they could pin a butterfly on their board. I'm told they've succeeded. Of course, I can't be sure they've got the right name, and that makes it even more tricky. Imagine if I dropped by the White House and raised hell. People we both know would ask unwelcome questions, and if they've got the wrong man I'd have to tell them and probably blow our guy sky high in the process.'

'We'll come to that.' Saviour was speaking even more slowly, giving the impression that he was engaged in some serious background calculation even as the words came out. 'First, how did you come to hear of this?'

'I'd call my source a friend of the embassy,' Flemyng said with a straight face, speaking just as carefully as Saviour and deliberately catching his good eye.

Saviour returned the ball at top speed. 'So it can't be the old rogue that a little bird tells me you had here for lunch the other day.'

Flemyng didn't let his shock show.

'Surely, he wouldn't count as an embassy intimate?' Saviour went on. 'Please reassure me, Will.' Flemyng almost said aloud how revolting it was to see him licking drops of wine from his lips.

But he spoke quietly. 'Angleton, you mean?'

Saviour was smiling happily. 'James Jesus himself. I didn't know he was ever seen out and about these days, but seen he was. Right here, so I'm told.'

Flemyng had no option but to dissemble, laughing as he made it up. 'There was a word from him, I'll admit to you, that I was able to put together with some other hints and nudges I'd picked up around town. You know how it is, Roland. These things never come complete, neatly tied up with a pink ribbon.'

Watching him carefully, Saviour said, 'So what did you talk about? I'd be fascinated. A man I've never met, except as a character in some of the stories I've heard.'

Flemyng said he wouldn't be surprised to hear that they had delved into the Philby story, and that gave them both an excuse to relax into reminiscence for a few minutes, a pair of dogs returning to lick a favourite bone.

But eventually Saviour came back to the point. 'What exactly did he say?'

'That he feared the name would leak to Moscow. Of course, it's what you would expect from him. Betrayal is his stock-in-trade.'

'Did he know the name?' Saviour asked.

'No – at least if he was telling me the truth. Just that it was out and about in the Agency.'

'It's damnable. There's no doubt about that,' Saviour said. 'Are you assuming the worst?'

Flemyng smiled at him across the table. 'That's been the way of things for so long that I feel I was born to it.'

'Any recent evidence of leaks from the Agency?' Saviour asked him.

'Nothing I'm aware of. I'm speaking to a couple of people at the White House and State this week and I can probe a little, without giving anything away. I'll watch for any signs of alarm.'

Saviour was refilling their glasses. 'So let's get down to it. Do we tell our man?'

Flemyng spoke as if he were back in his old game. How

important should it be for them to be open with him? Their duty, surely, was to warn him. But the price could be high. If he wanted to run, get out, take a chance with a new identity in the west with guards for the rest of his life, then they had to help him – fulfilling the promise they'd made from the start. 'After the first conversations in Copenhagen nearly a decade ago, I think?' he said, with a question in his voice, and Saviour nodded.

Again, Flemyng was certain he was covering up his ignorance. But, he went on, it would mean putting an end to an operation that might be about to reap its greatest reward, with a presence inside the citadel when its walls were starting to shake. The change they'd waited for half their lives. 'We'd know it all,' he said, 'at a moment that might turn into revolution. Can we afford to throw that away?'

And there was the question of how much he'd done for their status. Saviour didn't need to be told, he said, that credit in Washington didn't always come cheap. 'Our man's currency here is pure gold, and you could say he keeps us solvent.'

'So which wins – moral duty or our own self-interest?' Saviour said.

Flemyng picked up. 'The story of our lives. We can't separate them. I think we've got a moral obligation to know all we can, because it will help us make decisions that are right. That's in our interest, and a good thing. So we keep him in place. But I also think we have a duty to care for him. I've been on the other end of it – less spectacularly, I admit, but the principle is the same. You need to believe trust is absolute, especially when danger comes visiting. It's the only thing you have when you're alone.'

He understood that Saviour would be wondering where his line of thought was leading. Perhaps even preparing some questions that would take him onto territory that he wanted to leave unexplored in this conversation. Yet neither did he wish to stop. Liam had been in his mind when he had lain awake in the early hours, because a sense of anxiety – he tried not to think of it as foreboding – was rising in him. He had already decided to send Keane to New York for another rendezvous, a conclusion he'd reached after talking to Mungo. It was not a mission he could undertake himself, but he was now convinced that it was necessary, to take them round the next corner. He had planned out his conversation with Keane in detail. With Saviour, he found himself musing about the difficulty of reconciling the obligation to keep their man safe after all these years, and their duty not to abandon the quiet fight they'd been trained to pursue to the end.

'Let's think of it in practical terms, without waffling too much about moral dilemmas,' he said.

Saviour smiled. 'I most certainly approve of that.'

'We have the advantage in where he's serving right now, as we both know.' He watched for a sign of agreement, and Saviour duly bowed his head in acknowledgement. He wondered if he'd gone too far, but pressed on. 'Therefore if he had to run, it would be easier. Certainly compared with Moscow. I know some of the details, and it's just about the hairiest escape plan anyone could think up. I know who put it together, and it certainly seemed clever at the time.'

Flemyng could see by his expression, because Saviour had not been blessed with a poker face, that he was a step ahead.

'It allows us to be straight with him, straighter, I think, than we might be if he were embedded somewhere in Moscow. We can explain the risks, urge him to stay in place, with the promise that he could be easily extricated if word got back to his people and he sensed danger. Or unusual danger, I should say, because he's lived with a mighty risk all these years. I think he'd give us credit for being open, which is after all what we've always promised to be. With any luck, it would persuade him to stay in place.'

'And there's the benefit that he rather idolises our friends in this town,' Saviour added. 'So I'm told. I suspect he would think it unlikely that betrayal would emanate from here. I'm assuming, of course, that he hasn't provided us with any indication of penetration of the Agency by Moscow.'

Flemyng was careful not to make it obvious that Saviour was having to catch up with his own thinking. 'You're right, Roland, and I agree. I think we can be certain, because I would know. But it would be useful for us to get him to revisit the question, which he will do with some urgency if his own future – his life, let's be clear – is at stake. And if he did discover anything about sources they might have in Washington, it would be a jewel beyond price for us. The greatest bargaining chip of them all. Because, let's face it, we live in a marketplace.'

Saviour had taken a plate of cheese from the side table and was assembling a platter for himself. He laid the pieces out in a semicircle, in order of strength. He sniffed at some Pont-l'Evêque. 'So, shall I set things in motion?' he said, breaking the end off a long baguette and crushing it in his hand.

'Am I right in assuming that you might prefer to keep your nose clean on this one?'

Flemyng, who had been thinking the opposite, said, 'I'd suggest giving ourselves a little time. By which I mean days, no more. I can test the waters here, see if I can confirm the story, and perhaps cast a fly about Russian recruitment here and there. I wouldn't expect a quick bite on the line, but you never know. Then we can decide how to move. Does that make sense?'

Saviour could find no objection that would sound reasonable, so he folded. He acknowledged Flemyng across the table, waving a crust towards him. 'Of course you must stay on the case, as you suggest. It's so lucky for us that you're here, with all that cunning we bred into you.' He raised his glass.

'Well, Roland, I think it's less cunning than a curiosity that can't be satisfied. Anyhow, let's see where we are by the time you're ready to leave. For the moment, we say nothing.'

Saviour pointed out that he had a White House meeting the following afternoon and was due at Langley to talk to the Agency immediately afterwards.

Flemyng suggested caution. 'I think it might be wise for you to keep this off the table. If we were both seen to be asking questions around town, we'd be sending out alarm signals. I can operate on my day-to-day rounds without causing a fuss. An ambassador's life.'

It was his turn to smile patronisingly.

He took Saviour to the terrace. There was a decanter of brandy waiting for them, and they stood with their nightcaps looking into the dark. Late planes were following the course of the river from the north one after the other, and dipping down towards National. Sirens sounded from two cars coming up the hill, just over the wall. A helicopter passed low overhead. 'They say it's New York that never sleeps,' Saviour said, looking up.

'I wonder who that was, and where he's bound. Everything in this town is the same. You see as light movement, hear a soft word, and ask what it means.'

'Yes,' Flemyng said, 'and sometimes the significance

is elusive. You realise what you've seen or heard long afterwards.' Saviour turned towards him in the dark, sensing a more personal tone. 'The trick is not missing it in the first place. Puzzles are easier to solve that way, but too often we choose the harder path, and have to come from behind.'

Because his antennae were sharp, even when he had an empty brandy glass in his hand, Saviour picked up the unintended cue. 'We haven't talked about your brother this evening, thanks to your important piece of news, but I do want to do that in the course of this week. Talk about *both* your brothers, I should say.' He faced Flemyng directly, and suggested another brandy.

'You have endured a tragedy. Do you know what happened yet? *Really* happened.'

'No, I don't,' Flemyng said. 'But I've learned enough, I think, to be sure that it may bring more trouble.'

Saviour's silence was painful, because Flemyng knew that, despite all his preparation, he had made a mistake. He cursed himself.

'Let me explain another time,' he said out loud. 'Of course, I can wait,' Saviour reassured him, putting a hand on his arm. He drank up, said how much he was looking forward to their White House expedition, and wished him goodnight.

Flemyng stepped back onto the terrace. He was filled with regret.

Standing alone, he found that instead of the calm that he thought might come with the dark and the quiet there was a rising turbulence, stirred up in the previous few minutes, that he couldn't suppress. He reached into his jacket pocket and found the piece of paper on which he'd written the New York number Liam had given him in Chicago.

Flemyng had said he wouldn't use it himself, because of

the danger to them both. The evening's conversations had changed his mind. As a matter of self-defence, he argued to himself that a quick call on the secure line – untraceable from the other end – would be safe. If he kept it brief, and if Liam was there.

He went to his desk. Considered the words he would use. Dialled.

There were seven rings. He counted.

'Hello.'

Flemyng spoke.

'My young friend is coming to New York tomorrow. He'll ring at six.'

Liam said, 'I'll have interesting news for him, too.'

Eight seconds. Flemyng replaced the phone.

He went upstairs to bed, wondering what Liam had for them.

Twenty-seven

AT DAWN, MARIA COONEY TOOK HER FIRST WALK IN Washington for more than a year.

She kept a house behind Capitol Hill, and late in the evening the cab from Dulles had dropped her outside, where she spent a minute or two on the sidewalk before stepping towards the yellow door. A bright stripe of light between the curtains at the ground-floor window told her that the friends who were renting it, always keeping a room ready for her on short notice, were in the room she loved most. A colourful den, with thick rugs and vivid wall hangings that gave it a rich closeness that was personal. Aztec face masks and Native American pots, scarlet and turquoise beads on the mantelpiece, a gnarled piece of driftwood she'd taken home from Cuba. Icons from eastern Europe. Even from outside the house, with a sharp breeze bringing coolness to the night, she could breathe the warmth.

When she rang the bell to announce her return, she relaxed.

And now, at first light, she was on the move, taking a favourite route along the canal. Georgetown was above her, and on the other side of the cycle path the brown river slipped southwards at its lazy pace. The sun was behind her and she pushed into the wind, stepping out to get as much energy as she could from the scene. Exhilarated, she speeded up. Her black hair flew behind , giving her the look of a much younger woman. The passing years didn't trouble her, and as she walked she thought of her old friend whose birthday wasn't far from hers, and in the same year. She hoped that Flemyng in his mid-fifties, despite the rank and formality that came with the embassy, still had the flash of the glistening blade she'd first known in the streets of Paris when the world was young.

Home for a shower, and a call to his office, first thing. No delay.

Abel was in her head. She saw his sharp, dark features and heard his voice. Most of all, she remembered his eyes. Black like his brother's, with a shine that gave him sparkle even when his downward features projected gloom. His humour was often unexpected, and Maria remembered that in times of trouble – as when their young friend Joe had died in London, alone on his secret battlefield – Abel could discern light in the darkness. Late, lying in a nest of her cushions, they told the tales no one else was allowed to hear, and loosed themselves on their adventures.

It brought her back to Flemyng himself. On the line from Chicago she'd felt his pain as sharply as if she had been holding him. So the thought of seeing him for the first time since he'd arrived in Washington lifted her. Impatiently, she checked the time. The embassy day started early, to catch up with London.

It was seven thirty when she rang the switchboard, getting straight through to Lucy.

'Remember me?' Maria said. They laughed together.

Lucy asked for a number and said he would call back. On the secure line, the phone was picked up immediately. 'My dear old friend,' Flemyng said.

Before she spoke, they shared a moment's silence. He knew it was in remembrance of Abel, an acknowledgement of the presence they wouldn't know again, and it marked the start of a new chapter for each of them. They were drawing breath, aware that the conversation was a signal of trouble. It had always been like that. When their lives came together, a dangerous expedition lay ahead. Yet there was no regret in that truth. Not having to explain their shared excitement, they enjoyed the moment and breathed easily.

'Tell me how you are,' he said, softly. She spoke about travels and her absorption in work. Poland, and the whole glistening carpet of middle Europe. Stories, events, thoughts about tumults to come. Of her real task, the one that fired her up, she said nothing. That could wait. 'When?' she asked.

'Come here,' he said. 'Journalists are always welcome in the embassy.' Maria laughed at that.

He added, 'Five o'clock this afternoon,' and she understood the urgency.

'I'll be there.'

'The residence. You'll be expected.'

Although he was aware that he was dispensing with the caution that governed so much of his life, Flemyng felt the anxiety flee. It had been more than fifteen years since their escapades in Paris had first brought them together, in a beautiful throw of the dice. Their relationship had helped him keep open a channel to Abel, and he believed that if it had not been for Maria's position by his side in the L Street outfit, all

THE SPY ACROSS THE WATER

his brother's secrets might have been kept from him. She had helped to open the door a little.

Flemyng and Abel's sense of duty was unusual, because it involved a benign deception. Each was devoted to his professional life, and they had agreed, without any formal conversation to negotiate the pact, that neither would cross the line without permission. Each knew more than he should have done about the other's business – no outsider could have guessed at their insights – but although they had shared information when necessary, in operations where they were thrown together neither had ever pushed for access to the whole story.

Their duty to their own people meant the distance between them could never be properly bridged.

Maria was go-between. In Paris she and Flemyng had first found themselves engrossed in the Cold War intrigues that followed a puzzling death, comrades in the struggle. Flemyng understood a personal secret that Maria had to keep safe – the woman she loved was working in official Washington – and Maria knew that her cherished Abel could never reveal the full story of his life to the man to whom he was bound by blood.

To her, the brothers had carried the weight of what they knew with surprising vigour, as if each was proving to himself as much as to the other that there was a point to the intimate secrets governing their lives.

Even when Flemyng took himself to politics for a few years and found a decent foothold on the ministerial ladder, old rules with Abel still held sway. In the affair that had destroyed one of his colleagues, and which shook a government to its core, Abel couldn't reveal the extent of his involvement, even while offering help. Flemyng suspected, but couldn't ask. It was more important that they survived.

Now, as Maria spoke to Flemyng, she knew it was over. Abel was dead.

'I've been through it a dozen times,' she said.

He shook his head. 'I know. I've been to the place. As miserable as you'd expect. Dirty and bleak. That's why I was in Chicago. Come today, and we can talk.'

'I have more for you,' she said before they rang off.

Just before eight o'clock, with the morning light streaming across his desk, he summoned Keane.

'Early call, Patrick.' No apology. 'Could you come now? You'll be travelling today, by the way.' Keane, recognising his tone for what it was, didn't ask why.

Flemyng was due to have a breakfast conversation with Saviour in less than hour, by which time Keane would be well briefed and out of the way. Not only would they discuss Liam, and Flemyng's plans, but he had decided in the night, sharply aware of all the irritations of the previous evening that hung in the air like a persistent shower, to tell Keane more of the story of Maria. But he would keep her well away from Saviour – an encounter was unthinkable – and talk alone. It cheered him to think of happy times, especially in Paris, and in his journey towards the truth about Abel, his death and what lay beyond, there could be no better companion. He wondered what news she had.

He was clearing the overnight telegrams when Keane knocked.

He was well scrubbed and shining, and Flemyng wondered whether he'd squeezed in a haircut the previous afternoon. 'What's up, boss?' It was as if he'd been taken in hand. His blond curls seemed more under control. He was smart, in a midnight-blue jacket and cream shirt, and had polished shoes. Eager. Events were having their effect.

'You look fresher than I feel,' Flemyng said. 'But there's business to be done. Late last night I had the briefest of words with Liam. You'll ring him at six tonight in New York, which is where you're going.'

Asking no questions, Keane said he'd already worked that out. 'I keep an overnight bag in the office.'

'Good,' Flemyng said. 'I expect you'll stay over. Liam has news for us, he says. I think we can assume it matters.'

Keane was on the sofa, already used to the library as a place where the unexpected came to life.

'There's a complication I want to explain first,' Flemyng began. 'And an obligation – a happy one. You won't be surprised to hear that Saviour is the complication. We spoke last night. Mostly about the fallout from Angleton, and we had our awkward moments, but you'll be glad to know that he has no inkling of our doings in Chicago. His interest lies in what he thinks is the bigger picture. Let's keep him there.

'But we should be careful. I don't want him wondering what you've been up to, not that it's any of his business. However, he's got that young minister coming out – maybe even today – who's a pain by all accounts. Calls him Arty, God help us. His new remit covers the Barracks as you well know, not that I suppose they tell a junior minister much of what really matters, unless things have gone downhill since my day. Watch your step.

'The obligation I mentioned is quite different. I told you the other night about Abel's friend Maria. She's coming here later. I want you to meet her when you get back from New York, and I promise you'll enjoy her. One of a kind.'

'I'll relish that,' Keane replied. 'What exactly do you want from Liam?'

'I'm making progress in my own head with the Abel story,' Flemyng said. 'I have an idea what he was trying to do. Something that he believed would be helpful to me. But I need to tell you again, Patrick. This is dangerous, for you as well as Liam. We're dealing with people who're on the verge of panic. You didn't get that wound by accident. And given what's at stake for them, it means that if things seem to be unravelling they'll fight their way out of it, with whatever it takes. Anyone in their position would do the same. Be aware.'

Keane said the Viking had convinced him of that. 'But I'm still in the dark. Take me down the road.'

'I'll tell you where my interest lies, and Liam is the key.' Flemyng spoke with urgency. 'It won't be the whole story, but it will help. Get anything you can get about their internal arguments.'

Keane turned over in his mind what they had learned in Chicago. He told Flemyng about the chaos on the night Abel died. He was assumed to be a spy of some description, burrowing into their dollars-and-guns network. From Keane's own conversation with the Viking, he did wonder if it was true that no one was sure who fired the shot. It had happened, but all of them could plausibly deny personal responsibility. And did it matter who? It couldn't change the outcome.

Having reminded them both of that brutal fact, he said, 'I'm sorry to put it like this, but I know there's something you're not telling me. None of this is enough for you to have taken the risk of ringing Liam in the middle of the night to tell him I'm coming. You could have sent me, with warning, and I'd have made contact on the phone without all this rush. Why?'

Flemyng was still in one of the serious moods that they

knew so well. The morning sun was bright, but he was dark. His lined face created its own shadows. His mouth was set as if he was holding himself tight. For a brief moment he relaxed at Keane's question, and managed a smile.

'You're right. But sometimes it doesn't make sense to give a complete answer, even to you. It will come out better in the end – I'm convinced of that, and you'll have to believe me – if I don't take you all the way right now. That would make it more dangerous for you, I'm sure.

'So I'll say this. Liam isn't just someone who's worried about being fingered even by the flimsiest rumour as a contact of ours – for the rather good reason that it would cost him his life – but about something that's bigger than him. If you knew, I think he'd sense it when you talked in New York because he's got a sixth sense, one I know well. So better that you don't.' He added, 'Yes', as if he was still trying to persuade himself.

'I want you to explore. Get from him as much as he's willing to pass on about what's going on in Belfast. Then you and I will try to work out what it means. OK, done?'

Flemyng could see that Keane had lost the relaxed perkiness that he'd brought into the library a few minutes earlier and wasn't convinced. He was restless, anxiety showing in the movement of his hands and on his face. It was more than a natural concern to carry out the New York operation with care and look after himself, but an obvious feeling – so familiar to Flemyng – that he was being denied the part of the story that would allow him to do the job well. And, probably, give him some protection from the dangers that Flemyng had taken so much trouble to point out to him.

As he turned to leave, Flemyng made his move.

'One more thing. Can you ask Liam why he thinks they

made that visit to Mungo? It sounds obvious, I know, but I want his version. In Chicago he knew nothing about it. He'll have an idea by now.

'So, the simplest question. Why?'

Keane smiled again, although puzzlement showed through. The assault didn't seem mysterious to him, just a textbook threat. Predictable. 'I will,' he said. He closed the door behind him.

Satisfied, Flemyng stretched himself in front of the window, enjoying the sun. Then he turned to his papers, though the pages were blurring before his eyes.

Twenty minutes later, he had breakfast with Saviour, who was ticking off his appointments for the next two days and listing the coming conversations one by one. He read them as if he were reciting a league table. Then he sat back, evidently ready with a declaration.

'Decision,' he announced. 'Duty demands it. I'm going to follow up the leak of the name.'

Angry, Flemyng said he needed a few minutes in his study before they talked about the White House visit. As he walked along the corridor, Saviour's words stuck in his mind, and took him away from the embassy. That simple phrase – 'the leak of the name'. When he got to his study he left his papers alone and stood at the window.

And there, just before nine, he took a call from Keane, at Union Station.

'I'm sorry, but I panicked.'

'Again?' Flemyng said, aware of the cruelty.

Keane, feeling the sting, confessed that anxiety had caused him to call Liam, too early.

'From a payphone – to make a plan. I know I should have waited, I'm sorry.'

Before Flemyng could answer, and bawl him out, he added, 'But there's news. He's going home. Belfast.'

'His own decision?' Flemyng asked quickly, forgetting everything else.

'No. He was told his help was needed. He described it to me as an order.'

'But you'll still be seeing him?' Flemyng was anxious.

'Yes, he's booked on a flight tomorrow night to do a job for them in Amsterdam over the weekend – meeting a contact, I think – then going home. We have our arrangement for tonight.'

'Ring me on the secure line afterwards. However late. What was your feeling about his state of mind?'

'Anxious as hell,' said Keane with no hesitation. 'Apprehensive.'

'Amsterdam?' Flemyng repeated.

Keane said, 'That's where he'll be until Sunday night, then Dublin and straight up north.'

Flemyng was massaging his scar again, a serious look on his face. 'I think an idea may be taking shape. Bloody risky, but there we are.'

He told Keane that in his blundering phone call – he used the cruel word – he'd found a way forward, without knowing it. 'So I have a message for you to pass to Liam. Simple, and he'll understand.

'Tell him to take both his passports.'

Twenty-eight

A FEW MINUTES LATER, KEANE WAS STILL NERVE-WRACKED.
He'd taken care to get to Union Station early, and it was while he was filling himself with black coffee that he decided to make the call to Liam. He was lucky to have his regret at doing it almost wiped away by the news from Liam that he was able to pass on, because he'd not enjoyed confessing his near-panic to Flemyng. Now, walking towards the platform where his train was filling up, he was taken aback.

It began as a tingle of curiosity that turned quickly into shock.

A face in the crowd was familiar, but he couldn't place it. The man wasn't a friend, he was sure. But he recognised him, and wondered if he was some minor public figure he'd met – a semi-anonymous congressman maybe? – or an official whose path he'd crossed. Almost immediately, he decided not. As he walked, he tried to clear his mind.

Where was he from?

He was carrying a striped bag that looked to be packed with clothes. It was a cool morning, so he wore a dark-blue anorak, and he had a black knitted bonnet pulled down on his head. Stocky but fit-looking, he reminded Keane of someone. Square-faced with a ski-jump nose, he would stand out in a crowd. Where had he seen him? Or was he a lookalike?

Within the two minutes or so it took for him to get from the concourse to Track 9 and find his seat, he decided. Somewhere in his socialising they had been in a crowd together. And he concluded that it was in an Irish bar in Washington where he'd spent some happy evenings with acquaintances who liked to go there. A place where he picked up useful Provo-talk. Yes, surely. In his mind, he could see the throng at the bar, hear the band, see the face. The stranger was from the Four Green Fields.

Coincidence? That he should be going to New York to see Liam, and a character from that part of his life should materialise alongside him?

Like Flemyng, with whom he'd often spoken about coincidences, he didn't believe in them. Or at least, couldn't afford to.

Had he seen him before? Anywhere, apart from the bar? Keane thought not. He took simple precautions around Washington, without worrying too much about surveillance. It was natural to pick up a figure who turned up too often, or someone who was behaving oddly nearby, but he'd never had reason to worry. At least in his experience, not that kind of town.

So was it an artificial response to the Abel affair that caused him to be taken aback so suddenly? The chances of eventually seeing someone from the bar crowd in the street or at a station or the airport were reasonably high. Surely. But he was not in a mood to believe in luck.

He slowed down a little on the platform and watched

the stranger. He showed no sign of being aware of Keane, and there were none of the telltale signals that he might be watching him – checking the window reflections, finding excuses to look behind him, and all that – but the more Keane thought about him, and he was able to glance in his direction as he walked along, the more convinced he became that this was someone who'd been physically close to him, and more than once.

Therefore, full alert.

In the train, he sat by the window in a pair of airline seats, with an empty place beside him. He had watched the man climbing aboard and kept walking to be three coaches ahead of him.

When he made a check after Baltimore, making his way back from the café-bar near the rear of the train, he saw the striped bag on the overhead rack. He must have been slumped in his seat, because his head wasn't showing. But he had changed coaches to be nearer Keane. That was certain.

Act normally. Don't walk past his seat. Show no interest. Wait.

Keane read his thriller and placed the page with the crossword in the *New York Times* on the seat beside him, with a pen.

Wilmington, Philadelphia, Newark. Three and a half hours. Nothing.

He scanned the Manhattan skyline when the city slid into view and thought about Liam. The line looped eastwards and sloped towards the tunnel.

As the train passed under the river on the approach to Penn Station, he zipped up his overnight bag and made a plan. He'd walk forward to leave the coach, without looking behind him. At the station, he'd go to the bookstand, from where he could survey the concourse. On the last part of the train journey, through the industrial wasteland that stretched flat towards the shoreline with its watery trails of muck and smoke, he'd decided that he would give his companion a chance. Rash, but it was the only way to find out more.

He was certainly not in the crowd just behind him on the short escalator from the track. From the bookstand, where he browsed through some of the latest paperbacks on the table in the middle, he couldn't see him moving with the crowd towards the main exit, and wondered if he'd gone.

No. There he was at a ticket machine in the corner, apparently having difficulty completing a transaction. Wasting time, deliberately. So he was doing a job, and he wasn't a complete amateur. Keane bought two magazines and stopped in front of the bookstand to put them away in his bag. He wouldn't admit it to Flemyng afterwards, but he could feel his pulse quickening.

He walked towards the escalators that led to the street. He'd forget about a taxi and walk to his hotel, which was ten blocks north. He didn't stop at any shops, just enjoyed the city life crowding in on him and the swarms of yellow cabs honking at each other like angry hornets. At 43rd Street he took the crosswalk to the east side of the avenue and, sure enough, a block behind him on the same side he could see the striped bag swinging back and forth.

Was he a threatl? Or did he want to make contact? It was a measure of Keane's edginess that he found it impossible to decide.

Keane's hotel was another block east on 44th, and from the reception desk he watched the door. Nothing.

He took a chair in the lobby, picking up the crossword and apparently waiting for a friend to arrive. Still nothing.

He had checked in under his real name, which wasn't always the case. Again, Flemyng might disapprove of the lack of precautions when he was travelling for a purpose that had to be kept from others, but as it had turned out – the second stroke of luck that morning – the decision might prove useful.

'I'm expecting one of my colleagues to call on me,' he said to the friendly woman behind the desk. 'I'm not sure which one it will be. But if anyone asks for me, please just call my room.'

'I certainly shall, sir. Have a nice afternoon.'

Looking through the open elevator doors to the street, he saw nothing. They closed, and he was alone.

In his room, he unpacked a few things, had a shower.

Freshened up, in jeans and a sweater, he filled the little coffee machine on the desk, and thought through his day. Liam had asked on the phone if he could ring him at 7.30 – said the time must be precise – and he would be given details of their meeting place. It was now nearly two, and he had to decide how to prepare. Should he show his skirts again, as Flemyng would put it, or not?

He had to know, so the answer was yes.

First, he finished the crossword, and checked that his passport was locked in the safe on the shelf in the clothes closet. He made sure the room was clear of anything personal, and headed for the elevator.

Double-checking at reception, he was told that no one had made any enquiries about him. There had been no callers.

The lobby was empty except for a family of three, looking through a pile of tourist leaflets.

On the pavement, he spent a minute or two checking the contents of his wallet. He took some coins from a pocket and stepped into one of the two old-style payphones with folding doors that stood on the corner of 6th Avenue a few yards away. He looked around. Still no sign. He placed a call to the secure line in the residence and, when Flemyng answered, read out the number of the payphone, and no more.

Within a minute, the phone rang softly.

'I'm being followed.' He described what had happened.

'But what if he wasn't a threat, but wanted to get close to me? I walked to the hotel, so he had the opportunity. Not a peep.'

'Start at the beginning,' Flemyng said.

'A face I knew at the station, that was all,' he said. 'Pinned it down, eventually, in my mind. Somebody I think I've seen at the Four Green Fields. The pub way up Florida Avenue.'

'... where I can't show my face...' Flemyng said.

'Quite.' Keane said. 'I'm now certain that he doesn't want to make contact. I gave him the chance. Made it embarrassingly easy, and there was nothing doing.'

Flemyng picked up. 'Which means it's more dangerous. There's no message. He's watching, and passing it on.

'So what's your plan? I assume you've got one.'

Ignoring the edge to the question, and wondering why Flemyng seemed more anxious than intrigued, Keane said that he would tell Liam in their arranged call to see if it made any sense to him.

'And if it doesn't?' Flemyng asked.

'I think we have trouble,' Keane said.

Flemyng agreed. 'There's danger. Have you been followed anywhere else recently, as far as you can tell?'

'No, I'm as sure of that as I can be.'

But how, Flemyng asked, could someone have known of a trip to New York that had only been fixed that morning, when Keane arrived at the embassy? It had been quick work, and therefore important. Who else knew? No one in the embassy, because Flemyng had decided, alone in the night, that he would despatch him to the city and had told no one.

'It must have come from Liam's end,' he said after a moment's pause for thought, 'and that's worrying. But you've still got to see him. Must. Ideas?'

'Not yet, to be honest,' said Keane. 'Give me an hour or so and I'll call you back.'

He stepped out with a feeling that he wasn't in the solid surroundings that he knew so well but in some foreign capital far away, with the sound of guns in the distance and rubble in the streets. He seemed to have been transported from the familiar to a threatening and uncertain place. He walked two blocks south through the cacophony of Times Square and turned east along 42nd, past the Central Library square on Bryant Park. Watched the traffic streaming south on 5th, turned and looked up towards the park, and wondered how the city could take on such a patina of danger so quickly. But it had. Somewhere, his follower was waiting – perhaps handing over to a comrade – but had no interest in making contact. They wanted to know why he was there, whom he might meet, and why.

So, what might he be expected to do? He took out a dollar and caught an uptown bus on Madison. Within fifteen minutes he'd be in the Met, where he could lose himself for a while.

From his seat by the window, he scanned the pavement as the bus bumped towards the park. Was he there? He saw nothing.

Before going into the museum he spent a while walking

around Turtle Pond, where he could watch and think about the evening.

He had already decided not to ring Liam again – his obvious nervousness ruled that out – so he spent some time considering how news of his journey had spread. It was a conundrum he couldn't solve.

Liam was as secure for them as it was possible to be – any evidence that he was in touch with anyone at the British Embassy would be catastrophic for him. Fatal. And there was another objection to the idea that the tip-off about Keane's movements had come from him. Flemyng had said it was late in the evening when he rang New York with the news that Keane would be coming. And Liam hadn't spoken during the call.

Why would he deliberately tell someone else, who passed it to the man with the ski-jump nose, and all in double-quick time? It didn't add up.

He searched for an explanation, calling up a picture of the Four Green Fields in his head. He imagined being in the singing, flowing with the crowd. But where had his pursuer been standing? Could he bring him to mind in that setting?

Not quite. He juggled the images, but they weren't right. Which meant...

Keane was walking more quickly now, circumnavigating the pond and trying to keep his concentration going. He put the stranger's face against several different backgrounds in Washington, and couldn't make him fit. He was certain, having dismissed everything else, that he had seen him in a bar. Recently. And in a moment, from nowhere, the truth hit him with a slap.

Chicago.

Seeing him at Union Station, he'd been misled into placing

him in Washington, and he'd been roaming over the wrong landscape ever since. Forget the Four Green Fields: he'd seen him in the Old Cork, in the crowd with the Viking.

The shock stopped him dead. The conclusion was surely clear, and staring him in the face.

Any remains of the cover he'd used in Chicago had gone. If it had been a chance sighting, Mr Ski-Jump-Nose would surely have approached him to remark on the coincidence of meeting again. That he didn't, and that he'd followed him towards his hotel, meant that this was an operation.

But how had they found out where he would be?

As he walked towards the Met, still planning to spend at least an hour and a half with the manuscripts, stained glass and sculptures in the Medieval Treasury room, he was experiencing a mixture of self-congratulation and the kind of alertness that invited fear. In no doubt now that they had placed him at the embassy, he was on hostile ground.

Yet why hide away? Keane had a natural instinct for turning a problem on its head. It was why he had loved playing with numbers as a child. Faced with a difficulty, he could always change his angle of vision. He did it now. Instead of running from the stranger, why not seek him out?

There was nothing to be lost. He couldn't undo the fact that they, whoever they were, knew who he was. The confrontation would come, one way or the other, unless he simply ran from New York. Unthinkable. If he controlled it, he might yet find a way of creating an advantage for himself.

Assuming he hadn't been followed to the Met – and there was no sign he had – the obvious way to lure him back into the ring, or meet a colleague who'd taken over from him, would be to return to the hotel. Openly, even brazenly.

He took a bus down 5th and walked calmly along 44th. At

the hotel, he spent a minute or two on the sidewalk, leafing through a booklet he'd picked up at the museum. He looked as if he was waiting for someone. Inside, he sat in the lobby with a coffee and waited.

Nothing.

Keane waited, a sitting duck.

It was five o'clock: the hour of Maria's arrival at the embassy.

She walked the last three hundred yards up Massachusetts, preferring not to deal with the taxi in sight of the guardhouse because she liked to be in control of all her movements. She gave her name, and was shown straight to the library. Her escort knocked twice, opened the door and said, 'Miss Cooney, sir.'

'Immaculate timing as ever,' he said, as he came to the door. They held each other warmly. He was remembering the last time they'd been together, three years ago in London, when they'd spent a happy evening taking themselves back to old times in the fray. 'So good to have you here,' he said. 'I need you again.'

'And me,' she said. 'Let's talk about him.'

He ordered tea.

They spoke a little about eastern Europe while it was brought in. Warsaw and Prague. The Berlin he'd once known so well, and hadn't seen for more than a decade.

When they were alone, he said without wasting a minute, 'Tell me.'

She had the story ready for him and she told it without any hesitation or sign of puzzlement. This was what she knew and they could deal with mysteries afterwards. She hit him between the eyes.

'I was responsible for sending him to Chicago. Did you know?'

He shook his head, astonished...

'I had a source running in Prague. Deep among the reformers. Let me get a glimpse of the way it might work out. And – just like half the Poles I knew in Gdansk, going back a few years – there was an American connection. Cousins, friends, you know how it is. So I got the office to use Abel, at my direction, to be a go-between. The details hardly matter now, but he needed to befriend some Czechs in Chicago, which is their outpost over here.'

'It explains the beer,' Flemyng said, managing a smile.

'He made three or four trips. In and out. Nothing dangerous, just the kind of subtle probing that he was brilliant at. Getting messages that I could use in Prague. We got together in Berlin two months ago – I remember it so clearly. An icy wind, snow on the pavements, and Abel in a fur hat when we walked in the Tiergarten. Precious for us both, and now in my memory. I can see him now, feeding the birds. He told me how something surprising had come his way in the Windy City.'

Flemyng was following her words intently. She didn't prompt him to ask questions, because her story was going to be quick, organised, clear. Then they would talk.

'He stumbled into a gang of my fellow countrymen.'

Maria's Boston-Irish background had always given their relationship a distinctive character. In the hours they spent together, unpicking the stories of their lives, which had come together in their Paris adventures in the summer of '68, it was inevitable that when they would speak of the Troubles, too. She recognised in him an understanding of the past that she thought rare in London, and it was one of the reasons why their bond was so strong. She'd confessed to him more than once that with Abel it had taken longer, maybe because he'd been away from home for a long time.

But he got there in the end.

'Don't ask me how, but he began to pick up stories. Oh, there were hints of gun-running – but, to be honest, that wasn't what fascinated him and he wanted to keep his hands clean. He passed a few bits and pieces to the Feds – maybe a name or two, I can't be sure – but you won't be surprised to know that it was the politics that gripped him, the factions vying for control. He picked up gossip as clearly as if it was being passed around in the Falls Road. Names, bulletins from the front line, and he was maybe entranced a little bit. So hard to understand, so difficult to let go. You know how it is.'

Flemyng nodded, said nothing.

'He made a few trips to Chicago. Don't know how many, but enough to keep up contacts. There was a problem, though. You.' Pointing at him playfully, she went on, 'Naturally no one there knew there was a connection between him and the top Brit in our nation here – he was as American as apple pie. But, more to the point, I know that he didn't want to set up some channel with you on these matters. Breaks all our rules. He would wait until he had something special for you.'

It was characteristic of Flemyng that he declined to rush her, refused to push her towards the end of the story. He wanted every word, and although he was sitting in his favourite chair in a room where he was always the commander, she was allowed to keep the floor.

'He gave me a good idea of what he'd learned,' she said. 'We're talking here about the last few months. They knew a lot about the London–Dublin back and forth. Obviously, anything with your government's stamp on it is always going

to be suspicious. A deception operation, or something. Cover
for more hardline stuff in the North. But he was surprised
– cheered up, too – by some people he found who liked to
try to see past the moment we're in. Not like the ones still
celebrating the big bang in Brighton, and waiting for the next
one, but the others.

'He was on the trail of something. Promise.'

She leaned back, dealt with her long black hair, smiled at
him in the old way. Her legs were curled up on the sofa and
they both knew that in the short time they'd been together
they'd re-established the intimacy they'd known in the years
gone by. Briefly, in Paris, Flemyng had wondered if might
become a different kind of intimacy. But he learned that with
Maria it could never be like that, and part of him was relieved.

They spoke simply like the oldest of friends, with a trust
that wouldn't be broken.

'The tragedy,' she said, 'is I think he was nearly there.'

Flemyng had remained still throughout, concentrating on
every word. Now he spoke.

'What was the destination?'

'I think it was a person,' she said.

Abel had told her that in his outings with the group he'd
come to know he'd picked up the distant sound of dissent
that went far beyond the day-to-day argument about a failed
operation or a new tactic. He described it as being like a faint
radio signal that pulsed quite strongly for a moment or two
then faded almost to nothing, then returned more clearly
than before. Frustrating, but hypnotic. He'd waited for the
moment when everything would be clear, the hiss and crackle
gone.

The atmosphere was heavy with emotion. Maria, who had
loved his brother, said that she wished – every night before

she went to sleep – that she could have prevented it. Warned him when they met in Berlin that he had gone far enough, and that he should pass on what he had learned – the people he knew in Chicago – and get out. But he was Abel. Always wanted to finish the game, deliver checkmate with a flourish.

'I think it cost him his life.'

She asked Flemyng how much he knew from his own people in the Washington machine. Or even, she asked him gently, from his own expeditions to Belfast an age ago, of which she'd known a little.

'Not quite enough,' he said. But briefly he told her about Mungo's unexpected visitation. The shock and the mystery.

But first he had to worry about the here-and-now. 'We have a London visitor who, frankly, I could do without, except that he's not someone you can avoid. Sir Roland Saviour. You know what he does?'

'More or less,' Maria said.

'I'm going to do you a favour and keep you away from him. Unless, of course, you want otherwise…'

She was smiling again. 'Oh, I definitely want an encounter.'

'Let's talk. There's a dinner here tomorrow night. If you can…' His face showed his surprise.

'We'll have to break off now. I have a meeting. But there's someone I certainly do want you to meet. One of my youngsters.'

Maria said she remembered the time when he was one of them.

He got up and put an arm around her shoulder as they went to the door. 'He's got the old spirit. His name is Patrick Keane.'

★ ★ ★

At that moment, in New York, Keane was taking to the streets. His pursuer had not appeared at the hotel, but he was convinced that he or someone else would attempt to track him again. Otherwise, why follow him from Washington?

He felt like a strange kind of streetwalker as he patrolled 44th, stopping at the theatres along the way to check on tickets. There was nothing odd about that. He could see others doing the same.

Still nothing, but when he got back to the hotel, the receptionist beckoned him over.

'A friend left you a note, Mr Keane.' She held it up.

He sat in a corner of the lobby and slid a finger under the flap of the envelope, deliberately taking his time. It was not a moment to rush.

Plain card. Liam's writing.

'Don't call. Come to McSorley's on E 7th after 9.'

Twenty-nine

'THE MINISTER'S HERE,' LUCY ANNOUNCED.

Flemyng brushed the shoulders of his jacket and tightened the knot of his tie. Walking into the hall, he saw Arthur Livesey being shepherded from the street by Lucy, and, to his surprise, Guy Cotton behind them.

'Welcome to Washington, Minister. We're glad to have you with us.'

'Thanks, Ambassador. It's good to see you again. And, incidentally, as you know, it's Arty to friends.

Flemyng looked him over. He showed no signs of wear and tear from his flight. He must have changed his suit at the airport, because it was uncreased, sharp. Fresh blue shirt, bold tie. But it was always his hair that marked him out. Honey-blond, he'd heard it called, and it sprang from the centre of his head, so that he seemed to have two fountains of silky hair that he kept longer than the fashion in government, as a gesture of some sort. Unkindly, Flemyng recalled a piece of advice he'd been given by one of his more traditional elders in the office, early on – 'never trust a man who blow-dries his hair'. Well, Arty certainly did, but Flemyng was determined to give him the benefit of the doubt, at least for two days. It went against the grain, because all he'd heard about him raised his suspicions. But graciousness was expected and that's what he'd get.

'Tea, coffee, something more bracing?' he said as he guided the minister to his study.

'Strong coffee is fine,' he said, 'but I'll raid your cellar later, if I may.'

'Be my guest. It is yours, after all.' Flemyng was exuding charm. Lucy, who could see behind the façade, was amused.

'And Roland is well settled in, I'm sure,' Livesey said, leaving no doubt in their minds whom he saw as the source of any power he had. And his likely benefactor in government in years to come. 'Such a formidable presence, wherever he goes.'

'Indeed, as I saw in the White House this very afternoon,' Flemyng said. 'I left him in the West Wing, in fine fettle and in his element.'

Livesey said he could no doubt tune into some summit conversations in the following two days, but he had business of his own. 'I'll touch base with opposite numbers, of course, but some raw politics, too, you'll not be surprised to hear. The party chairman has asked me to run the rule over some of the campaign techniques they're polishing up over here. A new age, really, despite the administration appealing to the past in so many ways. Interesting, don't you think? We've got a lot to learn.'

And a lot to lose, Flemyng thought.

They took coffee by the window. Flemyng gave him a quick account of pre-summit conversations, and said he'd find a proper analysis in his room that had been put together in Chancery only the previous day specifically for him. 'In your honour, you might say,' Flemyng said.

'Steady on,' Livesey said. 'Give me time.'

Lucy could see that Flemyng's poise concealed the instant dislike Livesey had kindled in him. Was it the hair, the perfect teeth, the expensive-looking tie? Maybe the drawl that spoke of money, and conceit. She knew Flemyng too well to expect trouble, but she knew, too, that he'd be cast down by the experience of turning his easy charm into a chore. As if Saviour wasn't enough.

Livesey was talking about his new responsibilities. 'I know I'm not supposed to bandy names around, but I gather that I can rightly call one of my responsibilities your old patch. I'm allowed to know that, aren't I?'

'Foreign Office a long time ago, Arty. And here and there... liaison, you know. That kind of thing.'

'It would be good to get your perspective. An old boy's view.'

Lucy wondered how much Flemyng would be able to take.

He changed the subject to the dinner the next night. 'The Royal Shakespeare Company is in town, as you know, and we can put on something appropriate here. We'll have a good crowd. You'll have pride of place, if you want it. And, please, the performance beforehand, if you can. *Henry IV Part I.*'

Then Livesey surprised Flemyng. 'That lovely line – '*I can call spirits from the vasty deep.*'

Flemyng couldn't resist. 'And isn't it the scene made by Hotspur's retort?' He quoted it perfectly.

'*Why so can I, or so can any man. But do they come when you do call for them?*'

Lucy saw them for a moment as a pair of schoolboys. Willy-waving, as Keane would put it.

'Ambassadors are there to make the impossible happen, aren't they? It's what you're for,' Livesey said.

Flemyng put out his hands in mock supplication. 'When the Fates decree it. Otherwise, we simply do our best to keep the show on the road. *Your* show, Minister.'

'Indeed. And we have some fine new productions on the way, as you know. The summit. Ireland, we hope, later in the year. The atmosphere here on that one?'

'Much better than before,' Flemyng said. 'I hope the embassy is helping. A more realistic view I'd say, and understanding. But never easy, for reasons we all know.'

He said he would be happy to brief him properly, and he could meet the men and women of the station, for whom in some way he was now responsible. 'Patrick Keane is the acting head. Out of town, back tomorrow. I'll get us all together.'

Livesey responded, 'And of course I've met Guy Cotton. Good man. Exceptional, I'm told.'

'Of course,' said Flemyng, and gave Lucy a look with which she was familiar. On cue, she stood up and said, 'Ambassador, there's a prearranged call with the senator around now. I wonder...'

'Don't let me hold up the work of Her Majesty's servants,' said Livesey. 'I have reading to do, and perhaps a nap.'

'Supper at eight thirty if you're in the mood,' Flemyng said. 'Nothing formal tonight.'

'Promise me some White House gossip,' the minister said as he left.

Flemyng wondered when Keane would ring.

McSorley's Old Ale House stood against everything that was happening in the Bowery, where they were cleaning up old blocks and brownstones, and casting the curse of Wall Street on the area around Cooper Square, now colonised by the finance houses. But the dusty old bar, with a thick smell of malt that hung in the air, was still the place that had banned women, along with raw onions, until only about a decade before. It served only its own beer and no hard liquor.

Keane had heard tales, but had never been through the doors.

He wondered why Liam had suggested it, because surely there was a severe danger of recognition. Just before nine o'clock, he turned onto E 7th. It had wire mesh over the windows, dim lights inside, and a crowd that might have been marooned there for twenty-five years or more, because they looked and sounded like men who wanted to leave the world behind. Through the gloom, Keane headed for the bar. From behind a pillar, a hand reached out.

Liam said, 'No one I know comes here, and I had to visit before I go home. A risk, but who knows if I'll be back?'

He brought two glasses of beer to a corner near the window.

'For me, it's a farewell. You follow?'

His face was thinner. The beard had grown a little bit, but seemed even greyer. Liam's blue eyes were attractive because they were unavoidable and took you behind his expression even when it was fierce. In the dull light they looked like bright gas jets. He didn't have to do anything to hold attention, and in Chicago Keane had watched with some envy the way women reacted in his presence.

'You'll imagine this is nostalgic. Emotional, you might say.' Lowering his voice, he said, 'But I'm weary, Patrick. Done in.'

To his surprise, Keane realised Liam intended to talk about himself in those surroundings. They were tucked away from the main crowd, but there was still a risk. But he had made his decision. He needed the place, because it spoke to him in the language he wanted to hear. Keane had imagined them walking along a shoreline in Brooklyn, empty and bleak, lighting cigarettes in the dark, and spending an hour in the shadows. Then taking different subways to get away. Instead, he was crammed into an old bar that was half filled with regulars who knew each other and would pass on news of an unusual sighting, and passers-by who were crowded into every corner except theirs.

Keane's realised McSorley's on that evening represented what had become of Liam. Beaten down. Exhausted. He needed to bolster his emotions for the journey home. So he'd stepped back into McSorley's world, full of grey-faced smokers, sticky beer stains and memories. Of who'd once come there; of the stories they'd told at the bar; of Joe DiMaggio's streak in 1941 commemorated in a ragged photograph on the wall; of all the people who'd hung their chicken wishbones on the hook beside the lamp near the bar, one of the most unsavoury but weirdly touching collections in the whole city.

Liam was giving himself a vaccination against everything that might come his way. Keane wondered if he wanted to forget everything, except the moment he was in. Then Liam interrupted his thought.

'You were followed.'

'How did you know?' Keane showed his surprise.

Liam spoke more intimately than before. 'Did you doubt me?'

In his confusion, Keane felt the pieces falling into place. 'I should have known.'

Liam was sitting with his back to the bar and with Keane jammed into the corner he could talk quietly without being heard. And his face was away from the crowd. It was safe, with the hubbub behind leaving them alone. 'The guy you saw at the station is a good friend, none better. Sean.

'You saw him in the Old Cork. He drank with us all. I tried to make sure he wasn't too close to you. I doubt if you had a conversation, did you?'

'Definitely not,' said Keane. 'So you had a plan?'

'Just taking a precaution for the future,' Liam said. 'He's a Washington man. That's where he's happy. He's with me on certain matters, that's all I'll say. You'll meet him properly, never fear.

'When your boss rang me late the other night, he was an anxious man. Don't forget how long I've known him, since he was a baby in his queen's service, as you might say. So I knew he was in a state. He made the arrangement for us, said you'd be taking the train to the city in the morning.

'Well, there was a good reason for sending Sean at your back. He knew your face from Chicago – I'd made sure of that – and he understood how careful we have to be. I had to be sure that no one else was taking an interest. And, of course, I had to know your hotel, so he followed you all the way. For the moment, that was all. There was no real mystery. I was keeping you safe, making sure we could get together. More of Sean later.'

He was smiling as he had only a few times in Chicago. 'Did it put the fear of God into you?'

'For a little while,' Keane said, lifting his tumbler of beer.

'Patrick, I need to know why Will wanted you here so quickly.'

Straight out. Liam was frank, and he owed him the same.

'First of all, a picture of what's going on in Belfast. Mood music. Attitudes to what the two governments are up to. All that.'

Liam said that was no reason to scramble him to New York. When Flemyng had given Keane his mission, he hadn't heard of Liam's summons back to Belfast. So there was something else. What?

Keane took a moment to prepare. 'You know from the boss that his brother in Scotland had some unwelcome visitors. Your boys. He's not well – recovering from a heart attack – and it was alarming, dangerous. Now he's under guard. It hit the boss very hard. He wants to know – why?'

Liam was watching him carefully, a young man who'd no doubt met a few dangers already along his chosen path, but who'd probably never seen combat. Not the formal kind, and certainly not the dirty sort of street fighting where the blood took you by surprise, and the agonies of wounded boys on pavements and back greens and in burned-out cars would cast long shadows across the future. He'd wrestled for more than a decade with his own nightmares. The deeds he'd done, the people he'd betrayed, the perils he'd brought on himself. Friends lost.

'How do I start?' he said. 'The struggle never ends. And for believers it *mustn't* end. D'you see? More than a cause, it's a life. You have to start with that.

'It means everything can be justified. Think about your Flemyngs. Two brothers were spies, leaving the other one sitting happily in an estate in Scotland doing his history, and living a decent life. I've met him, incidentally, just briefly – more about him in a minute – and I know it all. To my boys that family's not just fair game, but irresistible.

'So it was natural to put on the pressure. What the hell was a Flemyng doing in Chicago? Was he going to blow apart a useful network? Nobody knew of his connections until after he was dead – you'll be aware of that – and the awful truth is he might have been protected if people *had* known. Your Will couldn't have been surprised that somebody was sent to his other brother. Easy enough to track him down.'

'There was a threat to his wife, too,' Keane said. 'She turned up on a list.'

'I'm sorry to hear that,' Liam said, obviously startled, and leaned across to touch him lightly. 'Truly. I can only say that some of these lists are more for show than anything. For boasting to the lads. But still...'

Keane took his hand. Liam went on.

'As it happens, as far as brother Mungo is concerned, I do know a little, and you can take it back to Will.'

Keane noticed that in the course of a few minutes Liam had started to call Flemyng by his first name, which he hadn't heard him do before. His decision to inject himself with the atmosphere of McSorley's, and to introduce Keane to the drug, was having its effect. Keane's astonishment at Liam's arrangement to have him followed had already passed. There were so many shocks that they were losing their sting. Calmly, he felt himself coming closer to understanding Abel's death, and the hand that Liam had been forced to play. He knew he'd soon be there.

'There was a decision,' Liam said. 'In your game you'd say it came from the highest level. Brother Mungo had to be squeezed to find out what he knew about Abel and Chicago. Was there some kind of operation being run from the embassy that threatened everything over here? The cash, the guns. You've got to appreciate the panic, Patrick. The alarm bells were clanging like they were in a bloody cathedral. Remember – the American operation is our spinal cord.'

He paused, obviously thinking about how to frame his words.

'Will knows that there's rough politics at work. Different groups – and don't forget, we're all armed – wanting to command. Watching. So it's brutal, and people get hurt. Sometimes disappear. He'll know – I want you to give this to him just as I say it – that operations aren't always what they seem.

'It depends who's in charge at a particular moment, pulling the strings. When he's thinking about Mungo, Will should remember that. I have one question for him, as an answer to his own. There's a name he and I both know that would mean nothing to you. Was it used when Mungo was threatened? That's a question for him, because I think Mungo the historian would have reported it accurately. Memory is his business. If Mungo did hear the name, you can tell Will that he should draw his own conclusion about the operation – why it unfolded as it did. He'll understand.'

Liam sat back, watching Keane as if he might be making a judgement about how much he'd understood. 'Are you giving me the name?'

'No,' Liam said, and when he laughed Keane remembered who was in charge.

'I'll report as faithfully as I can,' he said, without asking for more explanation. Then, 'What of you?'

Liam said he'd been given a message that he was needed. Full stop. There was a go-between he had to meet in Amsterdam at the weekend. He'd be picked up at Dublin airport on Sunday night and driven straight north.

Keane, emboldened by Liam's spirit as if the warm and heavy odours of McSorley's had turned it into an opium den, asked, 'Worried?'

'Apprehensive, I suppose,' Liam said. 'Wouldn't you be?'

His blue eyes followed Keane to the bar, where he got two more beers and came back to their table.

'I said I'd come back to Sean, didn't I? Well, now you know him by sight. You'll be seeing more of him. That's my promise to you. He's a good friend of mine, and will be yours too. Leave it to him. He'll be in touch in his own good time.'

After a short silence, Keane asked how long Liam expected to be away.

He laughed. 'Haven't a clue. Maybe for good. I'll hear more tomorrow.'

'How?' Keane said.

'Fergus Sullivan has called one of his meetings. Not a happy man these days, as you can imagine. I'll be there, helping to mop up the mess.'

He smiled across at Keane. 'And if you were there, you'd see an old friend.'

Keane waited.

'The Viking's in town.'

Maybe it was because of the headiness around them – Keane couldn't remember when he'd last been in a bar that still insisted on having sawdust on the floor, and a big, cracked jar where people threw in the money for their drinks – but at the same moment he and Liam put their heads down, almost touching, and nearly laughed.

'What the hell are you going to tell me next?' Keane said. No one seemed interested in them, but to any onlooker they would have appeared a happy pair, old friends on a catch-up night out. Certainly not talking about armed men in the streets, and a manhunt.

'After that night in Chicago, they'll be trying to identify you.' Liam said. 'I hope I'm wrong, but I think they'll send someone to find your student house on the South Side campus. If they do, they'll discover it's a fairy tale. But I doubt if they can make a direct connection to your place of work. There's nowhere to get hold of photographs of embassy people, is there?'

Keane shook his head. 'Not easily, no.'

'So be careful, that's all,' said Liam. 'I'll hear things at the meeting tomorrow. I'll muddy the waters as best I can. Stay here in the city and we'll meet. Sean's going to be here until you go back. Sullivan's meeting is at two. If you get the LaGuardia shuttle to DC at six, I can meet you out there at the little bar near the gate. An airport's a good place to bump into somebody. Almost as good as Union Station...' The old smile was back.

'And then I'll be off to JFK and away to Amsterdam.'

Keane said. 'Thanks for everything, Liam.' He held his hand tightly, even more than before.

'I'll go now,' his friend said.

'There's one more thing,' Keane said. 'A message from Will. Take both your passports. He said you'd understand.'

Liam stood still. A photograph of the moment would have shown their eyes locked together. Keane at the wooden table looking up, his hand still in Liam's, which seemed to be about to pull him to his feet. His friend looking down at him, with an expression as if he'd been interrupted suddenly, and had turned back.

As he broke away, Liam smiled. Leaning in, he said, 'I think I understand you.'

Five minutes later, Keane left the bar and crossed Cooper Square, taking 8th as far as the subway at Broadway. Steam rose from the grating under his feet on the steps down. He enjoyed the rattle of the trains in the caverns with their rusty pit props, the noise on the rails blocking out everything as surely as McSorley's had given him and Liam what they needed. Everything was crashing around him, an express whizzing past without stopping and leaving a rough echo in its wake. There were two buskers along the platform, and an old man with a tin cup was backed up against the wall. He found some coins.

In the noise, with the darkness of the tunnels feeling like the dangers he was having to confront, he was able to keep his head, as if it was the very chaos enveloping him that kept him cool and organised. Alone with his thoughts. Ready.

The Q train screamed to a stop. He got to 42nd Street, walked to his hotel through after-theatre crowds and rang Flemyng straight away, through the embassy switchboard. With a flicker of guilt, he realised he hadn't checked the street for a watcher. The Viking? Don't be ridiculous, he thought.

When Flemyng rang back on the secure line, Keane was lying on his bed, but as alert as if he'd just sprung out of the pool after a swim.

'Take your time,' Flemyng said.

Keane began with news of the tail-that-wasn't. Playing by the book, secure line or not, he didn't use Sean's name – that could wait – but he knew Flemyng would be able to interpret from what he said the inheritance that Liam had promised them.

Then, the Viking.

'He's in town. At Sullivan's meeting tomorrow, for sure. But I'm going to get an account of that before I come home. I'll take the shuttle at six.'

'So you'll miss the play, but make the dinner,' Flemyng said.

'And Liam's confirmed his trip,' Keane told him. 'Amsterdam

tomorrow night for the weekend, then to Dublin on Sunday night.'

Keane thought the silence on the line filled his ears as completely as the noise of the subway trains.

'I gave him your message.' he went on. 'He understood.'

Keane gave an account of Liam's words that was accurate to the last phrase. His description of operational control, of the factions that clashed in their hideaways. The panic about Abel after Chicago. Then – his question about the name that might have been mentioned to Mungo, and his confidence in Flemyng drawing the right conclusion if it had been.

Flemyng didn't ask for more information, just gave a sigh, and Keane recognised relief.

'We'll soon be there, and let's have a late, late nightcap after the dinner. Keep an eye open in the city, and stay away from the Bronx, there's a good boy.'

'Don't worry about that, boss. I'll take myself out of circulation.'

He asked how things were at the embassy.

'The usual,' said Flemyng, his anger suddenly breaking through. 'Saviour's buggering everything up.'

Thirty

MARIA WAS BACK ON THE CANAL AT FIRST LIGHT, WITH
company. When she locked her bike outside the new
condominiums alongside the canal below M Street, she ran
for half a mile then walked northwards. Eventually she saw,
ahead of her in an anorak, chinos and bright-red trainers, Her
Britannic Majesty's Ambassador. Behind him was a figure
trying to hang back, but she recognised him immediately
as security. Tony Pringle, his bald head shining like a bullet,
couldn't be anything else.

He had objected strongly when Flemyng had woken him
at around midnight. 'There's someone I have to see. It will be
early, and deserted. If you must, you can hang around nearby.'

'I don't like it one bit,' Pringle said. 'Everyone's still on
alert at home.'

Grudgingly, he had the car waiting outside the residence
soon after dawn.

Flemyng wondered if Pringle was assuming it was a
different kind of assignation. Surely not. But he had more
important worries. They parked not far from Key Bridge, and

clambered down to the waterside. He walked south along the canal to the stretch where Maria had promised to run at the appointed hour, and there she was.

Breathless, perspiring but smiling in her running pants, she leaned on him for support for a moment, then they stood together at the waterside. The flight path overhead was busy with early traffic, noise bursting above them every ninety seconds. She wondered why the birds didn't fly away, why they preferred to stay in the city. She and Flemyng watched some waterfowl on the canal. A mother and chicks, untroubled, steered a steady course towards the far bank. But for the planes, they might have been in a rural backwater.

'Peaceful,' she said.

'Apparently,' said Flemyng. 'I'm sorry for this fuss, but we did need to talk away from the office. Incidentally, come to supper tonight, please. And to the play first if you can, at the Kennedy Center. Lucy will fix it.'

'Give it to me,' she said.

'There's a bit more on Mungo, but first I want your reading of a tricky problem that's landed on me, which has just been stirred up some more.'

'From the beginning,' she said, and they sat on a bench together. Pringle watched from the next bench along the canal, about fifty yards away. There was no one else on the path.

Flemyng explained there was a point beyond which he couldn't go, even with her, as usual. But he was willing to push the boat out. She might know that there was a British source, as secret as secret could be, who'd been invaluable in getting both London and Washington inside the Soviet mind. 'We've benefited hugely, for years. You'll know, probably, how some of the stuff was so good it went straight to the

Oval Office. Once in a generation everyone gets a source like this, and it's been our turn.

'But he may have been uncovered. Not by one of our turncoats, though we've had our share of them, but by our own allies. The name is out and about in Langley, I'm told.'

Maria's happy-go-lucky demeanour had gone. She understood the summons.

'Now,' Flemyng said. 'I've no doubt the highest folk in this town would assure us that it's kept under lock and key as you would guard crown jewels, if you had any. But you see the worry. Fundamentally, it's not your secret but ours, and there could be loose talk. Or a leak from someone who's been turned. Our man would be done for. The gold seam exhausted.'

As he knew she would, Maria wanted to know his own source.

'Well, I'm afraid it's a strange answer. Angleton.'

Despite the seriousness with which she'd listened to him, she laughed out loud, with a bark that made Pringle stiffen on his bench along the canal as if it might be a call to action.

'My, oh my,' she said. 'The old magician still up to his tricks.'

Flemyng told her how Angleton had also revealed that it was he, in the dark days of the sixties, who'd set up the L Street outfit, and therefore – at a distance, admittedly – had been a kind of godfather to Abel.

'And to you,' he said, gently.

She was looking down at the water. 'I don't usually think of our place in that way, but you're right. We were his idea. He was getting more and more obsessive about penetration – disappearing into his files for weeks on end, the blinds down in his eyrie and no one allowed near. But his mind was brilliant before it was taken over by conspiracies. Once upon a time, they say he did see clearly.'

Flemyng, with a smile, made the ritual confession of guilt about Philby a generation ago, and how it had turned Angleton into the man he became. On the trail of betrayal, night and day.

'My question is this,' he said. 'What if he's right?

'He says the Soviets have been looking for new recruits without looking for converts. None of your Philby stuff. This is treachery for money, and lots of it. Now, if there's one bad egg – all it takes is one, as we know – who's somewhere in the system and hears that name, off it goes to Moscow and we're fucked. Sorry for that.'

She waved his apology away and asked what he wanted.

'How widely the name is known, that's all. And quickly.'

Being Maria, she replied with a question for him. 'You say it's been stirred up a little more. How?'

'Why do you think I came?' he said. 'I mentioned Roland Saviour to you. Well, despite his reputation as a master of dark arts, he seems to have screwed it up royally.'

She saw the anger. His face was set, he was staring straight ahead, and one hand was clenched. 'I tried to warn him, but he sailed off to the White House yesterday. Meetings with three or four people, then over to State, seventh floor no less. The Pentagon today in the secretary's office, God help us.

'And from what he tells me he repeated to at least one of his confidants exactly what I've told you.

'Which presents us with two quite serious problems. Firstly, more talk around the place about what's happened. If there is a rotten apple, news will reach him or her and the leak will follow. But right now, he's created a fuck-up of his own. There's already been an exchange of telegrams – I saw it last night and it's horrendous. A ding-dong about who's to blame. My office at home blaming more or less everyone here except the president, and your lot blaming us for being precious and not sharing the guy from the very beginning. It's the last thing we need.

'And our friend Saviour is a favourite of you-know-who. He'll be running the summit for Her. And, frankly, he's never been a fan of mine.

'I could strangle him.'

'Don't,' said Maria, and put her arms round his neck. Flemyng did get some amusement from watching Pringle further along the canal, whose interest in them was now obvious.

She promised to take soundings, and report back. 'I'll be at the play, never fear.'

He said, 'Remember, I want you to meet our Patrick, too. One of us.'

Then she asked about Mungo.

'There's something odd about what happened at home, at Altnabuie. They could have killed him easily. It would have been a piece of retribution for what Abel had found out – or, rather, for what they *think* he'd found out. But they didn't. They took care. Mungo himself told me that it seemed they wanted him to live to tell the tale. So I asked myself why. I may have the answer, and frankly it makes things more difficult, not less.'

Maria was studying him. 'You probably can't go much further, but why?'

'It's about my past life. Across the water – the smaller pond, the Irish Sea. There are precious names and I've got to guard them. With my life, I suppose.'

She knew it was time to go. Flemyng waved to Pringle and

he walked quickly towards them. 'An old friend, Tony. Maria
Cooney. A journalist these days. Prague, Berlin, you name it.
We had to catch up.'

'Nice to meet you, ma'am,' Pringle said. 'A good time to
have a private chat, and a lovely spot in the morning.'

They all smiled, and Pringle led him away to the car.

His last words, whispered, were, 'See you tonight.'

Pringle pretended not to hear.

There was no danger of Keane venturing into the Bronx.
Liam had only told him where he could find the Star of Sea
and Sullivan's gang in order that he could steer a wide berth.

He walked first to the Central Library, where he could
roost happily for the morning. Finding a table with a window
nearby, he settled down with a catalogue and identified some
volumes he'd lay hands on for the first time.

At the same hour, Flemyng was dealing with the Saviour
fallout.

He composed a telegram for London which he thought
sounded just the right degree of alarm, but demonstrated for
the record that he was not an ambassador given to panic.
There was enough tucked in between the lines, however, for
anyone senior in the office to realise that Saviour had screwed
up. As Flemyng had put it to Lucy when he got back from the
canal, he was the bull who carried his own china shop around
with him.

He acknowledged the embarrassment caused by the
Americans' successful identification of the name but did
all he could to suggest that the circulation would be highly
restricted. He knew it would be nothing like the Barracks,
where the walls around this one source were as thick as the

Tower of London's, but he stressed that he saw no reason to assume that it would become widely known. Moreover, he was willing to state confidently that there was nothing to suggest – after exhaustive enquiries with helpful officials – any suggestion of a penetration that would put the security of the name at risk. This was clear, he said, because he knew for certain there were no investigations going on into breaches of security. Therefore, so his thin argument went, matters could be much worse.

Flemyng was perfectly aware that he was writing a highly optimistic note for the file, and that it was full of holes. But it would be passed around to calm nerves. To amuse himself, Flemyng counted how many people would see his telegram, best guess eight. And at least five of them, including the Boss herself if it reached her, would not know the name itself.

Saviour's irritation at knowing less than him, Flemyng surmised, had driven him on his verbose tour of the White House and State, which was unforgivable. But it was also, he admitted to himself, hilarious. The man would suffer for it in some way, and was as yet unaware. Some of his glitter would flake off, like so much used confetti.

If his legendary skills were deserting him, so much the better.

Now he had to deal with Arty, whom he was confident was a minister with thin long-term prospects. Not a fool, of course. That would make him easier to deal with. But he was a bird of passage who was showing off his plumage in his brief time in the sun. Earlier he had told Lucy that he saw in Livesey a vision of the future that depressed him.

'I know we've got our old warhorses, from another time. But if you get rid of the ballast, all that's left is bluster and fluff. Livesey's spending most of his two days floating around with the consultants who're all the rage. Political whores, picking up any candidate they can. Half of them don't even care which party it is. They have their moment, charge a massive fee and move on. Of course, if it goes horribly belly-up, they're paid to come back and write a report on what went wrong.

'They're breeding a race of automatons. Twenty years from now you won't be able to tell one congressman from the next, except by the colour of his tie. We'll have the guys produced by the machine, and then the nutters. That's all.'

'Steady on,' said Lucy, 'you're getting carried away.'

'With good reason,' he said. 'It's Livesey's world. It turns him on, and the melancholy bit of me thinks he may be right. At home we'll soon have serried ranks of little Liveseys all over the place – never mind the party – who know all about the mechanics and the polls, and nothing else. Am I becoming an old fart?'

'Not quite yet,' Lucy said. 'Give it time.'

'Wheel him in at noon, anyway,' he said. 'I'll do my duty.'

And now he was here.

'So, Arty,' said Flemyng, trying to sound relaxed. 'What's your temperature reading in our town today?'

'I don't know anywhere with a love of the political game like this,' he said. 'It's exciting, because it's real. People think about power the whole time. How to get it, how to keep it.' He paused. 'And, naturally, the ways of exercising it for the best.'

'Of course,' said Flemyng. He wondered if Livesey might ask him what he thought, but no.

'I'm writing a report for the party chairman to take home. I know that's not your side of the shop, but of course it touches on policy areas that affect us all. I see this place as a laboratory. They try things out here, and eventually they reach our shores.'

'Indeed,' Flemyng said. 'And not always for the best. Sometimes the ideas are only half made up.'

He tried to tempt Livesey onto a wider stage. 'It's always good for the likes of me to get a feeling for how ministers see the drift of politics right now. Where the tide is going to run. What do you think?'

Livesey was sharp enough to allude to Flemyng's own ministerial career, brief though it had been. 'You're someone who can give the likes of me a lesson or two.'

Flemyng knew he didn't mean a word of it.

He was stroking his hair. 'I'm still an innocent at heart. But I must say I have the advantage of the lens that your old office provides. I think I can say that, can't I? The Barracks, as the old guard still calls it. That gives me a tiny bit of an advantage over some colleagues at my level. A different vista. You know what I mean?'

Flemyng asked him to paint a picture of his vista, and listened for a few minutes to a routine, reasonably competent summing-up of current international problems, and security questions, that displayed no trace of original thinking.

'We're looking forward to tonight. I'm always pleased when we can bring Shakespeare to Washington, and give him a cheer,' he said, to move Livesey on. 'The riddles of power, don't you think?'

Livesey had clearly done some homework. 'Yes. You're always wondering whether it will fall for the king or the rebels.'

'Which side are you on, Arty?' Flemyng asked.

'Oh, the king's. Continuity's the thing. Unreliable man, not a monarch to write home about, but he does keep the ship of state afloat, doesn't he?'

Flemyng said, 'Just. Government as we know it from the inside. Divided loyalties, moral conflicts.'

'Maybe,' Livesey said, changing the subject. 'It's Falstaff I'll enjoy most.'

Flemyng risked it. 'We have our own one with us this week, don't we? Roland. No – I shouldn't have said that. A joke, I promise you.

'I mean physically, not in any other respect.'

'I shan't breathe a word,' Livesey said, half smiling. 'Now, Will, the chap I'm seeing across the river this afternoon you say is reasonably senior. Anything I need to know?'

'I'd say things are chugging along quite smoothly,' said Flemyng, blandly.

Keane came out of the library with his mind whirring. He'd delved into a volume of Spanish manuscripts and found an image that resembled something in his own collection that he had never been able to identify. Exciting enough to carry him through the day.

To refresh himself further he went to a bookshop he'd been told about near the park, where they kept a room bulging with old prints. Nothing old enough to satisfy his special interest, but he found an etching of Dutch New York that he looked at for half an hour, on and off, and decided to buy for less than $100. He told the shop he was flying, so they packed it well for him.

Keeping an eye on the streets as he walked, he strolled back to the hotel and got his bag ready. He would get to the airport by three. Who knew if Sullivan would wind the meeting up in record time? If so, Liam could easily get from the Bronx to LaGuardia in twenty minutes.

A message was waiting for him at the hotel desk. Ring Lucy.

Her instructions were brief and clear. When he saw their friend – she didn't use Liam's name – he was to ask him to ring Flemyng on the following afternoon as near to four o'clock as he could manage, from wherever he might be. It was important. Keane was to give him the number of the secure line.

'Anything else?' said Keane. 'The boss will explain when he rings,' Lucy told him. She ended the call, and composed a message for the Barracks, bypassing Keane's embassy colleagues, which she could do because of Flemyng's fishing rights in that quarter. He wanted to speak to someone in Operations, immediately.

As he packed up, Keane puzzled over Flemyng's request for Liam to call from Amsterdam. What was he up to?

And then, in the corner of the lobby, he saw Sean. Mr Ski-Jump-Nose himself. Sitting alone, expressionless, and making no move to greet him. Keane walked across.

'I'm Liam's friend,' the man said.

'Sean, I know now. Hello.' He had a soft smile. 'Do you want to talk?'

'I have to give you one piece of information before I leave,' he said without preamble. 'And that's all for now. I'm taking the train, just like yesterday. The word is that Cathal Earley is going home, right now. May already have left. The Viking, I should probably call him. Good news for you.'

Keane's mood lifted. He thanked him and left, hardly bothering to check the street before climbing into the first cab in the line outside the hotel.

'LaGuardia. Quickest bridge if you don't mind.' He was an older driver, and steered his way admirably through the afternoon traffic. In only fifteen minutes, Manhattan was behind them.

To speed himself up in DC, he was going to keep his bag with him on the plane, and his print, taped between two sheets of cardboard. All the way to the airport, he was thinking through the implications of Sean's message.

He was at the terminal by three, and found a perch at the little bar nearest the shuttle gate. On a corner stool, he looked like one of the passengers who stole some drinking time before a flight. The man next to him, in a seersucker suit and yellow tie, was reading the *Chicago Tribune* and cradling a Scotch-and-something with a cherry on a plastic stick.

'I need a Bloody Mary,' Keane said to the hostess, who was dolled up as if she'd been doing duty on flights from the South. A belle with piled-up hair, and caked make-up that couldn't disguise the years that were etched on her. Constant travels over two decades or more. But she was a delight. Got Keane his drink, had a friendly word and left him alone. She knew what she was about.

For about an hour he stayed put, letting one drink last the course and watching baseball on the TV above the bar. He was conscious that wine would be flowing freely at the embassy later, and started to plan tactics. He'd have time to change at home, just. He'd miss the performance, but could be in place when the throng arrived. Perfect. And he knew he was bound to be able to see Flemyng in private afterwards.

Just after the hour, he saw Liam approaching the bar from the side, having materialised from nowhere. There was no one on the next stool, and he climbed aboard. They spoke as if they were strangers thrown together, just as they had in the station in Chicago.

After Liam had nodded a greeting, Keane leaned towards him. 'Sean found me. Told me the news. And I have something for you. Ring Will from Amsterdam, tomorrow at four o'clock our time. On the dot. Don't miss it.' He passed him a piece of paper with the number of the secure line.

'Now, what did they say about Chicago at your meeting?'

Liam's eyes took on an intensity that held him, and he felt again the apprehension that Sean had produced at the hotel.

'You know that there's always been a rule that there's no heavy stuff in public on this side of the water. No one's going to shoot you.' He smiled.

'They think you're connected with the consulate – I suggested you'd let something slip to me. Probably just a friend who's keeping an ear to the ground for them. But be careful. It's going to be different from now on.

'There's some good news, though. The Viking flew home last night, so Sullivan said. He'll be needed for something, I expect. Sullivan will know – but he wasn't saying. He's funny about the Viking, Describes him as a psycho, but a good man as well.

'Work that one out.'

Keane said, 'Sean told me, at the hotel.' Liam said it showed their relationship was up and running.

Then Keane asked if the Chicago night-time chase had come up at the meeting.

'Thank God, no.' Liam said. 'What Sullivan's heard, who knows? Not me, for sure. But at least I've got a clearer picture of the shooting. Will's brother was told to go to the warehouse by the Viking. He delivered a message to his hotel. They trusted him enough to have him there – remember he hadn't been asking questions about guns and money. So he was invited.'

'Fine, but what happened with the police?' said Keane.

'It's obvious,' Liam said. 'We'd done the deal with the Latin Kings. The guns were in a pick-up truck and off and away, and then the cops arrived. How did they find out? Well, to the Viking and the lads the obvious culprit was the Stranger in Town. Panic! He was the outsider and the natural suspect. In the melee, someone shot him. I don't know who fired, to this day – the Viking still hasn't come clean.'

So, Keane said, they were still left with the problem. Abel wouldn't have alerted the cops. 'He knew he'd inevitably be blamed, and he'd every interest in staying as part of the group, to learn more. Letting the gun deal be done, without any mishaps, suited him. It would prove that he could be trusted, so he turned up.'

'Exactly,' said Liam. He was playing with a napkin on the bar, and winding it round a finger.

Keane was shaking his head. 'He died because the cops came. So who called them?'

Liam's eyes turned away from him.

'I did,' he said.

At the embassy Flemyng was preparing for the evening's show. A performance in every respect, he felt.

Livesey had returned from Langley, bursting with eagerness. 'Much to pass on,' he told Flemyng. 'I think I connected.'

'I do hope so,' Flemyng said.

And Saviour was full of his Pentagon visit. 'I'm sure our little spot of trouble is going to prove to be a passing squall, no more. An embarrassment among friends. Natural enthusiasm on their part to solve a mystery, of course – but, Will, I have promises of maximum security. Exceptional measures.'

'Exceptional. Good to know,' Flemyng said.

He went through the running order. 'We leave for the Kennedy Center at six forty-five. A glass of wine for our guests, then the play. And after the Battle of Shrewsbury' – Saviour clapped his hands to salute Flemyng's reference – 'we all return, and supper will be waiting. Friends from the Hill and State – White House, too, Roland – and of course, King Henry and Hal, the Percys, old Falstaff and the rest of them will join us, cleaned up and ready to party.'

'A fine treat,' Saviour said. 'We're in your debt, Will.'

Flemyng went upstairs to change. He could identify his own tiredness in the mirror, and the signs of ageing that he would have denied only a year earlier. He shaved with the thought that he was putting on a fresh face. The clock on his bedroom mantelpiece showed him that Keane would be taking off soon. What had he learned that afternoon, and where did it leave them?

Keane, pleased to have a pair of seats to himself near the back of his plane, was playing, uncomfortably, with the same question about his own afternoon. Where did Liam's revelation leave them both? There was a long wait before they lined up on the runway, the usual palaver at the end of the business day, and then they were over the city on a flight that might get them to National at seven o'clock. Just as Flemyng was thinking of him, so Keane's mind was on the boss. About how life would be different around them, and what he had learned about Chicago. What had happened to Mungo at Altnabuie.

Most of all, he thought about Liam's farewell. A handshake lasting longer than any they had known. In their eyes, an understanding of what they now knew of each other, and on Liam's face, a picture of sorrow.

Turning his mind, with difficulty, to the rational problem in front of him, he was convinced he was close to putting everything together. But it was a puzzle that still had to be rearranged, turned around in some fashion before it made sense.

He watched the New Jersey shore leading them south, got a glimpse of Philadelphia spreading out and, catching a glint from the sun, the line where Sean's train would be rolling south.

His eyes moved over the clouds and caught momentary glimpses of the landscape below. The outskirts of DC were somewhere below them, and he was nearly home. But his mind was lost in the clouds.

How was he going to tell Flemyng?

Thirty-one

As Flemyng arrived in the hallway to lead everyone to their cars for the Kennedy Center, Lucy eased him aside. She wore a straight black dress and a serious face to match. Leaning close, she said, 'London, just now. They want you home, soonest.'

'Good,' he said, smiling to his guests all the while. 'I dropped a firm word.'

Lucy said she had booked him on his usual flight the following night.

As guests began to arrive, he whispered to her. 'Does anyone else know?'

'Not from me,' she said.

It was a happy gang. Saviour had picked a flower from the garden for his buttonhole. Livesey was in a blue velvet smoking jacket and cravat. The embassy high command was in good order. 'We have some interesting guests who'll be joining us,' Flemyng told them. 'And those among the cast who survive the battle, as well as some who don't.'

The company laughed.

He named a couple of senators and their wives, four members of the House, including Charlie Farrell, and a Supreme Court Justice who maintained close ties with the embassy. Two reasonably ranked White House men, an assitant Secretary of State, and the Italian ambassador, who was a particular friend.Maria had arrived in good time, looking more like a Washington socialite than a journalist, which is how she would be introduced to everyone.

'Enjoy yourselves.' He swung round and led them outside waving an RSC programme, like a tour guide holding up an umbrella to rally his troops.

Keane was just landing at National as they left. He'd have time to change properly and get himself ready for a late evening performance that he couldn't persuade himself he'd enjoy for a minute.

At the theatre, Pringle was first out of the lead car and directed everyone through the side entrance to their private room. As Flemyng passed, he leaned over. 'Please ring the switchboard, sir.'

The embassy had made sure that there was a phone line in the room, and a technician was on hand. 'Not entirely secure, sir, just so you know,' he said.

Lucy watched a look of surprise come over him. He mouthed to her, 'Mungo.'

If he was ringing at midnight from Perthshire, something unusual had occurred. Mungo hated to bother the embassy at any time.

Flemyng listened to his brother. 'It's Babble, I'm sorry to say. He's taken a bit of a turn. The ambulance was quick, and apparently it's a stroke of some sort. Not necessarily catastrophic... but... you needed to know.'

Shaken by news that took him home so suddenly, Flemyng

asked after Mungo, too, checked that his Special Branch officer was around for him and told him to make sure that Babble knew he was thinking of him, far away. There and then, he made the decision to tell Mungo of his plan. Keane could wait.

'Mungo, I can give you some news. I have to fly home tomorrow and I'm coming north on Saturday morning. I have a couple of days in the office at the start of the week, then I'll be back with you for a few days. That's a promise.'

He knew when Mungo spoke that he was struggling to keep his voice under control. 'Thank you, Will. Of all the things to hear tonight. I'm thrilled.'

'Sleep well, old friend,' Flemyng said. 'I'll soon be back with you.'

He took Lucy to one side. 'I've promised to take the rest of next week at home after I do my office stuff. Clear the decks, would you? I'll explain later.'

He plunged into the throng.

A pink-bow-tied Whealdon from the FBI was a guest, and Flemyng was relieved. 'A bit of a flap, Jack, as I'm sure you know.'

Whealdon said he did – he'd seen one of the telegrams – but thought it all unnecessary. 'Hold your finger in the wind, will you?' Flemyng said. 'I'm heading to London tomorrow night. An up-to-the minute picture would be helpful.' He arched his eyebrows. 'Courtiers!' He nodded his head towards Saviour. 'They can't leave well alone.'

Whealdon laughed. 'We all have 'em.'

Wondering whether he looked as tired as he felt, Flemyng spotted Maria and took her to meet Charlie Farrell. They'd never spoken. He was wearing a Red Sox pin in his lapel, which helped, and they were off. She knew his district from top to bottom, and within a few minutes they'd identified mutual friends.

Then he took Saviour aside. He'd decided since arriving at the theatre that if news of his forthcoming trip came back from London and it had been kept from Saviour, it would be another irritation that he'd carry home like a pocket grenade. So he turned it into a confidence, offered as a gift.

'I've just heard in the last few minutes, Roland, that I have to go to London tomorrow. So I'll be in the office Monday and Tuesday, I expect. A range of things, as ever. The summit, and no doubt more reassurance about our little hiccup here.

'Which flight are you taking?'

When Saviour told him, he realised that Lucy, dear Lucy, had taken the trouble to check and had booked him on one that was far enough apart from Saviour's that they wouldn't even have to travel to Dulles together.

'That's a pity. But I'll see you in cabinet office on Monday,' Flemyng said.

Saviour gave a formal little bow, which he did so often. His calling card. 'And we shall make you as welcome as you have made me here. First, I'm looking forward to a riveting performance.'

Surveying the crowd, Flemyng saw Guy Cotton in conversation with Livesey, and moved towards them. 'Arty, I hope the play is as good as it should be. Guy – a quick word in the morning? Good news, I think. By the way, Patrick should be back in town about now. All being well, he'll join us for supper.'

The buzz from the auditorium was growing louder. A chime sounded. Flemyng clapped his hands. 'Let's go. Battles are about to commence.'

The stage was dark. Gradually, dim light stole across,

revealing the shadowy outline of a palace chamber. There was a gleam from rich hangings in red and gold, and within a minute most of the gloom had lifted. The King and his retinue walked on in a huddle, into an explosion of colour. He spoke.

So shaken as we are, so wan with care,
Find we a time for frighted peace to pant,
And breathe short-winded accents of new broils
To be commenced in strands afar remote.

Frighted peace indeed, Flemyng thought.

His mind turned to the remote strands, in Scotland and across the water, where he and Liam had first met. What news from Keane, he wondered. Looking along the row, he saw that Lucy and Livesey were together. She would produce a full report. Every word.

He settled back content, and let the lines flow.

Falstaff appeared, larger than Saviour, and everyone laughed.

At the interval, the company mingled in the private room, with Flemyng managing to have a few minutes with Charlie Farrell. 'You were kind, Congressman. That meeting in Chicago was friendly and useful. I'm grateful.'

'You're most welcome,' Farrell said, evidently relieved.

'Sorry you're having to watch a King of England strutting his stuff, but there we go,' said Flemyng.

'I'm fine with history, as you know, Will.' He slapped him on the back.

Lucy was signalling from the phone. 'Don't worry. Nothing more from Mungo. That was Patrick. He's back safely, but he needs some private time later. Not tomorrow – tonight.'

Flemyng said that he should come to the residence with
Lucy and Maria. Saviour might linger for a while after
supper, but, however late, they would gather together when
he'd disappeared to bed.

'Reassure him. Is he OK?'

Lucy said that he was perturbed. Not an emergency, but
still...

Flemyng returned to the theatre in a state of uncertainty.
In the dark before the first interval, he had been thinking of
Mungo and Babble and their long friendship, now probably
drawing to a close. But it was Keane who preoccupied him.
He had panicked surprisingly before leaving for New York,
ringing Liam at a time that hadn't been agreed. Now he was
sending an alarm signal. What could it be?

Flemyng loved the history plays, always had. They spoke
to him about power – its elusiveness, the passing moments
of glory. The hopes of what might come from conflict; the
relentless struggle to survive. He listened to the King,

The trumpet sounds retreat; the day is ours.
Come, brother, let us to the highest of the field,
To see what friends are living, who are dead.

The words lodged in his mind. When the posse of cars bore
them back to the embassy, and they were turning through the
gates, he heard them again. What friends are living, who are
dead?

Keane was in the lobby, and when he had ushered the
guests through the door he turned back to him.

'What's wrong?' Flemyng said.

'Nothing that can't wait until after supper, but we'll need
to be alone. That's all.'

320

'Understood,' Flemyng said. 'Enjoy yourself first.'

Perturbed, Lucy had warned him. He could tell.

There was champagne and cocktails in the reception room while they waited for members of the cast. The group was high with excitement, and Lucy wasn't required to interrupt him. They reached for their canapés, and drank.

He clapped again.

'May I introduce the King, Prince Hal, Percy, Falstaff and sundry dukes and earls,' he said, to applause. 'The archbishop, too, of course. Some of them back from the dead.'

Falstaff was thin again, and ready to eat.

Each of the six tables for eight was lit by candles, and the ceiling chandeliers were dimmed. There was loud conversation as they took their places in the flickering light. Someone said they might as well have been on stage.

Flemyng rose without notes, as was his habit, and welcomed them all. He was careful to follow protocol with a Supreme Court Justice and a British minister in the room. But everyone – senators and congressmen, officials and the others – was placed in perfect order. Saviour would have nothing to complain about his introduction, which was warmer than Lucy had expected. The embassy staff – notably Keane and Cotton – were not identified by name.

Most of all he found words for the actors without leaving a single nose out of joint. All of them who'd been on stage knew how difficult that was. Well-nigh impossible, said Falstaff to his dining companion.

Flemyng apologised for the absence of Francesca at home, and spoke of her regret at not only missing the play but the company gathered in the residence. There were a few words about the old relationship between their countries symbolised by the building, but Flemyng was accomplished in knowing when to stop. Long enough and smooth enough to do the job and no more.

They ate, and he talked at his table as if there was nothing on his mind except the company, the actors and the play. When the time came to rise, he thanked the embassy staff and looked forward to welcoming everyone back. 'To *Part II*, next year,' he said, and raised a glass.

Charlie Farrell led the wobbly procession back to the reception room where there was whisky and brandy, with actors in hot pursuit. A few guests took their leave immediately, but the others settled down for what they hoped might be a good hour of night-capping, although it was well after midnight.

Flemyng made a point of urging people to stay, slipping away for a moment after about forty-five minutes to make a phone call. London would be up and about.

He got through to the chief clerk's office, where the overnight shift had just handed over. 'A quick one. I got the message earlier, and I'm flying home tomorrow night. Could you let the foreign secretary know that I'll keep Monday and Tuesday completely free. Best wishes from all of us here.'

Returning to the room, he watched Keane. He was smart in his Chicago-bought blazer and a bright shirt for the theatre. Polished shoes. But he didn't look happy, and Lucy had picked up his mood. What would he say?

Flemyng was satisfied to see that Livesey was a drag on proceedings. An elderly senator, who should have been in bed, was wilting fast, and Flemyng had to signal to Saviour to rescue him. 'Arty is a man of enthusiasm,' Saviour told the senator. 'Exceptional enthusiasm. But even with his disturbed sleep pattern – he's only just arrived, you see – we have to respect the hour.' Glaring at Livesey, he looked not towards the clock on the mantelpiece, but at the stairs to his bedroom.

And so the last guests left, and the high doors at the end of the pillared hall were locked behind them.

A bottle of whisky was on the library table, and Flemyng gestured to the gang. Lucy and Keane, and then Maria. Drinks were poured, with water for Keane, and they were left alone.

He introduced her. 'Patrick, my old friend Maria Cooney. Abel's friend. What more can I say?'

And they began.

Thirty-two

THE GATHERING IN FLEMYNG'S LIBRARY WAS A TRIAL FOR everyone, despite the instinctive bonhomie with which he swept them in when the others had gone. For Keane, who'd arrived carrying a burden that he feared might drag him into the depths, for Maria because it brought her face to face with her friend's death, and for Lucy because she feared that Flemyng was dangerously reckless in what he was proposing they should discuss, and how he encouraged them. Above all, for Flemyng himself, because the parallel loyalties he had to protect were painfully and permanently entwined. He couldn't cut the knot.

Maria began with the necessary question that reminded them of the strangeness of the moment.'Should I be here?'

'Of course not,' Flemyng said. 'But you are. If something comes up that offends my sense of propriety, I'll ask you to step out.'

His response made Keane feel even more uncomfortable. Were there boundaries that he had to observe? He felt he had to ask. 'I'm going to talk about some aspects of Abel's life and our own work,' he said. 'This is classified. Highly.' He added 'sir', because Maria's presence had unsettled him. 'Have we authority?'

'I've decided,' Flemyng replied, without indulging his anxiety. 'I'm waiving the rules, like a fifteenth-century king, you might say. So, like any monarch, I can change my mind as I please. If I think we're swimming into deep water, I'll invent a rule to shut us up, and Maria will leave the room. OK?'

Lucy recognised Flemyng in a mood she often enjoyed. Fired up by Saviour, no doubt, he was in command, and argument was pointless. He knew that neither she nor Keane would object seriously, nor that either of them would breathe a word outside the residence. If he went too far, she would clear up behind him. But it would be a rigorous ride.

'Patrick,' Flemyng said, without warning, 'tell me the news you have from New York, which is obviously worrying you.'

Keane couldn't conceal his nervousness. 'It's directly connected with Abel's death,' he offered, looking around.

'Go ahead,' Flemyng said, as if he'd never expected anything else.

Keane decided not to use Liam's name, as a gesture towards the embassy regime, which made for a hesitant start, when he had hoped to be decisive and give Flemyng the news without accoutrements.

'This is personal, sir.'

Flemyng stopped him. 'We're friends together. Boss is fine, but sir is a non-starter.'

Keane took a deep breath.

'Our contact, whom we met in Chicago, has explained to me why your brother Abel died. Not how, but why.'

The three others looked at Flemyng. The boldness of Keane's statement hit home.

'I intend to use his name, Patrick. It means nothing to Maria,' Flemyng said. 'You're referring to Liam.' He stared at him.

Lucy stiffened.

'I suppose I am,' said Keane, sounding miserable.

He plunged on. 'I met him in New York yesterday and again today. This afternoon, after we'd discussed Chicago, he explained to me the sequence of events. I'm sure he was telling the truth, and it upset him a good deal. As you know, boss, he's travelling home, and I can say that he's apprehensive.'

Keane looked at Maria, as if he might dry up. But, breathing hard, he ploughed on.

'Here's his story. As we know, his group in Chicago had no idea who Abel was. His identity was only revealed to them – by a police informer – after he died. So they had no reason to treat him in a special way, nor worry about him unduly. He'd worked his way into their circle over a period, winning their confidence sufficiently to be asked to be with them at a handover of guns from a Chicago gang. I suppose it was a kind of test for him. It was the man I call the Viking...' he glanced anxiously towards Maria again '... who delivered the details of the handover. To his hotel..

'But our man Liam was planning to help us by trying to scupper the arms deal. He'd done it before, and this time there was an unusual opportunity that presented itself. He knew that if the operation was blown, they'd blame Abel, the outsider who turned up as a hanger-on with their gang. And he was also worried, privately, that Abel was asking questions about the Provos' internal political battles, touching on the presence of potential informers.

'We can understand why that alarmed him.'

Flemyng remained silent.

'So blaming Abel – under a different name, obviously, and his identity unknown to Liam-- was a double bonus for him. He didn't bargain for the violence.

'Here's what happened. The Viking explained in his message delivered to Abel's hotel exactly where the handover of guns was going to take place, and Abel turned up. Why not?

'And on that same evening,' Keane said, his voice dropping, 'Liam made an anonymous phone call.'

Flemyng, who had been listening with an expression on his face that had hardened suddenly, now showed symptoms of distress that Maria and Lucy each recognised. He knew what he was about to hear.

'It was Liam who rang the police?' he said, to get it straight out.

Lucy could see his right hand trembling.

'Yes,' said Keane, who could hardly believe that he had been spared the task of breaking the news himself, 'and they were late getting there, as we know. They hadn't arrived to stop the handover before it happened, so there were guns everywhere. Result – chaos and a shoot-out.'

Maria spoke for the first time since Keane had begun, 'And Abel died.'

Lucy, who knew about Mungo's call earlier and had lived with Flemyng's anxiety after the Provos' arrival at Altnabuie, understood like no one else there – including Maria, whose own relationship with Abel preoccupied her – what it must have meant to Flemyng to utter the words.

He had protected them, had given them both the kind of loyalty that he had spent half a lifetime of discipline to master. Liam's ignorance about who Abel was, and his anxiety to protect his own secret bond with Flemyng, had now destroyed a brotherly relationship that he had believed would reach its natural maturity when they both laid down the swords of their trade and could talk, once again, like old friends. They would have their time in the sun, as they hadn't had since they were boys together on the hills and on the loch.

All gone, with Abel, into the ground.

Lucy knew Flemyng was thinking of Liam. He'd seen in Chicago how the strain of the years had marked his friend's features. Greying hair, the sharpened cheekbones, longer lines across his brow. A worn profile. When they spoke together in the hotel, he'd tried to reassure him how much strength he got from a relationship which could never be thought normal to an outsider, though it allowed them to find in each other reserves of trust as great as any they had shared with anyone else. They argued, on two occasions violently. But they had understood what held them together – a vague, half-constructed hope that, between them, they might help to bring it all to an end.

'Patrick, both Lucy and you know what I feel about Liam. Maria knows enough about me, and some of the strange couplings we've made over the years, to understand it in the same way. I'd be pushing the truth of this event away, out of my mind. Maybe I knew that this was the explanation. I've probably known all along, and feared that it would touch on my own role. Which it does. Not a vicious, planned execution. Just a moment when everything went wrong. It's common enough, but this time it hurts very much'

Maria spoke quietly. 'For those of us who fight in the dark, this is our fate.'

Lucy could see that Keane was finding the conversation hard to take. She passed him a glass of whisky and a large tumbler of water.

Flemyng managed a smile. He moved them on.

'Now, I asked you, Patrick, if you might ask Liam to give you his version of the attack on Mungo. You've told me what he said.

'Yes,' said Keane. 'Accurately, I hope.'

'Can you repeat the gist of it for everyone?'

Flemyng said he was going to prepare Maria. They might be venturing into territory where it was possible, despite what she had already heard, that she might be asked to absent herself.

But first, Flemyng took Maria through the events on the night that the Provos came to Altnabuie. The balaclavas, the guns, the effective kidnap of Mungo and Babble – whose stroke only a few hours earlier had surely been a direct result of the assault – and his own puzzlement about the way the operation was conducted.

'It's why I asked Keane to listen to Liam's account.'

'It boils down to a name,' Keane said. 'Did the men use it when they spoke to Mungo? He said that if you knew, boss, you'd draw the right conclusion.'

In the whole unravelling of the story, Flemyng knew this moment might be the most important for the three others in the room. But he knew, too – because of the presence of Maria, who was innocently affording him some protection at this moment – that even with the openness that he'd permitted them to exercise, it was not the moment to take the last step.

But he could lead them to the edge.

He spoke. 'Here's the mystery that always puzzled me. They scared the life out of Mungo and my dear friend Babble. It could have killed them both, but didn't. It would have taken only a little violence. I'm sure the two visitors had done it before – that's why they were chosen. I couldn't quite understand why they spared Mungo, because they could easily have done him in. But they made it easy for their two victims to loosen the ropes.

'Remember Mungo's words. They wanted him to live to tell the tale.

'Here's where I have to be careful. Liam asked through you, Patrick, whether I knew if a certain name had been mentioned when they were bombarding Mungo with questions. Well, thanks to his memory, I can say that the answer is yes. It's a name that didn't tell him anything. I told you Lucy, when you heard it a few days ago, that it meant nothing, and yet everything. What I can let you all know, and I hope I can go further in the next few days, is that it's a codename that Liam and I dreamed up. Pretty clever in its way, I think. It's the key to everything. If it's blown, we can't survive this, I promise you that.'

Keane asked why they could have imagined that a name out of the blue might mean anything to Mungo.

Flemyng's dark eyes sparkled. 'Good man.'

He took them a little way down the road. 'Long years ago, when my relationship with Liam began as a slow and up-and-down affair. Of course, because we know how it goes, Maria. But on one occasion – an important one – we spent a couple of days in the hills at Altnabuie. A weekend when our relationship was properly forged. I like to think so anyway, and so does Liam. I now think I know why the visitors were sent to Mungo, and what their instructions were.'

Pulling himself together like a fighter ignoring the blood on the floor, he seemed to get a second wind. 'Time for bed.'

However, as they all prepared to leave, and the car was summoned to take Maria home, he said a few quiet words to

Keane. First, he made sure that he'd passed Liam the private number and the instruction to call from Amsterdam.

Then, 'You're going to see this through with me, Patrick.'

'Of course, I am,' he said.

Flemyng drew him close with an arm. 'I'm not sure you follow me.'

'Sorry, boss...

'You're coming home with me.'

Keane looked lost, bewildered.

'If you can't fix that,' Flemyng said, 'I'd be mighty surprised. Sleep well.'

He left him alone with his astonishment.

The news that he was going to London banished any thought of sleep for Keane. He felt as if he'd taken a pill that kept him alert. There was one task that might have waited until the morning, but that he would take care of now. He went back to his office, using the key on his belt to enter the secure area, and found himself alone. It was dark except for his own desk light. Quiet as the grave.

He wrote a message, and marked it for Johnny Silvester in Belfast. Checking the protocols for cables to the security service, he looked at what he had written.

'Cathal Earley, nickname the Viking, back in NI, probably Belfast.Close to Fergus Sullivan. Possibly on a mission. Good luck.'

Going to a secure telex machine, he sent it himself.

Time for bed, indeed, and Lucy.

Thirty-three

THEY ARRIVED TOGETHER IN THE MORNING, AFTER LITTLE
sleep. Friday notwithstanding, it was a day of preparations.
She set to work on Flemyng's schedule, Keane cabled his
office and, with a pot of strong coffee, opened the envelope
of photographs from New York that had been delivered to his
desk from the overnight bag

He had confessed to her in the night that he was a touch
hungover, which she hadn't needed to be told. But he was
soon awake. The spread of pictures brought his desk to life.

He saw Sullivan arriving, in his smart suit with the familiar
briefcase at his side. Most of the arrivals were the usual gang,
of whom the library had thick files of portraits, but he paid
particular attention to Liam, who arrived late. He was bent,
and looked as if he was fighting against a strong wind though
it had been a fine day. He struggled with the door of the bar.
Keane saw what had been lost.

But the pictures afterwards held his attention even more.
Unusually, Sullivan had conversations in the street. After
most meetings they dispersed one by one, and left quickly.

Yesterday had been different. When Liam came out, nearly the last to do so, Sullivan was waiting. They had words, and neither looked happy in the photographs that Rodden had taken with his motor drive that produced an image every half-second.

Keane saw that they were arguing. A small group gathered, seemingly most of those who'd attended the meeting. Five men, and, in the middle, Sullivan and Liam. If it had been a home movie, you'd have expected them to take a swing at each other in the next shot. One of Sullivan's sidekicks stood behind, smoking and looking on with a scowl.

Keane had never seen such a group hanging around after a meeting. In one of the shots, the older men looked as if they were a group of guards. It reminded him of a couple of the scenes in the play the night before, when a rebel was about to be despatched or a king's man banished. Liam was in trouble.

Even in the still photographs, which he placed in a line so that the development of the scene was obvious, you could tell where the power lay, and at whom it was being directed.

Keane thought back to Liam's arrival at the airport, less than an hour after the pictures were taken. He'd recovered his bearing. A hard life had taught him how to do that, but looking at his confrontation with Sullivan he could see how much of a recovery he had made. The sadness on his face as they parted was explained. For whatever reason he was going home, it was not to a hero's welcome.

Liam was bent down again and left alone.

Keane looked through them once more and typed up a note for Flemyng. He enjoyed putting words to pictures and telling the story. Disciplining himself to let the photographs speak for themselves, he found it surprisingly easy to make sense of the scene and to reach his own conclusions.

Then he rang the Barracks from the secure room in the station. The controller with whom he worked was aware of his trip to New York, to service a source. He'd taken care in the previous two weeks to make the case for a slightly disordered schedule. Chicago had interrupted his routine, now New York. He had his story ready.

Flemyng had requested that he make some visits with him in London, he said. There were Irish matters and, as a few senior figures in the Barracks were aware, a difficulty with the Americans over Moscow material. He would visit the office on Monday, perhaps Tuesday, too, but there was no doubt that he was required in London.

Ten minutes later he had permission. A week at home.

He knew he could have booked a flight on his own authority, and explained it afterwards, but the uncertainties over the outcome of Flemyng's trip were great enough to have persuaded him to take precautions in advance. He would be on the same flight as the boss, and happily only a little further back in the plane, because he had successfully had it classified as an urgent trip that couldn't be delayed.

Guy Cotton, meanwhile, had his appointment with the ambassador.

'I'm a bringer of good news,' Flemyng said. 'Not official yet, but there's a promotion on the way for you. You know that I hear some things from the Barracks that aren't strictly my business, and this is one of them. You've been carrying a lot in the last couple of weeks, so I thought I'd let you know. It's station chief for you, though I can't stay where. I'm told you'll hear next week. Congratulations.'

Cotton knew exactly what was happening, but took it gracefully. He thanked Flemyng, who said they'd organise a fine farewell party.

'Do feel free to tell Roland,' Flemyng said. 'He'll be delighted, I'm certain.'

'Thank you, sir,' said Cotton as he turned away.

A lively morning in the station.

Flemyng turned on the phone to Whealdon, who'd promised an update. They arranged to meet for lunch, downtown.

The staff meeting was brisk. Flemyng would be gone for a week. He gave them a pep talk on summit preparations, but mentioned nothing of the matters that were occupying all his thoughts.

A couple of his colleagues expressed their pleasure that he'd be seeing Francesca for the first time for three weeks, and his response was genuine. The next two days, despite some of the extra security, were going to be a release. The boys were doing fine at school, and he relished the thought of being together. Two days to him now felt like a month.

He and Lucy spent an hour together on his schedule. Monday morning in the office, and an hour in the late afternoon in Downing Street, perhaps longer. She had prepared a list of officials elsewhere who wanted to see him. And she needed to remind him to ring Mungo later. Then, before leaving for lunch, he rang Maria.

'Thanks for your frankness last night,' he said. 'I appreciated it. Having to put on a happy face, and then deal with all that.'

'You knew, didn't you?' she said. 'About your friend's call to the police.'

'I hadn't realised until that moment that I'd worked it out. Afterwards, I thought – yes, I did know. A funny trick that the mind plays on you. An understanding lurks underneath, then pops up, fully formed.'

'I have to see you before you leave,' she asked him.

Flemyng had no doubt that she was anxious. 'I'll drop by after lunch'

Keane also had reason for alarm. He got a confused call through the switchboard. The voice didn't use a name. 'Have I got the right number? I'm not sure. But I thought we might have a cup of tea in the middle of the day, where we met last time. But I think it may be someone else I want. Sorry to have bothered you.'

Sean without doubt. Hardly the most elegant clandestine message, but he'd got away with it. Noon at Union Station. Keane would have to leave soon.

Compiling a list in his head of the preparations he'd have to make for the airport, he went to the street to hail a cab.

Meanwhile, Flemyng had made his own list of questions for Whealdon, and one for himself. Should he speak to Angleton again? No harm could follow, he concluded. And he'd see Maria first.

As he prepared to leave, Keane arrived at the station. He went to the gate where he'd boarded the train for New York and there was Sean, alone on a bench reading the *Post*, with his striped bag on the floor beside him.

They acknowledged each other discreetly, and walked through the arches to the central concourse, where they took a table below the dome and ordered coffee.

'That was quick,' Keane said, smiling.

'Had to be,' Sean said. 'Trouble.'

'Tell me,' said Keane, aware of the trust Liam had placed in this man. A public place, a quick summons. He was taking a risk, much bigger than Keane's.

'I'll keep it brief. Sullivan's on the warpath, if that's not a stupid word.' He managed a smile. 'I don't know if you're aware of this from Liam, but Sullivan's been convinced for a while that we've been penetrated. The Chicago business, and other things. That north London disaster has got them crapping themselves in the North, so everybody's on edge, and he's obsessed with the FBI because he says there's hostility that didn't used to be there.

'He's convinced your ambassador's brother was working for the Bureau.'

'Funnily enough, that's helpful,' Keane said, 'because it's complete bollocks.'

'I think Liam's OK, which is what you need to know. Sullivan's no fan, I can tell you. But Liam does have a couple of bigger friends at home, who'll try to help. He wants you to know that it's bound to be rough.

'Something else for you. There's another active service unit on the go, planning a big one, and he asked me to pass it on. It's an airport. London, but not Heathrow, and they're on the scene getting ready. Somewhere near a runway. He knows no more.

'And he wants you and me to set up a system for communicating. I'm not going to make another daft call like the one this morning, I promise you that.'

Keane had a plan ready. He explained how it would work, and took a handwritten card from his inside pocket which he handed to Sean, who explained to him in turn how he could be contacted safely.

'I wish you luck, Patrick.'

'You, too,' said Keane. 'And what's written on that card will work for Liam, too, if he gets the chance.'

They passed a few minutes together on sport, and White House politics, then shook hands firmly before they parted. Keane took a cab back to the embassy and picked up the phone to Belfast within five minutes. His security service friend, Silvester, whose rehabilitation apparently continued apace, thanked him for the second time.

He'd seen Keane's cable about the Viking's arrival. 'We're getting him on the radar.'

Flemyng was sitting down to lunch as Keane finished his call. Whealdon and he indulged in a plate of oysters, succulent and fat. Splashing the tabasco as if it was ketchup, Whealdon told Flemyng what he knew.

'They're as happy as sandboys over the river at having cracked your case. Took them nearly two years. But they're certain. Copenhagen was the clincher, I'm told.'

He looked for a response, but none came.

'I'm told that it's restricted in just the way you'd want. Tight as a duck's sphincter.' Whealdon squeezed a lemon, shooting a stream of juice over his last oysters.

'My own take is that there's hardly any chance of a leak. Nobody in my building has a hint of the name – most of them don't even know that the hunt was on. So, if I were you I'd relax. Old Jim, as you well know, has Soviets on the brain. If they were as good as he thinks, we'd all be fried to a crisp by now. Or have ourselves a president with a Moscow money stream.

'At least there are some things we'll never see.'

Flemyng talked about Ireland. 'We're getting there, I think. What our Chinese friends would call a Great Leap Forward. When you see the detail you'll be less than astonished, but it's going to change the set-up, more than people think. Two governments agreeing to do business together on the same territory.' He clasped his hands tightly to make the point. 'We've got years of this ahead. But if we don't start somewhere, it's never going to end.'

Then he said, 'We're told the money boys over here are worried about how much we know.'

'I hear they're paranoid,' Whealdon said. 'Which doesn't mean they don't have a point.'

'Just look at Jim Angleton,' Flemyng said, laughing.

'Sure,' Whealdon said. 'Even a quack medium in a circus tent sometimes guesses right.'

They finished their glasses, and Flemyng saw Pringle stepping from the car outside. On the way, he considered the curiosity that although the two cases occupying him were in such different spheres they had so much in common. Names that couldn't be spoken. Deceptions that had run their course and, at the end, the same fateful summons home.

The thought gripped him, and he wondered if Keane was getting there, too.

He had given Maria's address to Pringle and they pulled up at exactly the time he had predicted. The car stopped about a hundred yards away, as she'd requested, but Pringle insisted on getting out and standing sentinel by the car as Flemyng walked a block to the yellow door. He only got back in the car, grumpily, when he'd seen Flemyng go inside.

They hugged.

'What a night,' she said. 'I like Patrick.'

'You're right. He's being blooded quite quickly,' Flemyng said.

They spoke for a little about Abel, and he told her about his worries for Mungo. 'I'll be there next week, as you know. Patrick's coming with me.'

She smiled at that.

'I should be able to put all this to bed,' he told her. 'The Angleton stuff, anyway.'

'I wouldn't be so sure,' she said, pouring from the teapot

she'd produced. 'You said you'd heard there were no security alarms at the moment. Not true.'

So many of the times he'd been with Maria flashed into his mind. There was hardly one when she hadn't been able to deliver a sharp arrow, straight and true.

'No proof,' she said. 'Nothing. But Angleton was right when he told you that there's money flying around. We're going to see much more of it. Now, Will, someone on the other side has told us they've had some success in recruiting in the last year. It may be nothing big, some low-grade guy in Agriculture or Voice of America. But not necessarily.

'Here's what's happening above a certain level. There's a bunch of people whose household bills are being pulled apart. Cars checked. Their holidays, where the kids went to summer camp. Anybody who's been splashing out funds that they don't appear to have is going to go through the wringer. Big time.

'That's what I know.'

'But no one's been fingered yet?' said Flemyng.

'So far,' said Maria.

'But the place is on alert,' he said.

'Correct.'

Flemyng thanked her. It was another message he hadn't wanted to hear but strangely welcome. As with Abel, he believed he'd known it all along. He knew what he had to say in London.

For an hour or so, because he'd cleared his diary for the trip, they spoke about old times. Paris on fire. The Cafe Tournon! A man called Kristof, who'd led them into a maze. Grace Quincy, the writer whose memory Maria still adored. Then, years later, Flemyng in government, caught up in the kind of crisis he thought he had left behind. Abel had been part of it, and he'd discovered – as Maria always said he would – how much more he preferred life in the shade.

'Still?' she asked him.

'The joy for me now is I can have it both ways,' he said.

Before he left, they made an arrangement. Dinner at her place, with old friends, two Fridays hence.

In the car, Pringle ran through their timings. 'We leave for Dulles at seven sharp. I've told Patrick. I'll collect your bags from the hall as usual. Airport formalities are all done and we have your passports.'

'Thanks, Tony,' Flemyng said. 'I'm going to make a few calls to tidy up things. Then I'll feel released.'

He waited alone for Liam's call, which came from Amsterdam on the stroke of four. Flemyng told him briefly but meticulously of his plan for the weekend. What he had prepared with the help of the Barracks, and what Liam had to do.

Startled, Liam thanked him. But he said, 'You're happy taking this risk?'

Sitting in Washington, thinking of home, Flemyng said, 'Your call. If you're game, I am.' Liam told him not to worry about that.

Then Flemyng dialled a number in Arlington, Virginia. It was answered after a few rings. They spoke for about five minutes.

He read a few papers from his red box, leaving Lucy alone, until it was time for last preparations. He turned the key in the box and slid it aside.

He was smiling when he arrived in the hallway of the residence for their departure, and Keane wondered what he'd heard. 'We'll have a moment in the library before we get in the car,' Flemyng told him.

He told Keane briskly about the requests he had made to the Barracks without telling him – he offered no apology for pulling rank – then the instructions he'd given Liam in their phone call. Finally, he described in detail, as if reading from a script, the role Keane would play over the weekend. And where.

They left for the airport in a mood of exhilaration. Keane's head was spinning.

Thirty-four

IT WAS DARK WHEN THEY TOOK OFF. FLEMYNG HAD TAKEN Keane into the VIP lounge and confirmed with airline staff who knew him well that his companion could be moved to a seat next to his in first class, which was thinly populated. An ambassador's privilege. Even then, in what he acknowledged was sheer schoolboy excitement, Keane enjoyed persuading himself that it would always be like this.

An hour into the flight, they were served dinner at a table for two that popped out between their seats. The steward clipped it into shape and laid a white tablecloth. When he'd left them, Keane took the chance to brief him on Sean. He'd sent the information through the same route as the tip-off about the north London gang, so once again it would bear no Washington fingerprints.

'Sean's showing us he's the real thing,' Flemyng said.

There was no one close, so they were able to converse without anxiety. Flemyng spoke seriously.

He explained to Keane what Maria had told him. There was a hunt on. Maybe leading nowhere, but gathering steam.

He believed he was going to have to ring a loud alarm. It would contradict Saviour, of course, who would certainly arrive in his office on Monday with reassurances that the name was safely under lock and key at Langley. Flemyng would have to be the party pooper, yet again. He told Keane that Whealdon had let slip over lunch a piece of information that he shouldn't have known – that the Moscow source had been recruited years earlier in Copenhagen.

'That tells me too many people know,' he said. 'I can see no alternative to warning him,' he said. 'Then it's his choice. Come over now, or wait and take a helluva chance.

'It's not a choice I'd like to make. But I've never lived with that kind of weight on my back, year after year. Difficult moments, of course. Danger, I suppose, quite a few times. But never the storm that you know won't pass; the one you know is going to take you away in the end.'

'Like Liam, when you think about it.' Keane said. 'I felt sadness – much deeper than I'd expected – when I said goodbye at the airport. I can't imagine what it must be like to wake up every morning knowing that it can't last.'

They were two hours out from Dulles, over the ocean. Although it was dark, they left the window blinds up and could see the stars. The steward left them alone, their dinner cleared away, with half a good bottle of claret left for their enjoyment through the night. The steady roar behind them and snoring from one of the back seats in the cabin where a large figure was stretched out, inert under its blanket. And lying between them was the knowledge of a confrontation with the unknown.

Flemyng said, 'You know now, Patrick, how odd it is that in the two problems we're unravelling – in Moscow and

Belfast – there's a weird similarity. You've touched on it. No direct connection, but symmetry of a kind.

'I suppose you have a name for it in maths.'

'Lots of them,' Keane said. 'I've been thinking the same. A name that hardly anybody knows. Back-to-front puzzles that are hard to crack. And two individuals running for their lives.'

Flemyng told him, 'You and I are cut from the same cloth. Thank you for that.'

So Keane asked if he would take him on the last step of the road leading back to Chicago.

'Certainly in the next few days, I promise,' Flemyng said. 'But how far have you got?'

Keane's nerves were jangling. 'I understand the span of your relationship with Liam. At my age, it's difficult to think what it's like to have a source that takes you back so far. The long gaps, picking up from nowhere, working out how to rekindle the old flame. I understand your fear that it can be snuffed out in a moment. Gone. But if you're asking me to lay out this whole operation – how the parts fit together – I can't be sure, if I'm honest. I think I know what gets you about the attack on Mungo, though.' He paused, thinking it through again, step by step.

'Go on,' said Flemyng.

'They let him survive, you've pointed out more than once. But I don't think there was anything fake about the questioning. The name that Mungo had never heard before, their interest in anyone who might have visited you at home.'

'Now finish the thought,' said Flemyng. 'You've got the pieces in your hand.'

'Part threat, part warning,' Keane said.

'Not unfriendly?' Flemyng asked.

Keane said he was losing him, so Flemyng's black eyes gleamed, like Abel's when he was excited. 'Patrick,' he said, 'it's all as clear to me now as the morning sun that we're going to see out of the windows of this plane before too long. But everything depends on tomorrow.'

They settled down and flew into the night. Keane didn't sleep. Flemyng dreamed of the hills.

Thirty-five

THE BARRACKS MAN WHO HAD BEEN DESPATCHED FROM
Brussels to Amsterdam by his controller arrived at Schiphol
at almost the same time as Flemyng and Keane were making
their approach into London in the early light, with patches
of mist lying on the fields. His instructions were to conduct
a simple observation at the airport and report back. On no
account should he intervene. He had Liam's picture, and
the name in the passport that had been arranged for him by
Flemyng eight years earlier. He didn't know his real name,
nor the reason for his journey.

He located the check-in desk Liam would have to use,
found a table at a café-bar that gave him a view of it and
checked his watch. He had at least an hour before Liam was
likely to arrive, so took the chance to ask the airline if his
flight was on time.

It would depart on schedule at 10.30, for Edinburgh.

He had been given two tasks. Confirm that Liam boarded
his flight and establish whether he was being followed. He'd
been left in no doubt about the importance of the message of

confirmation he had to send to London, despite his ignorance of the background. Nothing unusual in that: his life was full of it.

At Heathrow, Keane rang Operations at the Barracks from the lounge where he and Flemyng could spend an hour before walking to the gate for their own flight north. He was told their man was at Schiphol, but as yet there was no news of Liam. Keane said he would ring again from Edinburgh.

Then Flemyng produced a surprise from his hand baggage. He gestured Keane across and they went to a table near the window where he laid out a well-worn Ordnance Survey map of the Central Highlands. It was of the old cloth kind, with deep creases where it had been folded and refolded on hill walks and picnic expeditions over the years. There were even a few spots circled in ink where, years before, the boys had camped or spent an afternoon by the water. Flemyng ran his hands over it when he had laid it out, to show Keane the territory that he would soon be able to explore for himself. He stroked it as Keane might have touched an early manuscript, though more gingerly, enjoying the closeness.

'This speaks to me of happy days,' Flemyng said.

He picked out the spot where Altnabuie lay, worn away on the map by the pressure of countless fingers over the years, and pointed to the curving road down into the glen, the faint line of the driveway to the house and the tiny patch of light blue showing the water beyond the garden. He identified the hills around, touching them in turn, and showing Keane how their contours opened up passageways to the mountains in the west, and the wildness to the north.

'You'll see it this afternoon for the first time,' he said. 'I'm excited for you.'

The map pre-dated by many years the improved main

route from Edinburgh, but Flemyng showed him where he would branch off after taking the motorway west from the airport and then north up the A9. He traced the route past Pitlochry, pointing out that it was almost certainly the way the Provisionals' unit had taken when they went to confront Mungo. A tiny square on the map was the Pole Inn, high above the glen, and then he followed the lazy circuit round the last hill before the long run towards the house took you down and through the trees to journey's end.

'You'll do it in three hours. Don't rush, but don't stop along the way. Stay secure. This beautiful stuff mustn't fool you.' He placed a palm on his treasured map. 'There's danger here, for all of us.'

'By now, I think I've learned how to enjoy without relaxing,' said Keane.

Folding away the map, Flemyng said he knew what he meant. He gave it to Keane to put in his bag, pressing it flat with care between his hands. 'I wonder how much Liam will remember.'

He added, 'If he comes after all.'

When Lucy had asked the office to book their tickets, she had made sure they were seated apart. From the moment they left the lounge at Heathrow they would be separate travellers. Flemyng would find a government car waiting for him, while Keane went to pick up the rental car arranged for him by Operations. They wouldn't speak again until they were behind the gates of Altnabuie.

As Flemyng showed his boarding pass at the door of the aircraft, the captain stepped from the cockpit. 'Good to have you on board, sir.' They shook hands. 'We'll get you home safely.' Keane was already tucked away in the second row from the back.

Operations got a call from Schiphol as Flemyng and Keane's plane was taking off. Liam hadn't appeared. Boarding for his flight in Amsterdam would close soon.

Scanning the check-in area, the Barracks man could see no sign of watchers. No one lingering for no obvious reason; no one replicating his own inspection of the whole area. He was certain he couldn't have missed Liam, three of whose updated photos, just received from Washington, he'd studied in the Brussels station the previous evening. No one resembling him had turned up at the desk.

It was nearly ten. He could see the check-in staff preparing to close up. One of them was checking the stubs of the boarding passes she had issued, so in a few minutes he would have a story for London. No-show.

10.05.

Then Liam came through the door in a rush. He was almost running, moving fast enough to reveal his anxious state. He dashed across the floor to the desk, and the Barracks man could see him apologising, evidently pleading to be allowed onto the plane. There was a exchange between two members of staff, both looking at their watches. But they would know it was the only direct Edinburgh flight of the day, and he was carrying only a small overnight bag. Nothing had to be checked through.

There was a quick transaction, and one of the staff accompanied him, walking ahead fast, to whisk him through. Liam skipped along.

The Barracks man was walking to the payphone when he stopped, noticing a passenger emerging from the shop selling books and newspapers who was now approaching the desk where Liam had been helped a few moments earlier to catch his plane. He was a tall, dark young man dressed in anorak and jeans and carrying nothing but a newspaper. Well-groomed, he looked like an easy-going business traveller who was used to it all.

He spoke to the check-in clerk who was closing up at his desk, apparently in friendly fashion. In answering him, the clerk gestured towards the departure gates and smiled reassuringly.

She made a sign with her hand showing a plane taking off.

The Barracks man was in no doubt that she was confirming Liam's imminent departure for Edinburgh. The young man turned away, raising an arm in a signal of thanks, and walked straight to the doors leading out of the terminal.

Operations at the Barracks received their man's account within five minutes, and a detailed description of the young stranger. Liam was on the flight, but he had been watched.

After Flemyng and Keane landed in Edinburgh they took fifteen minutes to retrieve their bags. The government driver, whom Flemyng knew, would be parked in his usual spot, where police never disturbed him. But he decided to pause and talk to Keane after all. Was it Flemyng's sixth sense that caused him to wait until they had contacted London before getting in the car? Or was it simply that in the course of an operation devised and executed by him, the tiniest detail was important? No longer passengers keeping apart, they went together to a payphone.

Keane spoke to Operations, and asked for the news from Schiphol.

'Trouble,' he was told. 'He seems to be on the flight but our man thinks he was watched. He's all but certain your chap had a tail – someone taking an interest in him, checking he'd got away. It wasn't one of ours, you can be sure.'

Flemyng could read the message on Keane's face. Hanging

up, he led Flemyng outside the terminal where they could stand alone. 'Bad news. He was followed. We've got to assume they know.'

'Damn,' Flemyng swore quietly.

Keane expected what came next, because he knew how much emotion Flemyng had invested over the previous two days in the coming encounter with Liam. More than an operational fix, it was a commitment he couldn't break.

'We stay with the plan.' Flemyng's expression was set. 'Special Branch can double up. They can arrange to have the main road watched, so there's protection. I'll ring Mungo's minder immediately. You know there's now a secure line at the house? So I'll go north, wait for Liam and you, and behave as if nothing has changed. Don't alarm him unnecessarily. Say nothing about all this unless he's panicking, or asks directly. Get on the road as soon as you can.'

'Shouldn't we warn him straight away?' Keane said.

'In our own time, I think,' Flemyng said, walking to the payphone to speak to Mungo, who would pass him onto Alex of Special Branch.

'This changes everything, doesn't it?' Keane said.

'Of course,' said Flemyng.

His call to Altnabuie took five minutes, and he left to find his driver. Keane picked up his rental car and got it safely into the car park half an hour before Liam was due to land.

His excitement at the unexpected trip north had been bolstered by the sense of being back in the field, engrossed in the work that lifted his spirits. But the news from Schiphol brought back the memory of his chase in Chicago, the fear that it had planted, and the dark truth that if his position in the embassy had been compromised, he was going to remain in danger. The Edinburgh manoeuvre might only be the beginning. He touched his cheek, where he now had a thin scar.

If Liam had been followed to the airport, what else did they know?

He took an escalator to the first floor and found a lounge with a view over the runway and, from the windows on the opposite side, across the city. He could see the bumpy outline of Arthur's Seat above the city, and the contours of the castle on its rock, dark grey against the sky. He had hoped that he and Flemyng might be able to get into the streets for a while, but these brief days were going to give them little time for history.

Except for Liam's own.

Walking across the lounge he watched a couple of planes dropping out of the low cloud towards the runway, and tuned into their rhythm. He could see the red girders of the Forth Railway Bridge not far away, and rising beyond them in the distance the first of the hills that would soon be drawing them northwards.

Checking the arrivals board, he saw that Liam was due in five minutes. Going back to the window, he waited until his plane appeared through layers of cloud, wheels down and almost home. A puff of smoke on the runway as it touched the ground, a screech as the pilot pulled it up, and soon it was wheeling round and rolling slowly towards the terminal.

He went to the arrivals hall where he had to wait only a few minutes, though it seemed an eternity. Mothers and babies came through the doors first, a group of student travellers, and only a few businessmen because it was Saturday. It was towards the end of the line of passengers that Liam appeared, walking slowly. He looked as weary as Keane had remembered him in his lowest moments in New

York, without the stiff determination he'd shown when they had said goodbye at LaGuardia. They had been draining days for him, and now they showed in every step.

Their reunion was happy. Neither wanted a public display of affection that might attract attention, but there was warmth and understanding in their eyes. They knew they were on a risky, quick adventure , and a dangerous one. The fact bound them together, and as they exchanged greetings on the short walk to the car, Keane felt strengthened. They'd be together through it all.

Swinging out of the car park and heading towards the airport exit and the motorway, they relaxed for the first time. Keane asked about the flight, and checked there had been no trouble with the passport.

'No,' Liam said, smiling at him. 'The only problem was that I screwed up my timings getting to Schiphol. Got the wrong tram, and it was a nightmare. Just made it, so I spent most of the journey calming myself down.'

'Which I hope you're managing,' Keane said. 'We'll have a good day.' Noticing that it was approaching noon, Liam put his watch back an hour and spoke about how he looked forward to seeing Altnabuie again. 'We'll be talking a lot, I know,' he said, 'but I'll also have some memories that are happy for me. The time there was so short, but it's still there in my mind. Will's going to be there when we arrive, I'm thinking?'

Keane explained that he was maybe an hour ahead of them and would have had some time with Mungo before they arrived.

'I'm not sure how much he said to you on the phone yesterday, but you know Mungo isn't being packed off anywhere, don't you? He's obviously unaware of who you are – doesn't have the slightest idea – but he understands that your visit has to stay private. He's used to it.'

'Will told me not to worry about the police officer,' Liam said. 'You'll understand that's a bit strange.' He laughed at the thought. 'But he's probably been given a story that I'm a diplomat or something. Or undercover, which of course is true, but not in the way he imagines. Anyway, I'm trusting your man and we can't go back on this now.'

Keane got him to take Flemyng's old map from the glove compartment, and asked him to find the route they'd take when he left the motorway. They settled down to the drive, and Keane believed that the conversational pace they set – gentle, with long pauses where they remained silent and let the landscape take them away – was the preparation that Flemyng had hoped for, to settle them down.

But he knew it couldn't last.

Flemyng had arrived home at Altnabuie to find his brother waiting for him at the bench near the garden gate. The clouds had lifted, the sun was out and there were fresh spring breezes playing in the trees.

Mungo stood up. Warm, rounded, smiling. Looking better, wrapped happily in his favourite tweed jacket, than Flemyng had dared to expect. There was moisture on his cheeks when they hugged. 'You're home,' said Mungo.

'Don't I know it,' said his brother.

Flemyng stood beside him and they looked down to the loch, the water brightening before them in the splashes of sun. The sounds from the wood were loud. Birds were clustering in the birches, there was distant barking and a tractor and chainsaw at work not far away. Two young dogs appeared round the gable end and they raced into the garden. The brothers followed as if they'd been summoned.

The clouds coming in from the west were moving fast, so that pools of light fell on the hillsides and shadows chased them one after the other across the landscape. Mungo said there was weather on the way; rain in the afternoon. But there was nothing dull about the colours around them. The tapestry had light and shade, the dark foliage of the pines and spruce in the wood standing out against the vivid greens and yellows on the hillside. The water on the loch was swept with sun, then blackened again when the lines of light disappeared.

Everything on the ground and above them in the sky seemed on the move.

Flemyng said to his brother, 'It still calms me, this world turning around us. See the water. Look at the hills, as famijliar as friends.' He turned back towards the house, and his eyes followed the undulating line of the roof from west to east and the crooked chimney, then down to the window of his mother's studio on the first floor where Mungo still kept her easel and a few canvases she had never finished. The spirit was intact. Flemyng looked along to the window of his own room, directly above the front door, and the years fell away from him. He could feel the change.

Without saying much, they walked up the slope towards the house and the open door. Through the hall, Flemyng turned into the drawing room to go to the orrery in the corner. Mungo said he should set it going, and he pushed the lever. The planets began to move in their orbits, rising and falling in the unchanging patterns that had always given him solace.

He sat with Mungo for a few minutes. They spoke about his health, about Babble away in hospital, and the house itself. The stories, and its resilience.

After a while, Flemyng said gently. 'Mungo, I'm going to have to speak to Alex, the policeman. There are concerns. I'll tell you more when I'm done.'

Mungo saw his brother disappear towards the kitchen, and the back quarters where Alex had established himself. He knew it was time to take himself away while they spoke, and he joined the dogs in the garden.

'Sorry to land you with a problem without warning in that call from the airport,' Flemyng said to Alex. 'But I had to let you know immediately.'

'Don't worry, sir, two colleagues will soon be here from Edinburgh. They'll be discreet, keeping an eye on the road and so on. We know the place now, so you'll be secure. The watch on the ferries has been stepped up, too.' He didn't ask who Flemyng's visitor was going to be, having been instructed from above that Flemyng would tell him what it was safe and proper to know and no more. Alex was aware that it would be, to use a favourite phrase of his boss, a weekend that hadn't taken place.

'We can't know if this is a false alarm or not,' Flemyng said, 'but you'll be used to that. We've got to assume the worst. I can't tell you who's coming, but take it from me that we're in national security territory here, so strictest rules please. I'll say as much as I can, but no more. OK, Alex?'

'I understand, and you're in charge,' said the young policeman, who had been well briefed by his superiors about Flemyng's background and reputation. 'My guest will be here until tomorrow, and my colleague from Washington, Patrick Keane. He's only a touch older than you, I'd say, and I'm sure you'll get along fine. He's as secure as they come, just so you know.'

Alex understood what he must be.

Flemyng then spoke about Mungo, thanking Alex for the friendship he'd shown through a time when there was continuing concern about his health. 'He doesn't get unduly anxious, but I'm obviously aware his recent experience weighs on his mind – and that it came about directly because of me. So you'll realise how determined I am to protect him.'

Flemyng had known Alex for all of ten minutes, but the policeman could see how events had caused him to cast off the protective diplomatic gear he was obliged to wear. 'You see, I feel sadness at what he's going through.

'And guilt.'

Before Alex had to come up with a reply, he was relieved to hear a car crunching to a halt on the drive. Flemyng asked if he might step outside alone, and he got through the back door in time to see Liam and Keane standing together at the side of the house, taking in the scene in silence.

Liam turned to him, and Keane knew they would embrace. They stepped towards each other with arms outstretched.

Why was it that the more fearful they were, the closer they became?

The three men walked to the front of the house. 'It's all coming back to me,' Liam said. He hoped they might take the boat onto the loch, and walk the high track behind the woods.

In the distance they could see the figure of Mungo at the lochside, the dogs running close by him.

'Of course we will,' Flemyng said. 'We'll get out this afternoon, and then we'll have the morning before we need to get you back. Time to talk, to remember, and to think ahead.'

Liam's gaze was faraway, as he looked over the water to the light-splashed hills beyond. Flemyng fixed Keane's eyes and gave him a look that was as sharp as the question that lay behind it. Keane shook his head. He had told Liam nothing.

Pointing Keane towards the rim of the hills, talking about the pattern of the tracks leading in every direction and showing him the trees they'd planted, explaining how the loch had a capacity for peacefulness like nowhere else he knew, then turning him to face the house itself, Flemyng prepared them both for the day and night to come.

Putting a hand on Liam's shoulder, he led them both inside.

'Let's sit together for a while. We need to talk about our troubles.'

Thirty-six

'You were followed to the airport. Somebody knows you're here.'

Flemyng was in one easy chair by the fireplace, with Liam across from him in the other. Keane had taken to the house so quickly that he was relaxed on the corner of the sofa in a way that suggested he'd always known it. There was a pot of tea on the table, and shortbread from Mungo's store. The room was a warm response to the clouds that were thickening, and promising a rainy night. In the corner was the orrery, shining in its glass case. One of their mother's paintings above the fireplace was a meditation in deep shades of blue and purple, where Flemyng always identified hidden faces that seemed to be different each time he came home.

'You were watched, Liam,' he went on. 'See anything?'

Liam looked to Keane greyer than before, his face longer, the hard angles sharper. But he showed no agitation, only a tighter expression as if it was fixed in place. His self-discipline was always arresting. 'No, nothing. I'm surprised. No one could have known I was taking that flight.'

'Exactly,' Flemyng said. 'Let's go through it. You rang me from Amsterdam yesterday at ten o'clock in the evening, your time. I told you my plan. I take it you didn't pass it on?'

'Hardly.' A twitch of a smile, but Keane saw the fear.

Flemyng said, 'And in Washington only Lucy knew, until I told Patrick just before we left for the airport. So, apart from one guy in a certain office in London that's as secure as you can get, it was the four of us, full stop.'

Keane joined in, smacking a hand on his knee as he started. 'It follows they must have been watching you in Amsterdam from the start – even before the boss hatched the plan to get you here. It's the only explanation. What exactly were you doing there, anyway, Liam?'

Flemyng's eyes narrowed. No, Patrick, please.

But Liam seemed relieved to tell them. In the half-world he occupied, he had to choose so often what to pass on and what to hold back. It was the only way, he said, to manage some kind of balance between his loyalties. 'There's no rational sense to it. But emotionally, it's all I can do. I can't abandon everything – just can't – so I'm stuck with my private trade-offs that nobody else would understand.'

'I do,' Flemyng said. 'Always have.'

Liam said he was ordered to make contact with a go-between in Amsterdam, whose precise role he didn't know. 'I passed on a message to him – it had to be in person – and I got a reply that I had to send on to Sullivan in New York, because it's his show. News of a shipment, but I don't know all the details. That's usually the way of it.'

'Now consider this,' Flemyng said. 'Had Sullivan started to doubt you enough to ask someone to have you trailed?'

Liam thought not. 'That's not how it goes. Fatty Sullivan is a big guy in every respect, but operationally he's not in the loop day-to-day. It's just too dangerous to have detailed stuff discussed in transatlantic phone calls. You, of all people, know why.'

Flemyng was smiling.

'So, who?

'It would worry me a lot if they shadowed me on a job like this one. It just doesn't happen. They're solo. It's a rule.'

Keane saw that Flemyng had slipped into a mood he had seen so often before. He was completely still, not shifting in his chair nor making any gestures. His hands motionless. Determined, quiet, but ready to spring. Like a fisherman who feels the first tug on the line, he knew the endgame was beginning. Keane was conscious of learning as much about Flemyng himself – his disciplines, his worries, maybe the shafts of self-doubt he'd never spoken about – as about Liam's story.

Flemyng said Keane should think back to the airport when he had spoken to Operations at the Barracks after they landed in Edinburgh. 'Remind us of the description of the man at Schiphol. I've just been thinking about it.'

Liam's bright-blue eyes were alert, moving between them.

Keane was clear. 'Young, tall, dark. Anorak and jeans. Looked natural in the airport, and our man described him as neat and well groomed. Carrying a newspaper, nothing else. Could easily have been a business traveller.'

Flemyng was upright in his chair. 'Let me take you both back to this very room, where Mungo and Babble were questioned, tied up and all the rest of it by their two visitors two weeks ago tonight. Mungo described the guy who was in charge. I told you what he said, Patrick. Remember?'

Keane closed his eyes to remember. 'Young and dark, you said, six feet plus. Mungo said he could have been one of his students. Unlike his friend, who was rougher – calloused hands and so on.'

Flemyng said, 'Well done, Patrick. You've only missed one detail. Mungo noticed – he said the little things struck you in a moment of panic or fear – that his nails had been carefully filed. It seemed incongruous. Now we find someone, Liam, who's trailing you to Amsterdam airport who's described by an experienced watcher of ours as neat and well groomed. Young and very tall.

'I don't want to make too much of a leap. But...'

'Coincidence?' Keane said. 'We don't believe in them, do we?'

'Hardly ever,' Flemyng said. 'So think why this same young man might have turned up twice.'

As Flemyng told the story, Keane began to see the pattern that had been woven over the days they'd all experienced, and Liam heard for the first time some of the details of what had happened to Mungo in the room where they sat, and what Flemyng's conclusions had been. Outside there were lowering skies now, but Keane, surprised to find himself in one of his heady moods, knew that light was breaking through at last. They were drawn together, all three, even closer than before.

Flemyng was speaking with confidence. 'I'll take you back to the question of why, when they came to this house, they didn't injure Mungo or, frankly, do away with him. They surely knew he had been ill, because they would have done their homework, and he could easily have been pushed over the edge. Instead, they tied the ropes loosely and, as Mungo put it more than once, they seemed to want him to live to tell the tale. That was perceptive.

'It's the most important point. Liam, when I got Patrick to ask you in New York why you thought they had been sent here, you gave him a question to ask me in return. Typical you.' Keane saw the smiles they exchanged, as if to remind themselves how long it had been. 'Had a certain name been mentioned to Mungo, though it would mean nothing to him? A name, because of his famous memory, that he would certainly pass on to me.

'The answer was yes, of course. He did tell me the name they'd put to him, and as I said to you on the plane coming over, Patrick, I understood it to be a friendly message. It was a reassurance to me, communicated in an ingenious way. In other words, Liam, I did draw the conclusion you expected. Three people know that name – you, me and one other, who was letting me know that it still matters to him.'

He waited for Liam.

'I can't know for sure, but I see it the same way,' he said, carefully. 'I asked the question because I wondered if the whole business had a purpose beyond Mungo.'

Flemyng was smiling in agreement.

Again, Keane raised the objection that bugged him. 'It still confuses me, boss. They wouldn't organise an operation like that – driving across Scotland, effectively kidnapping an ambassador's brother, risking a shoot-out, not to say a murder – just to send a convoluted message like that. You're right that it's ingenious, but also bonkers. Too ingenious, to my mind. Why do it that way? I can't get my head round it.'

Flemyng, without moving an inch, opened a door for him.

'Let me explain my suspicion. The assault on Mungo wasn't organised in the first place to pass the message. It was a genuine attempt to find out what he knew about me, and to put pressure on me by threatening him. Maybe, for all I know, by killing him. They were panicking after Abel died, don't forget. But after it had been set up, someone intervened to use the operation for a different purpose.

'Mungo was allowed to live to tell the tale, and the name that only Liam and I know was passed on to him, in the knowledge that he would remember it and tell me, when I interrogated him – sorry, questioned him – as I was bound to do. And only I would understand its significance – who it came from.

'Someone turned the assault on Mungo to his own ends. And the person he used to do it...'

'... may well have been the young guy who turned up at Schiphol on Liam's trail,' said Keane.

'Which would mean?' Flemyng asked.

'That he was watching over me, as protection' Liam said, with a sigh.

Flemyng said it was only a thesis, a possible explanation of events. But wasn't it plausible? The young man had been sent to Amsterdam by the same person – or persons – who took control of the Altnabuie operation to use the planned assault on Mungo as a means of sending a message to him. With a young man who'd been instructed to let Mungo live, and to pass on a name that meant nothing to him, but everything to Flemyng.

'It makes sense to me,' he said. 'What about you?'

Liam was leaning forward, almost out of his chair. The worry lines on his brow were deep, his hand was scratching his cheek and he looked to Keane like a man sinking under a heavy weight.

'I'm not aware of this youngster. But I know what we're dealing with.

'I suppose it makes it easier for us here. They're not going to summon up an assault on us if my watcher in Amsterdam was sent by a friend.'

'Just like Sean and me in Washington,' said Keane. 'A relief.'

Liam shook his head and leaned back. His answer didn't surprise Flemyng, but hit Keane hard.

'Think about it, will you?' he said.

As if he was in acting in slow motion, Liam looked at them both, deliberately, in turn.

'If someone feels the need to protect me, someone else is out to get me.'

There was silence.

'We'll resume this later,' Flemyng said, to change the mood. 'But we can relax tonight. I picked up a couple of venison pies in Pitlochry on the way up here and stocked the boot with wine in case Mungo is running low. Some decent cheese. So we'll have a happy supper here tonight. First, I'm going to say – we walk.'

With that, he led them to the bootroom and they kitted themselves out for the hill. Both Flemyng and Liam took long crooks topped with deer horns and they took tweed bonnets from the hooks in case of a shower.

The curtain had come down on their conversation, and Mungo joined them, in his cape. He would be slower, he said, but he wanted to see them down to the loch at least. They set off under a darkening sky.

'Spring unsprung,' Mungo said. 'But that's the Highlands for you. Our weather comes and goes faster than you can track it. Look yonder.' He pointed with his stick to a patch of bright light breaking up the grey sky, far beyond the hills around them, somewhere over the mountains. Sunshine was breaking through the clouds, making pillars of light that touched the mountains, and they could see two of the high tops gleaming in a sun that wasn't reaching them in their garden deep in the shadows of the glen.

'It could go either way this evening,' he said. 'You never know. But I smell rain.'

Flemyng and Liam walked a little ahead, and by the time they were all down at the water the two old friends had taken a turn round the loch so that they were at the foot of the steep path that led up past the woods, with open fields stretching out on the other side, to join the high track that would take them on the long way round and back to the house.

Keane knew his place. He stayed back and sat with Mungo on a bench at the wooden jetty where the boat was rocking gently in water that was picking up the quickening wind. They felt a few spots of rain, and across the surface, spattered like tintacks, the patterns traced the showers that were arriving overhead. For Keane, a city boy for whom the occasional ramble was a virtual safari, it was intoxicating to feel the presence of the circling hills, to watch the wind take the tops of the trees and bend them to its will, see the colours around changing with every shift of the light as the clouds parted and then came together again, and to look northwards from the water to the house itself, where the sun lit up some of the windows and the rest remained in shadow. Understanding Flemyng had become a necessity as well as a fascination for him, and he had never been so close to cracking the code that was his life.

This was the source, and everything led back here.

Mungo was talking. 'That's always been our favourite walk.' He gestured to the path where they could see Flemyng and Liam bending into the slope as it got steeper. 'When you reach the top, everything opens up on the other side, and when you have clear skies you see into the high hills in every direction. On the way down you get an angle to the house at its best. I always think of it as the place where the intimate meets the wide expanse of our little world here. You get the feeling when you're on that track that you could walk forever.'

Together, they rose from the bench and faced the house to take the path round the other side of the loch towards the garden and home.

Keane said, 'It's magical. But remote in winter, I imagine.'

Mungo looked at him with a smile that Keane knew had some pity in it. 'Och, not at all. It's just a different kind of magic. And if we're snowed in for a day or two, or a week, why not? We sit around the fire, and all is well. Winter doesn't change the place, it protects us. In the spring, over the next month or so, everything comes back to life. You always feel the cycles on the move around you here. They're not something you have to learn, they're always with us.'

They walked for about ten minutes, Keane letting Mungo take the lead. Eventually, they passed through the gap in the dyke at the foot of the garden, and as they took the gentle rise towards the house Mungo showed him the results of his planting in the last few years. 'Problems with deer, of course. They'll eat anything that grows. Did you see that young one loping into the woods just now? But we survive. The fruit trees over there – they've been producing happily year-in-year-out since we were boys.'

Keane was quick to pick up, though unsure if it was fair. 'You must miss Abel so much. I'm sorry.'

'I do, desperately. He was his own man, but ours, too. D'you understand me? The three of us learned everything here, how to live, really. Now, I don't know exactly what happened to bring his life to an end, but I'm sure – aren't you? – that it's what they'll be discussing on their walk along the high track up there.'

'I wouldn't claim to know,' Keane said, 'but I think you may be right.' Flemyng's purpose in bringing Liam to the north was surely being laid out as they walked together, out of sight behind the woods.

'Not my business,' said Mungo. 'But if home is the place where it's done, so much the better.'

He asked nothing about Liam, who he was or where he came from.

As they approached the house, Keane looked up to the high point of the wood, the treetops blowing back and forth against the clouds, and imagined the two friends somewhere on the path behind, looking out to the hills, where he could see sun shining through a heavy rain shower in the distance. It was moving closer. Perhaps they were sharing a time of silence on their walk. More likely, they would be deep in their own histories and, he thought, trying to comfort each other.

It came to him as a shock to realise that they both needed that solace.

He scraped mud off his boots as he reached the front door. From inside, Mungo said, 'Let me show you some books I think you'll enjoy.' He took Liam to his study.

Three-quarters of an hour later, weary and a little damp, but exercised in body and soul, Flemyng and Liam reached the house and stood together for a few minutes at the door, watching the heavy skies and the arriving rain pattering on the roof.

Then they parted. Everyone would be alone for a while. They would meet round the table later.

Flemyng sat beside his orrery, its shiny brass and copper

orbs and spindles picking up the light. He slid the lever gently, and one by one the planets joined their stately dance.

Alex took charge in the kitchen. Mungo was enthusiastic about the evenings they'd spent together by the stove and the table in the previous two weeks. Who knew when it would come to an end, but the young officer was evidently determined to enjoy Altnabuie while he could. He was content, at Flemyng's quiet request, to stay away from the conversation at the table, and even happier to provide their supper.

As he went to open some wine in the early evening, Flemyng found him peeling potatoes. 'All sorts in Special Branch these days, I see,' he said. They spent a cheerful few minutes, and Flemyng said he might be able to give him some information in the morning. But not now.

Alex, fair-haired like Keane, but with a build more like Flemyng's, spoke to him about the warmth he felt in Mungo's company. He was learning a lot. 'My gratitude is immense,' Flemyng told him. Alex, taken aback by signs of emotion that had appeared suddenly on Flemyng's face, took his leave to set a fire in the drawing room.

Drawing the curtains together, he could hear steady rain on the terrace outside.

For Mungo, the circumstances of the gathering had slipped from his mind. A brother's death, a visit from gunmen, and a house surrounded by police, even the obvious alarm that he detected from Keane – all of it gave way to the prospect of a table where they could enjoy an evening of talk and contemplation. He'd been asked by Flemyng to be prepared for any lapses from the others that might let loose a stray word he'd be asked to forget. The trust between them was strong enough to allow that to be said without Flemyng feeling guilt nor Mungo any unusual unease.

Flemyng had suggested to Liam in the last few minutes of their walk that they should have Mungo with them at the table, and he'd said it would be fine with him. 'When you've lived my life, it's hardly a problem to survive one supper, is it?' Flemyng laughed with him. 'I hope not. If anything slipped out, I suppose I could always strangle my brother...'

Content, they all sat down to plates of smoked salmon and Flemyng poured wine. They could smell the pies.

Keane wondered how the conversation could flow around Mungo without bringing them trouble.

Liam led the way. 'Altnabuie...' he said. 'I understand it, naturally. In Irish we'd usually keep it as "buidhe" in the spelling, and I suppose it would be the same in your Gaelic, would it?

'Indeed,' Mungo said, 'though I'm not a native speaker, of course. What would your translation be?'

'Much the same as yours, probably. "Alt" in the placename is a stream or a burn, though the word's spelled originally with two "ll"s, and "buidhe" for us would be blond or yellow. Maybe, touched by light.'

'But here we have a secondary meaning – "glad" or even "lucky",' Mungo said. 'That's nice, isn't it? Appropriate.

'"The lucky stream." That's my choice, and who's to deny it? I often think of it when I'm down at the loch and watch the water rushing off the hill.'

Keane admired Mungo's ease around a table where he knew secrets lay, and Liam's, too. Navigating away from the alarms that had rung in his ears for days, he emerged as a conversationalist who could turn from Flemyng to his brother without awkwardness, for whom a life in which he had to deal with the likes of the Viking might have been a world away. He even engaged Flemyng in politics.

The depth of their relationship became obvious to Mungo and Keane. Asked to describe the Dublin negotiations, Flemyng knew what he had to keep back, but he understood how far he could go. They spoke for a while about the passionate resistance from Unionists who were watching for a sell-out and also – both Keane and Mungo sat up as he spoke – those Republicans who saw too much soft diplomacy as a threat to the primacy of the armed struggle that was a kind of birthright. Flemyng was fluent and confident, steering easily round the rocks and shoals that could have diverted them, and led them into trouble. And then, Liam.

Mungo asked him, with deceptive simplicity, to describe his own concept of identity.

Flemyng's face showed nothing. Keane's eyes were flicking from him to Liam and back again.

'We spoke about the language a minute ago,' he said in answer to Mungo. 'It's a terrible thing when your tongue is taken away from you, and you're silenced. I'd say that's what it's been like in the North. But I'm a fair man – Will knows that, I think – and I'd say this, too. People like me – practising your own faith, Mungo – and believing in one Ireland, were sold out terribly cheaply by too many people Dublin when they agreed to partition with London in the twenties. That's been a soreness for generations. We were forgotten and cut loose by our own government – the one we had to fight so hard to get in the first place – and then discriminated against in the North by your people. Viciously, I may say. Beaten down. So we were locked up, and sitting on a tinder box at the same time, weren't we? A place where a spark can always set things off.

'And everyone gets burned.'

Mungo said amiably. 'And there I was, thinking you'd mention Cromwell. He's not celebrated very much up here either, you know.'

Liam smiled. 'Ah well, we don't even have to go back that far. And, of course, there's an English army in the North again now.'

'Hardly English,' said Flemyng.

'So you want to claim a part of it, Will?' Liam said. 'Well, good luck.'

Keane was finding the experience disorienting. He'd expected anything but politics at the table.

'I want it to end, that's all,' Flemyng said.

'I wish you worked for a government that really agreed,' Liam said, his eyes focused on Flemyng. They were staring at each other across the table.

'And I wish everyone on your side was like you,' Flemyng replied, unblinking.

Keane looked at Mungo. What would he say?

'My younger students sometimes imagine history dictates a single course of action. Of course, the opposite is true. It's bound to be disputed because our experiences are different. It doesn't matter where you are in the world.' Keane could see what was happening. Mungo was rescuing them from what might come along when Flemyng had poured more wine, as he was about to.

Within a minute, using Flemyng's Washington perspective as a happy excuse, he'd taken everyone back to the American Civil War. Simple by comparison, Keane thought.

And they were happy. They laughed and ate and drank for nearly two hours, Alex coming and going with necessary supplies. By the fire, the brothers told stories of evenings in that room. Liam spoke of his boyhood in countryside that they would recognise, and Keane even engaged them for a while with talk of monastic illustrators who laboured in scriptoriums – he was proud to employ a diplomatic touch – in much the same way on both sides of the Irish Sea.

Flemyng had assured Keane that the Highland air would be an anaesthetic. After an afternoon by the loch and on the hill, he promised he would sleep the sleep of the just. But when they went to bed, Flemyng to the room that would always be his, and Mungo and Keane to the floor above, all their minds were alive to what they had said and done, and they lay awake for a while, listening to the rain outside, thinking of each other before they slept.

A stranger arriving on a late walk from the loch at that hour and looking towards the front door, would have seen through the rain one last movement in the house before the lights went out for the night. A young man, blond and casually dressed, and with the bearing of someone fit and trained, was standing sentinel at the door, looking into the dark. Told he was a policeman, the stranger would have wondered what he was thinking.

As he looked into the night, listening to the hiss of the steady rain on the roof and the terrace, Alex thought he had seen and heard enough to ask himself the question that he was sure would be troubling Flemyng as he lay in the dark.

Where would it end?

Thirty-seven

When Mungo went to his window in the early light, he saw a figure down by the loch. His brother was standing by the jetty, alone and still. He didn't have a fishing rod, or even a stick. Mungo wondered how long he'd been there.

Then, a moment later, he saw Liam on the path in front of the woods, making his way back to the house. They must have been together, perhaps soon after dawn. The rain had cleared, leaving a diamond sheen on the grass, and the signs pointed to a bright day. Liam walked steadily, with none of the weariness that had troubled Keane the previous day, and Mungo watched him turn through the stone gateway to the garden and pause to look towards the house. Flemyng had started his own walk back, striding up the other side of the water.

Mungo saw them come together in the garden, turning as one to look to the hills. Flemyng was pointing out a distant summit that was showing itself as the clouds rose and thinned out. With a wide wave, he was describing the whole panorama, as if pulling back the curtain on a painted scene.

They spoke to each other as they came together and stepped to the front door where they were lost to Mungo's view as they came inside.

Keane had awakened to the smell of Alex's breakfast cooking, and was first at the kitchen table, buttering his rolls. Within a few minutes they were all together again, and the chatter was about the weather, the coming sun, the freshness of the garden and the trees. The birds that had awakened them early, the scent of spring. They ate bacon and eggs.

After a little while, Flemyng turned business-like. 'I'm being picked up at ten, I'm afraid. The good news for me is that Francesca will be in London tonight, so we'll be together in the flat before I hit the office tomorrow morning.'

Liam was tentative. 'Is she all right?'

Alex was in the room, and Mungo knew nothing of the alarm sounded by the target list. So, caution all round. 'In great shape, thanks. We're looking forward to being together again this evening.'

Keane joined in. 'Liam, you and I will leave for Edinburgh an hour after the boss, and that's going to get you to your flight in good time. You'll make your evening connection to Dublin. A long way round, but...'

Nearly over.

'But it's not quite nine yet,' Mungo said. 'Time for a last stroll. I know you've been down to the water, Will, but let's step out, shall we?'

They left. Alex cleared breakfast away, then watched them all from the front door.

Flemyng and Keane strode out together, and ahead. 'We may not get another chance to speak today,' Flemyng said. 'Liam and I have had a goodtalk. The best. I know where we are. Thank God I did it like this. We can discuss tomorrow. One more thing. I promised Mungo from Washington that I'd return here later in the week, and I shall, maybe on the sleeper. Timing's not certain, but Lucy will sort it out.'

He stopped, and Keane knew it mattered.

'Rest assured, I have the whole story now. You'll get it.'

They progressed towards the water. Mungo and Liam were catching up.

'I'll remember this,' Liam said to him. 'You're a lucky man.'

Knowing that he would always remain at one remove from what had been discussed over the weekend – settled, left in limbo, who could say? – Mungo didn't want to ask a question of the man about whom he knew so little. He said simply, 'You'll always be welcome here.'

The four were together, and Keane took Liam aside for a moment.

'To reassure you, we'll have a Special Branch guy at the airport, keeping an eye. He has no idea who you are, just that we need to be clean. I'm told he'll spot anything suspicious at a hundred yards.'

'I've heard that before, Patrick,' said Liam, smiling. 'But thanks. Protected by the British constabulary, whatever next?'

Keane was moved when, just as they turned to rejoin the others, he felt Liam's hand come hard onto his shoulder, giving him a friend's grip.

The last half-hour was edgy for them, although Flemyng appeared relaxed, and smiled all the while. He said nothing about the importance for him or Liam of the hours they'd passed together. Keane's mind was preoccupied with the airport delivery of his human cargo, and he was unsettled by worries about a wrong turning on the road to Edinburgh. Mungo, though happy to know of his brother's return later in the week, was worried about them all. He had the natural anxiety of a sensitive man who had been unable to tune in fully to the conversations and the relationships that he'd seen develop around him. For Alex, who was with them as they prepared for the arrival of Flemyng's car, it was an enticing scene. As someone trained for the unexpected, with a feeling for careful planning and observation, he'd seen the weekend as a confirmation of his chosen path. He wasn't troubled by the fact that he might never know the reasons why.

Flemyng's familiar driver, who knew the house, swung into place just before ten. Alex took the bags out, and Keane went through the hall to the front door where he'd just seen the boss and Liam stepping out to enjoy the sun that was lighting up the landscape at last. As he stepped through, past the dinner gong, he saw them standing together side by side on the steps outside, Flemyng's arm across Liam's shoulder. In a moment of sharp recollection he pictured them against the window in Flemyng's room at the Blackstone in Chicago, at that electric moment of reunion after so many years, drawn back together and looking into the night. Now they were facing the light, but Keane had a near-overwhelming feeling, coming at him with unexpected suddenness, that he would never see them together again.

They turned, and there were short and apparently easy goodbyes. Liam stood back from the car. Everything had been said. They all waved as Flemyng was swept through the trees, onto the drive and away. Liam's was the last of the arms raised in farewell to come down.

Mungo said to Alex, 'You'll get to know Will better later in the week. We'll have a fine time.'

'I know it,' said Alex.

The rest was quick.

Keane and Liam left bang on eleven, and there was no problem with the route. The old map came out, for the sake of it, although they didn't need it.

Keane easily spotted the SB man in Edinburgh, stiff in his suit with none of Alex's ease. But there was no alarm. Liam's plane was on time, and he would have two hours at Schiphol before his late flight to Dublin and then the drive north, where no one would know where he'd been. Almost.

They said goodbye with no fuss. Not a hug, no confessional talk, but a simple wish for safe travels, and a look between them that absorbed everything they hadn't said.

When he reached the door to departures, Liam turned and waved. For a moment he stood still, as if he wanted to remember Keane when he'd gone. He had his broad smile back, and Keane felt a surge of affection as he saw the door slide shut and he disappeared. A friendship he could never have expected, and which he knew would always perplex him. He turned away to deal with his car, check in for London and prepare for the next day at the Barracks.

But on the plane, he thought of his last sight of Flemyng and Liam together at Altnabuie. Tiredness was overtaking him in a rush, the shades coming down, and he reminded himself that when he got to London he must ring Lucy. How would he best describe that memory from the house? A call to arms, a truce, perhaps even the strangest of family photographs? A farewell?

He slept for a little while on the plane, and in his lightning dream the day just past came back to him, clear and unchanged. He saw the hills, heard the rain. Waking up, he pictured Liam in Amsterdam. Waiting, watching for the young man who might still be tailing him.

He wondered if they might talk. And, if they did, what Liam would hear of the fighters he was going to meet once more at home.

Thirty-eight

LATER THEY WOULD AGREE THAT DESPITE ALL THE suppressed emotion, and the nervousness flowing strongly underneath, they'd been lifted briefly out of the turbulence. Even in the rain, Altnabuie had done its work.

Flemyng arrived in Whitehall on Monday morning like a man who had lost five years. Fit and straight, his skin clear, his hair trimmed in the way that he liked it best. Keane, taking the Tube to his own office, even found the London air more invigorating after the Highlands, just because its smells were different. His senses had sharpened. The streets had their own sounds, and when he'd walked in the south London park near where he was staying with friends he'd enjoyed the contrast with Washington. The city had its own trees, its own pulse, a noise that couldn't come from anywhere else.

Their spirits, refreshed by a weekend in the hills, prepared them for difficulties to come. He knew, however, that although he was ready for storms, he was also trying to forget his calculations about what lay ahead.

Flemyng, as always, had a plan. But first he had to deal

with Moscow matters, and that helped because he was ahead of the others.

He would make sure that Saviour, who had to be given his news face to face, would not be alone. He had sent messages at breakfast time on that Monday to two of the half-dozen most senior figures on the patch to see if they could join him with Saviour at eleven. Both of them knew of the Moscow operation. Only one, he was fairly sure, the name itself.

They met in a secure room below ground, Whitehall above them.

He was warm with Saviour, and when the others arrived they told them the story of Thursday night. 'Memorable performance. Exceptional entertainment at the embassy,' said Saviour. His wayward eye settled on Flemyng, probing. What was coming next?

Flemyng took the floor. 'Thank you, Roland. Now, I'm afraid we have a difficult decision to make. I shall explain.

'I've been told at a high level – like you, Roland – that the name we are anxious to protect, more than any other, I dare say – is safe with the Americans. They did discover it, by efforts which I think we can understand, even if we don't approve. They cracked it, not by subterfuge, but by patient elimination. We can't help that now. The difficulty is the safety of our man. They told us – Roland and I – that the circle of knowledge was intimate, not as tight as here at home, I'm sure, but still restricted to an unusual degree. But I'm afraid I had a disturbing conversation on Friday, with someone I have reason to trust absolutely, and there's another side to the story that's been withheld from us.'

Saviour was shifting in his seat, which made him seem even bigger than usual.

'This person tells me that there is alarm in Langley and elsewhere about Russian money and recruitment. The point has been reached where officials with access to sensitive material above a certain level are having their lives pulled apart, almost routinely. Every item of expenditure. Family budgets, friends and even cars, the works.'

'Dear God,' Saviour said.

'It is rigorous in the extreme,' Flemyng went on. 'I'm told that nothing has come of it yet. They haven't found a cipher clerk driving a Maserati yet, but I'll put my own money on the table. An exercise like this wouldn't be taking place unless they had a fair suspicion of a successful Soviet recruitment, somewhere. Whether that affects the security of our man's name we can't tell, and to be frank I'm not sure we'd be told if it were. But I bet it does.'

Flemyng had deliberately left it to Saviour to raise Angleton's name, because he preferred not to invite ridicule, and Roland obliged.

'This was a panic all got up by Angleton, the old obsessive. I hope you haven't been talking to him again, Will.' He sat back.

Undisturbed, Flemyng said, 'My source for this latest information was absolutely not Angleton, I can assure you of that. But I did speak to him after I'd had the conversation I've described, because it was in our interest, and he was able to provide collateral evidence.'

'Such as?' said Saviour, showing discomfort.

'A list of names of people whose finances are being put under the microscope. He's obsessed with such things, as we know. And this isn't his imagination, for once. It can be checked. We have the people who can do it. And if it's confirmed, we know there's a hunt on.

'Therefore we must assume the name we have to protect isn't as safe as we'd like it to be.'

One of the other two men, from Defence, said, 'Safety first, then?'

'I'd say so,' Flemyng replied. 'I can't see the case for keeping our man in the dark any longer. He may have to run quickly. We need to protect him, and what he knows. Methods, people, everything. Now it may be that he can stay in place, but he has to be told that if something threatening occurs – a recall to Moscow is the obvious one – he'll have to run.'

'Are we ready?'

'Yes,' said the fourth man at the table, who had come from the Barracks.

'It's dodgy,' he went on. 'Very risky indeed. But he'll have a chance.'

The question, Flemyng said, was whether they'd let him come over immediately, as a precaution, despite the cost in lost intelligence.

'That would be my preference,' the fourth man said. 'Because, as you may be aware, Will, there are reasons why it would be easier for him to come across if he did it now. Physically simpler, let me put it like that. But let me take the thought away.'

Quite quickly, they parted. It was out of Flemyng's hands, but he had no doubt that he had changed the game. Duty was involved, and he had discharged it.

He spent the afternoon in office meetings about the summit, and heard no more from Saviour. His Downing Street visit had been postponed to the next day, and he would swot for that in the evening at the flat. He had spared Francesca most of his anxieties, but she knew he was fighting against some fast-running tide. They'd talk about her return to Washington, which he hoped might be with him, after he'd been back to Scotland.

The morning was cheering him, though he was aware of the burden he'd dropped in the laps of those who'd have to handle the plans for their Moscow man's escape. They would be dusting down the plan again. That was the life he'd known.

Now, he'd arranged to see Keane to find out what he'd learned at the Barracks. They would take a walk.

'St James's Park,' he'd said, smiling into the phone. 'For old times' sake.'

They met by the lake in the late afternoon.

'News,' said Keane. 'Not public, but they've rolled up an Active Service Unit that was sitting near Gatwick. A quick operation, apparently. Didn't take long for the boys to find a bunch of crude rocket launchers in a back garage. Ramshackle – looked as if it had been put together in a hurry.

'There was no fuss. Nothing will be known until the court appearances, a long way down the track. 'Anything else from your place?' Flemyng asked.

Keane was smiling. 'I was congratulated. Apparently the American money operation is having problems. A couple of newspaper pieces about fundraising, which they don't like one bit. They're about to do a duck-dive, apparently. Sullivan's in a state about internal disputes and leaks. All good, and does the embassy no harm.

'But I'd take the Barracks view with a barrel of salt. The boys are not always right, as we know.'

As they walked, Flemyng made Keane a promise. He'd know everything soon.

'I'm due to hear something from Belfast a little later,' Keane said, 'and I'll ring you at the flat if it's worth passing on.'

They enjoyed the afternoon sun, and walked towards

Victoria, where Flemyng set off for Pimlico and Keane got a south London train. A little later, Francesca was taken out, for the first time in a month, to a Vietnamese restaurant round the corner from the flat, where she had the longest conversation she'd had with her husband since it all began.

They went home to bed. But just after eleven Keane rang, apologetically, in a state of alarm.

'I'm sorry, boss. Big trouble.'

'What is it?' Flemyng's mind was in a whirl.

'Liam. He's disappeared.'

Thirty-nine

The gloomiest day.

The news had come from Sean in Washington in a risky call, but one he'd felt compelled to make. Keane's consolation was that Sean and he were at work together, and he could be confident it would last. Keane established a post in the Barracks, and spent the morning on the phone to anyone with a connection to a network that might pick up Liam's movements.

Sean had been a man close to despair. 'I'm told something's happened, but nobody knows what. He's disappeared under the waves.'

Keane was lucky. His security service friend Johnny Silvester, recipient of his golden tips about two active service units and news of the Viking's return, was eager to repay the favour. He knew nothing of Keane's presence at home, let alone his weekend adventures, but when he heard through one of his own sources that there were rumours of a Provo purge, and an American link, he picked up the phone to

Washington. From the embassy, Keane got a message to ring Belfast.

The information was sketchy, but enough to alarm him further. Sean had been right.

Silvester reported that there was panic among the Provos about the security of their American operation. Sullivan in New York was spooked by extra FBI activity, and there had been an embarrassment in Chicago – something to do with an arms deal – that they'd had to work hard to keep out of the papers. An accretion of problems. And now, so Silvester had been told, the finger was pointing across the Atlantic, to someone who'd recently come home. Senior guy, so it was said. Decorated in the field, as you might put it. But an enemy of Sullivan's. In the current atmosphere, a target.

'Word is, he can't be found,' he told Keane.

'Name?' Keane hardly dared to ask.

'Maybe Liam something. Best I can do.'

Keane spent a full hour in torment. Helplessness overwhelmed him. They could do nothing overnight in Washington, but at least both he and Flemyng were on the case. Had he run? Got on a flight back to the States? Been taken?

Flemyng put up storm cones. They knocked on every door, got colleagues to squeeze every source. Keane's friend promised to get everything he could from his side of the shop. Flemyng, who'd been enjoying the only pleasure of the day in cancelling his meeting in Downing Street, went to the Barracks, and straight to the top.

The man to whom he spoke was one of the few who knew a little of his relationship, and what it had delivered down the years. He knew Flemyng was already in despair for a friend.

'We've all experienced something like this, Will. I admit

not on this scale – over this time, and with the stakes so high. I promise you we'll scour every corner of the place. Use every informer we've got. We'll find out.'

During the day, Flemyng thought of the success he had in the Moscow affair. Among the few in Whitehall who were aware, it was his name that would always be attached to the case. How odd to think of it, with all its weight, as a distraction. Out of his hands now, he thought the right decisions were probably being reached, and Saviour's unfounded optimism had been squashed. Their man would be given the chance to run if that was his choice, and a promise that the escape plan was ready if he decided to stay.

He was alone with his decision. They could do no more. Meanwhile, with luck, he'd continue for a while at least to let them see into the new regime through a clear lens. The chance of several lifetimes.

Back home, Flemyng had to think of the other loner. Liam had become the strangest comrade and friend. Unbending and hard when he still believed he should be, but honest with Flemyng too, and resolute in defence of the decision he'd made to divide his life and complicate it to the end.

Flemyng wondered whether it had been impossible from the start. He calculated the number of times when Liam's information had helped his enemies on the battlefield, and wondered if it would have been better for him to stick with the cause, and do his worst. Had he never juggled with the moral choices that brought him pain, and burdened his years, he might have been happier. Who could say? They would have fought on until someone won, and someone lost.

Instead, they had revealed so much to each other. About their masters, but mostly about themselves. And each time they came together, Liam's guilt surged back. A friendship of torture as well as balm.

Flemyng knew at heart that the betrayal game couldn't have a happy ending.

And then, just after lunchtime, when he was about to ring Keane at the Barracks, he was stricken by a realisation that came on him unexpectedly, but with the force of a storm.

He was thinking about Liam and speaking about him in his head, in the past tense.

For half an hour, he sat alone in the gloomy room in the Foreign Office where he was allowed to perch, and sank into misery. At the end of it, he rang Lucy – told her everything. The warmth of the weekend, the connections new and old that it had made, the reassurance it had given. She understood his feeling. Francesca, too, though he had to speak in a private code that only she could understand. Mungo would have to wait.

Then Keane was on the line.

'Have you heard anything?' Flemyng asked.

'Only that everyone's talking about some kind of power struggle. But it's like the bloody Kremlin, most of it's guesswork. The big guys are still in charge, we're sure. But below them there's carnage. Literally, I wouldn't be surprised.'

Flemyng told him, 'I'm going to the flat. You'll find me there.'

He knew it would come.

At five o'clock exactly, because he could hear the pips from the radio in the kitchen, Keane rang.

He began to speak. Stopped. Then he was sobbing.

'I'm so sorry. It's taken me badly. He's dead.'

Flemyng couldn't speak for what seemed to them both for a long time.

'Tell me.'

'It depends whether we believe what they say. Here's what we know. There's a statement with the usual Provos' codeword saying that Liam, described as a Republican of renown, volunteer and a gallant freedom fighter etc. etc. – the traditional trumpet sounds – has been killed in action. No place or details given, but it claims at the hands of British forces.

'I've done a quick check here and at Defence, and there's nothing.

'Our people think it's a cover story. We can't be certain yet. But the betting is that he died in some other way. They can't admit it because he's a senior man, and their American guys wouldn't want the spotlight to fall on them any more than it is at the moment. So that's where we are.

'But here's no doubt that he's gone. He's getting the full funeral. Milton Cemetery, the parade and all the rest of it. Firing squad at the graveside.'

'I wonder if it matters how he died?' Flemyng said, miserably. Keane heard his despair.

'I can't bear to think of him being blown up by accident,' Flemyng went on. 'Shot, or beaten to death in some bloody cellar by his own people. Or being taken out by one of ours. But right now there's no difference is there? It's a life gone. We want it to be set right and it can't be. Just like Abel. He's away, and it's over.'

Into his mind, as powerfully as if a bright image had flashed on his eye in a darkened room, came the picture of Liam's face looking from the car window at his brother's funeral.

Flemyng wept.

Forty

'YOU KNOW THAT I'M GOING NORTH AGAIN, BUT YOU'RE coming with me.'

Keane got the call from Flemyng very early. It was barely light. His sleep had been broken and it seemed to him as if the weariness he'd felt at the end of the day, and the sadness he'd shared with Flemyng, had continued uninterrupted. He'd had no respite in the night.

How did Liam die? Where was he lying cold now?

Flemyng sounded tired, and his voice had lost its vibrancy. 'I've asked Lucy to fix the sleeper for you. We'll get the Inverness train to Pitlochry tonight. It'll feel like home to you, already.'

'Why take me?' Keane said. 'I know you said you'd go back to Mungo, but what use can I be? Better here, surely.'

'No.' Flemyng was emphatic. No argument.

Then he said, 'I need you. I can't see this through alone.'

Keane could find no words.

They would eat together before the train. Francesca was going back to the country. Flemyng said they should each try to find out more about what had happened, and they'd exchange stories on the train.

'I'll tell you everything,' he said.

I've heard that one before, Keane almost said, but thanked him instead. 'I'll do my best today. Shake down everyone I can.'

He took a walk before catching the train into town. In the park there was a runner, two old men propped up against a tree with bottles at their feet, some kids cycling early to school. Keane was stricken by the knowledge that he'd never see Liam again. How long had they spent together? Only a few hours – a fraction of one minuscule portion of their lives. Yet it had brought them closeness, trust, a kind of friendship like some shaky, makeshift bridge across the gulf between them.

They were more alike than either of them could have expected.

Imagining Flemyng's sadness, he knew it was incomparably deeper than his own. He pictured the two men side by side as he'd seen them at the front door at Altnabuie, silhouetted against the light, still and together. So much between them unsaid, because it was understood. That was giving Flemyng strength even now.

But as he'd learned in his own life already, there would be guilt. Had Flemyng led him to his fate?

Shaking himself so hard that two passers-by stepped away from him as they approached, he was determined to throw himself into work at his desk, and leave the ruminations for later. He had to find out what had happened.

Flemyng, too, spent an hour on practical matters. He rang the Barracks to make sure the passport used by Liam on his journey to Scotland was cancelled but kept in the system, so anyone trying to use it would be picked up. He confirmed in a message to be sent to Lucy that he wouldn't return to Washington until the beginning of the following week, and he spoke to Saviour's office to inform him that personal matters meant the chance of a rescheduled Downing Street meeting that afternoon had disappeared, sadly. He couldn't face it.

Then he spoke to two old friends, one who still walked the secret byways and another who'd laboured with him in government. He didn't think they could solve the puzzle, but he was reaching for helping hands. It wasn't odd for him to be seeking reassurance without being able to tell them why. He'd done it so often before, and they understood.

Some day he might explain.

Then he and Francesca spent two hours together, before the car came to take her away. Washington next week, he promised. They embraced.

By lunch, he was exhausted so in the afternoon he walked to the Tate and spent some time with pictures he loved, taking a walk along the Thames before making his way back to the flat. The river was calm, with little traffic. The pleasure boats hadn't started their summer season, but from Vauxhall Bridge he watched two barges moving slowly downstream, keeping their distance as they passed Westminster one after the other, leaving a wide wake. He could hardly hear the traffic on the Embankment. His senses were soothed for a while by the river's pace and the gentleness of the movements on the water.

A police launch disturbed the scene for a few moments with a roar, making a crescent in the water as it turned back upstream. It raced under the bridge beneath his feet and was gone.

Turning up his collar against a freshening wind, Flemyng strode towards the flat.

Less than a mile away, Keane was talking on the phone to Silvester in Belfast. Johnny would meet a contact later who might know a little. The history of these moments suggested that sooner rather than later a couple of versions of what had happened would start to circulate. Then they could begin to search for the truth. 'You've got to prepare for the possibility that it was a punishment,' Johnny said. 'It happens.'

Keane picked up. 'I'm well aware. And that would mean that we're all in deep trouble, because it would tell us how much they know.'

Johnny Silvester understood little of the relationship between Liam and Flemyng and the secrets they shared, but he suspected, because of his trade, that Keane and his boss were tied somehow to a friend's fate. 'I hope you see it through,' he said.

'Don't worry,' said Keane, who knew that if it was true that for alleged crimes against the cause Liam's people had executed him – there was no other word for it – it would be over for Flemyng, because it would tell them that the story of the spy across the water was known. He'd be brought home from Washington to a life under guard. And Keane himself? Even his natural optimism couldn't conjure a happy ending.

Pushing the thought away, he rang a friend at Defence, and walked the corridors of the Barracks. Nothing.

In early evening they met at Flemyng's club, where Keane had to borrow a tie from the porter. They ate quietly, hardly talking about Liam, but thinking of him all the time. They picked at shrimps and two shrivelled lamb chops, and took time over a small carafe of wine.

'I have to know,' Flemyng told him. 'And not just for our safety.'

Before they left for the station, Keane took the chance to

ring a colleague at the Barracks. He was in the phone booth in the club hallway for five minutes, and came out to find Flemyng looking at his watch.

'There's word,' he said. 'A first snippet. I'll ring again from the station.'

He did, and after they'd settled into the berths, they met in the lounge car as the train got up to speed.

'We won't be able to confirm this until the morning,' he said. 'But it's not good news. The story of an army ambush is rubbish, as we thought. There's been nothing in the last few days that fits. Whatever happened was internal, if that's the right word.'

Flemyng's face was reflected on the window, long and dark. 'A punishment killing would mean the end for us.'

'I know,' Keane said.

But Flemyng said, as if turning away from that prospect, 'Here's what's gnawing at me. What were his last thoughts? Words?'

'How did we get here?' Keane asked, mainly to himself.

'That would take a whole lifetime to answer,' Flemyng said, 'and we only get one chance to play with it.'

They turned in quietly in their adjoining cabins, and neither had much sleep.

They didn't bother with breakfast, only drank tea in their berths, and waited for Pitlochry. Keane lay on his bed with the blind up, watching the hills getting higher as they pulled north. It was sunny now, the weekend rain long gone, and he was eager to make the drive again. As they snaked round the last bend and rolled through the trees along the course of the river and into the station, there was a loud knock. Flemyng was ready with his bag, and at the train door by the time they drew up.

Alex walked towards them on the platform, smiling.

Clearly, briefly and without embroidery Flemyng explained to Alex as he drove them home that their friend from the weekend was dead. 'In Northern Ireland, circumstances unknown. I'll simply say, Alex, that I'd known him a long time, which will have been obvious to you. I can't say more.'

At the wheel, Alex expressed his sadness, and asked nothing else. Flemyng liked him.

Swinging through the gates less than an hour later, they saw Mungo ready and waiting at the back door. Flemyng hugged him and, leaving his bag for Keane to take in, he led him into the garden. How much he would say, Keane didn't know, but he was certain that Mungo would be brought into part of the secret and he he would be able to complete much of the story.

For his part, he would settle down with the secure phone and dig for more information.

An hour later, he had news.

Flemyng was reading in the drawing room. He had left Keane to his work, and they had planned to walk later. When Keane found him, he'd put his book down and was sitting in his favourite chair staring at the window as if there was nothing he could do but wait. Events had moved beyond him, and he was at their mercy.

Keane approached, unsure whether or not he was bearing good news.

'Boss, there's something. I'm told – this is reliable – that whatever happened it wasn't a punishment beating that went too far, and definitely not an execution. I've also heard what may turn out of be the most interesting bit of the story.'

Flemyng was sitting as he might in his own office, now leaning forward with elbows on the arms of the chair, hands together with fingertips touching, almost in an attitude of prayer. He waited, refusing to hurry Keane.

'It seems as if the Viking has disappeared. Silvester tells me they've pulled out the stops since I told them he'd come home, picked up some footprints and they're now convinced something's happened to him. They're also hearing there was a bust-up at a Provo rendezvous on a farm near the border on Monday. A panic meeting about American leaks and the FBI. Sullivan's been sending hysterical messages, apparently. Banging his drum.

'Silvester's seeing somebody later – his best source, he says. May even have been there.'

Silence. Liam was in both their minds.

'At least we'll know,' said Flemyng. 'Now, time to walk.'

They put on boots, needing no hats against rain because the sun was lighting up the landscape as they headed down to the loch. Keane was hit by the familiarity of a place he'd seen for the first time only four days earlier. The high pines, rowan and willow by the water, the hilltops above the wood. A heron took off from the waterside at their approach, dipping his wings as he floated silently and peacefully away.

On the bench, with no sound except the gentle slap of the water against the jetty, Flemyng told his story.

'You see, Liam and I shared something more than our curious relationship. A secret that we had to ourselves. I'd been trained never to ask someone for something they hadn't the power to give, and I've followed that rule. So we got to know each other's limits and respected them. The result was trust between us, against all the odds. We were combatants who discovered how we could sit down together, alone. It was because of that trust, built up over a long time, that we got our secret prize. Someone else.

'Patrick, we found another.' Keane felt all the weight of the moment.

He knew that the last veil was finally being pulled aside. He was looking over the loch, where birds skittered across the water, and crows were cawing from the branches that hung over it. The hills in the distance made a hazy blue rim against the sky and closer to them he could see rolling slopes brightening with new growth. The trees were coming into leaf, and when he looked up the slope and followed the line of the wall through the garden to the house, he absorbed the place that had shaped Flemyng, every crease on him, the expression on his face, each tilt of his head, the swell of his emotions.

All this came to Keane in a moment, and he felt no time passing. Only stillness.

Flemyng continued.

'Liam was an agent who operated with courage and skill. He was a constant. Helping us when he chose, standing back at other times. And still serving his cause in his own way, which I couldn't deny. I accepted all the contradictions because there was no point in pretending they didn't exist. Spare me the luxury of moral purity. There were benefits, that was all, and I knew the line he wouldn't cross. That was the price of the trust between us.

'The other figure I'm talking about was – and remains – different. Not an agent in the same way, but someone playing a longer game. A bigger one, too. We haven't asked for what he can't give, but only what might be possible one day. I have reason to know he respects us for that.

'The consequence is that help may come when the time is right. If the agreement they're wrangling over does get signed, for all that it will be scoffed at for being mostly hope and limited substance, with a bit of luck we could be on a road leading to that moment. Nothing matters more.

'You can see now why the coincidence of the Moscow business and Liam's crisis coming along at the same time gripped me, mystified me – even scared me. The secret names, the deception, the running for cover. And, in each case, a man left alone.

'Like me.'

Then Keane watched a quick flash of anger cross Flemyng's face, a rush of shame at the hint of selfishness he'd displayed. He had his wife and family. Everything Altnabuie had given him. His life. Liam, with whom he'd walked the treacherous path and trusted, had nothing. He was gone.

Flemyng rallied, and picked up the story, glad to have Keane at his side. 'Think about the collision of these two cases. They represent so much of what our lives are about. But you wouldn't expect to come across two episodes on this scale, of this importance, at the same time. By chance, we did.

'And a wicked stab of fate brought Abel down along the way. You'll see now that Liam acted the way he did in Chicago not just because he suspected they might be onto him – he'd lived with that for long enough. He feared they'd gone a step further – and discovered we might have an even bigger fish in play.

'He told me straight out in the hotel room in Chicago.'

Keane was watching the picture coming into focus. Looking out to the landscape, he said, 'The one whose codename we wouldn't recognise. The name they let Mungo hear.'

'Exactly,' said Flemyng. 'The name invented by us, for Liam and me, and the person to whom it refers. Someone we'd hardly ever name, even to ourselves. But who knows

– whether he admits it to himself or not – how much is invested in him. Let's call it hope.'

Keane, because he felt it was right, spelled it out. 'So he was the one who managed to turn the assault on Mungo into a message for you, using our unknown friend, the tall young man. And he sent the same youngster to Schiphol to watch Liam. I bet he knows Sean, too.'

'You've got it,' said Flemyng. 'A friendly, hidden hand, and a powerful one.

'Abel's misfortune was that he sensed the movement under the surface. That was always his gift. He realised there was a group – only a tiny handful of people, but determined – who were starting to shift the strategy, to move beyond everything that the likes of Sullivan believe. He knew it might help me. But his presence in Chicago sounded an alarm. They put his questions together with the FBI's activities, and the balloon went up. Abel had stirred up a panic that threatened to ruin our whole game, because it could have exposed the people we're going to depend on some day.

'Witch-hunts are never good news, whichever side you're on.

'Our family has had a tragedy. So has Liam's. Abel died trying to get to the truth – and it's my belief that he came close with his listening and his questions to stumbling on our real secret, without knowing that it had been mine from the start, the one I could never share with him. And Liam had to help to get rid of him, not knowing that he was my brother – a man who shared his own friend's blood.'

They walked up the slope to home in silence. Keane spent fifteen minutes on the secure phone, then joined Flemyng in the drawing room, closing the door behind him. He stood for a moment, in silence. The light from the window was shining on the metal orbs of the orrery, Flemyng was sitting under one of his mother's paintings, and the room was a picture of peace.

The clouds parted.

'I've got it all,' he said, walking across to Flemyng's chair.

'Johnny Silvester's come good, with payback for me. It was a meltdown, a summit about the American leaks. The Viking gave the Sullivan version, screaming at them all. High as a kite on some stuff he'd been taking, Silvester's man is sure, and out of control. Which seemed good news for Liam, who was calm and strong when he was accused of helping the FBI. Laughed it away. The big guys warned the Viking, because they believed Liam.

'But it turned into a fight outside – in a farmyard, for God's sake, on a hillside in Tyrone – and the Viking, wild as a dog, pulled a gun. Went mad, according to Silvester's contact.

'Shot Liam. He died half an hour later. A hero, in the end.'

'And the Viking?' Flemyng said, hardly needing the answer.

'Taken away. We'll never hear tell of him again.'

Flemyng stood and Keane followed him to the door. Looking towards the sun, Flemyng said, 'We live with our history, but it can kill us.'

'If you're right,' Keane said, 'he died protecting what's to come.'

Flemyng turned to him, his black eyes glistening. 'That's why I cried last night.'

He went to give Mungo a version of what had happened. 'I'll be as honest as I can,' he said, putting a hand through his hair as he left the room.

Keane sat alone for a full hour.

In the late afternoon, Flemyng asked him to join him for a drive in Mungo's car. He took him over the hill and along the winding road towards the west, opening up blue vistas into the hills and discovering the mountains beyond, revealing stretches of water that were hidden unless you knew the right turnings. High crags in the distance stood out against a clear sky, with shadowy glens below that guarded their own stories. Keane was dazzled, then comforted.

Just before five, Flemyng pulled up at the little church on the promontory that looked along a west-reaching loch, with steep rocky sides and holly and rowan trees clinging to the slopes. A stream tumbled from the heights and splashed into the water below in a glistening shower. Alongside them at the church, the sun brought a pink sparkle to the stones around the door.

'This is exactly the hour when we got the news. I thought it right to come here now,' Flemyng said. 'A family place.'

He pushed the door back and led Keane in. It was cool, musty, intimate. There were a couple of plaster saints, a stone baptismal font, and on the small altar a green and white cloth ready for Sunday. Dusty beams of light came through stained glass windows that told the old stories in pictures. They heard a car pull up outside and went to the open door. It was Father MacNeil.

'I saw Mungo's car, but Will, it's you!' He had aged since Flemyng had seen him last, his back bent and hair turned white, but in the folds of his lined face was all the old warmth.

'Father – Aeneas, dear man – this is a happy surprise for me, too,' Flemyng said.

The priest put a hand on his shoulder. 'A red-letter day for us, and at the church as well.'

Flemyng introduced Keane, and turned back inside. The others stepped quietly behind him.

He sat in silence for a little time, his hands together.

Father MacNeil, sensing his sadness, spoke softly. 'Can I help, Will?'

'I'm fine, Aeneas, thank you. Private thoughts.' Keane looked at Flemyng's profile in the half-light, his head not bowed but held up. His eyes were open, fixed on something far away.

'Tell me what's on your mind, if you would like to,' Aeneas whispered.

Flemyng turned his head, and spoke gently to them both, his dark eyes full.

'A funeral, of course. I wish I could be there.'

Afterwards

In November 1985, the British and Irish governments signed a constitutional agreement on the future of Northern Ireland that was a tentative but significant step on a path away from the Troubles. The IRA campaign continued for years, but by the early nineties the British government and senior IRA figures were discussing seriously how the 'armed struggle' might end. After stop-and-start clandestine negotiations over several years, and with many setbacks, the Good Friday Agreement signed in 1998 provided a framework for peace, instead of the conflict that had cost around 3,000 lives over three decades. There were dissident voices among Republicans and Unionists alike, but the agreement won overwhelming popular support in referendums on both sides of the Irish border. Sinn Féin, the political wing of the IRA, entered government in Belfast.

In the spring in which *The Spy Across the Water* is set, the CIA also learned the identity of Oleg Gordievsky, who had spied on the Soviet Union for the Secret Intelligence Service (MI6) since the mid-seventies, despite the British government's determination to keep his name secret. Fearing a leak to Moscow, SIS offered him the chance to defect from his position as KGB *rezident* in the Soviet Embassy in London, to which he'd just been appointed, but he chose to stay in place. However, when he was recalled to Moscow the following month, he realised he had been betrayed. He was drugged and interrogated by the KGB, but eventually managed to send a signal to the British Embassy, and escaped from Moscow to the West in July by means of a long-planned and risky 'exfiltration' – codenamed Operation Pimlico – which, after a perilous journey, delivered him across the Soviet border into Finland, concealed in the boot of an SIS officer's car. Washington later concluded that he had been betrayed by Aldrich Ames, a CIA officer who had offered himself as a Soviet agent for financial rather than ideological reasons. In 1994, Ames was sentenced to life imprisonment for espionage. He had learned Gordievsky's name after American intelligence decided in the early eighties to establish the identity of the British spy who had proved a more useful source than any of their own.

In this story, Ambassador Will Flemyng, the other inhabitants of the British Embassy in Washington and their friends, the IRA fighters and their supporters, all the civil servants in Whitehall, and even the mayor of Chicago, are fictitious. None of them ever existed. James Jesus Angleton, who died in 1987, is an exception. But, as with the others, his words and actions here are imagined, not real.

About the Author

JAMES NAUGHTIE is a special correspondent for BBC News, for which he has reported from around the world. He presented *Today* on BBC Radio 4 for 21 years. This is his third novel, and his most recent book is an account of five decades of travel and work in the United States – *On the Road: American Adventures from Nixon to Trump*. He lives in Edinburgh and London.